The Cadet of TILDOR

The Cadet of TILDOR

 **ALEX LIDELL**

DIAL BOOKS
an imprint of Penguin Group (USA) Inc.

DIAL BOOKS

An imprint of Penguin Group (USA) Inc.

Published by The Penguin Group

Penguin Group (USA) Inc., 375 Hudson Street, New York, NY 10014, U.S.A.

Penguin Group (Canada), 90 Eglinton Avenue East, Suite 700, Toronto, Ontario,
Canada M4P 2Y3 (a division of Pearson Penguin Canada Inc.)

Penguin Books Ltd, 80 Strand, London WC2R 0RL, England

Penguin Ireland, 25 St. Stephen's Green, Dublin 2, Ireland
(a division of Penguin Books Ltd)

Penguin Group (Australia), 707 Collins Street, Melbourne,
Victoria 3008, Australia (a division of Pearson Australia Group Pty Ltd)

Penguin Books India Pvt Ltd, 11 Community Centre,
Panchsheel Park, New Delhi - 110 017, India

Penguin Group (NZ), 67 Apollo Drive, Rosedale, Auckland 0632,
New Zealand (a division of Pearson New Zealand Ltd)

Penguin Books, Rosebank Office Park, 181 Jan Smuts Avenue,
Parktown North 2193, South Africa

Penguin Books China, B7 Jaiming Center, 27 East Third Ring Road North,
Chaoyang District, Beijing 100020, China

Penguin Books Ltd, Registered Offices: 80 Strand,
London WC2R 0RL, England

Book design by Mina Chung • Text set in Adobe Jenson Pro

Printed in the U.S.A.

1 3 5 7 9 10 8 6 4 2

Library of Congress Cataloging-in-Publication Data

Lidell, Alex.

The Cadet of Tildor / by Alex Lidell.   p. cm.

Summary: At the Academy of Tildor, the training ground for elite soldiers, Cadet Renee de Winter
struggles to keep up with her male peers, but when her mentor is kidnapped to fight in illegal gladiator
games, Renee and best friend Alec struggle to do what is right in a world of crime and political intrigue.

ISBN 978-0-8037-3681-8 (hardcover)

[1. Military cadets—Fiction. 2. Military education—Fiction. 3. Schools—Fiction. 4. Adventure and
adventurers—Fiction. 5. Crime—Fiction. 6. Political corruption—Fiction. 7. Fantasy.] I. Title.

PZ7.L61613Cad 2013   Fic]—dc23   2012026612

 **DEDICATION**

To my dive buddy, riding partner,

and best friend

Lady Renee de Winter turned her back to the parlor, where her father's clerk counted gold crowns into the visitor's waiting palm. The coins' melodic ring turned her stomach.

"Please thank my lord Tamath de Winter for his donation," the visitor said, bowing. "His generosity keeps the roads well guarded."

Renee wondered how long the man practiced that sincere voice, or how her father's clerk tolerated the farce. For that matter, whose benefit was the show for at all? Calling extortion "charity" fooled no one.

She knelt on the carpeted floor and opened her travel trunk. With luck, the visiting thief would see her Academy of Tildor uniform packed inside. Once she graduated, these Family thugs would think twice about making their demands on the de Winter estate. Or on any other estate.

"Your pardon, my lady." The approaching maid worried her skirts, waiting until Renee shut the wooden lid. "Your father wishes for you to address the tenants tomorrow."

Renee closed her eyes. He knew she was leaving for the Academy today, just as she had done at the end of every summer since turning ten. Renee wanted to protect Tildor, to serve its people and the Crown. Her father wanted her to stay home and count goats. In gods' names, they had discussed it—again!—over breakfast that very morning.

Blood boiled beneath her cheeks as she stalked down the wide hallway to her father's study and slammed the door hard enough to topple accounts books from their shelf. "The Family's demands will only grow if you keep indulging them, my lord."

Lord Tamath dipped his pen into the inkwell and continued writing. The dark wood of his furniture matched his strict woolen tunic. "With a mere boy now holding the throne, the danger to us doubles." His pen scratched over parchment. "It costs less to give coin than to lose wagons. A fact of which you, of all people, should be well aware." He didn't look up, didn't even acknowledge the sting of his words.

Ten years ago, a Family-rigged accident crushed a wagon carrying Renee's mother and older brother to a market. It would have carried Renee instead of Riley, had she not fallen off a horse that morning. The scar on her palm pressed her to honor their memory; Lord Tamath honored it by feeding their killers.

"Recheck the crop figures before tomorrow, if you please," he added.

Renee took a breath to steady her voice. "By tomorrow, Father, I will be in Atham, in the Academy barracks, preparing for classes. Surely this isn't news."

He dipped his pen again, as if meeting her eyes was beneath him. "Your desire is not news, no." His curled mustache twitched. "This is." He held out a folded sheet of parchment with a cracked Academy seal, his lips pressed into a taut line.

She tugged down her tunic, took the three paces from the door to his desk, and tried not to seem as if she reached for a poisonous snake.

> *Cadet Renee de Winter,*
>
> *The Academy of Tildor has reviewed your record and found that your competence in the Combat Arts Track falls on the borderline of acceptable levels. As such, the Academy will scrutinize your performance in the coming year and, should we find a lack of sufficient progress, dismiss you from the program. Consider this your Formal Notice of Warning.*

Signatures followed the text. Renee looked away, her world trembling. She trained every day. Each and every one. And she was so close. One last year in the Academy's schoolrooms and two in a field trial and then she would be a Servant of the Crown. "I will work harder, Father," she said quietly. "During meals if I must. I will get stronger. You know I will."

Lord Tamath snorted. "No quantity of training will make a wolf from a cockroach. You're sixteen. If you had any hopes of growing strong enough to compete with the men, you would have by now." He jerked the letter from her hand and nodded with satisfaction. "I have indulged this Servant of the Crown fantasy long enough. No, you will not attend the Academy. You will remain here, pursuing an occupation that you have some chance of not failing. I will not have you disgrace these estates or my name."

Renee swallowed. "The Academy does not require a father's permission, my lord." In point of fact, the Academy was Tildor's sole establishment to ignore lineage. Noble or not, all cadets studied together and graduated—or not—on merit alone. A Servant's uniform could not be bought. "You cannot stop me from going," Renee said.

He did look up then, and the fire blazing in his eyes threatened to burn through her. "I can stop you from coming back." He rose, bracing his palms on the table, and spat his words at her in short, venomous breaths. "Should you ignore my wishes, do not expect a welcome here." He sat back down and resumed scratching with his pen as if he had not just stuck a dagger into his daughter's life. "Either come to your senses or live with the folly of your choices. That will be all."

CHAPTER 2

Cadet Renee de Winter strode down the long corridor of the Academy barracks, each step carrying her farther from home. She trailed her fingers along the walls, enjoying their cool, uneven surface.

Hanging lanterns bathed the hall with dim, yellow light. Soon the walkway would fill with dozens of rushing cadets, future Fighter and Magistrate Servants of the Crown dressed in black uniforms with the colored trims of their career tracks; magistrate red, fighter blue. Black and blue, yes, that fit Fighter Servant cadets well.

As in any army, most of Tildor's warriors were common soldiers; uneducated weapons-bearers who'd never lead units. Officers—whose skills and studies reached beyond weapons-handling to strategy, law, mathematics, and more—were *leaders*.

And then there were Servants of the Crown.

A unique type of officer, a Servant attended a school—*the* school—the Academy of Tildor, instead of apprenticing in the field. The very few cadets able to endure the Academy's rigorous regime and fortunate enough to graduate formed an elite cadre, destined for the most vital assignments and missions. Servants were the Crown's champions. As Renee strove to be. Would be.

Renee took a breath and pushed her father's ultimatum to the back of her mind. What was done was done, and she had at least been able to carry some coin away with her. Enough to survive the year. Many were less fortunate.

Renee halted by the most beautiful sight in the building, her name etched into a wooden nameplate mounted on the door. Her door. Tucking an escaped wisp of brown hair behind her ear, she fumbled in one, then another pocket for the key. It had to be somewhere.

She was searching still when the door swung open, and a tall, grinning girl let her inside. "I recognized the footsteps. No one in their right mind has so much energy."

"I never claimed sanity, Sasha." Renee laughed, embracing her roommate. "Try spending a summer with my lord father, if you wish to know why." She stepped inside and groaned. Books already lay scattered everywhere, a natural hazard of rooming with a magistrate cadet. Not that sharing quarters with another fighter remained an option; the cuts had left two girls in the fighters' senior class, but the other had developed mage's Control last spring. A late bloomer. Renee did not know where the Mage Council placed the girl.

Renee maneuvered around a teetering pile of books and dropped her bag on her bed. "Did you rob the library, Sasha?"

"Being the Crown's cousin has its advantages."

"You are a corrupt abomination."

Sasha picked out a leather-bound tome and held it so its title,

Battlefields of the Seventh, was visible. "You do not want this, then?"

Renee snatched the treasure from her friend's hand. The book's thin pages bent under her touch. Seven years ago, the Seventh's leader, Korish Savoy, was a fighter cadet her age. He trained in the same salle, worried about the same exams, followed the same rules. Maybe he opened a book like this too and counted the days to the year's end, to the two years of field trials, to turning nineteen and graduating. Maybe in another seven years, some other cadet would open a book about Renee. If she made it.

A knock interrupted her musing. Her best friend loitered awkwardly in the open doorway, his hands buried in his pockets. For him, this was positively outgoing. "Alec! The door is wide open."

"Mmm. Didn't notice." He bowed to Sasha before stepping inside.

Renee ran up and hugged him, rising onto her toes to get her arms around his neck. The differences in their physiques had grown pronounced within the last year, when soft curves shaped her previously boyish body. The summer apart accentuated it. Resentment pricked her before she could stop it, and her father's words bubbled in her mind like a disease. The boys grew. And she did not. Even Alec, who once had looked wide-eyed at her superior swordsmanship, started powering through her parries last spring.

He lifted her off the ground for a momentary hug and then retreated to hide in a corner.

Sasha smiled like a cat with a bowlful of cream. "Your new instructor will come a week late." She cut her gaze at the book on Renee's bed. "You may have heard of him."

Renee looked at Sasha blankly until her roommate chuckled and mouthed the name.

Savoy. Servant Commander Korish Savoy. Renee closed her eyes, sending a thank-you to the gods. Her heart beat faster. At least one cadet would be cut after midyear exams, and she would not let it be her. If anyone could hone her skills by then, it was Tildor's top swordsman. "How did you find out?"

"I have my birdies." Sasha nodded toward *Battlefields.* "Make certain you return that. I may have forgotten to obtain Master Librarian's permission."

Alec shifted and stared at the floor.

Renee frowned at him. "What bothers you?"

He glanced up, rubbing his arms. "With Savoy in charge, everyone will be watching us."

"True." Sasha scratched the side of her nose. "Having the commander teach cadets is like, well, asking the palace's mage to Heal scraped knees. If Savoy's here, someone wanted it so."

Renee shrugged and resumed her search for the missing door key. The Academy always pulled instructors from field duty. Even those permanently stationed at the Academy split their time between teaching and other work. Headmaster Verin, a Servant High Constable in rank, was the Crown's top military advisor, while Servant Magistrate Seaborn, the cadets' favorite law teacher, regularly addressed real cases. But Sasha would look for hidden meaning if the kitchens served pudding in place of custard. All magistrates did. The lack of a door key presented the more immediate problem for Renee, since reporting it lost would doubtlessly trigger some official inquiry. She checked her pockets for the third time.

"I know a smith in town," Alec said quietly.

Sasha cleared her throat and rose, placing her own key on the bureau. "If you'll both excuse me, I think I will indulge in an extended bath before Lys's welcome address. My dear cousin the now king will be sweating enough for all of us."

A smile tugged Renee's lips. It was good to be back.

By the time Renee and Alec had copied the key, a slow breeze cut the warm afternoon. The trees surrounding the Academy grounds rustled companionably. Inside, servants scurried about the main courtyard, adding final touches in preparation for the Crown's speech. Curiosity tickled the air. King Lysian III had ascended to the throne barely two months earlier, following his sickly father's passing.

Before them, a small boy and his dog ran circles around the dais now mounted on the manicured lawn, while Guardsman Fisker, his horse-face pinched into a scowl, watched from a distance. Renee sighed. Fisker had left his position at the Academy a year ago for a new assignment as a Senior Guardsman in the Palace Guard—much to the delight of most cadets. The man would hunt down anyone who even *thought* of breaking the rules, if he could. He was likely here to safeguard the king, which meant they'd be rid of him soon. Renee sighed again, then staggered back as the boy's dog, an enormous wolf-like creature, made a dash for Alec.

Alec dropped to one knee to greet the disaster. The habit was bound to get him bitten one day, but that day stubbornly refused to come.

"Khavi likes you." The boy, no older than eight, cocked his head, blond hair ruffling in the wind. He was eleven hands tall or so, temporarily matching heights with the kneeling Alec.

"Most beasts do," muttered Renee, staying clear of the dog's muddy paws. "The courtyard is closed for the ceremony," she said pointedly.

The boy crossed his arms. Green eyes came up to meet hers. "How can grass close?"

Alec turned away in an apparent coughing fit, leaving Renee to conjure a response. "What's your name?"

"Diam." He held out his hand. "I'm gonna be a page and then a cadet and then a Servant."

"Young." Alec rose to stand beside her but continued scratching his new furry friend's ear. "Few students come before ten."

"Korish Savoy came at eight," Diam shot back.

Renee smiled. "Are you our next Commander Savoy?"

He stood up straighter. "I am."

"Well, be careful, Master Savoy, because the real one will soon be here," said Alec.

"I know. He's got a huge horse named Kye, who is all black and can kill a man."

Alec whistled. "You know all that?"

"More." The boy opened his mouth to say something further, when Fisker approached waving his four-fingered hand to banish them from the yard.

"You let that beast bite anyone, and I'll cut its head off myself," Fisker grunted, throwing Diam and his dog a dirty look.

"Bloody gods, the man's skull has grown even thicker since getting posted to the palace, and a promotion to boot. You'd think he has half the army—not ten junior guardsmen—under him," Alec mumbled when they parted paths with the boy and headed to barracks. "What security breach were we possibly creating?"

Renee chuckled. Fisker's perfection crusade was not the true cause of Alec's irritation. "I'm certain the dog will play with you again tomorrow," she told him.

Alec blushed.

"Is it strange seeing your cousin as the Crown?" Renee asked Sasha, while wrestling into her dress uniform.

"Like watching an unbroken colt saddled." Sasha settled a magistrate's burgundy shawl on her own shoulders. "You can't tell whether the horse will give or the rider will break his neck." She shook her head. "The first thing Lys did was arrest three Viper lords, Renee. I'm holding my breath to see what comes of it."

"Besides three less violent criminals in Tildor?"

Sasha snorted. "Gods help me, you're just like him. If it was *that* straightforward, the Crown would have done it years back." She dropped her voice. "The evidence was broth-weak and now the Vipers' Madam is pouring underlings into Atham to put the new Crown in his place. A new king's position is tenuous enough without goading enemies into confrontation."

Renee winced. The Vipers had emerged as the Family's top rival about ten years ago, dragging violence wherever they stepped. They'd be an unwelcome addition to the capital. Still, taking decisive action against criminals was a strong opening move, and a good message to send to the Vipers and Family both. Renee liked Lysian as king already.

By early evening, the late summer breeze played across the Academy courtyard, tousling the flag of Tildor and the cadets' uniforms. White marble buildings, like soldiers, lined the two sides of the lush lawn. A peaked shadow from the temple at the east end of the yard stretched toward the library in the west, slicing into the students' formation.

As a senior, Renee stood in the front and felt, rather than saw, the whole complement of the school gather in ordered rows behind her. The Crown's welcome address would hold little content beyond a call to attentive studies, but his visit was a tradition. Most officers and officials pledged to serve Tildor; the fighters and magistrates who graduated the Academy pledged loyalty to the *Crown*. Personally. And when that day came, the young new Servants of the Crown would all have met their liege. The Academy took pride in that.

Trumpets called the courtyard to attention, dipped and rose again as King Lysian III strode out from behind the temple mound. His footsteps kept time with the Hymn of Tildor, which filled the air, the last step and note ending exactly at the erected dais.

He was five paces in front of Renee.

Lysian was young. Renee blinked at the absurdity of her surprise. Of course he was young, he was nineteen, just a few years older than she. For a moment, standing so close, he was an attractive blond boy whose large blue eyes, so like Sasha's, reflected the apprehension and excitement brewing within Renee's own chest. But then he spoke, and the boy in his eyes disappeared behind the steel voice of the Crown.

"My champions." King Lysian's gaze swept them. "For years I've stood at my father's side as he offered you words of encouragement and challenged you to great deeds. Tradition tells me to do the same." He swallowed. "But I must set aside the luxury of tradition. Tildor is sick."

The eyes of an advisor standing by the dais widened as the king put down his notes and drew a breath.

"A decade ago, we fought off a Devmani invasion. The Servants and others rallied to my father's call, buying our victory with their blood. Many fell. Too many." He paused and Renee could see his jaw tighten before he drew breath to speak again. "After our victory, too few swords remained to protect Tildor from its own disease. Now Vipers steal men and children from the streets and cut women's throats for pleasure and boast. The Family robs the purses of our merchants and nobles while fattening its own with sale of veesi leaf. Today, I wager that there is not one of you who stands before me who has not lost a friend to the violence of a Viper, or coin to the corruption the Family spreads."

Renee's fist clenched, fingernails digging into her scarred palm.

Lysian raised his chin. "My armies guard our borders, and my soldiers strain to keep our roads safe for commerce. Some of you will join and lead those troops. But it is the disease of crime on which my reign opens. I will fight it. And you are the champions who will fight beside me." He paused. "Please, study. Please, train. The Crown needs your Service."

Trumpets hurried to catch up with the king, who had turned and left without waiting on applause.

The crowd of cadets twitched, necks straining to watch the royal departure and catch the eyes of nearby friends. "What did you make of his words?" one cadet whispered to another while instructors ascended the dais to read schedules of classes and exams.

"What did you make of his words?" the question came around again.

I pray I'm here long enough to give my pledge, thought Renee, and closed her eyes, wondering how she would survive the coming year.

CHAPTER 3

Servant Commander Korish Savoy tilted his face to relish the pouring rain. It streamed down his cheeks and neck, washing away dust, sweat, and blood. The horse beneath him pawed the mud and whinnied into the damp morning air. Savoy petted the stallion's quivering shoulder before nudging him under the shelter of the sprawling trees.

"A victory worthy of minstrels' songs, would ye not say, sir?" Cory, a young sergeant, trotted up on his bay, his grin untroubled by the bandage binding his brow.

Savoy leveled him with his eyes. "If I hear it, I'll know whom to hold responsible." The latest string of victories was boosting the Seventh's confidence to dangerous levels. Pride was one thing. Invincibility was another. "Anything useful to report?"

The boy's grin, of course, didn't falter. "Aye, sir. Half the bandits had Viper tattoos, plus several thousand gold crowns' worth of veesi leaf between them. Someone's head will fall for this."

Savoy nodded. The Vipers' Madam was not known for mercy—rumor held that she had executed her son's father for producing an offspring who fell short of her standards. Whichever Viper lord was in charge of the operation the Seventh had just uprooted was unlikely to survive the week. And neither would the lord's family.

But seeing Vipers this deep into the countryside, and with veesi to boot, bothered Savoy for other reasons. "Vipers on the Family's turf?"

Cory scratched his horse's ear. "Maybe the bastards will kill each other off. I'll nay cry if they do."

"Or they use us to do it for them." Savoy ran a hand through his hair. The information of the hoard's location came from a birdie, not the Crown's own scouts, and snitches had their own agendas. "What else?"

Cory pushed his soggy bandage behind his ears and pulled a folded square of parchment from his coat. "Messenger returned from Fort Ellis. I dinna know if they're more grateful or embarrassed for our help, but they'll be sending men to collect the prisoners. And a personal message for ye from the capital."

Savoy rubbed his temple. Good news from Atham was as likely as raccoons talking. "We'll rest a day here, then move out to drill in the mountains." He slid a dagger blade under the envelope's seal. "The boys still have most of their blood inside them?"

"Aye." Cory frowned, then added with some reluctance, "Mag's hoping you won't notice his limp, but that's all."

"Should I notice his limp?"

Cory shrugged.

"Fort Ellis has a mage Healer. You and Mag will volunteer to help take the prisoners there." He held up a hand to ward

16

off protest. "And I will continue thinking that bloody bandages around sergeants' foreheads are a fashion to attract women." Letting Cory blush in relative privacy, Savoy unfolded the message.

A wave of nausea gripped him as he read and reread the text. When the words didn't change, he stared at the neat handwriting, watching the raindrops smudge the ink. Someone played a jest. Savoy had created the Seventh, handpicking and training each man in it. It had to be a jest.

"Sir?"

Savoy schooled his face and voice. "Belay my previous orders, Sergeant. The Seventh will go up to Ellis as a group. And stay there." He refolded his orders before slipping them inside his jacket.

"How long, sir?" Cory's voice was carefully flat.

"Until you get other orders." He looked up to meet the young sergeant's wide eyes and hardened his own. "I've been reassigned."

Four days later, Savoy guided his mount past Atham's city walls, into an ambush of scurrying pedestrians and bellowing merchants. "Fish! Fresh fish!" a woman shouted into his ear. He could taste the rot from the stench alone. The closest fishing pier was a three-day ride west. He managed to get past the fish lady only to have a small girl block his path.

Her bare feet toed the ground inches from his horse's metal-shod hooves. "Can I pet your horse?"

A warhorse. She wanted to pet his warhorse. Savoy rubbed his temple and pulled Kye to a halt to avoid trampling the future cavalrywoman. "He's trained to kill people."

"Oh . . ." She rubbed the sole of her right foot against her left calf. "Do you kill people too?"

"Of course he does," said a boy's voice. "He's got a sword."

Other voices joined in with their opinions. Behind the buzz of the children's speculation brewed a wave of adults' quiet comments.

"Is that him?"

"No, Savoy isn't coming."

"The Crown ordered him."

Stopping had been a mistake. Someone reached a hand toward Kye's flank and the stallion snapped his teeth.

"Get your animal under control, Commander," said a familiar voice. Its owner, leaner and more gray-haired than Savoy remembered, guided his own horse through the crowd. He sat tall in his saddle and his eyes scrutinized Savoy from head to toe, as if he were a boy caught after the curfew bell. "The mount oft reflects the mood of his rider."

Savoy swallowed his thoughts and bowed to Verin, Servant High Constable of the Crown's army, the Academy headmaster, and for several years, Savoy's foster father. "Hello, sir."

"Supply problems at Fort Ellis?" Verin asked mildly.

"Sir?"

"I presume your lack of uniform reflects poor efforts of the quartermaster. My apologies for the inconvenience." Verin nar-

18

rowed his eyes, glaring at the onlookers and arousing a flurry of activity. No one wanted to upset a Servant of the Crown. Verin's voice softened. "The cadets look to their teachers for example, lad."

Cadets. Savoy's hands tightened so hard on the reins that Kye tossed his head, earning a sideways glance from Verin. *Cadets.* He was being made to trade the Seventh for a gaggle of children. Savoy forced his fingers open and continued the journey in silence. The familiar sights of the Academy's stone-walled barracks, trimmed-grass courtyards, and imposing buildings welcomed him with the hospitality that shackles greet a prisoner.

"I arranged a corner stall for Kye, on the chance he is as intense as other warhorses I've had the pleasure of knowing," Verin said as they reached the stable where two handlers awaited.

Savoy nodded. Kye hated stalls.

"I will see you in my study. You spent enough time there to remember the way, I believe?" Verin's lips twitched in a suppressed smile as he walked away.

The stable hand reached for Savoy's reins. "Sir?"

"Don't go near Kye." Savoy unsaddled the stallion himself and bent to clear rubble and sewage bits from the horse's hooves. This assignment wasn't just ridiculous, it wasn't right.

A half hour later, Savoy, in full uniform, came to attention in front of Verin's desk. The office had changed little since Savoy's cadet years, when he and his friend had stood in this spot too often. A few more lines creased the old leather chair, a few more volumes filled the oak bookcase. Even the smell was the same—sealing wax, old books, and jasmine tea. He tensed despite himself.

"Sit, lad." Verin waved toward a chair. "For once, you are not here for a reprimand." Crow's-feet wrinkles accented the corners of his eyes when he smiled. That was new too.

Savoy stayed standing. "Why am I here, sir?"

"To teach." Verin's weathered hand took an iron teakettle off the tray and filled two cups.

"I'm a fighter, sir, and the Seventh is a combat unit. I know as little of children as my replacement knows of my men."

Verin's face hardened. "You are a Servant of the Crown, sworn, if memory serves me, to obey said Crown's wishes."

And if King Lysian even knows of my assignment, I'll eat a goat intestine raw. Savoy caught himself in time to guard his words. It was not beyond Verin to take him up on the suggestion. "Is this an exercise in administrative policy, sir?"

"It is an exercise in fortifying our Servant officer cadre. The Academy believes that a year of teaching cadets is an investment worth making." Verin pulled up his brows. "It is a compliment to your skills, lad. One that I am proud to support."

"It is a farce, sir. I fight in real battles, with real swords, and real consequences. I will happily demonstrate all that to whichever puppeteer arranged this ludicrousness. I—"

Verin's palm slammed the table. The resulting din reverberated off the walls and rippled the surface of the jasmine tea. "You are twenty-three and behave like a sullen child."

Savoy swallowed.

"The Academy is a living institution. We all carry out duties beyond these walls." Verin leaned forward and the High Constable pips on his collar caught the light. His tone took a familiar note of steel. "You may reclaim your command and re-sharpen the Seventh after dispatching your current obligations. I am not suggesting that task to be simple; I am saying it is one you will address at a later date. For the time being, your responsibilities are to your students, Commander Savoy. You are in the service of the Crown and are called to serve here."

Savoy said nothing for a few moments. Ridiculous orders or not, if not for fostering with Verin, he'd be a guest in a prison instead of an officer in the Crown's champion troop. "What do you expect me to teach them, sir?"

"They are the upcoming officer elites. Teach them what you think they need."

"Experience."

The headmaster bored his gaze into him.

Savoy strained to keep the discontent from his voice. "Yes, sir."

Leaning back in his chair, Verin allowed the silence to linger. Finally, he sighed. "You may go."

Savoy bowed and braced to attention once more before starting for the door. His hand was already on the handle when he turned back and asked softly, "Why am I here, sir?"

Verin sipped his tea, silent.

As Savoy walked away, he could not help but wonder how he would survive the coming year.

CHAPTER 4

To an outsider, the practice courts might look like the bastard children of the spotless Academy. Tucked at the far west end, away from the main courtyard, past even the stables, the handful of wood-fenced corrals circled a barn-size building called a salle, a large room with a sand floor. To Renee and the other fighters, this was the Academy's soul. Rules carved into a wooden plaque hung above the door. She couldn't recall anyone ever reading them, but they belonged here. Just as she did.

The morning sun flowed through the salle's windows, lighting the Academy of Tildor crest, which was painted at chest height on the opposite wall. Its sword and scroll shimmered in the rays full of swirling dust motes. The blue mage flame, a remainder from the days when mages ran the school, proudly held its ground. It was an old drawing, one that nobody seemed to notice any longer on the wall.

When she was little, like all children, Renee wanted Control. She had seen mages walk in shrouds of respect and glamour, Healing wounds with a touch of their blue flame, and answering summonses to work on secret projects for the Crown himself. She wanted it most upon turning thirteen, when the Academy dismissed many of the girls and weaker boys in her class. Even the smallest, scrawniest mage could contribute to a battle, she told herself at night when she imagined waking up one morning to discover herself a mage and suddenly able to sense the Keraldi Barrier. What must it be like, she wondered, to reach toward a friend and feel the invisible shell holding his life energy as surely as if she were touching real skin.

"The mage's ability to feel and Control life energy manifests when the body matures," Headmaster Verin had told her upon finding her in the chapel. "You cannot make yourself a mage any more than you can make yourself taller. But, to each strength is a cost." He had sat down beside her, looking straight ahead, as she did. "Do you know why we have no mage Servants?"

Renee had shaken her head, and he'd glanced at her then.

"The Servant's oath. It must be given freely. A mage has no choice, either in who she is or what specialization the Crown's mage council selects for her. And, since she already belongs to Tildor, there is no oath to give." He had smiled. "Plus, mages only support armies; they do not lead soldiers or wield weapons themselves."

Renee had crossed her arms. "Tildor has battle mages, they wield weapons."

"They do not. They *are* weapons. Dangerous weapons that someone else wields." Headmaster Verin's voice softened. "Very few mages have both the strength and the training to make a meaningful difference in battle. Even if you were one, at most, you might use mage energy to strike a target someone else selected while a team of fighters tries to protect you from the enemy's arrows. Is that where your heart lies?"

Renee did not want to be a mage after that.

Now she traced the painted sword's edge with her finger. This was her choice. "What do you think Commander Savoy's like?" she asked, feeling a presence behind her and turning to glance at Alec.

"Ruthless." Alec leaned his back against the wood-planked wall, arms crossed over his wide chest and gaze fixed on the door. The other students, fewer than twenty left in the senior class now, milled about, speaking in hushed voices and rechecking gear. They were early. A smart thing to be on the instructor's first day.

Renee shook her muscles loose. The tension in the room was growing, feeding on itself, and she sought comfort in the familiar sights. The large, rectangular hall smelled of sweaty leather and old sand. Spare gear, dusty and ill-fitting, spilled from the bins in the corner. Outside the window . . . She blinked as a pair of curious green eyes on the other side of the glass met hers. The eyes widened and disappeared, replaced by a dog's white muzzle.

She chuckled, earning annoyed glances from the boys.

Alec sighed. "Try and keep your head down, for once. You don't need Savoy riding hard on you any more than he will anyway."

"Where's your strategic mind?" Renee raised her brows. "The more attention he gives me, the less he gives you."

He rolled his eyes. "Yes, I'm certain the commanding officer of the Seventh is able to make only one person miserable at a time."

"Scared?"

"Sane."

The door swung open before she could retort, and everyone raced into formation.

Korish Savoy was not, as Renee imagined, big as a blacksmith. He was average height, and his lean muscles underscored agility, not bulk.

Renee's heart beat in her ears.

"Pads. Practice swords. Now," said Savoy.

So much for an introduction. They scrambled.

Savoy swung a bag off his shoulder and began strapping on worn leather pads. He moved like a cat, the gear pliant in his hands and conforming to the familiar shape of his muscles. Renee admired the economy of his motions until she realized he was ready and waiting. Cheeks hot, she sprinted through the rest of her buckles and laces.

Alec held her weapon out to her. "What's holding you?"

"Nothing."

"You're warmed up?" Savoy drew a practice sword from his bag and moved toward the center of the salle.

The cadets exchanged glances. No one spoke.

Savoy ran a hand over his hair. He pointed his blade, singling out Alec. "Answer."

Alec shuffled his feet.

Renee hid a wince. The last time Alec looked that miserable in front of an instructor was at age twelve, when he was summoned to explain the contents of his pockets to Headmaster Verin. Granted, he hadn't sat too well after that, and he never again earned so much as extra work duty.

"No, sir. The class . . ." Alec drew a breath. "The class just began now, sir."

Savoy massaged his temple. He was but half a hand taller than Alec, and not as broad—but seemed bigger. "Was that a surprise? Did the gods miraculously summon you all here, at the same time, with bags full of gear, and without any idea of what we might be doing?"

He caught the eyes of each student in turn. Renee tensed when his gaze met hers. How could anyone know what he expected before he told them? *He raises standards,* she told herself. *Certainly the Seventh warms up on its own.*

Withholding further comment, Savoy separated the students into pairs. He joined the cadets' lines instead of ordering them about from the sidelines like their past instructors had. Alec, who now faced Savoy, had the grim look of someone preparing for the gallows.

They started with a single attack-parry drill. Instructors always started with boring moves. Renee made herself focus, determined to make a good impression. She adjusted her stance. Parry left. Reset. Keep back straight. Push off the back foot hard when lunging. Attack left. Parry right. Relaxing, her body fell into the drill's rhythmic motions, punctuated by the even clacks of the wooden blades.

"Rotate!" The order brought Renee to a new partner. In her peripheral vision, she watched Savoy face off with Tanil, a thin blond boy who darted to and fro, trying to stay ahead of the instructor's blade. In contrast, Savoy's movements looked leisurely to the point of boredom.

Rotate. The drill changed to single combination attack.

Rotate. Alec.

"You're the only one not breathing hard," he said, adjusting his grip on the sword.

She shot a glance at Savoy. "Not the only one."

Alec shook his head in warning.

Rotate.

Renee looked into Savoy's eyes and smiled.

He did not smile back. He attacked, sword sailing at her head. When she blocked, the vibrations from the impact ran through her body. The blow hadn't looked that forceful. They reset, and she lunged to attack left. His blade materialized in her way. Renee blocked the next blow and attacked again, their swords beating a comfortable cadence.

Savoy looked bored to tears. She shared the sentiment. Gathering her courage, Renee reset a little quicker, attacked a little harder and faster. No rebuke came. He met her blow for blow, always hitting the perfect center of her blade, always parrying with the center of his. Hot blood urged her on. High block. Left parry. The clacking wood sounded like a drum roll.

She caught his eyes and, seeing a twinge of interest, pushed the speed further. The reset pause disappeared, the drill's rules a memory. *Clack-clack-clack.* Her body danced. Low block. Attack. Right parry. Attack. Parry again. In a flash of inspiration, Renee added a feint before her next advance. Savoy blocked, unfazed by the ruse. He countered and she hurried to block his high attack.

Except, he did not do a high attack. She watched him change the strike in mid-motion, while her blade continued up to block an assault that no longer headed that way. Savoy's face said he saw it too.

He did not pull the blow. The blade struck Renee's right forearm so hard that the thud of wood hitting padded leather made all heads turn toward them. Air caught in her lungs and pain seared through her arm, spreading into her side. Burning, then numbness, shot down to the small fingers of her hand. Her grip failed. The wooden blade slipped, thumping against the sand-covered floor.

Swallowing, she forced herself to straighten in silence. Her eyes met Savoy's just in time to see the calm on his face while his blade rose again. It landed on the same spot.

She cried out. The world swayed. Cradling her arm, she knelt to the floor. Looking up, Renee saw Savoy swing his blade for a third time and grimly braced herself. The blow stopped an inch short of her neck.

"You are dead," he told her before pitching his voice over the salle. "That will be the last time anyone here lets go of a weapon." He looked down at Renee. "Am I understood?"

"Yes, sir," she whispered, drowning in disgrace.

He extended his hand and pulled her to her feet.

The rest of the period passed in silence. Alec abandoned his partner for Renee, all the while fixing Savoy with a look of promised vengeance. The glare failed to make an impact, so far as she could tell, but Savoy didn't separate the pair. For the first time in her life, Renee couldn't wait to leave the salle.

Savoy stripped off his pads while his fearless followers silently escaped the salle. After the last cadet vanished, a fat middle-aged man squeezed through the doorway. An annoying, if not unexpected, visit.

"Lord Palan," Savoy said without glancing up. "My training is not a show."

The man puffed, either from indignation or else from the exertion of hauling his own bodyweight, and opened the top clasp of his shirt collar.

"You have stood by the side window for the past quarter hour." Savoy straightened and looked into the man's little eyes. Nothing had changed in seven years. Palan's dark, intelligent gaze still tirelessly weighted everything it touched, making Savoy feel as if he held fire beside straw. "Let me save you the trouble," Savoy offered. "My sword is still not for sale. I serve the Crown." *Unlike you.*

Lord Palan cleared his throat and gestured toward the Servant's crest on Savoy's tunic. The jeweled rings clamped around Palan's sausage fingers caught the light and shimmered. "Yes, Commander, I'm quite aware that tempting Verin's foster son lies outside my omnipotence." He chuckled, a smooth, bitter sound. The graying hair around his temples curled in droplets of sweat. "You were but a lad then, and a troubled one at that. I offered you employment and fair pay. Was such a proposal unjust?"

Savoy twirled his practice blade before placing it in his bag.

"I hear the gods blessed your parents with a second child?" Palan continued, undeterred.

"Eight years past."

"Expensive to raise children nowadays. If ever—"

"You employ little boys now, Lord Palan?"

"How dare . . ." Lord Palan's nostrils flared. He took a step toward Savoy, but stopped himself, his face transforming into a mask of nonchalance. "My apologies, Commander. You misunderstand. I had only stopped by to check up on my nephew's progress."

Savoy raised an eyebrow, admiring the flawless transition from failed negotiation to plausible fiction.

"Tanil. The thin blond youth?" Palan adjusted an expensive ring. "Don't distress. People's ignorance of my family members is common. Tanil assured me that he kept up practice all through the summer."

"I assure you he hasn't." Savoy slung his bag over a shoulder.

"Now that we have pacified your concern, I expect you will find no further need to grace my class with your presence?"

Lord Palan's mouth tightened at the dismissal, but he offered a slight bow and did not press the issue.

Renee followed the narrow trail that snaked from the barracks, down the hill, and into the adjacent woods. It ran for about half a league, stopping at the edge of Rock Lake, so named for the boulders lining its circumference. The water's vast, calm surface belied the danger of the lake's uneven bottom, but reflected the surrounding world with looking-glass accuracy. A bird perched on one of the boulders cried to its mate, and the call echoed from the stony outcroppings. There were no people.

At the lake's sole beach, a small sandy clearing to the left of the trail's mouth, Renee settled into a fighting stance. Practice sword in hand, she watched her reflection while coaxing the weapon through five basic parries. Her movements were hideous. Just holding the sword made her arm throb. A lighter, junior blade lay inside her bag. In the solitude of Rock Lake, she considered reaching for it to soothe the strain on her arm. *No.* The boys put away such childish things two years ago, and the enemy seldom waited until injuries healed before attacking. She swallowed and forced her shaking hand to keep trying.

"Looks awful," said a voice behind her.

She startled but managed to conceal the surprise behind a bow. "The arm or the parry, Master Seaborn?"

"Both." Connor Seaborn, a magistrate instructor who taught

Renee's law and history course, cleared the trail's mouth and leaned his tall frame against a boulder. He set down his bag and cocked his head to the side, awaiting an explanation.

"It was deserved, sir." Renee sighed, lowering her sword tip to the ground. "I didn't parry Commander Savoy's attack very well."

He nodded. "Most people don't parry his attacks very well. That's why the Crown sends him and the Seventh where it does." He frowned and leaned forward. "Renee, had you expected to win against him?"

"No." She shook her head. "No, of course not. But . . . " A chuckle tickled her chest, easing shame's weight. "It would have been nice, no?" She cleared her throat. "Are those practice swords in your bag, sir?"

"They are. An old classmate of mine is here. Speaking of missing parries . . . " He grinned toward the rustling leaves that signaled an impending arrival.

A moment later, Savoy stepped out onto the beach. He glanced her way but offered no greeting. It was a request to dismiss herself, but it wasn't an order.

She moved away to give the men as much space as the small beach allowed, the resultant twinge of guilt unable to compete with the chance to watch a hostile species in their natural habitat. Plus, perhaps Savoy'd be pleased to see her practicing.

He sat on the sand and folded himself over an outstretched leg. The back of his shirt outlined shifting muscles. "Why is my lord Palan still puffing around the Academy?" Savoy's hair fell to cover his face and he shook it off with a practiced motion. Renee blinked. If not for the unregulation length of the blond mane, he could have been a cadet savoring a free afternoon.

Seaborn reached back to plait his own red curls into a short, thick braid. "Largely on account of being the uncle of one of your students. And, he is petitioning the Crown to take the offensive against the Vipers, suggesting an assault on their stronghold in Catar City." Seaborn winced at a bird's shrill call, then jerked his thumb in the direction of the noise. "Remember him?"

Savoy snorted. "I remember you missing a shot by three paces. At least."

Seaborn cleared his throat. "Because the bow you made broke, and I landed on the back of my skull."

"Yes, well, there was that." A smile touched Savoy's face. He uncoiled and came to his feet with a smoothness that his friend could not match. "Most anyone with a decent mind and ties to Atham knows Palan runs the Family. Since when does the Crown entertain criminals' petitions?"

Seaborn chuckled. "I challenge you to find one shred of evidence implicating Palan in a crime. Any crime. Until that happens—and it won't; he's careful—he's just another conniving noble and can petition all he wishes. Officially speaking."

Savoy sighed. "I suppose I could kill him. Wring some good from this posting."

Seaborn tensed and picked up his practice blade. "Renee, could you give us the beach?" A forced smile tried to soften the demand.

There was nothing to do but bow and trot to the trail. She had been lucky to keep her ground as long as she had. Several paces into the woods, she paused, drew a breath, and ducked behind the foliage. The pounding of her heart threatened to give her away. Seaborn spoke again once she was hidden from view.

"Some good from this posting? You're teaching cadets!"

"A waste of my time and theirs."

"Give them a chance. Speaking of which, the girl's forearm is blue, and double its size. What was her crime?"

"Attempted suicide." There was a pause and a rustle of equipment before Savoy spoke again. He sounded annoyed. "Stop scowling, Connor. It works."

"Yes, I remember Verin doing it to you. Made you a golden child."

"Made me a living child," said Savoy, then raised his voice. "De Winter! Either don't eavesdrop or hide better."

Swallowing, she sprinted away.

CHAPTER 5

Academic Quarter. Palace Court. Mage District. Southwest.

Of the four sections in Tildor's capital city, only one was unworthy of a real name.

Alec blended into southwest Atham, where narrow streets of torn-up cobblestone rarely saw parades of uniformed guard. Here, pickpockets, workmen, children, all went about their business not with the forbidding glamour of the Mage District, or the philosophical wonderings of the Academic Quarter, but with the sharp eyes and skeptical ears of the slums.

He rounded a corner and walked down Orchard Street, a dirt field on the left and a mesh of shops and drab dwellings on the right. It was evening, but still light, and a gang of barefoot boys chased a ball around the field, sending up clouds of earth and cheer. There were fewer children than usual, but enthusiasm balanced the numbers. One boy leaped into the air flipping head over heels. When he landed on his feet and proclaimed himself the master of a jumping-tumble-of-doom, Alec clapped along with the others.

Southwest lacked money, not life—just like the small cottage his grandmother raised him in. He doubted his mother ever saw that. When he became a Servant, he'd find her and ask.

A few yards ahead, a boy stepped out of a shop whose sign proclaimed it a meat market. "Greg says to tell you he's got fresh pies," he informed Alec. "You want pies?"

Alec sighed. Greg must have changed his boys again. "I want corn."

The boy shoved his hands into his pockets. "Pies be better. You want pies."

Shaking his head, Alec ignored the boy's dirty look and went inside. Here, several trays of ground meat slop lay on a shelf beyond the customers' reach. A potbellied butcher in a smeared white apron stood behind the counter. He scrutinized Alec as if they'd never met. Carelessness killed people around here. "Yes?"

Alec pulled a gold crown from his pocket, twisted it in his fingers, and let the coin disappear. "Need to talk, Greg."

Nodding, he let Alec behind the counter and guided him through a side door, whose oiled hinges slid in silence. They entered a crossbreed of a bedroom, storeroom, and office, so common for this part of town. A narrow bed tucked into the corner, and shelves, burdened with clothing, foodstuffs, and other items, crowded the space. The reek of garlic made Alec's eyes water, but he did his best to ignore it and took one of the two wooden chairs guarding a bare table. Greg settled into the other.

"Don't have much corn, lad—an ear, maybe two, of anything decent. Expand your horizons. Try the pies." Greg drummed his fingers against the tabletop.

"Why the deficit?" Alec hid his concern behind a mask of professional curiosity.

"Spent the summer away, cadet?" Greg snorted, not bothering to conceal his contempt. "The babe we've got on the throne threw a tantrum and nabbed the wrong Vipers. Now the Madam is taking a personal interest, and it's trouble for everyone." He shook his head. "Two of my lads vanished last month. I'll wager you a gold crown the Madam's got them in some Predator lair, being fattened to fight in the arena for the Vipers' gambling pleasure. We'll have trouble with the mages next. You heed my words, boy, Vipers always stir up the mages, registered and dark ones both. It's a dangerous thing, overactive mages."

Alec slumped back in his chair and turned his coin between his fingers. Mages trying to avoid registration had to hide *somewhere*, and Vipers offered a place to go and paid good coin for mage skills too. "Doesn't answer my question."

"Think I'm cheating you?" Greg licked his tooth. "Wish I was. Our Viper guests took a Family's veesi shipment down just recently—a major one. Killed the merchant, and killed my supply. Most leaf on the street now will make you sick. Wouldn't sell that to you. Greg saves the good bit for you, boy, you remember that."

Alec nodded his thanks—the Academy Healer would notice veesi poisoning in a moment—although he doubted the dealer's concern came from anything but self-preservation.

The news worried him, though. The Vipers did not belong in the capital. Their clashes with the Crown and the Family would spill on to bystanders. Already had, if Greg spoke the truth about lads disappearing. Accepting an ear of corn, Alec edged back the leaves and twisted at the tip. It snapped off, revealing crumbled orange leaves packed into the hollowed stem. The fashion of concealing veesi in corn was gaining popularity. He sniffed the goods, feeling a familiar nausea grip at his throat.

After paying for the leaf and ignoring Greg's attempts to saddle him with other wares, Alec headed back toward the Academy. One would think that after four years of buying nothing but veesi the man would get the point, but no one was immune to coin.

He was almost back to the Academic Quarter, two ears of corn secured between the lining and outer fabric of his jacket— evenings chilly enough to get away with wearing it were precious few in the summer—when shouts turned his head back toward lower Atham. He gasped despite himself. Rising above the rooftops, a tower of black smoke spiraled to soil the dimming sky. Bodies, small as ants from so far away, scurried from the flame. A barefoot boy with the savvy look of a street rat and soot around his ears trotted past. Alec called to him and tossed a copper. "What burns?"

The boy caught the coin with one hand and crammed it into his pocket. "The registration post in the Mage District."

Alec sighed. It seemed Greg had been right.

The boy cocked his head. "You be needing a message ran?"

"No." Alec waved the boy away. The message was quite clear. Only the Madam would dare burn a mage registration post in the capital city itself. The desecration was the Vipers' calling card to Atham. *We are here,* it said. *And we have demands.*

Renee awoke to a thud. She had stayed up strength-training well past the midnight bell the previous night, and now opened her eyes to see the chalkboard a few paces away. Seaborn stood by her desk, which vibrated from a large book that had just landed on it. Her cheeks heated.

"See me after class," he said quietly and then pitched his voice over the classroom of fighter cadets. "Three centuries ago, before the rebellion wars, we were slaves to mages. What's stopping a repeat performance? Alec?"

Despite a liking for history, Alec looked at the floor. He always did when required to speak in class. "The mages used to be stronger," he said finally. "In addition to higher Control ability ratings, they also knew more, and, being the ruling class, they already had a government infrastructure in place."

"For example?" Seaborn prompted when Alec fell silent.

"For example"—Alec's words forced themselves out in a semi-mumble—"mages imposed a *vitalis* tax, forcing non-mages to submit to a draining of a measure of their life energy. The mages then used non-mages' energy for their own projects and power."

"Very good." Seaborn rubbed his arms, then straightened, folding them across his chest. "There is little to dispute here: Centuries ago, mages did bad things. So bad, it took a war to put an end to their domination. After the bloodshed, the new Crown destroyed many mage instructional texts to prevent a repeat of history. Even much of Keraldi's own work was burned. Later, mandatory mage registration was established as both a safety measure and as a means of reconciliation and coexistence." He lifted his brows. "In short, today's laws address a three-hundred-year-old problem. Are they still relevant?"

Renee crossed her feet while the rest of the class fidgeted in silence.

Seaborn sighed. "Let's consider this scene: It's next year. You, now seventeen, have finished the Academy's classwork segment and are on your field trial, stationed, say, on the western border near our less than friendly—which neighbors? Tanil?"

"Devmani Empire."

Seaborn nodded. "Near our Devmani neighbors. The invaluable asset that you are, you find yourself dumped off in a small, isolated town. Your commander orders you to keep out of trouble until he gets back from a mission. Sound about right thus far?"

The cadets laughed.

"One of the soldiers in your company falls ill. The helpful townspeople fetch the medicine woman, who you realize is an unregistered mage. Issues, my friends?" He didn't wait for hands. "Renee, please."

She rubbed her eyes, hoping the grogginess of her head wouldn't seep into her voice. "The woman avoided registration, thus committing a high crime against the Crown. I would arrest her."

Seaborn put his hands into his pockets. "Depriving the town

of its Healer will cost many lives, including that sick soldier of yours. Still want to do it?"

Renee frowned. "That's the law, sir. Mages must register and submit to education and regulation. I'd have no choice."

"Yes, that's the law. But what does this law mean for us *today?*" Seaborn eyed each student in turn. "Does it matter?" He crossed his arms. "Healer Grovener has a young apprentice this year. The boy is interested in Healing and hopes the experience with Grovener will sway the Mage Council to keep him in that vocation once he turns thirteen and registers. It may work. Or, the Council may find the boy's aptitude or Tildor's needs better served by training him as a thermal mage. Or a battle mage. Whether the boy is allowed to Heal others and stay safe or forced to kill and risk his life, is not up to him. That is Tildor's law." Seaborn rocked back on his heels. "Yes, you are fighter cadets, not magistrate cadets. But, you will kill more people with the law than you will with the edge of your sword. Understand it, my friends. Know its reasons. In fact"—he smiled—"write about it. Five pages before week's end. Dismissed."

That last did not apply to her. Renee stayed seated until the last of her classmates cleared the room, shook her head at Alec, who waited by the door, then rose to strike attention before Seaborn. Her stomach clenched.

He sighed and rubbed his chin. "Up late with your sword, cadet?"

"Yes, sir. I'm—"

"On probation in combat arts. I know." He sat on the edge of his desk. "I am not down-rating you this time, Renee, but this is your warning. No late assignments, no missed classes." His voice was gentle. "A cadet will be cut at midyear and a down-rate in academics will affect your class standing. I don't believe such would help your predicament and do not wish to do such things. But I will. You understand?"

Only Seaborn could issue an ultimatum that left *you* feeling guilty. She nodded.

He patted her shoulder. "Dismissed."

Renee started to leave, but a thought scratched at her mind. "Sir, Vipers want to end mage registration. They even burned down an official post three days ago. But . . . Why do they care?"

Seaborn smiled and held the door open for her. "A group that enslaves fighters into Predator pits demands freedom for mages. Ironic." He paused. "But can you think of a better way to recruit mage support? The Vipers' Madam is ruthless and blood-lusting, but unfortunately not stupid." His face grew serious. "There are now more unregistered mages allied with the Vipers than there are unregistered mages in all the rest of Tildor."

Renee swallowed. The Family caused enough heartache on their own, without Vipers and their illegal mages dragged into the melee. *A disease of crime.* King Lysian was right.

CHAPTER 6

Renee aimed her blow at Alec's head. He blocked late and their blades locked a hand-width above his forehead. Her arms shook from the strain, sweat stinging narrowed eyes, but he shook too. With her sword pressing down and his up, the advantage was hers. They both knew it. She had practiced the attack all summer.

"Halt!" Savoy's voice broke them.

Renee's jaw tensed as she obeyed the order, stepping away without seeing her score connect.

Alec gave her a minute bow, conceding the match despite its premature end. He never begrudged her her victories, not even in junior years when they were of a size and she beat him nine of ten bouts.

Savoy rubbed his temple. "He outweighs you by three stone. What in the Seven Hells are you doing, de Winter?"

Winning. She clasped her hands behind her back.

"You think you can overpower him? Or anyone in this salle?"

Her knuckles tightened. "Yes, sir. If I create the right circumstance."

Savoy raised his head, pitching his voice over the salle. "Class halt! Push-up position. Knuckles and toes, backs straight, eyes on me. Hold." He lowered himself directly in front of her. "Start creating."

A minute passed. Two. Three. Renee's shoulders trembled. Sand had scraped the skin off her knuckles and now grated into the sores each time she adjusted her fists. Sweat dripped into her eyes, slid to the point of her nose, and fell to a puddle forming on the sand. Her right arm cramped in inevitable surrender. Her knees sagged toward the sand.

"Recover!" Savoy called a hair before she failed. He held her gaze, driving his point deeper while the class around them reclaimed its footing. Girls and weaker boys didn't belong among Fighter Servants. They weren't worthy of becoming the Crown's champions.

Renee drew a breath and held it. Savoy was testing her resolve, goading her to work harder, to be better. She would.

The door creaked. At Savoy's nod, Seaborn slipped inside. "Commander, when you finish, Master Verin requests to see us."

Savoy's face tensed for an instant before he collected his feet under him and rose. "Dismissed," he called, dusting his hands against his britches.

Renee stared at the backs of her classmates who poured out the door, Tanil at their lead. By Savoy's tradition, anyone who failed to finish an exercise owed two hundred push-ups. She hadn't technically failed, but they both knew why. She didn't need favors.

She swallowed and, before she could change her mind, claimed a spot by the wall. Her muscles protested the renewed abuse and she worked her fingers, staring at her raw knuckles. She could lay her hands flat. *No.* Erring on the side of honor, Renee planted her fists into the sand. The discomfort would thin once she started the exercise. Two hundred. Given enough time, anyone could do two hundred. Hells, anyone could do two thousand if they stayed at it long enough. Up and down. Small, easy steps.

She managed twelve.

Collapsing every dozen moves, she did not realize Savoy was still there until he dropped down beside her. His push-ups, easy and controlled, rose and fell in unison to her rhythm. "How many left?"

"One hundred forty."

"Korish . . ." Seaborn's voice trailed off when Savoy held up a finger without breaking form. Seaborn sighed, pushed away from the wall he had leaned on, and headed out. "Very well. I will tell Verin you will join us shortly."

Savoy nodded and kept Renee's pace even when she could manage no more than two or three at a time. The companionship scrubbed the exercise of shame, turning soreness from misery to challenge. When they finished, she rubbed her arms and looked up at him, trying to hold on to the string of connection that mutual suffering forged. "Thank you, sir."

He extended a hand to help her up. "You're weak."

The string broke. Renee bowed quickly, hiding her face.

"That wasn't fair, sir." Alec stood by the door, his hands buried deep in his pockets and shoulders slouched as if bracing

45

against a storm. He lifted his face. "You're not treating her fairly."

"Fair gets you killed." Savoy dusted sand from his hands. "Your friend thinks she can do the same things you do." He picked up his bag and slung it over his shoulder. "She's wrong."

In Renee's head, her father nodded with satisfaction. *No amount of training turns a cockroach into a wolf.* Her fist tightened around her scar. She should have died with her mother at the Family's hands, but she had not. She was a fighter cadet for a reason. She would be a Servant. And she would *correct* weaker muscles, not surrender to them. She would beat the boys on their terms. She just needed to work harder.

"He's an unreasonable horse's ass." Alec pushed a branch out of the way, letting Renee walk ahead of him down Rock Lake Path. The wind whispered in the canopy above them, as if wishing to weigh in with its own opinion. They were just past a month into the school year, the air only slightly cooler, yet the summer days of liberty already seemed far gone. "He tries to break you."

"He tries to see *whether* I'll break. That's different."

"He's singling you out."

Renee angled to face him. "Last year, the Seventh rescued three hostages from the Family, found five weapon caches, and tracked down an unregistered mage on the Vipers' payroll. And that's just from the missions we know of. If the commander of the Seventh wishes to single me out, he's welcome to do it."

"He—" Alec cut off as noise reached them from the lake below.

"Madam is displeased," said a low voice. "Your pup lost. Payment came due three days ago."

"Tell her to credit it against the next win," answered a whiny tenor that Renee recognized as Tanil's. A slap sounded, and the whine turned to a whimper.

Madam, pups, payment. Tanil was betting on *Predators?* The Vipers forced their captives to fight for sport, and here a Servant cadet was actually laying wagers to line the criminals' pockets? Renee was incredulous. King Lysian had spoken of the disease of crime, and here it was, lurking on Academy grounds.

Alec's hand tightened on Renee's shoulder. "Don't." He sighed, attempting a reasonable tone. "What will you accomplish besides earning yourself enemies?"

She detangled his grip. "Bear witness and report them."

"On what evidence? Did you see what happened when the Crown tried it?"

He meant the Viper attacks terrorizing Atham ever since Lysian's arrest decrees. The Crown took decisive action, and criminals responded with violence, trying to cow the king into passivity. It wouldn't work. There or here.

"I need time," Tanil protested. "No. Wait. Look here." There was a rustling sound of a bag opening.

The voice laughed. "Put that away. In lack of coin, Madam will again accept information. That much you can scrape up, can't you? The Family must have another corn merchant somewhere. One week." Twigs crackled under receding footsteps.

If she hurried, she might catch up. Renee shoved passed Alec and headed toward the sound in the woods.

"Gods," he whispered under his breath, but came up beside her.

They made it several paces when a child's shriek stalled their retreat.

"Filthy spy!" Tanil shouted.

There was a splash. A yelp. Then growling. The noises sounded in rapid succession, freezing Renee in place. Taking a breath, she turned again and sprinted down the hill—

And skidded to a halt in the middle of the beach, where a large white dog bared his teeth at Tanil. He backed away, his eyes glued on the salivating fangs. Meanwhile, in the water, Diam struggled to keep from drowning. Rock Lake had no waves, but its banks dropped abruptly close to the shore, creating deep, hidden pools. The boy's choking made a sickening harmony to the dog's low rumble.

Teeth flashed in the sunlight. The dog crouched, ready to pounce on Tanil.

"Khavi, down!" Alec shouted, stumbling onto the sand while Renee dove into the lake.

Air caught in her chest, and her head rang from the cold as she lifted her head and took her bearings. On her right, Diam flailed, sucking in more water than air. She swam toward him. Boots dragged in the water and she reached the boy just when the lake closed over his head. "Diam! Take my hand!"

The boy seized her like a python. And pulled her down.

She screamed for him to let go but he held on, squeezing with all the strength his thin arms allowed. Drawing a breath, Renee dove under and twisted to pry off the boy's hold. Ice water poured into her ears. Her leg cramped. Finally, and much too slowly, Diam's grip failed under the pressure and she maneuvered them both to shore.

"What . . . in . . . the Seven Hells?" She braced her hands on her knees, gasping between words while Diam coughed his way back to consciousness.

"That mad animal attacked me!" Tanil pointed to Khavi, who snarled despite Alec's grip on the collar. It was a good accusation, and one Tanil's bleeding calf supported. The Academy frowned on pets and would not tolerate dangerous ones.

"That's not what happened." Diam wiped his mouth and rose to his feet. "You grabbed me!"

"Shut your trap."

"Shut yours," said Renee.

Tanil's eyes snapped to her, then to Alec. He winked at the latter and stuck his hand inside a pocket. Something crinkled, like dry leaves breaking against each other. "Go back to the barracks," he said, still looking at Alec. "I scratched myself on the rocks. No harm done."

Alec sniffed the air and paled. "Let's go, Renee." He reached for her shoulder.

She jerked away. "What are you talking about?" she demanded, but he would not meet her gaze. "He torments a boy half his age and you want to walk away?"

49

"Renee. Let it be," Alec repeated.

Tanil grinned.

She cocked her fist.

The grin froze on Tanil's face. "You don't wish to do that." He reached into his coat and threw a small sack onto the sand. Veesi leaf, the lifeblood of the Family business, spilled from the open top. "If we return with bruises, Master Verin will ask all sorts of questions, won't he, Alec? And we all know what will happen if Verin catches you with veesi again."

Alec's pallor turned green.

Renee's eyes widened at the shameless lie. Alec hadn't touched the stuff in years. "None will believe you," she said, stepping next to her friend. "Our word will count over yours."

"Will it?"

Alec cringed. "Tanil's right. I'm the only one who's ever been caught. They'll never believe it wasn't mine." He lowered his eyes and added quietly, for Renee's ears alone, "And I can't have them search my room. You shouldn't have pushed it."

Her stomach sank. "You promised me, Alec. Bloody gods. You promised." She looked at him a few seconds longer, wondering how she could have missed the signs. Her ignorance stung as much as his lie. She turned toward Tanil. Her arm ached to punch his smug face. "Go." She stuck her hands inside soggy trouser pockets. "Go care for your scratch."

Tanil collected his bag of filth and offered a mocking bow before departing.

She stood silently, watching him disappear from view, then

walked to Diam. The boy shivered, wet, sandy clothing sticking to him in patches. She needed to get him warm, to get them both warm. "Let's go up."

Diam shook his head. "Khavi hurts."

On cue, the dog lifted his head and whimpered.

"Easy, boy." Alec crouched and ran his palm over Khavi's fur, wiping away blood. "Tanil caught him with a stone." He kept his head bent. "I'll care for him."

"I know," Diam said.

The certainty in his voice made Renee stare at the strange little boy before holding a hand out toward him. He slipped his small, cold palm into hers and they picked their way up the trail, sodden boots squeaking with each step. They had almost made it to the pages' wing when a familiar voice hailed them.

"De Winter! Savoy! Stop. What happened to you two?"

Renee froze and turned toward Verin. She didn't see Savoy. "Ah, I don't know where Commander Savoy is, Master Verin."

"I suggest you find him."

She frowned. "But, sir, you just said—"

"He's talkin' to me," piped the small voice beside her. "I'm Savoy. Diam Savoy. Why do we gotta find Korish, Master Verin?"

Verin gave the boy a severe look. "So that he can sort out whatever mess his student and his brother got themselves into."

51

CHAPTER 7

Brother. Savoy's little brother had heard the exchange at Rock Lake and now held Alec's secret in his eight-year-old hands. Her eyes flickered down to where her fingers wrapped around Diam's, and she fought off an impulse to jerk away. As if reading her thoughts, the boy squeezed tighter and tugged her toward the instructors' quarters.

The Savoy who opened the door to room fifteen scarcely resembled Renee's training master. He panted, sweat dripping from his hair onto bare shoulders and sliding along muscle grooves. His worn-out breeches never belonged to a Servant's uniform, and the blade resting in his hand voiced a threat so powerful that Renee took a step back before catching herself.

"Ah, M-M-Master Verin ordered us here," she stammered, justifying their intrusion.

"I see." Savoy swallowed, catching his breath. He rested his sword against the wall and reached for a discarded shirt. A tangle of long, thin scars crisscrossed his back. He dressed and stood aside, letting them in.

The room was larger than a cadet's, and seemed even more so owing to the exile of all furniture into a single corner, leaving a clear space in the middle. There were no pictures or mementos. Weapons hung on otherwise bare walls, and smells of oil, leather, and flint filled the air. A travel pack stood beside the door, like a saddled horse awaiting departure.

Savoy cleared his throat, and the events of the past hour rushed back to Renee's head. Her heart raced. She couldn't tell Savoy anything, not without sacrificing Alec. What if Diam told? She needed a moment to think. "Did we interrupt your training, sir?" she asked. "Why don't you practice in the salle?"

"Why don't you two tell me why you're dripping all over my floor."

So much for time to think.

"'Cause we're wet," Diam said, and reached for his brother's sword.

In one smooth motion, Savoy intercepted the intruder and sat him atop the bureau.

The boy muffled a cry of glee, but pleasure danced impishly in his eyes.

"Diam." Savoy crossed his arms and scowled. Now face-to-face, the brothers startled Renee with their likeness. Although the solid, athletic Savoy dwarfed the skinny, squirmy Diam, the two had matching green eyes and identical stubborn expressions.

The boy fidgeted. "We helped the stable hands water the horses and got into a water fight, and got wet."

Savoy raked his hand through his brother's blond curls. "And the sand?"

"I fell on the practice courts when we walked back."

"You fell. Did de Winter fall too?"

Diam glanced at her. "No, she didn't fall, but she helped me stand up, so she got all sandy too."

"Which is why she has sand all over her clothes?" Savoy turned to her before Diam could answer. "All right, de Winter, your turn. And before we continue down the same path, I remind you that I am your commanding officer."

The warning eliminated the option of lying. "We took an unplanned swim in Rock Lake, sir."

"Do I wish to know details?"

"Probably not, sir."

He crossed his arms and stared at her, his green eyes penetrating yet revealing nothing of his thoughts. "Very well."

She blinked. "That's all?" The words left her mouth before she realized she was speaking.

"I will not punish you for playing rough or getting wet. Is there a reason why I should give you misery?"

Hearing no sarcasm in his voice, Renee swallowed and dropped her gaze, the deception gnawing at her.

Diam came to the rescue for a second time. "No, no reason. I'm cold!" he declared from his perch atop the bureau and scampered down using the drawers for footholds. Grabbing her hand, he towed her to the door. "Let's go change!"

A voice stopped them as they headed out. "De Winter."

She turned, met Savoy's eyes once more, but said nothing.

He nodded. "See you in class."

"Yes, sir," she mumbled, bowing and turning away once more. Savoy's unexpected laxity unsettled her.

A few hours later, everyone gathered in Sasha and Renee's room. Khavi vaulted onto Renee's bed, demanding attention. She ruffled the dog's fur and found a thin, healing cut in place of what had seemed a vivid gash a few hours back. Alec had done an excellent job sewing the wound.

Sasha crossed her legs and swept the group with a glance. A magistrate to the core. "So, Tanil caught Diam watching a compromising situation and tried to scare him into keeping his mouth shut." She said the words with small-talk ease that Renee didn't mistake for nonchalance. "Then you two showed up and he turned to blackmail."

"Exactly like Tanil to get brave when someone's too small to fight back." Renee stuck her hands into her pockets.

Sasha bit her lip. "Lord Palan is of the Family. High up too. What's his nephew doing talking to Vipers?"

"Gambling." Alec shook his head and glared at Diam. "You never said you were Savoy's brother." The anger in his voice startled Renee. All heads turned to him.

"I didn't tell on you," Diam shot back.

"And you, Alec, promised to dump the veesi," Renee stepped in. "So, worry about yourself right now."

"If Tanil knew about Savoy, he'd never have started with Diam," said Alec. "None of this would have happened."

"And if you'd dumped the veesi like you promised, we could

55

have . . ." She rubbed her forehead. What was done was done. "You need to get rid of it."

Silence loomed until Alec lowered his face and swallowed. When he spoke, the words barely broke a whisper. "I can't."

"Like hell you can't. The stuff makes people stop caring. Idiots destroy their lives because nothing concerns them." She ignored his flinch. "And they destroy other people's lives in the process."

He lifted his gaze to meet hers. "You see me stop caring about anything or destroying my life?"

Renee paused. He didn't show the lethargy and nonchalance of a veesi user. "I see you destroying your career this minute. Correction, I see *it* destroying your career."

Several moments passed before Alec spoke again. "It has no agenda. You make veesi sound evil."

"It is."

"It's not," said Sasha, drawing startled looks from both of them.

Renee glared at her roommate. "Taking his side?"

"Taking the facts' side. Veesi masks pain," she said simply. "That makes it dangerous, not evil."

Renee rolled her eyes. Sasha would assign degrees to evilness next, and write an opinion essay on it. "I'm not talking Healers' salve. Dolts chew the leaves, get high, and dance off to do stupid feats while the Family or Viper coffers gain. It—"

"Veesi doesn't give you a high," Alec cut in, the voice of experience. "It relieves emotional pain the same way its salve takes pain from a cut."

"And your life is oh so painful, right?"

"I heard the guard talkin' about using it," said Diam.

Sasha nodded. "The guard uses it to control mages in custody. It inhibits their ability to Control."

"Does it make them happy?"

"No, it makes them nauseous," said Alec. "Like chewing something that makes you blind, only worse."

Diam crinkled his nose. "Mean."

"How about a guardsman binding a prisoner's hands?" Sasha said without missing a beat. "You can't use rawhide strips to bind a mage's Control, only veesi. It works as punishment too."

Renee frowned, caught off guard by the turn in the discussion. The last bit of information surprised her. "That's not right," she said after mulling it over. "Forcing someone to chew veesi isn't right."

Alec ran a hand through his hair and shrugged.

Sasha smiled. "Was it right for Savoy to hit you? That arm looked awful."

"That's different!" Renee rubbed her forearm, which tingled on contact. "He was demonstrating a point."

"Your career relies on your arm. A mage's career relies on his Control. Doesn't sound too different to me."

Renee found no reply.

CHAPTER 8

Savoy sat on a practice court fence and, seeing Lord Palan waddle toward him, braced himself for a headache. The sight of Diam trotting along the fat man's side turned annoyance to caution. The lord often appeared like this during Savoy's own time as a cadet and, despite Palan's unfailingly courteous manner, the encounters had always left Savoy feeling unsettled, as if he were a pawn in an unknown game.

"Korish!" Diam sprinted forward. "Look what Lord Palan gave me!" Bouncing on his toes, the boy produced a spyglass from his pocket and presented the treasure to Savoy. Sparks of excitement in Diam's large green eyes threatened to set the wooden fence aflame.

Savoy's stomach churned. Shooting Lord Palan an angry glare, he squatted to his brother's eye level. Diam stopped bouncing and tensed.

"You must give it back."

"No! Why?" The boy's face grew dark. "It's a present, isn't it, Uncle Palan?"

The old sense of a game returned. Savoy's jaw tightened. "*Lord* Palan, that's first. Second, Servants don't take gifts from nobles. Otherwise, we'd be Lord Palan's Servants and not the Crown's."

He reached toward his brother, but the boy pulled back. Refusing to look away, Savoy turned up his palm, demanding the sacred object. He received it via projectile. Diam shot him a hate-filled look and stalked off.

Watching the boy's receding back, Savoy took several breaths before standing up and glowering at Lord Palan.

The older man sighed and patted a handkerchief over his sweaty brow. "He's eight, Commander. It's a present, not a bribe. Next time, he simply won't tell you."

"Next time, he'll face Verin."

"Then don't tell Verin." Lord Palan's tone took on the note of frustration. "Though you never could learn than one."

"I'm daft. Now, my lord, did your visit have a purpose beyond giving me a headache? If not, I assure you that you've accomplished your task."

Something akin to disappointment flickered across Palan's face, but a fake smile rushed in to conceal it. "Of course. I only came to check on my nephew. The day seemed right."

"Tanil is cowardly, but works hard when cornered like a rat in a cage. Anything else?"

There wasn't, although the encounter left a sour taste in Savoy's mouth that clung for the rest of the day.

In the evening, after the last of the classes let out and with two hours of daylight left to spare, Savoy retreated into the back woods. The dense forest concealed many trails, clearings, and caves, luring cadets into exploratory voyages. The more courageous trekked farther than they should. At one time, Savoy and

Seaborn knew the woods better than its resident squirrels did.

Those were deceiving years, his junior ones at the Academy. With both parents mercenaries, Savoy had spent little time in one place—much less a place with children—before getting bundled off to the Academy. He'd seen more battles by age eight than most cadets did by graduation and, having survived those experiences, knew himself to be both invincible and, despite his smaller size, talented. The only uncertainty was in deducing how to extract the most amusement from his new school while suffering the least punishment and workload. Friends were never intended to be part of the equation. Seaborn just happened.

And he paid for it. They both did.

The grassy alcove where Savoy stopped saw little traffic. The surrounding evergreens, soft ground, and converging trails showed few signs of human intrusion. Kye cantered around the clearing, bucking the air to work off his pent-up energy while Savoy leaned against a tree. The second horse he'd brought, a bay gelding named Lava, showed more interest in grass-chewing than bucking, which was why Savoy chose him.

A birdcall disturbed the silence an hour past the appointed time. Savoy cupped his hands and responded with an identical tune. The poison of last-minute doubt crept through him, questioning the wisdom of opening old wounds. He shook it off. "You're late."

"My apologies." Seaborn entered the clearing. "A conversation detained me. It seems the City Guard found another corn merchant's body not far from Atham."

Savoy shrugged. Such things happened, and Seaborn somehow always knew of them.

"The attackers took his corn and left his purse, Korish. The two puncture wounds on his neck are a Viper signature, except I can make little sense of what Vipers may wish with corn." Seaborn scrubbed his face and leaned against a tree trunk. He was strong and athletic, like the fighter he should have been. "I'm here now, however. Why the secrecy? Please tell me you did not steal that horse."

"No, I learned that lesson quite well, I believe." Savoy hesitated. "An idea struck me."

Seaborn chuckled. "Good gods help me."

"I brought the gelding for you to ride."

The mirth faded from Seaborn's face. "I don't ride."

"You did. We did. I'll teach you."

"I've seen you teach, Korish. I think I'll pass on the experience."

"When did you become the fragile butterfly?" The words escaped before Savoy could stop them. The day two boys learned the limits of their invincibility remained imprinted in his mind, but this was the first time he challenged aloud Connor's choice to abandon the fighter track.

Seaborn's look could freeze flame, and Savoy felt a void spreading between them. He'd been a fool to try this. And he'd be a fool to stop. When Connor started to walk away, Savoy blocked the path.

"Move, Korish." Connor's voice was dangerously quiet.

Savoy crossed his arms.

"You wish to fight?" Connor met him stare for stare. "You think us fifteen?"

"Think you can take me?"

"No, Korish, I don't. And I'm all right with that. I have responsibilities that don't include one-upping you, stealing dessert from the mess hall, or going along with whatever suicidal idea enters your skull."

"Too busy reading?"

"Grow up, Korish." He paused. "I did." Saying nothing further, Seaborn walked around Savoy and left.

Savoy watched his friend disappear down the path, then twisted around and slammed his fist into the nearest tree. He struck again and again, seeing different faces appear in the trunk. Connor's. Lord Palan's. His own. That of the idiotic, unknown official who hauled him back to this cursed place.

A snort from behind got his attention. Kye had stopped frolicking and now pawed the ground, ready for battle. Savoy knotted Lava's reins and sent the gelding toward the stable before vaulting into Kye's saddle and, heedless of the setting sun, kicked him into a gallop.

CHAPTER 9

Lightning ripped through the early autumn sky, startling clouds into a downpour. Alec snatched the half-finished mapping assignment from Renee's hands and tucked it into his tunic. "Figures."

Renee shielded her face. "We can still memorize the pace count." Daylight had dimmed behind the clouds, and night approached swiftly through the rain.

Alec took her shoulders and turned them toward the main Academy grounds. "We'll finish it tomorrow. It isn't as if either of us has Queen's Day plans." He sighed. "That's it, isn't it. That's what's spurring today's masochism?"

Renee shrugged. Queen's Day was for family, and even the Academy suspended classes to welcome parents onto its grounds. Not Lord Tamath de Winter, of course, but he had been absent for three years anyway. It was for the better. She didn't need Savoy informing her lord father that all the failures he assigned to his daughter were, in fact, accurate. And her mother . . .

Alec squeezed her arm. His own family never came to Queen's Day, his grandmother being too old for the trip and his mother estranged since his birth. The situation seemed to bother him little, however, as, poking her shoulder, Alec offered up his miracle solution to most of life's issues. "Let's eat."

Despite having rolled her eyes, Renee found that a bowl of hot porridge did improve her spirits, enough even that after returning to her room and hanging damp clothes up to dry, she could ask Sasha's plans without fighting a hitch in her own voice.

"Palace." Sasha, who saw no reason to pull her nose out of the thick volume weighing down her desk, traced her finger down the page. "I'm going to tell Lys he's an idiot."

"Some Servant you are."

"As a Servant, I enforce his laws." Sasha tapped a line and picked up a pen. "As his cousin, I tell him he's an idiot. And tomorrow, I'm his cousin." She scratched out a note and looked up, her face flushed. "Do you know what he did when the Vipers burned down that registration post? He denied audience to the Madam's emissary and turned the arrest decrees into death warrants. That's . . . that's like lighting a match in a barn full of straw, Renee! Walks around like a rooster now, saying he won't bow his head to criminals."

The liberties Sasha took in discussing the Crown, though only in private, made Renee blanch even after years of exposure. "My father *pays* the Family to leave his wagons alone," Renee offered. "The price grows each year. You think that's better?" She fell back on her bed.

"Victory in war does not come from fighting battles. It comes from winning them." Sasha tapped her book. "Lys's just fighting. And you think that's great because you like the cause. And I think the Crown is about to get a bloody nose or worse!" She paused for breath and blinked, rubbing her forehead. "Speaking of tomorrow, I near forgot to ask . . . Would you be my Queen's Day dinner bodyguard?"

Renee raised her brows. The Palace Guard was responsible for palace security and hated outside interference, especially from the military. "The Palace Guard will never permit it." She could already see Fisker's face darken at seeing a cadet interfere with his work. "And why bodyguards at a family dinner to begin with?"

"A compromise. With the recent unrest, the guard captain wanted extra palace security in the dining room and Lys didn't. They finally agreed that Fisker's team will remain outside and each guest will choose his own bodyguard to bring inside. I asked that you be mine. If you don't mind, of course—"

Renee vaulted up to hug her friend, not bothering to muffle a cry of glee. She was going on her first field assignment. In the *palace*. With the Crown himself in attendance. "Do you know who will stand behind King Lysian?" she asked upon reclaiming some semblance of dignity.

"Last I heard . . ." Sasha made a show of rubbing her lip in thought. "Who was it? Oh. Right. Servant Commander Korish Savoy." She smiled. "He wanted you to come see him tomorrow. You two are the only ones coming from the Academy."

"The only ones?" Renee echoed, licking her lips. The only ones. Just her and the commander of the Seventh.

Excitement roused Renee from bed before dawn the next morning. Her sword, sharpened and polished, hung on her hip. She ran her hand over the pommel, engraved with the crest of the de Winter estate. The sword had been intended for her brother, but Lord Tamath had gifted it to her back when he believed her capable of graduating, when he thought she'd grow as strong as Riley had once promised to be.

Still, it was her blade now, and together they were heading to their first real mission. Renee smiled. Her uniform was pressed. Her boots polished. And, despite her stomach's rebellion at the thought of food, she was ready. She was not, however, suicidal, and thus confined herself to loitering outside Savoy's quarters instead of waking him.

She was still there when a whirlwind of a boy in a nightshirt raced through the corridor and vaulted past her into the room.

"Korish!" Diam's voice escaped into the hallway. "Korish! There's someone under my bed."

A pause. Renee held her breath.

The bed creaked. "Go kill it," said Savoy.

"I don't wanna kill anyone."

A sigh. "Ask de Winter to do it. She clearly has no better activity for this hour of the morning. Guarding my room notwithstanding."

Her cheeks heated. Taking the comment for invitation, Renee edged her way inside. With the furniture back in place, the quarters looked almost normal, except for the small boy curled at Savoy's side.

"There's somebody under my bed," Diam informed Renee gravely, then turned back to his brother. "A page said Mother and Father couldn't come today 'cause mercenaries aren't allowed."

Mercenaries? Renee kept her face still. Soldiers for hire held little reputation for honor.

"Horse shit." Savoy spoke to his brother but looked at her, daring a comment. When she made none, he extracted himself from the bed and tossed a blanket over Diam's head. "They don't come because they have a contract in the west, at the Devmani border, guarding a merchant caravan from unwelcome neighbors."

"Why?" The wool muffled the question.

"Because a new king is an appetizing target." He turned to Renee and sighed. "You're attending this evening's farce with me, aren't you? All right. One—eat. Two—it's Queen's Day *dinner*. Early is good, this early is ridiculous. The day is yours until the second afternoon bell. I will meet you by the practice courts then. Three"—he pointed to a weapon standing beside his—"you will carry that blade and not the club you've strapped to your hip."

Her heart sank. It was a junior sword, the kind carried by young cadets not strong enough to wield the real thing.

Half an hour before the appointed time, Renee pulled herself up on a practice court fence to await Savoy, who still spoke with parents and students. It was odd to hear his voice blending with dozens of others. Usually, when Savoy spoke, no one else did.

She stood to stretch her shoulders and froze. Walking beside two well-dressed nobles was her father. His gaze passed through her as if she were fog. She waited a few moments, but the group continued toward the main courtyard, quickly leaving the practice courts—and her—behind.

"Father!"

He walked on.

She called out again, starting toward him.

One of his associates pointed in her direction. Her father hesitated before turning. She slowed her step. This was her world, not his study.

They halted two spans from each other. Just two large steps, but it could have been a league. Renee didn't expect hugs and smiles. Neither did she expect him to look as if he had swallowed a leech.

She bowed formally at the waist, like an officer. "My lord father. Gentlemen."

Her father pursed his lip. "Cadet."

One of his companions cleared his throat. "Forgive my manners, my lady, I did not know to expect you." A smile spread over the man's face as he turned back to her father. "Why, my lord Tamath, I believe I understand how you were able to secure passage onto these grounds. And why you insisted we come today."

Understanding gripped her stomach. Her father wasn't here to see her at all. He was here to call upon the administration, likely in an attempt to sell the estate's crops. Lord Tamath had not so much as told his colleagues of Renee's existence.

He scratched his mustache. "My time is spoken for today, Renee. I do not wish my presence to distract from your training."

A chill settled over her.

The other of his companions, a short man with a trimmed goatee, rubbed a finger down the side of his pointy nose. "Tell me," he said, peering toward the practice courts behind Renee, "is it true that they allow commoners to enroll?"

She bowed to him. "Yes, my lord. No distinction is permitted among Servants."

He huffed. "Gods help me, Tamath, if the lady insists on playing soldier, why did you not simply purchase her a commission as befitting your station?"

Renee blinked. The man compared a purchased commission to an Academy education? A Servant *earned* her place. Not that the mustached tree trunk would value that. Very well. She would speak his language. "The two positions are not identical, my lord. Consider the Crown's top advisors, for instance," she said. "How many non-Servants do you see in their ranks?"

"You will use your . . . great knife . . . to cut a path to the Crown's favor, my lady? Your strength must be scarcely matched." He nodded at the junior sword Savoy had insisted she wear and chuckled. "Let us forgo today's business, my lord Tamath, for your daughter's grand plans will surely bring good fortune to our estates."

Lady Renee knew better than to enter into spitting matches with idiot lords. Unfortunately, Cadet de Winter, who happened to inhabit the same body, could not hold back. "I believe one can do more to protect Tildor's land by attaining a Servant's post than by rubbing gold into criminals' palms." She turned her face toward her father. "Although I understand opinions on this matter differ."

He slapped her.

Renee touched her tingling cheek, then made her hand drop away. It was her fault; she had gone too far. Now she struggled not to disgrace her uniform with tears. She felt the eyes on her, curious people waiting to see whether she would meekly accept the humiliation, or run off like a child, or start a scandal. Such things attracted an audience as surely as carcasses called to vultures. Tanil smiled from the safety of the crowd.

"Touch my cadet again, and I will break each one of your fingers," said a quiet voice behind her. "One at a time."

Renee swallowed as Savoy, in his midnight black instructor's uniform, stepped up beside her. He stood motionless, but nothing could conceal the fury spilling from his gaze. Around them, spectators stopped pretending to be otherwise occupied and stared openly. His words repeated themselves in her mind. She was his cadet. He wasn't her friend, he thought her weak, but he would stand beside her without asking what the quarrel was or how it came to be. Servants protected each other's backs because sometimes, too often, there was no one else.

Renee's father cleared his throat, indecision playing in his eyes. He was a good spokesman. Would he apologize that a trivial misunderstanding created such a disturbance? Or puff his chest in indignation? He squared his shoulders. "I apologize, young master. My daughter and I found a poor place for a family squabble."

"Servant," said Savoy.

"I beg pardon?"

"Servant." Savoy crossed his arms. "The proper address is Servant or Commander, not master. You seem to have forgotten where you are, my lord."

"Indeed." Lord Tamath bowed just deep enough to avoid discourtesy. "My partners and I have business to attend to. Please do not let us impose on your time further. Renee, come along and guide us to the clerk."

Savoy put his hands behind his back and shifted his weight just enough to give her freedom of movement.

She took a breath. "I am needed elsewhere, my lord. I will see you . . ." She paused, stumbling on the words. If there had been any chance of regaining a welcome to her father's estates, she had destroyed it. "I will see you at another time."

Savoy's weight shifted back. A small movement but unmistakable.

Alec's face appeared at the edge of the crowd and moved toward her. A moment earlier, Renee was a girl outnumbered. Now she had the whole Crown's army behind her.

At least until midyear exams.

A long table stretched down the palace family dining room. Flickering chandelier candles reflected in the polished wood.

King Lysian sat at the head of the table, his back to the door. The night beyond pressed at the glittering window across the room from him until Savoy opened the glass, reached out, and swung the shutter closed. Lysian sighed but said nothing.

With Queen's Day's emphasis on family, the guests were just that—people who were cousins and grandparents and uncles as deeply as they were esteemed members of the royal household. Sasha's parents sat together, holding hands like enthralled lovers despite their years. Renee swallowed and looked away. A large-eyed toddler clutched a wooden puppy doll and reminded everyone that her name was *Claire*, pointing a chubby finger at her chest and rocking her raised chair until Sasha tickled the girl into silence. Sasha's attempt to carry a political conversation over Claire's bobbing form earned shushing noises. Lysian inclined his head toward her. "This isn't the forum, cousin," he said quietly, his eyes as cool as Savoy's. The topic was not raised again.

Renee rocked back on her heels, studying King Lysian as he fed a scrap to a dog beneath the table. Although Lysian did not appear to remember her, she had seen him with Sasha a few times before, when he was a prince. Once, he had pulled his cousin's braids. Then he grew taller and pulled back her chair instead. Now he silenced her with a look. He was her liege and her cousin, like a gold coin twisting in midair, showing one face, then the other.

The room erupted in laughs at someone's jest. Renee wondered how soon Lysian's easy smile would become a relic, buried beneath duty. Her eyes cut to Savoy, who stood poised, like a stalking cat, behind his king.

By the dessert course, many of the bodyguards slouched where they stood behind the guests' chairs. Renee hid her dismay behind squared shoulders. Savoy, whose gaze roved the room, motioned her to come beside him.

"Something amiss?" he asked quietly.

She inclined her head toward the dozing woman wearing the colors of a wealthy local noble and theoretically protecting the royal grandmother.

Savoy shrugged. "A farce, as I said. Let us hope the Palace Guard outside know their duty. Most of the guards in here stand as marks of favor, not skill or experience." He frowned at a maid who had brought in fresh candles and now loitered by the large window that faced King Lysian. "Before you give your thoughts voice, realize that that is how you came to be here as well." He tilted his head, speaking quieter still. "Your friend's favor does not change your skills. You struggle amongst fighter cadets, but you would best most anyone here. You—" He didn't finish. Savoy's hand flew to his sword side, thrusting Renee away. His voice pitched clear above the bustle of the room. "Latch the shutter back up."

The maid froze, her face pale. "'Tis beautiful stars out tonight, Servant." She faltered, her fingers plucking her shirtsleeve.

Without warning, Savoy shoved the king's chair back from the table, spilling Lysian to the floor. A startled cry rose around the room. The king grunted, a trickle of blood forming where

73

his brow struck the chair's edge. The shouts grew, crackling with sudden panic. Renee took Savoy's action on faith and yanked Sasha down. A mug of scalding coffee doused them both. Renee's heart began to pound. The guests wailed, Claire's shriek rising above the rest. The dog streaked across the room, frenzied and baying.

"What's happening?" Sasha yelled into her ear.

Renee twisted in search of the danger that had triggered Savoy's action, but saw only a terrified maid fleeing from the window and the flushed face of King Lysian. He blotted his brow with his sleeve and blinked at the stain. Frowning, Renee readied to let Sasha rise.

Which was when the window shattered and an arrow meant for the Crown lodged itself in Savoy's shoulder. He staggered back, and the guests' screams changed.

CHAPTER 10

Shrill, frightened yells filled the air. Guests stampeded toward the door. Porcelain cascaded to the floor and crunched underfoot. Bodyguards, shaken from their trance, shouted to their charges, their raised voices blending.

"Close the window shutter." Savoy's cold command rose above the noise.

Renee spun toward the far wall. Glass fragments littered the floor beneath the broken window, its shutter ajar. Another arrow whistled inside, bursting a wine cask and feeding the panic. The royal guests pressed against the door, fists pounding the unyielding oak. Someone must have sabotaged the lock, Renee realized with indrawn breath. It wouldn't be long before the horde presented a target so large that even the most inexperienced shooter couldn't miss.

Sasha dashed to the exit with the rest.

"No." Renee grabbed her arm. "Get to a corner!"

Before they could move, a large man barreled past, growling and shoving bodies from his way. His paw caught Renee's head and threw her, like a rag doll, against Sasha. They stumbled back, knocking over lit candles. Sasha doused the infant flames before they nipped her dress, while Renee regained the balance a stronger soldier would never have lost.

A few paces away, Savoy overturned a side table and dragged a protesting King Lysian behind it for cover. The king struggled, but Savoy kept him pinned. Renee watched, dimly aware that she couldn't have done that either.

A chorus of wails rose beside the door. Half the bodyguards threw themselves against it, as if their shoulders could crack the heavy wood. The other half found cover for their wards and awaited rescue. No one worked together. Bloody gods, they likely had never even met each other before now. No wonder the arrangement had irritated Savoy.

Another arrow sliced into the room. And another. A woman's scream tore the air.

"De Winter." Savoy's voice was steady, almost bored. "The window." He was shielding the Crown and could not move a span without the young king attempting to escape.

Sasha grabbed Renee's shirt. "Don't leave me."

Renee swallowed. Savoy was right. "Stay flat," she whispered, untangling her friend's fingers. She slithered across the carpet. Bits of pudding and broken pottery riddled the floor. A sharp edge of glass ripped her sleeve and sank into her forearm. She reached the window and crouched beneath it. Sweat beaded on her lip. The arrows came fast now, a rain of shafts that poured into the marooned room. Most crashed into walls and clattered down. Some drew screams of pain. Renee took a breath. She had to close the window shutter. And to reach it, she'd bring her body into the line of firing. *Focus on the task. The window shutter. Close the shutter.*

Renee pulled off her coat and popped up for an instant to throw the cloth over the window's jagged remains. She crouched again as an arrow sliced in, shattering a vase instead of piercing her temple.

"Stay down," Savoy spat.

"I can't see from here."

"I can. The shutter swings in from outside. Extend your hand up and out to feel for the shutter's bottom. I will guide you."

Renee grabbed a napkin from the floor and wrapped it about her hand. She listened and moved, trusting his eyes to be hers. The orders were simple and calm, and she repeated each one in her mind. *Reach up. That's the base. Grip. Good. Now pull.* Nothing moved. Savoy repeated the command, but, reaching overhead as she was, Renee could not budge the heavy metal sheet.

"I can get it," King Lysian growled at Savoy. "Let me up."

Savoy ignored him. "You must grasp farther out for better leverage. Stay down until I say, cadet."

Renee crept to a new position, her face flushed with shame more than fear. Alec could have moved the shutter. Any of the guard—

"De Winter. Pay attention." Savoy's voice cut through her thoughts. "Rise and reach on my mark." Heartbeats ticked, arrows flew through the window, tickling the edge of Renee's vision, a drop of sweat dripped into the corner of her mouth. "Now!"

Rising to her full height, Renee reached out through the shattered glass, grasped the shutter with both hands, and swung it closed. It banged shut just as another arrow thudded against it. And another. And a third.

Renee blinked. Nothing more entered the room.

It was over.

She sagged to the floor, breathing hard.

Around her, the movement took on a pattern. Someone must have unjammed the door, because the guests were gone. Fisker's troop of the Palace Guard, and what must have been all other free guards in the palace, stormed inside. Someone escorted Sasha out. Tear tracks stained her cheeks. Renee wanted to apologize for leaving her, but by the time she found her voice, her friend had disappeared. Two soldiers who knew their business collected the king, covering his body with theirs as they ushered him out. A woman in a captain's uniform, the senior guardsman in the room, interrogated Savoy, periodically turning her head to issue orders.

"Strong work, cadet."

Renee blinked. The captain now stood above her, offering her a hand. Renee scrambled to her feet and stood at attention.

"At ease. You've earned it." The woman motioned to the door. "We seized the maid who exposed the window and stuck a bit of clay into the door lock. She had orders from the Vipers." A burst of yelling tore the captain's attention away from Renee, and she tilted her head to where Savoy stood smiling blandly at a ranting Fisker.

"Incompetent bastard." Spittle flew from the guardsman's mouth and he shook his four-fingered fist in the air. "I'll see you held accountable."

"Mmm." Savoy snapped off the arrow shaft protruding from his shoulder. "I tremble at your importance nowadays, Senior Palace Guardsman Fisker."

The captain rubbed her temple. "Excuse me, cadet, but I must prevent Servant Savoy and Guardsman Fisker from shredding each other to ribbons."

"They're acquainted?"

"Eh?" The captain pulled her gaze from the men. "Oh, them. Fisker claims Savoy cost him a finger."

Renee stared at the familiar scarred stump. "Did he?"

The captain chuckled. "I believe Junior Guardsman Fisker once fell from his horse and cut his hand because Cadet Savoy loosened the saddle girth. But it was embarrassment, not Cadet Savoy, that kept him from attending the Healer until the small gash festered to a problem." She shook her head. "Guardsman Fisker's duty is his life, cadet, and Commander Savoy has cost him his pride too often. Between Vipers, the Family, and Commander Savoy, I'm unsure whom Guardsman Fisker hates more. And," she added as Savoy grinned at Fisker's reddening face,

"that overgrown adolescent feeds the fire each chance he gets."
She shook her head. "Make certain the Healer checks you," the
captain said, nodding at the cuts on Renee's arm before turning
to prevent a brawl.

Overgrown adolescent. Renee almost laughed. Then grimaced.
You didn't laugh on the heels of battle. Did you?

Renee let herself out, wondering why her hands had only
now started to tremble.

CHAPTER 11

The news of the attack must have already reached the Academy. Alec ambushed Renee on her way to the Healer's office and followed her inside, toward the reek of salves and dried herbs.

Despite the late hour, Healer Grovener, a tall, dry twig of a man, looked as immaculate as his workspace. He pursed his lips, spreading disapproval between Renee and the hovering Alec, as if the twin assaults on her flesh and his workspace were a personal affront. He went to wash his hands.

Renee drew a breath, held it, and exhaled slowly. Injuries and Healings were facts of training for fighter cadets, but that didn't make the experience pleasant. Rubbing her face, she stared at the only spot of color in the room—a painting depicting a woman with a blue glow and an eagle perched on her shoulder; Keraldi, who first described the barrier to Healers, some thousand years back.

"I brought that." A boy in a Healer's apprentice robe smiled at her and adjusted his round spectacles. "It's Keraldi and her bonded mage bird, Talon. Once the bond took, they shared sights and feelings."

"Did they?" Renee raised an eyebrow. This was an old story.

Keraldi might have managed to *tame* a mage bird, yes, but more likely Talon was just an eagle. And for certain, the bond was a myth.

Alec shrugged. "There's some evidence for bonding being real. Mostly from before the rebellion, when mages were stronger and mage beasts more common . . ."

Renee grunted doubtfully, but little wanted to debate. "You know entirely too much mage history," she said instead, poking his chest. "But at least you're smart enough never to try to pet a mage beast." Lore held that only wild animals—and of those, only predators—showed Control abilities. The best to be said for animal mages was that they were mercifully rare now. "*Right?*" she pressed.

Alec smiled, but it failed to hide the worry from his eyes.

"I'm really all right," Renee told him quietly as Savoy entered the room. She bowed a greeting to the man, uncomfortably aware that despite an arrow cutting his shoulder, he had controlled the room and King Lysian both, while Renee had been pushed around and nearly failed to shift the heavy shutter.

Alec squeezed her uninjured arm and stepped away to lean against the wall.

"I saw a mage wolf once," the apprentice said. "Defending her cubs from a bear. The wolves will run usually, you know, but not this one. She had the bear writhing on the ground while she herself just stood a few paces away, hackles up and a stream of mage flame flaring. Added three hours to our trip, staying clear of her."

Grovener cleared his throat. "Have you divined a means of Healing without touch, boy?"

The apprentice blushed, hastily extending a blue glowing hand to Renee's shoulder. "May I? Healer Grovener gave his permission."

Renee nodded and the boy laid his hand on her, the hot brush of his energy sliding along her Keraldi Barrier. Despite knowing what was coming, she gasped as the mage nicked an opening and slid past it. From here he could exploit her insides as he pleased. Seaborn had said mages once made a practice of it. That the Mage Council would have the boy's life if he harmed her did little to quiet her heartbeat as his energy coursed beneath her skin. A few minutes passed before the flesh around the cuts on her arm heated and pulled, healing rapidly with the young mage's assistance.

"You seem all right. I found nothing beyond gashes on your arm, and they were shallow." The apprentice pulled back. "Did I hurt you? I tried not to."

"Not at all." She smiled at the boy and rubbed the pink skin now stretching the cuts' edges closed. "Are you far from home?" she asked.

"Half a day's ride, if you have a horse." His face said that his family did not. That would change once the young mage finished his training.

Renee turned to watch Grovener cut away the dirty remains of Savoy's shirt and mop a wet rag around the protruding remains of the shaft. The water in the washbasin reddened. "Do you know if the maid was telling the truth about the Vipers orchestrating the attack, sir?" she asked.

Savoy winced as the blue light shimmering about the Healer's hand touched the wound. "Yes. They issued demands."

"Quiet." Grovener stepped back. "I must remove the arrowhead and sew the muscle before Healing. But I can mend you, boy. This time." He reached for a small blade and hesitated, considering his patient.

"I'll be still," Savoy said dryly.

Grovener clasped the arrow while Savoy braced his good hand on the table's edge. Tinges of nausea gripped Renee under her jaw when the knife pierced flesh. It was ironic, she thought, that a man who trained his whole life to protect himself could allow another to cut him. Healer Grovener need not know attacks and parries to deliver a fatal blow. He could just do it. If he wanted to. And Savoy trusted that the mage would not.

Alec touched her between the shoulder blades and inclined his head toward the door. The warmth of his palm was welcome, like a blanket after a storm. She looked at Savoy.

He stared at the wall while the Healer addressed his shoulder, but he felt her gaze and turned his head. "It's not my first cut, de Winter. I don't need the company."

Blushing, she let Alec lead her back to the barracks.

The next day, early rays of sunlight pulled Renee outside. She hadn't slept. The previous day's assault reenacted itself in her mind all night. Would a stronger fighter, a boy, have done better? Would Sasha have been safer with Alec? Would the screams and blood and crash of shattered dishes ever stop flooding her thoughts? She shook her head and picked up into a run. Dew-covered grass and the shush of green and gold leaves gave the still courtyard and empty walkways a mystical feel. A pair of bickering birds and several early shift guardsmen spiced the silence. She sighed. The guard detail had doubled overnight.

Approaching the training salle, Renee frowned at the open door. Having never yet encountered company during her morning workouts, she secretly considered the room hers. Inside, Savoy flowed from stance to stance in an unfamiliar pattern. Sweat glistened in his hair and framed the angle of his jaw. The blade resting in his left hand slashed a deadly rhythm. He didn't greet her.

Renee's heart quickened. Feeling blood rush to her face, she turned her back to Savoy and claimed an empty part of the salle. She pulled a weapon from her bag, drew a breath, and commenced her routine, begging the movements to clear her mind as neither sleep nor willpower could. She finished one pattern and started another, and then a third, hurrying to get ahead of her thoughts. When she paused, a hand touched her shoulder.

She startled.

"Work with me?" Savoy switched the blade to his right hand and rotated the shoulder experimentally. "That was a request, not an order."

Her skin tingled. Renee brushed hair from her eyes. Rivers did not run uphill, arrows did not fly into the Crown's dining room, and Savoy did not issue requests to cadets. "Why, sir?"

"I'm bored."

She blinked.

He rubbed his temple. "My shoulder, de Winter. I need to work my shoulder and it's boring."

She blinked again. Yesterday he was wounded saving the Crown's life. This morning he was bored. Diam had a longer attention span. "Healer Grovener will be unhappy." She stepped into the center of the salle.

"And I'll know whom to blame if he finds out."

Squaring off with him, Renee saluted, hiding her concern over their lack of padding behind the leveled tip of her practice sword.

She needn't have worried. Savoy's game resembled nothing she saw in class. Instead of blocking her blows, he redirected them to slide off his blade. His attacks were gentle and deadly, a brush across her throat, a slide down her wrist. By the end of the bout she felt as if she were waving a club at a killer bee.

"You never showed us that," she said, panting between rounds.

"I teach the standard style. It works for most fighters most of the time."

"Why aren't you using it, then?"

He raised an eyebrow. "I can't." He extended his arm, holding the practice sword parallel to the ground. A few seconds later his arm began to shake. He retracted the weapon and massaged his shoulder.

"Sorry. I just thought . . . I apologize, sir."

His brows drew together for a moment and then he chuckled. "You thought I'd ignore it?" He nodded to himself. "Of course. That's what fighters do. That's what *you* do. Right?" His blade flashed to her neck, the wooden tip pressing into the groove just left of her throat. His mirth dissolved. "Why rip my shoulder smashing your skull when I can slice your artery? You are just as dead, and I am spared Grovener's rebukes. I fight to win. You fight to prove you're the same as the boys."

His practice sword pressed harder into the soft spot. Renee grew lightheaded and stepped away, blood rushing to her head again. She hadn't asked for the match. Or the condescension. With his reputation, Savoy could afford pet styles, moves that shied from confrontation and snuck in attacks instead of meeting their opponent on even ground. None would hold such choices against *him*. "I fight to prove myself worthy of the privilege of remaining at the Academy. Sir." The last word came out with a hiss she was certain to pay for. "May I be dismissed?"

He cocked his head, regarding her for several seconds. "No." The word was mild. He switched the sword back into his left hand. "Fight."

Fine. She skipped the salute and went for his throat.

The throat moved. And continued moving.

The harder she swung, the more Savoy slid, his very lack of force mocking her efforts. An urge to hurt him suddenly gripped her, and Renee threw her whole weight behind the blows, aiming for his ribs, his thighs, his hurt shoulder. If a blow connected, just one, just once, he'd feel her worth, her potential, he'd know she belonged here with the boys. Her breaths came fast, burning her lungs. The wooden blades quarreled, carrying on a conversation voices could not. The world blurred to a buzz. She . . .

Renee did not realize she had tripped until Savoy grabbed her tunic to steady her on her feet. She shuffled to reclaim her balance, her muscles trembling even at rest. She stared at him, aghast. "I—"

"Saw your first battle a day ago." He put away his blade. "You'll see more."

She wiped her face, realizing through a haze of exhaustion that her mind was quiet for the first time since the Queen's Day dinner. Savoring the tingling relief, she looked at Savoy and knew that he knew. She had needed that fight.

"Thank you, sir." She chewed at her lip. "Will . . . will you be bored again tomorrow?"

"Perhaps."

Renee bowed and drew herself to full height before him. "I *will* get stronger, sir."

"Save it for class. Won't be much use with me." He shrugged and turned away. "And if you plan to play strength games again, de Winter, don't bother showing up."

"Yes, sir." Renee bowed again. "I—I'll be here." One did not turn down a chance to train with the leader of the Seventh, no matter how impractical a style he insisted on teaching.

And, she noted with a smile, the muscles shifting beneath his shirt didn't hurt either.

CHAPTER 12

Tanil breathed shallowly. Southwest stank.

The man calling himself Vert leaned against the dirty stone building on the right side of the alley. Ignoring Tanil's approach, Vert inspected a box of finely rolled Devmani tobacco sticks that Tanil knew were only available in Tildor from a rare handful of Atham smugglers. "One box costs as much as a good riding horse," Vert said without looking up, "and they're bloody painful to find. But Madam likes what she likes." He smiled and secured the parcel inside his vest, the viper tattooed on his biceps dancing with the movement. "And she gets what she likes, don't she?" Vert raised his gaze, cocked his head.

Tanil wiped slick palms on his trousers. Vert was a lowly, stupid peon, nothing more. "Cover up that snake."

The man smiled and pulled his sleeve over the tattoo. "Better?"

Tanil's information had been good, hadn't it? It had to have been. He'd heard his uncle whining about the corn. Tanil gathered his voice. "What did you need, Vert?"

"Oh, Madam sends her compliments. Says your credit's good again. Pleasure doin' business. Come again. Can get you better odds if you place bets early. All that."

Blood rushed to Tanil's face. The moron risked a meeting to

toy with him? He opened his mouth to detail Vert's parental lineage, but caught himself. There was nothing gained in angering the man. "Thank you, Vert." He glanced at the dimming sun and collected himself. "Now, excuse me. Uncle awaits with dinner." And Tanil turned and walked away, ignoring the soft chuckle the Viper directed at his back.

Gutter manners notwithstanding, the Vipers understood something dear Uncle Palan's Family did not. Power needed exercise to grow. While Palan pranced around the capital petitioning—petitioning!—the Crown, the Madam took direct action. The Queen's Day assault stood proof to that, as did the charcoaled remains of the mage registration post.

It was a disgrace that Palan, head of the Family, the wealthiest man in Tildor, didn't acknowledge the truth publicly, always insulating himself from his orders and never dirtying his own hands. The man *liked* playing the mere noble, even when most everyone knew otherwise. The Vipers' Madam was different. She didn't inherit her throne as Palan had, she ripped it away from the old management, from the very Viper lord who had trained her as his assassin. And she was no coward denying her station. Madam didn't bribe people's silence; she took their tongues. Personally. How many mages stood on Palan's payroll? Three dozen? Four? The Vipers hid hundreds. Tanil snorted. Fear controlled Palan. Vipers controlled fear.

Back in the chandeliered dining room of Palan's estate, the sizzling aroma of steak filled Tanil's nose. He fidgeted, waiting for his uncle's sizable rear to get comfortable in the cushioned chair. The comfort-seeking rear end took its time. Palan savored such pleasures. One would think he'd show a little respect for Tanil, considering the deficit in kin.

Of the three Family brothers, the oldest had changed his name and disappeared decades ago with a band of mercenaries. The youngest, Tanil's father, fell into the Servants' hands and kept to the Family code of silence throughout prison and, ultimately, his execution. His sacrifice left the middle brother, Palan, in charge and with patronage of Tanil, however grudgingly the idiot gave it.

Just as Tanil reached for his fork, the room's heavy door swung open. A tall figure in a hooded cloak looked in from the hallway.

"An unexpected pleasure, Yus." Palan smiled. He drank deeply from a silver water chalice and daintily replaced the cup before speaking again. "News on our corn merchants? A single attack may have been accidental, but two . . ."

Yus nodded. "The Vipers learned our route, my lord. I have redirected the remaining veesi to other networks."

Tanil's stomach churned. Who knew the man would obsess over losses so petty? Plus, it was Palan's own greed at fault—if he'd granted his nephew a sustainable allowance, Tanil would not have been forced into alternatives.

The fat man frowned. "Keep at it, Yus."

Tanil ground his teeth. This obsession was breaching all bounds. Good gods, Palan likely expended more coin on the search than he had lost in product. Uncle needed something else to worry about.

"What else?" Palan asked Yus.

"More Vipers are slithering into Atham. I have men in place to thin their numbers."

Palan drank more water and pursed his lips. "No. They target the Crown, as the attack last week proved. So long as they stay off our assets, let them shake Lysian. They push hard enough and he shall welcome us with open arms and closed eyes. Or better yet, he'll send troops against the Madam's stronghold in Catar and it will cost us nothing." Palan smiled again. "The young king does not yet realize his error in so antagonizing the Madam. Once he does, he will be desperate."

Yus bowed low. "Yes, my lord. Might other matters impose on my lord's attention?" His eyes shifted between Tanil and his uncle, and Tanil relished the man's discomfort. The lieutenant was, after all, interrupting the dinner of two very important people.

"Excuse yourself." Palan's words singed the air.

Tanil began to smile before realizing that the order concerned him. Anger and embarrassment heated his blood. Him, the head's next of kin, discarded like a lackey! He glared at both men, but suppressed a futile protest. *Watch your step, Uncle*, he thought before pulling the heavy door closed behind him.

The serving girl appeared a half hour later to tell him that his uncle wished the pleasure of his company. Tanil's stomach growled. The steak would be cold by now. Forcing an appropriately humble expression onto his face, he reentered the dining hall. The cause of his recent exile had departed. "I wish you would permit me to remain and learn from you, Uncle."

"You have other duties, my boy. What of your classes?"

Tanil wanted to roll his eyes. The Academy was another of the coward's roundabout schemes. Servants of the Crown traditionally rose to prestigious posts, and Lord Palan wished to have his man fill such a role. "Savoy is a brainless sadist."

"Who won't flinch to fail you." The words carried no sympathy. The cowardly lord wasn't the one spending his evenings sore and bruised. "Do not trifle with the man."

You want a Servant on the Family books, not me. You deal with it. "He is a risk to our work, Uncle. I want to dispense with him."

"Out of the question."

"I didn't know the Family now fears Servants." Let his uncle explain his way out of that one.

Palan tented his fingertips and laid them atop the tablecloth. "Permit me to clear your misconceptions, boy. Your task, your only task, is to enter the Service of the Crown. Should you fail in that, I will no longer have need of your . . . labors."

Ice gripped the lining of Tanil's stomach. "But Savoy—"

"I don't care whether you polish the man's boots or train until the Seven Hells freeze over. Either way, you will pass and you will graduate. And, for once in your existence, you will fulfill this task independently. The Family needs leaders, not cripples who use my influence as a crutch." He rang for the servant girl. "Mari, pack Master Tanil's gear. He will be returning to the Academy early."

Tanil stared in a combination of disbelief and humiliation. Blood raced through his heart, heating and speeding. So, dear Uncle liked Savoy, did he? And to dare imply that Tanil did not work independently? That hunk of lard, chasing his tail about a sorry bushel of corn, didn't begin to know the connections Tanil maintained.

He fingered a key in his pocket, a gift from the gods found on the opening day of school. The key would ensure his success at practical exams, but that, Tanil knew now, would not be enough to regain peace in his life. He had no intention of spending the rest of the year suffering indignities from Palan *or* Savoy. Those two needed to occupy themselves—and each other—elsewhere. Yes, that was it . . . Let Savoy shift his sights to the dear lord coward. Tanil just needed to figure out a way of handling the bloody dog. One bite at Rock Lake had been quite enough.

He found a smile for his uncle and pushed back the chair.

CHAPTER 13

In the month following the Queen's Day fiasco, Renee's life reclaimed its old pattern, despite an increase in guards now patrolling the Academy grounds. She returned to the palace once to debrief with Fisker, who, as one of the first responders on the Queen's Day scene, was charged with overseeing the investigation into the attack. The man had opened the interview with a threat—no, a promise—to see her hanged for treason for colluding with the Vipers and kept her five hours while she first disproved the accusation and then described details of the attack. Despite knowing he used the same tactic with everyone, Renee had come out trembling.

Meanwhile, more children and young men disappeared from Atham's streets, likely snatched by Viper hands—Madam, it was said, had a taste for harvesting people and breaking them. Sasha confessed that King Lysian had now retreated a step in his aggression against the wanted Viper lords, deescalating death warrants to imprisonment.

"He bought time, but to what end?" Sasha said into the doom of unfinished homework that hung over the barracks. "Now Lord Palan is trying to take advantage of the Crown's troubles and dwindling treasury. Yesterday he offered Lys a purse to help address 'the Viper threat to the Crown.'"

Renee jerked up. "Palan runs the Family. Proof or not, you know he does. The coin is tainted."

"Of course it's tainted." Sasha waved her hand. "And Lys refused it, for now. You must admit, though, it was a wise move on Palan's part. The Crown could never accept a bribe from a crime group, but funds from a wealthy noble to help protect the *Crown* from Vipers, well . . . The residual benefits for the Family can almost be overlooked."

Renee sighed. The Madam tried to bend the king to her will while Lord Palan was luring him to his. At the end, it was the same thing. She glanced at the door. Alec should have been in by now. They had homework to start on. He appeared as if summoned by the thought, his cheeks the apple-red of outside chill.

"Where were you?" she asked.

He dropped his books to feed a log into the fire. "Library." Ignoring her frown, he found a chair and opened his journal to read Seaborn's latest assignment, their major one of the half year. "*Analyze the facts of the case assigned and discuss whether a thief's intentions should be taken into account before passing judgment.* Twenty journal pages due in six weeks. Have you started?" he asked her.

Twenty pages. Renee winced and shot a look at Sasha. As a magistrate cadet, she would have had this course a year earlier; the archives of her mind could save them hours of work.

"All right, all right. Hold on." Sasha pulled an old journal from her drawer and rustled through pages of her neat writing. "Here. In essence, two boys took a pair of the Crown's prized horses for a night ride. Bandits attacked, killing one horse and severely wounding one of the riders. The surviving boy took the blame, but swore that he intended to bring the horses back. Claimed he wasn't a thief."

Renee snorted. "Thieves always claim they had meant to give the loot back."

Sasha shook her head. "In this case the claim was true—all agreed the deed was a jest. The boy just wished to ride the stallion, not keep him. But, the guardsman—who was responsible for said horses and didn't take kindly to a pair of children making him look the fool—claimed that intentions are irrelevant. Said the boy was a thief and a heinous one, since he stole from the Crown himself."

Renee pulled her legs up under her and sat back against the wall. She was inclined to side with the guardsman. "What happened to the boy?"

"Court agreed with the guard. Ordered the boy flogged for horse poaching and sent to the dungeons for treason."

Renee blinked. With Tildor's economy bound to commerce, thieves received harsh treatment, but common reason separated a boy's prank from a criminal conspiracy. "How in the Seven Hells did two boys even get close to the Crown's horses to begin with?"

Sasha's smile confessed that she had awaited the question with some eagerness. She put her palms on the writing table and leaned over them. "They were Servant cadets—fighters—in this Academy."

Cadets? Renee jerked her head toward Sasha. Cadets weren't criminals; they were kids like her and Alec and Sasha. Moreover, they were kids training to do right by Tildor while others did right only by themselves. To scourge a cadet, much less shut him in a dungeon, was to violate . . . something. The word eluded her. The peasants on her father's estate pledged their obedience and lives to Lord Tamath, but he pledged to protect and care for them in return. Did King Lysian owe anything to the Servants who swore to him? Did he owe anything to Savoy, who took his arrow? "Who was it?" she asked softly.

"I don't know." Sasha dropped the journal back into the still-open drawer and shut it with her foot. Her lips tightened as if the lack of information was a personal affront. "The Academy precedes the anti-mage rebellion, so we can narrow things down to several centuries of students and closed records."

The logs in the fire began to crackle and the room filled with a savory aroma of burning hickory. Renee scooted closer to the flame and reached for her ink. The bottle tipped, spilling blackness over the blue trim of her uniform. The cap rolled mockingly under the bed.

Cursing, she righted the bottle, sprang to pull a rag from her trunk, and blotted the mess. At last settling back down, she grabbed another bottle from her desk. The cap slithered off in mid-motion, spilling ink over her hand. She cursed again.

Once an accident, twice . . .

Renee opened her drawer to find all the bottles identically sabotaged and glared around the room. One day she's in battle for the Crown's life and the next she must check her quarters for juvenile pranks. Wonderful.

"We didn't play jest with your ink." Alec held up his hands.

"Yes. Triple promise," a voice added from the doorway. Sloshing mud on the ink-stained floor, Diam and Khavi padded into the room. Beads of murky water dripping from the boy's once blond hair had turned him into a grinning mound of dirt.

Sasha threw a towel at him. "What happened?"

"I learned the jumping-tumble-of-doom. Wanna see?"

Alec stiffened as the equally wet dog rubbed against his side, sniffing his jacket and whining. "What if you go bathe Khavi instead?"

It was a worthy effort, but destined for failure. Diam cocked his head in Alec's direction, smiled, and sprawled himself in front of the fire. "No, we like it here," he announced. And fell asleep.

"You'll lose a student after midyear exams," Seaborn said, his knee testing a chair in Savoy's quarters. "Who do you think?"

"Tanil or Renee." *But you knew that before you asked.* Savoy watched his friend pry off the chair cushion and smack it, eliciting a dull thud. "Quit destroying my furniture."

"I think someone put a board inside the pillow."

"Yes. Me. Put it back."

"Life here too soft for you?"

Savoy perched himself atop his desk. His friend didn't come to speak of furniture. He came to talk about the only topic he cared about these days. Cadets. "Say it, Connor. Or don't say it. Make up your mind."

Replacing the cushion, Seaborn sat down, his eyes inspecting the floor. "I care little for Tanil's fate, but Renee . . . She's got the mind to make a good Servant. It would upset me to lose her. Speak with her about her academic efforts. Your words would do what mine cannot."

And Cory, the Seventh's sergeant, could speak on virtue next. "Connor, you wrote half my papers."

"Which makes me a dangerous evaluator."

"I'm a fighter, Connor. My job is to keep her alive, not to worry about her grammar."

"You are a teacher! Your job is to steer her from trouble and help her graduate. Are your morning sword games accomplishing that?"

"If she deigns to actually use the moves I teach her, they may guard her life." Savoy crossed his arms. "Whether she does, or how she balances time, is her decision."

"A teacher ensures his students make the right one, with books as much as with swords." Seaborn shook his head. "You work with her because you're bored, Korish. But you aren't here for you, and you aren't here to be her friend. Kids make choices based on your guidance. When you get it wrong, they pay the consequences. Stop this before you lead her into trouble."

"She is sixteen, not six, Connor."

"Wake up, Korish! With your looks and status, you could tell a sixteen-year-old girl to drink poison, and she'll want to." He drew a breath. "You don't even see how she looks at you, do you?"

"Bloody gods, listen to yourself." Savoy shook his head. This was the senior cadets' last Academy year, before their two-year field trials. By nineteen they'd take the Servant's Oath and make decisions in the Crown's name. They'd hold others' lives in their hands. And Connor feared granting them control of their own schedule. "Have you even ventured out of Atham in the past five years?" Savoy asked. "There is a world out there, you may have failed to notice. One where people must make their own decisions of what to eat for breakfast. And then deal with the consequences."

Connor sat down and laced his fingers together. He spoke with frustrating calm, as if addressing a magistrate in court instead of a friend in a barracks. "The Seventh, if I recall, primarily runs secret, highly tactical missions in hostile territories. Do you believe that platform gives you the full worldview you speak of? Do you even know the real purpose behind half your assignments?" His hands opened. "So yes, Korish, I seldom leave Atham, and I ride in a wagon when I do go. But I work with the law, which touches more people than the edge of your sword ever can. And I work with cadets, who will likewise touch others."

Savoy stared at the invisible wall of words that his friend erected between them. "You tangle in abstracts, Connor. I'm a fighter."

Connor raised his brows. "Abstracts? Like laws that treat children as hardened criminals?" His voice dropped and he leaned forward, bracing his elbows on his knees. "You hiding from everyone for two years did not make me blind. What happened to you—"

"Was what I deserved and what I needed." Savoy shoved himself away from the desk. "I went from hooligan to master swordsman. Don't fix what isn't broken, Connor. And sure as hell don't do it under my flag."

"Verin—"

"Saved my life." Heated blood rose to Savoy's face and he locked eyes with Connor, daring him to so much as consider contradicting.

Connor held up his palms. "Forgive me," he said softly, and dropped his face down before turning to the window. Outside, the wind ruffled golden leaves. The transition from summer heat to autumn chill had been as gradual as a cliff. "I heard the Crown recalled the Seventh."

A peace offering. Savoy swallowed, accepting the change in conversation and letting his heart reclaim its normal beat. His men were coming. Verin had handed him the stack of documents that morning, including permission for the Seventh to lodge at the Academy's guest barracks. For all his words at the year's start, Verin knew a unit worked best when whole. "Under guise of 'inspection and training.'" Savoy replied, and allowed a smile at Seaborn's snort. "Should be here toward autumn's end."

"A mission?"

"A precaution." Savoy stretched his shoulders. "The Madam ordered the Queen's Day attack. She is unlikely to give up after one bout."

CHAPTER 14

On the sand floor of the salle, Renee leaned into a stretch and shuddered against the chill of the morning. Beyond the window, red maple leaves lost their grip on branches and drifted to cover the stiff yellowing grass. Despite Alec's grumblings that she was wasting time learning moves she'd never use, Renee still returned to the salle each dawn.

Kneeling a pace away, Savoy bound his forearm with a string of thin lead weights. Healer Grovener had promised to skin him alive for overworking the joint, and Savoy swore to do the same to Renee if she reported him.

The weights unwound and slid to the sand. Savoy growled.

Renee rose to help, but he shook her away.

"Very well, struggle on." Remembering herself, she added, "Sir."

His face rose from his task, the corners of his mouth twitching, but then he cocked his head and frowned at the opening door.

Despite the early hour, Master Seaborn appeared in a dress uniform, his face set in grim lines. "Servant, cadet." He offered a small bow to each of them.

Renee tensed at the formality.

Savoy rocked back on his heels. "Skip the horse shit, Connor."

Seaborn sighed. "As the guardsman overseeing the investigative team, Fisker is charged with presenting the findings on the Queen's Day attack to the Board of Inquiry this afternoon." Seaborn handed a sealed parchment to each of them. "Your presence is mandated."

"Our presence?" Renee looked from one man to the other. She and Savoy had already been interviewed. Ad nauseam. "But we did nothing wrong."

Savoy glanced at her, his brows raised. "A room full of bodyguards lose control of the situation to a maid, and the royal family gets near massacred in the Crown's own palace. Do you *not* see a problem?" He turned back to Seaborn. "What else?"

Seaborn sighed again. "I'll be the magistrate running the proceedings."

Savoy chuckled.

"You think Fisker questioning you is funny, Korish?" There was something in the way Seaborn said the second "you" that caught Renee's notice. "Or that I wish to administer such an inquiry?"

A darkness passed over Savoy's face as the two men exchanged a glance that she could not interpret. Then Savoy shrugged and, taking up his blade, stepped toward the center of the salle. "It is as it is. De Winter and I have time to make something useful of the day yet."

Renee's shoulders tightened from the rising tension. Shaking herself, she slid away from Savoy's coming blow, which streaked through the air a bit faster than usual.

Tense, quiet chatter buzzed beneath the domed ceiling of the Justice Hall courtroom. The brown velvet drapes were pulled back to let in wide rays of sunlight. The Board of Inquiry, a four-man panel of judges pulled from the Palace Guard, the military, and civilian officials, sat with Seaborn at a polished wood table at the head of the room. These four would evaluate Fisker's conclusions and decide what charges, if any, were to be pressed. And against whom.

A gray-clad clerk herded Renee, Savoy, and other members of the protection detail into a roped-off area on the left, across from a gated witness box. A few paces from them, the palace maid wept into her hands. Renee settled into a hard chair and clenched her jaw. The woman cost Savoy an arrow in the shoulder and near murdered the royal family. There was no redemption for that, not by anyone's measure.

Beside Renee, Savoy tipped his chair back, balancing it on its hind legs and ignoring Seaborn's scowl. Spectators crowded the benches. Among the solemn bodies, Renee made out the anxious faces of Alec and Sasha, Verin's intense gaze, and Lord Palan's forehead. Dabbing his face with a gold embroidered handkerchief, Palan leaned down to speak to a bored-looking Tanil, who was not one to pass up a chance to miss classes. Palan sighed at his nephew, then heaved over to make room for another man. The two shook hands in greeting and Renee felt the hair stir on the back of her neck. The dark coat, the set of the newcomer's shoulders . . . The man turned and sat, drawing the breath from her lungs. Her father. What in the Seven Hells was he doing in Atham?

Before she could sort her thoughts, the clang of a bell swallowed the room. The proceedings opened. At Seaborn's direction, Fisker rose.

"Vipers are an abomination," Fisker announced to the Justice Hall. "An abomination that should be eradicated from Tildor's soil. And with them, all those who aid them, who heed them, who spread their seed. Vipers—"

"Guardsman." Seaborn rubbed the side of his nose. "If you would be kind enough to detail your findings on this case in particular?"

Fisker bowed, his face reddening, and continued in a more relevant vein. "While the Vipers undeniably orchestrated the assault against the Crown this Queen's Day past," he concluded, tenting his nine fingers, "the actions of several others, whether in assisting the Vipers or showing egregious incompetence in their duty, pose concerns the board may wish to address."

Incompetence? Renee caught a glance Fisker threw at Savoy and frowned.

Savoy grinned at the guard.

Fisker's eyes flashed, but he drew a breath and requested that the maid take the witness stand. Her hesitation bought her an armed escort.

"You are Mistress Olivia?" Seaborn's usually kind voice held a note of cold indifference that chilled Renee. He waited for Olivia's nod before proceeding. "Guardsman Fisker believes your words will help the Board of Inquiry understand what happened during the Queen's Day attack. He will ask you questions designed to show a fact pattern to the board. Note that the board may find *your* actions suspect. If it does, you will be charged with a crime and have access to a defense advocate. Do you understand?" Seaborn waited for another nod and gestured to Fisker. "Go ahead, sir."

Fisker brushed stray strands of silver hair from his long face. "You opened the window shutter in the palace dining room and, when leaving, obstructed the door lock, is that correct?"

"Yes, sir," she whispered.

"Why?"

"A letter." She twisted her hands in her lap. "The third of three I received, all with instructions. When I refused the first, my boy Jakie disappeared. He was a happy, healthy lad. Four years old and lively like a bumblebee." A tear ran down her cheek. "He was returned but a day later, too weak to lift his head by himself. I . . . I had a bit of savings and I scraped all I had for a Healer. My Jakie, he saw the mage fire around the Healer's hand and howled and howled, as if he knew what it was. And . . . he did know."

Nausea brushed the back of Renee's throat.

Seaborn waited a moment to let the witness regain her composure and prompted her to continue.

"The Healer said a mage violated my Jakie. Ripped his Keraldi Barrier and bled the life energy from him. Left so little that my boy could but breathe. A chill would end his life." She hugged herself. "I tended him and fed him soft food and a month later he sat up himself again. He is a fighter, my Jakie."

Renee bit her lip. A registered mage would never dare this, but the Vipers sheltered unregistered ones. And now they used their human weapons to close in on King Lysian. Mistress Olivia and her son were just pawns caught in the crossfire.

Olivia's eyes closed. "The day after that a second letter came, ordering me to add a powder to the king's drink. When I refused . . ." She broke into sobs.

Fisker cleared his throat and looked up at Seaborn. "Healer Grovener examined the child upon his return from the second disappearance. With the board's permission, I would like him to testify tomorrow to the boy's condition." He waited for a nod and turned back to his witness. "When you received the third letter, you followed its instruction, is that right?"

"Yes, sir."

"You knew you committed treason by doing so?"

"What choice had I, sir?" She straightened her back. "I will sacrifice my life for my son."

A bearded man seated on Seaborn's right shook his head. "Your life is yours to give, mistress. But you offered up the Crown's."

Sourness filled Renee's mouth. A rogue Viper mage drove Olivia to her task. And she would hang.

Fisker dismissed the maid and called the bodyguards from

the dining room to the stand one by one to relay what they'd seen. Renee stared at the witness box while they spoke, her heartbeat straining. Everything had happened so fast. Arrows flew, people screamed, wounds bled, porcelain crashed to the floor. She hadn't thought beyond the crisis of the moment, and could not have. But now, the board, sitting in the safe comfort of velvet chairs, would dissect it all. Would they find her incompetent? Images fluttered. The king jesting with his family. Sasha's gripping fingers, begging her to stay. Renee too weak to budge the shutter. Did she remember it right? Did—

"Cadet de Winter." Seaborn's tone said he was repeating himself. "Take the witness box, if you please."

Forcing her shoulders back, Renee took her place. She bowed, then clasped her hands behind her back and awaited Fisker's pleasure.

"You are the cadet who closed the window shutter, effectively ending the assault?" said Fisker.

Renee blinked. "At Commander Savoy's direction, sir, yes."

"But you recognized the danger first?"

"No, sir. The commander noticed it first."

Fisker made a show of frowning. "So Commander Savoy was the first to both recognize the danger and the solution, but left it all to a sixteen-year-old cadet?"

Heat rose to Renee's face. "He had closed the shutter before dinner, sir. When the maid reopened it and the assault started, Commander Savoy was shielding the Crown."

Fisker tented his hands again, his missing finger leaving a gap in the pattern, and held a pause. "You too had a protected that day?"

"Yes, sir. King Lysian's cousin, Sasha Jurran."

"How were you able to cover her while addressing the window?"

Behind her back, Renee clenched her hands together and glanced at Sasha. "I wasn't, sir. I left her on the floor."

"Did Commander Savoy order you to do so?"

She ground her teeth. "He instructed me to close the shutter."

"The shutter was made of heavy metal. Didn't you have trouble moving it?"

Her face flushed. "Yes, sir, I had trouble."

"I see. So, the commander ordered you to abandon your post to correct a problem that he knew you were not physically suited to handle . . . while he himself remained in the corner of the room?"

"He was guarding the Crown!" Renee turned to Seaborn in an appeal for reason.

"Answer the question, Cadet de Winter," Seaborn instructed. "Are the guardsman's statements accurate or not?"

Renee tensed, her gaze darting around the Justice Hall. Fisker awaited her answer, his eyes glowing with satisfaction. She wished no part of this game. It was unfair.

"Answer the question. Now," said Savoy.

"Servant Savoy, you will be silent or you will be removed," said Seaborn. His lips pressed together. "Cadet, answer the question."

"Yes, sir," she heard herself say, and was dismissed to her seat. In the audience, her father smirked beneath his mustache.

Savoy was called up before she could apologize. He smiled at his interrogator.

Fisker stepped back and cleared his throat. "Commander, you were the most senior, most experienced bodyguard present inside the dining room. Did you perform a threat assessment when you entered the room?"

"I did."

"Was the window there?" Fisker asked.

"It was."

"Did you recognize it as a source of potential danger?"

"I did," said Savoy.

"And you permitted the Crown to sit facing it nonetheless, did you not?"

Renee shook her head. Savoy had no more say in the seating arrangement of the royal family than he did in their choice of meal.

Fisker pressed ahead without waiting for Savoy's answer. "And later, when the maid opened the shutter, you begged others to shut it, is that right? You made no move yourself?"

"Yes," said Savoy, his voice calm.

Fisker leaned forward. "Tell me, sir, do you believe that had you acted, addressing the window yourself instead of making a child assume the task for which she was poorly suited and bear the risk herself, you could have stopped any arrows from entering the dining room?"

"I believe I erred earlier than that, guardsman." Savoy leaned forward in a matching motion. "Had I replaced your guard unit with twelve-year-old cadets, I would have had a perimeter team able to differentiate its ass from its elbow, and arrest the archer before he took the first shot."

Seaborn paled and the room erupted in shouts.

CHAPTER 15

"You'd think half the class would be here," Renee said to Alec, pulling herself atop the cold training yard fence. That morning had welcomed frost on her window and she'd had to dig through her chest for a woolen shirt. A few dozen paces away, the men of the Seventh, all lean and fit, checked laces and adjusted their packs while maintaining a steady roar of conversation. Savoy blended in with them, his face animated with talk and jest.

Alec snorted. "It's the Seventh's first day, not last. No one is coming at dawn on a liberty day to watch them do push-ups."

"But it's the *Seventh*. Isn't anyone curious?"

"Not at this hour." Alec stretched his back. "Has the Board of Inquiry finished deliberations yet? They've been at it for a week already."

"On everyone but Savoy." Renee pushed the memory of the sobbing woman from her mind before it seized her thoughts, instead relishing the memory of Savoy's final words. "Fisker indulged a personal grudge and painted a target on him."

"Grudge?"

"When Savoy was a cadet, he helped Fisker fall off a horse. A cut festered and ..." She waved her hand vaguely. "Point is, personal histories don't belong in the Justice Hall any more than Fisker's private moral code does. He had no call to single Savoy out."

"Well, Savoy was the senior officer in the dining hall. And the only Servant. He was responsible for the room."

She twisted toward him. "You think Fisker's right?"

"No." Alec held up his palms. "I think he might just be doing his job."

Renee opened her mouth to respond, but a tall young man, whose tanned skin and dark hair reminded Renee of a hawk, clapped Savoy's shoulder and pointed toward her and Alec. Savoy looked up, expressionless, while several others erupted in laughter.

Alec pushed away from the fence. "I've seen enough. Let's go."

Her cheeks heated. Alec was right. There was no reason to be here, watching other people train instead of working her own sword. More chuckles sounded, and when she glanced back, Savoy was studying the sky.

She slid down to the ground. Hawk was watching her again, eyeing her up and down. He was eighteen or nineteen, with broad shoulders, a flat stomach, and a smile that refused to surrender even at Savoy's sharp call of "Sergeant!"

She wondered if she should bow in greeting.

"We have an essay to write." Alec touched her elbow. "Something about thieves and motives that I know you've not touched in three weeks. Let's go."

Right. Seaborn's essay. Free time was scarce of late. Guilt

crept over her, and Renee rubbed her arms. Still, her probation was in combat arts, not academics. And she had to prioritize. Papers didn't save lives.

"Eh, you two!" An unfamiliar voice cut through the air. Hawk waved them over. "Come here."

Alec sighed and shot her a scowl, but there was nothing for it now. They trotted over to the group.

"The commander says ye're his students," said Hawk. He smiled like a boy hiding a frog in his pocket—a frog he planned to drop down a victim's shirt.

She bowed. "Yes, sir."

"He's 'sir.'" Hawk jerked his head toward Savoy. "I'm Cory Kash."

Renee blushed. The army reserved *sir* for commissioned officers. Common soldiers, including sergeants—as Cory's sleeve insignia named him—were not extended the courtesy. Since all fighter Servants were officers, Renee was unaccustomed to seeing other warriors on Academy grounds, so the slip of the tongue was understandable. But from Cory's perspective, she must seem either blind or an idiot. The Seventh could have only one officer—and Savoy was it.

She drew herself taut and bowed. "A pleasure, Sergeant Kash." At least the words came out crisp. "Renee de Winter, fighter cadet, senior class. My classmate Alec Takay."

Cory whistled at Savoy. "Next thing ye'll be wanting us to talk like that."

"I'd settle for you not talking at all," Savoy told him, drawing chuckles from everyone, including his victim. "Don't mind Cory, Renee. We try keeping him gagged, but he chews through everything."

Renee. That felt good.

"Can you run?" Cory loomed over her, his shoulders clearing her head.

She met his dark eyes. "Can you?"

His grin grew wolfish, like Khavi's, but he looked at Savoy before speaking again. At the latter's nod, he turned back. "Will you join our wee jog then, fighter cadets?"

Renee accepted quickly, before Alec could bring up homework once more. This was not an opportunity to let pass. He'd thank her later. Maybe.

The lightness of excitement faded within a half hour. Savoy set a hard pace up a never-ending, winding hill. The men ran in a shifting cluster and not, as she had imagined, a military formation. Cory paced her and Alec for a few minutes before speeding up to Savoy's side. Another man with a sergeant's insignia followed suit. Although she heard none of their conversation, she marveled at their ability to speak during this run and implored the gods to keep her from falling behind.

Her lungs burned by the time Savoy called a halt. The men dropped to the chilled ground the moment they stopped, and she too collapsed, gratefully gasping air. A sense of someone watching made her look up. The entire squad, including Alec, held a push-up position and waited, all eyes fixed on her. *Seven Hells.*

"Not yet," said Savoy. "But we'll get there."

Realizing she had spoken aloud, Renee turned deep red and scrambled to imitate the others. Alec chortled. She elbowed his ribs the next chance she got. Hard. But the remorseless goat only chuckled at her again. At least he was enjoying himself.

The "wee jog" Cory promised proved an exercise in masochism. Run. Stop. Drop to the ground and work. Run again. She soon discovered the contents of the men's backpacks.

"Sandbags?" she asked, crunching up and passing the sack to Cory, whose sweat-soaked hair stuck to his forehead. Her burning abdominals threatened to spasm. He nodded, did a sit-up with the burden, and passed it back.

"Better than rocks, aye?" His hand gently pressed on her shoulder. "Keep moving."

Renee lay back, uncertain she could rise again. Her body shook, fighting gravity.

"Move, girl!" someone growled into her ear. She turned to see the other sergeant, an older man with a shaved head, kneeling next to her, partnering Alec in the same drill. "Sit-up! Now!" Alec grimaced at her side. By now, he was keeping up little better than she was.

She sat up. And then did it again. And again. She ran, collapsed, got up, and ran more. She passed the sandbag. She carried it in her arms. She pulled herself up on tree branches. And, despite the agony of each motion, a deep happiness seeped into her bones. She and Alec were with the Seventh, and the

Seventh was not giving up on them. The toughest warriors in Tildor encouraged, shoved, yelled, but never dismissed either of them as the irrelevant tagalongs they were. When they returned to Academy grounds, Renee's prayer thanked the gods not just for the training's conclusion, but for its beginning. She lowered herself to the sand to stretch.

"You two keep walking another twenty minutes." Savoy's voice turned all heads toward her and Alec.

"We're fine, sir, real—"

Severe looks from several fighters dissuaded her from contradicting their commander and she swallowed the rest of her protest. The older sergeant stalked toward her, but Cory beat him to it.

"I'll come with ye," he offered, smiling and extending her a hand to pull her up. "Maybe you can show me this sacred Academy that trains you Servants?"

Hiding a smile, Renee suddenly didn't mind the prescribed cooldown.

Alec scowled.

"You should come back," Renee told Alec, who, despite her urging, had declined to return to the Seventh's morning training. The three weeks since the team's arrival had flown by in a rush of wind, and undone homework now hung thick in the early winter air.

"I get enough of Savoy during the day." Alec scrawled another line of his essay, assigned a month and a half ago and now, suddenly, due to Seaborn the following morning. "Extra time with him has given you nothing but blisters and moves you've no intention of using. Plus, I don't enjoy the same sights you do." The last was mumbled under his breath.

Renee's head jerked up. "Sights?"

Sasha chortled and answered in a singsong voice, "Cory and Savoy."

Renee threw a pillow at each of them.

Alec let it hit him, his head unwavering from his work. He had made no secret of disliking Savoy since day one, when the man had cracked his blade across Renee's forearm, but Alec's animosity toward Cory made little sense. Everyone liked Cory. Alec straightened and made a valiant attempt at a smile. "Go with the sergeant. Savoy isn't your friend."

She sat on the floor beside him. The heat from the fireplace warmed the stone, and they had spread a quilt atop that. "*You* are my friend," she said. "Are we going to work on the assignment or not?"

Five hours later, Renee rubbed her eyes. "I can't take much more," she mumbled, steeling herself for the all-night experience of transforming notes into paragraphs. If she forwent sleep and food, she would just make the deadline.

Alec peered over her shoulder. "Well, you but need to start and finish."

She scowled, but before she could reply, the door burst open and a pale Diam stumbled inside. She rose, but he sidestepped her and made a beeline for Alec.

"Someone hurt Khavi," Diam whispered.

When Alec remained seated, Renee frowned at her animal-loving friend and crouched by the child. "I'll come. What happened?"

Diam shook his head. "No, not you. Khavi wants *him*." He swayed and remained upright only by grabbing the older boy's shirt. "Please," he added, eyes shining. "He'll die."

Alec's head snapped toward Diam, and his face grew as pale as the child's. "Can't Renee—"

"No." A tear curved a clean path down his cheek. "You have to help. The way you helped when Tanil's stone cut him, remember? You—"

Alec hopped to his feet, cutting off the boy's words. "Renee, Sasha, stay here." He took Diam's hand and led him from the room.

Instead of wasting time arguing or responding to Sasha's speculations, Renee gave the boys a head start and, a few minutes later, followed them out of the barracks and across the courtyard. The wind rose and fell, shaking the naked branches, which grew denser as they walked past the Academy's edge and into the woods. Here Renee closed the distance, using the larger tree trunks for cover. She expected Diam to become hysterical as they approached Khavi, but he grew increasingly quiet, stumbling on flat ground.

They found Khavi on a tucked-away trail, blood soaking fur and earth. When Alec touched him, the dog lacked even the strength to whine. The arrow that had cut the animal's flank lay several yards away. Diam curled on the ground, whimpering.

Shedding secrecy, Renee sprinted to the boy. "Diam," she started to say, but Alec was there first, hauling the boy to his feet and ripping away clothing. "Are you hurt too?"

"My side," he whispered. "An arrow hit me."

"No, it didn't," said Alec. He scrubbed his sleeve over his forehead. "There's no blood, Diam. It . . . it hit Khavi."

"It hit *us*." Diam's voice faded, his body going limp.

Renee swallowed in confusion. "Alec?"

He looked at her, eyes searching. "I . . . I think they're bonded. That Diam will die if Khavi does." His mouth twitched. "I'm sorry," he whispered to her. "I'm sorry." Alec drew a breath and let it out, its mist dull against his glistening eyes.

"For what?" Renee stepped toward him, her hand reaching for his shoulder.

He backed away. A wolf howled deep in the woods, and Khavi lifted his nose just a little, as if trying to pick up the song, and failing. Khavi's muzzle fell. Taking another breath, Alec tilted his face to the sky. His shoulders opened as if surrendering to an energy that existed for him alone. His eyes widened, his arms trembling at his sides.

He was frightened, Renee realized. Her chest squeezed.

So was she.

But what—? She caught her breath. Alec's fingertips glowed.

His body tensed, twisted. And then, as quickly as it came, the tension melted away. His face flushed with relief and his palms flamed with blue fire that shimmered against the dusty brown of scattered tree leaves. *Mage fire.* The thought seemed to come to her from a distance. Alec stared at the glow and licked his lips.

CHAPTER 16

Renee staggered back. He was a mage. Alec was a mage. Her shy, steadfast, loyal best friend wielded the power to Control life forces. Her ears rang as if from a blow.

Alec turned to Diam. "I don't know what to do."

"Khavi does."

Alec nodded and knelt to grip the dog's shoulder. Blue mage light engulfed them both, pulsating like a beating heart and illuminating the forest around them. Diam groaned.

Renee gathered the boy in her arms. His small body pressed into her while sweat and fire consumed Alec and Khavi. When Alec's hand dropped away at last, his clothes soaked despite the cold, Khavi climbed to his paws.

"You Healed him?" Renee's voice sounded hollow.

"Yes. Well . . . no. It's simpler with animals, but I wouldn't know how to Heal a wound like that. I offered Khavi my energy and his body guided it." Alec sank to the ground. "I think it's instinctual with him . . . with the mage beasts. They can't Heal themselves any more than human mages can, but once I gave Khavi my energy, something in him took over." Wisps of blue flame scurried about his fingers like bits of lost lightning. Gasping, he clawed at the lining of his coat. The mage fire flared up over his hands, died, and flared again. He ripped at the cloth. "Help me," he whispered.

She knelt beside him and patted the jacket. Something inside crinkled in response. With the nimbleness her friend's fingers now lacked, Renee found the opening to a hidden pocket and suddenly knew what she was about to extract.

Dry orange veesi leaves crumbled into her palm. The bloody cursed leaves that affected mages so differently. She bit her lip.

"Please, Renee." Alec's shaking hand extended to her. "Please. I need it."

Renee stayed where she was, her jaw tight. It wasn't fair. He was making her a part of this and it wasn't fair.

"Renee."

She stood and flung the leaves onto his lap. "Take it yourself."

He did, trembling as he placed the orange bits into his mouth, cringed, chewed, and swallowed. Nausea contorted his face, but the blue glow died. His shoulders drooped in relief.

Renee hugged her chest and studied Khavi, now cuddling against his boy. *It hit us*, Diam had said. And Khavi ... mage animals were rare ... and wild. Hawks. Bears. Lions ... "He isn't a dog, is he?" Renee whispered. "He's a wolf."

Alec nodded. "He's so friendly, you wouldn't think it, but ... Maybe mage animals act different when they bond?" Alec chuckled without humor. "I guess they'd have to, if they are to keep from eating their partner for dinner, right? And the partner's family ... I guess we've proved bonding is more than legend." He offered Renee a weak smile.

Rene didn't smile back. "Is Diam too a mage then?"

"I think he'd have to be. He's too young for it to show yet, though." Alec's shoulders slumped farther over a bowed head. He prodded the dirt with his knuckle, bracing for the question they both knew she had to ask.

"How long?"

"Four years." He looked up, holding her eyes. "I've never touched a human. I swear, Renee! Never. Not once. I wouldn't even know how to get past the Keraldi Barrier in a person. Just animals, sometimes, sick ones who I can help a little. But almost never that even. I keep it down."

With veesi. An illegal drug to hide a power so dangerous, the Crown mandated its supervision. She kept her face blank.

"Now you know," he said, hushed.

"I . . . yes. Now I know." What should one feel upon discovering that her best friend is a felon? Betrayal? Sympathy? Fear? All Renee felt was a humming silence filling her mind with a single, monotonous note. She chewed the inside of her cheek. "Why?"

"I chose freedom." Alec's eyes strayed to the boy and dog curled up together, asleep on the ground. "But not at the expense of their lives." Alec's head shot up with borrowed strength. "I asked you to say behind!" he yelled, but the fight left him as quickly as it had come. He lay down in the dirt. "I asked you to stay behind." His gaze rested on the ground. "What will you do?"

Staring at him, Renee found neither the will to answer nor the desire to help him sit up. Debating whether to arrest a hypothetical mage in Seaborn's class was nothing like standing across from a friend. If she told, Alec would face a noose.

Her fingers curled into tight fists. King Lysian waged war against crime while Alec, the king's own Servant cadet, was himself a criminal. And Renee . . .

She had never thought herself capable of betraying the Crown.

She could not, would not, betray a friend.

And that loyalty meant treason.

Renee pushed herself off the ground. "Damn you." The words squeezed past her gritted teeth. "Damn you, Alec!"

"Renee . . ." His hand reached for her, but she stepped back, turning away.

A gust of wind blew in, howling through the trees. Renee walked into the wall of air, holding on to her jacket, trying to think of nothing but placing one foot in front of the other. The evening moved on, at a distance. The guards called *all's well*. A clique of cadets hurried to reach the barracks before curfew. A stray cat brushed her leg and scurried up a tree. Renee walked. Just walked. Nowhere in particular.

The midnight bell tolled.

"Renee?" Savoy, flanked by his two sergeants, turned into the small quad between the barracks buildings, where Renee realized she now was. With all the increased security, she should have known she was bound to run across an adult sooner or later. "Is all well?" Savoy asked.

Another instructor would have punished her for missing

curfew. He wouldn't, she knew. Savoy asked direct questions and took her at her word. And she was about to lie to him. Another betrayal. "I thought I saw a horse loose." She gestured behind her.

"All the way over here?" Cory's voice carried surprise, not doubt.

Her fingers toyed with the hem of her coat. Catching herself, Renee stuffed her hands into her pockets. Gods, how did Alec stand it, lying to everyone—lying to her—all these years?

"We'll check," said Savoy. He crossed his arms, his eyes penetrating hers. When she remained silent, he nodded. "Very well," he said, and they walked away.

Hanging lanterns illuminated her walk back to quarters, and unfinished notes welcomed her home. Alec's materials had disappeared. Sasha, asleep in her bed, pulled her blanket over her head in response to the creak of the door.

On the heels of the evening's events, the impossibility of finishing her essay by tomorrow throbbed like a drip of water against a wound, simultaneously trivial and unbearable. She chuckled bitterly. Seaborn would down-rate her, and the lowered academic standing would pull her further along the spiral toward losing an already tenuous hold on her Academy slot.

Renee walked to her roommate's drawer. There lay the assignment she needed. If caught, she'd still be down-rated and likely spend every evening for the rest of the year digging latrine holes. But the consequences of doing nothing were little different. The past four hours saw her become an accomplice to treason because of her friend's choices. It would serve nothing to jeopardize her own for the sake of a few sheets of homework.

After she finished copying Sasha's words, Renee spent the rest of the night washing the ink from her hands.

CHAPTER 17

Savoy knew he was sleeping, but it made the dream no less vivid.

The cell stank of blood and urine. Both his. "Is he alive?" His voice cracked, echoing against the stone walls. On his stomach, he slithered toward the bars. "I'm sorry!" The taste of copper filled his mouth.

The guard snorted.

A hand from the darkness grabbed at him . . .

Savoy gripped his assailant and threw him into the wall.

The foe grunted and stayed put.

Savoy vaulted from his bed into a defensive crouch and froze in place. Sun rays poured through the window to fill his quarters with light, and the man slumped on the floor beside the bureau was Verin. His long gray coat pooled around his body and his silver-streaked hair puffed out in disarray.

Savoy drew a breath. "Gods." Shaking away the last bits of sleep, he offered his hand to help the older man up. "I'm sorry, sir."

"I see you've grown a bit, lad." Verin's voice was composed despite its owner's sprawl. He climbed to his feet, leaning more on the proffered arm than Savoy had expected.

Savoy's head pounded still. If the headmaster wished to see

him, courtesy demanded a summons or, at the least, a knock. He was no longer Verin's foster to be subject to random intrusions. His gaze weighed the other man. Verin was still taller, of course—Savoy had outgrown his adolescent runtiness but still stood nearly a hand shorter than the other man—but Savoy out-massed Verin now and had the edge of recent battle on his side. He braced his hands on his hips. "You should not startle me so."

"Ah, my mistake then." Verin pulled down on his tunic, settling it back into place. His forehead creased. "I had been under the impression that I raised a self-controlled military officer and not a wild animal. I thank you for correcting the misconception."

Heat rose to Savoy's face and he turned away for a moment to let it settle. Behind him, chair legs scraped against the floor. He turned to find his former teacher and guardian seated in the room's sole chair.

"I've known several people who chose to leave their quarters unlocked," Verin said conversationally. "But you are the first to have removed the locking mechanism completely."

Savoy glanced at the door, where his handiwork had left several holes from the extracted screws. Locks had a way of trapping you in as fast as keeping others out. He shrugged. "A good sword bests a good latch, sir." Verin had taught him to fight, even if it had been decades since the now Servant High Constable was junior enough to wield a sword on the battlefield himself.

"Mmm. Indeed." Verin smiled, crossing his legs. "Especially

when someone else has another set of keys, eh?" A metallic jingle sounded when he patted his pocket and a bushy eyebrow rose in gentle amusement. "Were you afraid I'd lock you in?"

Savoy picked up a shirt and shrugged into it, letting the hem hang down over the battered britches in which he had slept. He started to pull himself up to perch atop his desk but changed his mind and walked back to the bed instead. With a few motions he tugged the woolen blanket tight and tucked the corners under the mattress. "Would you?"

The older man chuckled. "No. If I wished you to stay in your quarters, I believe I would have but to ask." He tented his fingers under his chin. "That is something that differentiates a man from a boy, don't you think? That he fulfills his obligation and follows his orders because they are obligation and orders, and not because he's forced into obedience." He cleared his throat to indicate a change of topic and inclined his head toward the bed. "Sit. Since I seem to have intruded on your sleep at midday, may I presume your night was otherwise occupied?"

Midday. Savoy glanced out the window for confirmation. "I drilled the Seventh until dawn, then herded cadets around the salle." The words held an unintended ring of excuse that he didn't care for. He scrubbed his hand over his face. The headmaster did not make social calls, so something was amiss. If previous experience was anything to judge by, the longer Savoy took to realize what that bloody something was, the worse the outcome. He sighed, remembering. The instructors' conference to discuss the midyear exams a few weeks off had passed without the pleasure of his company. He squared his shoulders. "My apologies for the ill planning, sir."

Verin nodded slowly before speaking. "I believe it was more a matter of priorities than plans. The needs of your men versus those of your students?"

It was a trap, but Savoy failed to see how he could avoid the bait. "A misstep for my fighters will get them killed. A misstep for my cadets will get them sent home to their parents."

"Your dedication to your men is commendable." Verin's fingertips tapped each other. "Your disobedience to my orders, less so. I seem to recall holding a similar conversation with you upon your arrival, but perhaps my memory is in error." His brows narrowed and he leaned forward. His smile faded, replaced by a steel-gray gaze that laid a heated rod along Savoy's spine. "Let me thus revert to more primitive methods: You will keep your commitments to this Academy, Servant Savoy, or you will find your team's behavior under a level of scrutiny they will not enjoy. Am I clear?"

The older man rose, waited until Savoy stood and bowed, and then headed for the door. He paused with his hand resting on the handle. "I know my words raked you, lad. That marks you a good officer. See that you are a good teacher as well."

Savoy stared at the door long after it closed, wondering how Verin had turned being a "good officer" into a liability.

The conversation still weighed on his mind when he met his sergeants, Cory and Davis, a few hours later for a surprise inspection of the Seventh's mounts. The men had drilled with the Palace Guard a few days ago, but until a specific mission arose, the team had little to do in Atham but patrol the city and the palace grounds, watching for misbehaving Vipers. The reserve status chafed his soldiers. And chafed soldiers found trouble. As glad as Savoy was for his men's company, he was beginning to reconsider the wisdom of the precautionary recall.

"How are the boys handling the tether?" Savoy asked.

The stable's lantern light glinted off of Davis's bald head. "We have enough mending, supplying, and training to do to keep them trotting a while longer, but once that ends . . ." He opened his palms. "I can't keep a sword sharp for you if I have nothing to sharpen it on, sir."

"Understood." Savoy drummed his fingers against a stall gate. The occupant poked her black nose over the railing and sniffed curiously until a crash of the stable door startled her into a rear. "Whoa, girl." Savoy grabbed her halter, restraining the filly lest she harm herself. He twisted to see the source of the racket and found a man who should know better standing a few paces away. "Easy near the horses, Connor."

"Get your hooligans under control," said Seaborn.

Cory and Davis stepped forward, hands hovering over sword hilts.

"Gentlemen." Savoy kept his voice low. "Give us a minute." He watched his men retreat, then stared at Seaborn.

"Either the back pasture grew a barrel of mead, or your men cannot tell a school from a taproom. I found two cadets stumbling around the barracks, losing their dinners."

"Mead any good?" Savoy rubbed the bridge of his nose. "I told them to stay away from the cheap brew."

Connor planted his palm against the wall near Savoy's head and leaned close. His voice, coming quiet from behind clenched teeth, was a growl. "Get your gang on a leash, or get them gone."

Savoy crossed his arms. He permitted Connor much, but disrespect toward the Seventh was beyond those bounds. While the Academy slept in the peace of high walls and pretty guardsmen, his men spent most nights with death guarding their dreams. "Put a damn leash on your cadets. Or teach them to drink. I don't care which."

"You are the guests here, not the kids. Behave or get out."

"You think I want to be here?"

"I don't care. The Academy exists for the cadets, not for you." Connor's voice dropped, sending a shiver through Savoy. "Break up the party or I will call Guardsman Fisker to do it. I'm certain he would make the trip from the palace for the pleasure."

The door slammed behind Seaborn, upsetting the horses again. Breath caught in Savoy's lungs, as if someone punched his stomach. When he forced himself to turn away, he found Cory and Davis leaning against the stable wall, their eyes boring into him.

"Move the hooligans and their mead into my quarters," he told them, and started toward the door.

"Where are you going, sir?"

Savoy paused, but did not turn around, not wishing his face to show. "To find a way to get you released from this dungeon."

"Am I still welcome?" Alec hovered at the threshold of Renee's quarters. They had not spoken in the two days since Alec had stood the world on its ears—two days that had left Renee's nails bitten to the quick and no memory of Alec unstudied. He put his hands into his pockets and hunched his shoulders.

"You are." She chewed her lip. One friend should not have to ask such things of another. "Gods, of course you are."

He closed the door behind him and lingered there for a few moments before sitting on Sasha's empty bed. He braced his elbows on his knees and interlaced his fingers, his head bent. "I'm sorry that you know." He spoke toward the floor. "But I'm glad too. And I'm sorry for being glad."

Renee's finger traced the rough texture of the bedcover. Two days earlier she would have sworn that a true friendship had no room for secrets. But secrets, it turned out, carried burdens. "Does anyone else know?"

"Gran may suspect." Alec took a breath. "She raised two mage daughters, she knows what to look for."

Renee fidgeted. Alec had never mentioned that before either.

"I didn't lie to you," he said quickly, as if reading her thoughts. "My *mother*"—Alec spat the word—"she tossed me to Gran and took off, like I've told you." He drew a breath. "Aunt Cayle . . . I never told you about her, but she taught me a bit. We didn't know whether I would Control yet, but she'd call me over and explain things—how Control works, mage history, some stories. The fundamental skills are the same for all mages, and

Aunt Cayle specialized in Healing atop that, learning bits and pieces as best she could in secret. She Healed my dog when he burned his paw. I didn't know it then, but she was trusting me with her life by doing it."

And now he was trusting her. Renee scooted to the edge of her bed, closer to him. She remembered his grandfather passing on a few years back and knew he little cared to speak of his mother, who had left long before that. That was all. Renee and Alec had been each other's family for years now, and rarely talked of other relatives. Now she knew why. "Your aunt isn't registered, then?"

"She wasn't. The guard hanged her eight years ago." He dug into his pocket and pulled out a leather square the size of a gold crown. The attached thong marked it a necklace, although Renee had never seen Alec wear it. He turned it over to show a small diamond stud worked into the center. An amulet. "She gave it to me when I feared the dark. I could touch it to make it glow."

Renee reached out and brushed her finger over the smooth stone. Nothing happened.

"It can't store the energy long. Giving me a candle would have been cheaper and much more practical. But . . ." He raised his shoulders and let the rest go unsaid.

"Why don't you recharge it? I don't think she'd mind."

He snorted. "Why don't you best Savoy with a sword?" His thumb rubbed the leather. "Healer Grovener probably could, but it would seem strange to ask."

She bowed her head in apology. Amulets were rare and expensive, but Renee had always assumed that the cost was due to the diamonds and regulation fees. It was easy to dismiss the skill and training involved in unfamiliar vocations. "Is your mother hiding?" That would explain why Alec spoke so little of her. Unwise to draw attention—to his mother and his own bloodlines, both. "Is that why she left?"

"No." He chuckled without humor. "No, she registered and went to a Crown's school. Not the Academy, but nicer than anything we'd have been able to afford. *Registered* mages have status and money, you know. At the expense of freedom." He snorted. "I was an accident that delayed my mother's graduation. When she finally received orders, well, I don't know if she couldn't take me or chose not to, but I have a guess." He spread his palms. "The Mage Council has her developing army tools somewhere. She sends Gran coin."

"At least you know she's alive." With a sigh, Renee leaned back on outstretched arms and studied the cracks in the ceiling. She recalled little of her own mother, but the memories she had were warm. "So, your mother is registered, your bloodlines are mage-filled, and you Control . . . And instead of skulking in the shadows of your village, you got yourself to Atham, defying registration under the Crown's—and Mage Council's—very noses. You're hiding in plain sight."

His jaw tightened. "But I'm not hiding. I'm making a choice to be a fighter Servant instead of yielding to a mage's impulse. You do the same, choosing to train instead of surrendering to your size or your father's decrees. Anyone can conscript as a common soldier or purchase an officer's commission, but becoming a Servant—that proves something." He rubbed the back of his neck. "All Servants have their reasons." A hint of a smile twitched across his face. "Even Savoy, I'm sure."

She smiled back. Alec was right. The Servants' code inspired her, but different yearnings drove different people—whether for opportunity, or challenge, or to uphold a family tradition. They all had potential to be good officers.

Alec shook his head like a dog and leaned back. "Where is the Seventh this fine day? You like running with them over training with Savoy alone?"

A knock at the door halted her growing blush. She missed the regular morning sparring, but Savoy still found an hour for her now and again. "Enter," she called instead of answering Alec.

A small girl in a page's uniform appeared long enough to say that Headmaster Verin wished Renee to attend him in his office immediately.

Alec's face was carefully neutral. He looked out the window.

Renee waited until the girl's footsteps receded. "I didn't say anything," she told him, her mouth dry.

His shoulders relaxed. "I didn't think you would, but . . ." He frowned. "Diam? I like him, but he's eight."

"I'll give you warning if they know." Renee leaned her forehead against the doorframe before stepping out. "It may be something else altogether." She headed out before he could ask what.

The late afternoon sky was still crisp and clear. The administrative building towered above Renee, casting its shadow over the Academy grounds. Its white marble steps, thick columns, and strict, smooth walls radiated grandeur and intimidation. No one, except perhaps for those who entered it daily, could walk inside without feeling the significance of her own existence dwarfed by the immensity of the institution.

Holding her breath, Renee pulled open one of the doors, so heavy that for the first few years as a cadet she couldn't open it by herself. Not that she had much practice. Mischief that sucked most of the boys into trouble and a headmaster's summons had politely avoided her. Until now. The door closed behind her with a puff of cold air, shutting out the courtyard noise and leaving her to climb the stairs in dooming silence.

From the top stairway window, she saw Savoy approach the building and forced herself to maintain composure. He'd expect that of her. He was near the entrance now and seemed unaware of Seaborn rounding the corner. Without warning, Seaborn grabbed Savoy and spun him around. A suicidal move. Renee held her breath.

Savoy stiffened, but allowed himself to be shoved.

Seaborn's finger jabbed Savoy's chest until the latter turned away and entered the building.

"Make no mistake about it, Korish." Seaborn's voice echoed up the stairs. "We both know who's responsible."

"Yes," Savoy answered.

Renee stepped farther away from the landing, as getting

caught eavesdropping was unlikely to improve her situation. Her thoughts raced as quickly as her heart. The exchange below shed little light on which of her recent misdeeds put her here. It was possible that Diam had told his brother the truth, and Verin now planned to force her into bearing witness against her friend. Or that Seaborn had realized the essay she turned in was not of her writing. Or . . . she clasped her hands behind her back to still them.

Savoy crested the stairs, looking as pale as Renee felt. Whatever had happened, he was unhappy about it. That made two of them. She forced a ghost of a smile to her face to encourage them both.

"Face the wall, cadet," he said.

It was as though he'd doused her with freezing water. Renee turned toward the wall, too humiliated to meet either his eyes or Seaborn's. Footsteps sounded behind her as the two men walked past, toward Verin's office.

"What about her?" Seaborn asked as the door started to creak closed.

"She stays outside," said Savoy. There was a click, and conversation became too muffled to discern.

Renee's palms were slippery with sweat by the time they came out an hour later, Savoy in the lead. He walked toward her, stone-faced, while Verin watched from a few paces back. "With me." Savoy tapped her writing journal against his leg and shoved her toward the steps. Seaborn and Verin followed.

CHAPTER 18

Renee stumbled as Savoy thrust her into the training salle. She slid on the sandy floor, catching sight of Seaborn and Verin taking posts at the wall while she regained her balance. Seaborn's slumped shoulders sank farther. *Seaborn. The essay.* At least she knew what it was about now. Her heart sped. "I'm sorry," she whispered toward him, but it wasn't Seaborn who rounded on her with disappointment, and something else, flaring in his eyes. It was Savoy.

He opened her journal, ripped out a fistful of pages, and threw the bundle at her. Paper separated in mid-flight and glided to the ground, fluttering in and out of the squares of late-day light that fell from the windows onto the sand.

"What in the Seven Hells possessed you?"

Blood drained from her face. She glanced back at Seaborn, but found herself unable to meet his eyes. Savoy towered over her. Swallowing, she bent to pick up the pieces of her essay. No, not her essay, just the one she handed in.

"I—I didn't have time," she stammered, containing herself to the task of collecting the rubbish. She wished the ground could open and let her disappear into oblivion.

"You found time to play with swords and the Seventh," Savoy

shot back. "I trusted you to act responsibly, de Winter, to act worthy of the office you strive for."

She straightened to face the sting of his words, finding none of her own.

Savoy grabbed the pages from her grip and ripped them apart, letting the shreds fall like bits of dirty snow. She watched them cover the sand, not looking away until she felt something hard shoved into her chest. Her hands gripped the proffered practice blade, her sweaty palms slipping on the hilt.

"This here is fun, right, de Winter?" His wooden blade struck her thigh. "Unlike doing your own work."

She flinched.

He struck again, landing the blow on her upper arm. "You plan on just standing there now? Did your sword turn into a fashion piece?"

She brought up her weapon but could not meet his gaze.

Savoy swung at her head.

His attack was too clean, too obvious. Renee raised her sword to block.

He circled her blade and struck her side, laying a welt across her exposed ribs. Blood pooled beneath unbroken skin. Renee gasped and clamped her free hand over the pulsing bruise. The instant she did, Savoy hit her crooked arm just above the elbow. Numbness, then fire shot up her shoulder and through her side. She hunched over in pain, knowing she was presenting her already throbbing shoulder for another blow. It came.

Renee backed away, staring at Savoy wide-eyed. The systematic savageness of the attack frightened her in a way sparring with him never had. He followed her retreat. A belly strike snatched her breath and Savoy's blade rose up again, his face promising this was but the beginning.

No reprieve. No pause. Granting her a sword had been a mockery. Savoy powered though her parries or else manipulated her moves to expose bruises. He branded new stripes over hurt flesh. *Good gods.* She whimpered. He ignored her cry. The attack kept coming. Forever.

Renee fell.

Savoy grabbed her tunic and jerked her up. "We aren't done."

Her stomach clenched. She suddenly cared for nothing except avoiding another blow. Not skill, not pride, not dignity. Nothing. This wasn't punishment, she realized through growing fear, it was humiliation. And it wasn't stopping.

Renee's legs buckled. She couldn't do this. Clutching her sword, she sank to her knees, knowing Savoy would force her up again, but shrinking back anyway. She was too weak to block, too small to attack, and too afraid to stand another moment before him. She prayed he wouldn't strike her unless she rose. And she never wished to rise again.

His hand reached forward and she flinched away, cowering into the sand. "Please," she heard her voice whisper, and breathed in shame.

No jerk came. Renee looked up at her teacher but saw his

eyes moving past her, toward the two men on the sidelines. She followed his gaze in time to see Verin nod.

Savoy's shoulders relaxed. He squatted by her and tugged at the practice blade in her grip. When she held on, he shook his head and touched the back of her hand. "Let go. It's done."

Renee searched his face for emotion and found none. "I'm sorry," she said again as he took the blade from her, but his face remained a stone.

She staggered up, her feet looking for solid ground. And fled.

Outside, Renee found Diam waiting by the door. His eyes locked on the tears running down her cheeks. Turning away, she headed to the well. A moment later, feet pounded the ground behind her, and a small hand slipped into hers. The boy did not ask what happened.

Despite the beginning of the winter cycle, the evening was the warmest they'd had in weeks, and the breeze felt good on the back of her neck. She ladled frigid water from the well-bucket, gulping and wiping her face. Then she sat on the ground, letting the wind dry her skin. The sun was setting over a bloody horizon as the evening journeyed toward darkness. Inside her, misery, shame, and anger battled with the ferocity of fire consuming kindling.

Diam plucked at her shoulder. "Cory's comin'."

She turned in the direction of the boy's pointing finger, but could not make out the identity of the shape moving toward them. Diam, scratching Khavi's ears, looked certain.

The shape materialized into the tall, dark-haired sergeant.

Saddlebags slung over his shoulder, he strode up to the well and paused, surprise playing across his face. "Dinna expect ye here," he said, setting down a lantern before drawing a bucket of water and gulping. "Just rode a patrol." He smiled in apology and drank again.

Diam wrinkled his nose and turned away, his face full of contempt. Renee heard him muttering something about kissing as he detached himself from them. If Cory heard Diam's prediction, he didn't let it show.

"So." Cory surveyed the dimming landscape. "I heard you have a beach here . . ."

The remaining strands of sunlight had disappeared by the time Renee and Cory picked their way toward Rock Lake. She had expected the tameness of the Academy grounds to disappoint a fighter like Cory, who practically lived on the battlefield, but he drank in each new sight with Diam-ish enthusiasm. The lantern in his hand swung to and fro, casting odd shadows on the uneven slopes. Branches, disturbed by the wind and evening birds, rustled around them.

"You all right?" Cory asked, offering a hand down a steep part of the trail. "You seem stiff."

Renee swallowed, grateful for the darkness's veil. The deep ache in her limbs moaned. "Stiff," she repeated, clinging to the word. "Yes, over-trained, I think."

He patted her shoulder. "Aye, been there meself. I know something that'll help."

The trees opened without warning, revealing a sky full

146

of stars. The glowing specks of light reflected off the lake as the last brown leaves floated from their tethers to drift on the water's surface.

Cory froze. "Och."

Renee smiled, the humiliation of the evening suddenly distant, left behind in some other time, some other world. With the trees blocking the wind, the warmth of the mild evening wrapped around them. "I know."

Without taking his eyes off the water, Cory settled onto the sand. Renee lowered herself by his side and the two sat in silence, drinking in the night. A leaf fluttered close, teasing the lantern light. Cory's hand reached out to catch it, and, failing, settled onto Renee's shoulder. Her skin tingled under his fingers.

Holding her breath, she reached up across her chest and touched her fingertips to his. His chin hovered just above the crown of her head, disturbing her hair. Warmth from his body hugged her like a cloak of thin wool. She lifted her face to find his eyes looking down into hers.

Cory leaned toward her. His lips touched hers with a brief gentleness that seemed impossible in a boy so big. When he pulled away, he smiled like a cat who stole cream for his supper and gathered her in his arms. "I promised something for stiffness," he whispered, his breath tickling her ear. A strong hand kneaded into the base of her neck.

"Mmm..." Renee leaned into his touch, her heart palpitating faster with each second. She sensed his grin.

He squeezed her shoulders, fingers searching for knots. Then his hand slid down her arm.

Renee jerked away, gasping.

"What's wrong?" He held her at arm's length. "Did I hurt ye, then?"

She shook her head, uttering denials, but he was already pushing up the loose sleeves of her tunic.

He lifted the lantern and whistled. "Och. Quite a sunset ye've got there." Shaking his head, he checked the other arm.

All energy left her. At a loss for words, she stared at the sky, awaiting the destruction of the night's enchantment. Cold nipped at her skin as he moved away. Shame rushed to fill the void. She had cowered on the salle floor and even now, her breath quickened with remembered fear. The camaraderie Savoy had extended her on Queen's Day, and while training with the Seventh—it had been a jest. The man she had thought her friend had, in but a quarter hour, reduced her to a crumpled, frightened heap. It meant nothing to him; his face had said so. He had never intended to let her keep a shred of dignity. And she had not.

Something rustled behind her, and Cory's warm hand returned to her shoulder. She leaned away despite herself.

"Easy." Cory showed her a small jar labeled *Bruise Balm*. His dark gaze caught hers, and a finger brushed against her cheek. "Just bought the wee thing from a peddler. Let's test it." Without waiting for a response he cradled her against him and spread the viscous substance over her upper arms. She doubted the balm's medicinal properties, but Cory's touch worked miracles on its own.

The toll of a late evening bell found Renee and Cory lying on their backs, staring at the stars. It would be curfew soon. But not yet. Renee smiled, her neck resting on Cory's outstretched arm. The near three hours they had spent together had whispered by.

"So, what did ye do, then?" he asked, breaking the comfortable silence.

"Hmm?"

He chuckled and rose onto his elbow, brushing a strand of hair from her face. "I wish to know what mischief tickled your fancy."

"Just sparring," she answered, glad for the darkness that hid her blush.

Cory laughed. "Och, aye." He tugged up her sleeve again, and traced the welts gently. "You dinna appreciate the finesse of these, but trust me, a wee bit in either direction and ye'd have broken bones in place o' yer bruises. Perfect shots. All of them are. And I know but one man who is that good with a blade."

He had known all along. A smile crept onto her face. "You have me there," she said, catching his hand in hers.

He poked her ribs. "So, what did ye do?"

"Not saying. Savoy was a bastard about it, though."

Cory stiffened. "I'm nay the person to say such to."

"What? I can't call Savoy a bastard?"

He pulled away. The familiar lightness of voice and poise disappeared. "Commander Savoy. And no, ye can't. Not in front of me, anyway."

Renee sat up, indignation bubbling. "You don't even know what happened. How can you choose a side?"

"I'm nay choosing a side, Renee. I chose it three years past, when I joined the Seventh."

"Savoy can do no wrong, then?" She hugged her arms around herself. "You just yes along with anything he says?"

"If I dinna agree with him, I'd tell him. Not you."

They sat without speaking. Clouds moved to cover the stars, and it started to drizzle, the rain disturbing Rock Lake's still surface. Renee stared at the colliding ripples.

"I need to get back to me squad," Cory said quietly. He put the lantern by her feet.

"You won't see the trail."

He pushed himself to his feet. "I just walked it a few hours back, and no one is shooting at me. If I couldna retrace me steps under these conditions, the commander would skin me alive."

"Right," she mumbled, and turned away to avoid watching him leave. Let him go if he wanted to.

Later that night, Renee curled herself in a deep cleft between man-sized boulders on the far shore of Rock Lake. The climb to get there, clambering around the lake and maneuvering over the wet slippery rocks in the darkness of night, had taken hours. Blissful hours of worrying only about finding the next stone and keeping her footing and moving farther into the shadows. The lantern had fallen and broken. She barely noticed.

The thought of facing Alec or Sasha, or worse, Savoy, nause-ated her. A fighter brushed away bruises as irrelevant hazards of the trade. What did it say of her that she could not? She pressed her forehead against the cool wall of her stone circle. The night grew colder and the boulders sucked up whatever heat her body had. A dampness hanging in the air broke again into rain that fell on her hair and face, soaking her already damp clothes. She curled into an even tighter ball, and, shivering, surrendered to fatigue and sleep.

"Wake up, kid."

Renee opened her eyes to find Savoy crouched atop the larg-est of the boulders. Her drowsy eyes widened, her back pressed hard into the stone. A pang of nausea gripped Renee, her eyes darting to his hands. She jerked her gaze away, struggled to clear her sleep-addled head, but it was too late, he'd seen.

Savoy shook his head and uncurled his fingers to show empty palms. "I am not here for round two."

Not even a pretense from him to guard her dignity.

Savoy took hold of the ledge and swung down, hanging on outstretched arms before dropping lightly into the stony hol-low. The moisture from last night's rain frosted the rocks and glistened in the faint rays of dawn.

Gathering her legs under her, she sat up and scooted away from him. Ache and cold clung to her like the wet clothes she wore. She balled her hands into fists and tucked them in her armpits for warmth.

He took off his coat and held it out to her.

"I'm fine, sir."

"It's not a suggestion."

Swallowing, she stripped off her damp tunic and pulled the coat over a sleeveless undershirt. The welts his blade had left on her arms had turned a deep shade of red.

"Still hurting?"

"Yes."

"Good."

She met his eyes.

His shoulders pulled back into a stretch. "You deserved what I gave you."

"Yes, sir." Renee drew up her knees, wrapping her arms around them. Disgrace filled her. And not just disgrace, she knew, as her heart drummed beneath the cold, but fear too. She knew what he could do now and, to her shame, knew she could not face it again. Holding her breath, she prayed that he would leave.

Savoy's brows narrowed as if in contemplation, but he shook his head. "It's done, de Winter, and they're just bruises." He ran his hand through his hair. "They'll heal. No one died for your mistake."

She studied her feet.

"You know the only way to never miss a parry?" He waited until she looked up. "Don't spar."

She blinked, rubbing her arms. A tear gathered rebelliously in the corner of her eye. Several seconds passed in a silent, losing battle for composure. Renee dropped her head to her knees.

"Please leave."

Clothes ruffled as he shifted his weight. "Stop. Crying."

Go *away.*

"Please." The plea escaped him through clenched teeth. "Do something else."

She looked up to find Savoy's own eyes closed as he sat with his head tipped back against the stone. She took a breath of cold air and wiped the back of her hand across her cheeks. "You don't cry."

His eyes opened. "No."

No, of course not. She lifted her face toward the open sky. The chill tingled. "What's the worst thing you've ever done?"

He startled, then shook himself. "You're out of line."

"Yes, sir." She closed the coat tighter and leaned back, trying to melt into the rock behind her. She did not need Savoy, she reminded herself, and rubbed her shoulders. She needed no one but herself. In the clouds above her, a gaggle of geese flew in formation, making a circle above the lake. She made herself think of them, forming a picture in her mind of how their ordered V reflected in the water.

"You know it."

She blinked as his voice disturbed her drawing.

"At least I presume you know it," he continued with an odd mix of nonchalance and resignation. "Unless you divined a way to copy text without reading it." He cocked his head to one side, an eyebrow lifted in question.

"I read it," she said. "Two boys took a pair of the Crown's

prized horses and got into an accident. The uninjured boy was charged with . . ." Renee jerked upright, staring at him. "With theft." An unlikely start for a decorated commander of the Seventh, especially since the boy thief had ended in a dungeon. She shook her head. "But you're here," she said dully.

"Thank you. I was wondering where I was." He sighed. "Verin left me in the cell for months before making his offer." His eyes took in the walls around them, but he spoke calmly. "He said he wasn't ready to give up on my sword arm yet, but he was not about to underestimate the limits of my stupidity either. If I fostered with him, obeying his rules, I could continue at the Academy. Should I graduate and become a Servant, I was free."

Sasha's essay had concluded the court's sentence unfair and, though the words had been her friend's, Renee agreed with them. She was glad to know that a generous offer had balanced the injustice. Renee leaned forward, bracing her elbows into her knees. "He was unable to save you the lashes?"

"They were his idea. I near got Connor killed, I deserved every one of those. Just ask Guardsman Fisker. It still chafes him I got off at all."

Renee scratched her nose. The two boys—it was difficult to think of them as Savoy and Seaborn—had run into bandits. The outcome of that struggle was no more Savoy's fault than it had been her mother's when her wagon had ridden into an ambush.

"That ride had not been my first exploit, or even my tenth," he said as if aware of her thoughts. "Verin was correct both about my fighting and my discipline." He glanced at her arms, now hidden inside the heavy woolen sleeves of his coat. His voice was that of experience, not speculation. "The worst of the soreness will ease by tomorrow, but you will wear the marks for two weeks or so."

She frowned at him. Perhaps he'd had no choice in her punishment. "Did Master Verin make you discipline me as you did, sir?"

"No." The crisp answer ensured no room for doubt. If anything, Savoy's intense gaze claimed the act as a personal boon. "I requested it."

Renee was silent. At last she understood.

Him. Savoy. The man she foolishly considered a friend, was just a bully who, having received a pounding from a larger kid, turned around to pass it on to a smaller one. She had stolen Sasha's paper, a dishonorable, shameful act that ate at her guts. But instead of leaving the matter to a poor grade and the school's routine discipline—down-rating, work details, quarters confinement, even a paddling from Headmaster Verin as younger students faced—Savoy had wanted to rub her face in her physical weakness, to make her surrender, humiliate her in front of others. Just as he had been. It was not discipline, it was retaliation. And it had come from the one person whose opinion she had permitted to matter so much. Too much. Alec had warned her. She should have listened and kept her distance.

Her face carefully void of her thoughts, Renee suggested they return to campus. Savoy's company kindled too great a disgrace to bear.

CHAPTER 19

Two days after Renee's night at Rock Lake, winter's full force slammed into Atham. Renee hid her bruises under heavy woolen tunics while she marooned herself in her quarters, burying her face in books when friends approached, and staring at the wall when alone. The Seventh left within the week, hurrying to ride out before the snow. She didn't come out to wish them farewell. When Savoy addressed her in class, she held his gaze but bowed in silence. On the heels of Alec's secret and Savoy's humiliating idea of discipline, Renee's mind pleaded for respite. Instead, it had life-altering exams to look forward to.

After a week of concerned glances and increasingly frustrated inquiries, Alec took action. "Renee," he called, jogging down the barracks corridor to catch up. Uninvited, he followed her into her room and pulled the door closed.

Renee tensed, then reached into her desk drawer for ink. Seaborn still wanted a paper. Twenty journal pages due a week post practical exams. She needed to find a topic. And materials. The library, she should go there. "I—"

Taking the ink from her hand, Alec set it aside and took hold of her shoulders. He held on until Renee lifted her face to meet his gaze. "Whatever it is, I will not ask," he said softly. "Neither will Sasha. All right?"

Renee's mouth went dry. She drew her breath for another denial, but Alec's eyes said none was necessary.

She pressed her forehead into his shoulder. It helped.

A few weeks later and with exams just six days away, the Board of Inquiry finally made its Queen's Day rulings. Returning to their room that evening, Sasha sat herself in front of Renee, who looked up from her push-up set by way of greeting.

"The board just issued Savoy a letter of censure." Sasha crossed her arms. "I heard all the evidence. They should have cleared him weeks ago, but Fisker kept pressing."

Renee suppressed a twinge of perverted satisfaction. The letter would slap Savoy's pride. It was unjust, of course, but in the colossal balance of pride infringement, it was somehow fair. If Fisker was hells bent on destroying Savoy's career in vengeance for childhood pranks, it was the men's problem. Her own career might face the gallows in a week. She had to focus on that.

"I think there's a history with those two." Sasha tipped her face to the ceiling. "It doesn't make sense otherwise. You'd think Savoy was a Viper or Family man, the way Fisker went after him."

Renee dusted her hands. They had a history all right, and Sasha knew it—she just didn't know that she knew. "They don't like each other." Renee shrugged, trying to evict Savoy from her thoughts, and lowered herself for more push-ups. "The captain in the Palace Guard thought Savoy had something to do with Fisker losing his finger."

For a moment, Sasha seemed as if she'd press the question, but then her brows twitched and she did not.

In the days to follow, exam anxiety loomed over all cadets—fighters and magistrates alike. For fighters, the midyear academic evaluation traditionally paled in comparison to the physical. That ratio would be reversed during end-of-year tests. At the moment, the end of year felt decades away, and so Renee disappeared into strength training. Only Diam and other young pages, who had taken to climbing the barracks' rooftop to launch snowballs at passersby, seemed immune.

"Get back to bed," Sasha scolded, waking during Renee's undesired vigil the night before judgment day. Fruitless advice. One student would be dismissed the next day, and Renee had more riding on the exam marks than did her classmates.

At breakfast, Alec forced two rolls and a slice of cheese into her mouth. "You'll see these again when I throw up," she warned him.

He only grinned. "I'd hate to see you forgo tradition," he said, shouldering his bag as they started back to her room to collect her equipment. "I think you've threatened to sick-up before every exam. And then passed."

They found her door unlocked. Renee pushed the handle and felt her hand curl into a fist. "What are you doing in here?"

Tanil jerked and turned toward her. "You startled me," he said, color creeping back into his pale face.

"How did you get in?"

He squinted at her. "Turned the handle, same as you. Didn't you leave the door open on purpose?" Digging into his coat, the boy pulled out a key and flicked it to her. "I found it on the ground and didn't wish you in trouble. Sorry. My mistake." Without waiting for a reply, Tanil turned on his heels and left the room. The door slammed in his wake.

Renee compared the new key to the copy she and Alec made on the first day of classes. "Looks worn." She surveyed the room for evidence of sabotage. "I think it really is the original. How long you think he's had it?"

"Long enough to do this." Alec held up her dress coat, freshly decorated with mud smears. "Do you have another?"

"No." She ground her teeth. With no time for cleaning, a dress shirt alone would have to suffice. Cold but still proper. She rubbed her arms and regretted it. They were tender still. Shaking her head, she grabbed her equipment bag and hurried to the training hall.

The salle had undergone its biannual morph. Several rows of benches appeared by the door at the west end of the room. A judges' dais draped with black and blue covers dominated the east end. Renee's gaze flowed over the ground, raked flat and neat. Several years ago a cadet ripped his knee after tripping on a clump of sand.

A cluster of junior students buzzed around a long wooden table, arranging mugs of water. Healer Grovener, immaculate as always, settled into his designated chair, drilling the examinees with a critical gaze. Tradition mandated disqualification to any student the Healer's hand touched.

"We have little time." Alec steered Renee toward the far benches.

She followed his lead, pulling pads from her bag and fitting them on. They looked odd. When she realized why, every muscle in her body tensed. The laces of her gear were all severed.

CHAPTER 20

Renee checked one useless piece of padded armor after another. Panic and disbelief made her hands tremble. Her gaze scoured the room for something she could use. Spare gear. The salle usually housed crates of old, but mostly serviceable, items.

"Where did the common pads go?" she asked, unable to find the stash.

"We moved everything out to the stable," a junior cadet volunteered in a cheery tone. "To give you more room."

Alec shot her a questioning look. His eyes widened when he saw the damage. "We run to the stable," he said, grabbing her arm and pulling her to the door.

They made it halfway to the exit before the bell sounded, ordering everyone to their place. Verin entered the salle and strode to the dais like a king ascending his throne. An elaborate blue and black velvet cloak trailed behind him, basking in its own dignity. Savoy and another Servant whom Renee didn't know followed at the headmaster's heels.

Renee lined up with the others in front of the judges and watched in fear while Verin took out a roster and began to call roll. No title but "Cadet" preceded the name of each student, noble or not—another reminder that Servants of the Crown made up a class of their own. When "Cadet Renee de Winter" sounded, she knelt on one knee.

"Did you develop a craving for broken bones, de Winter?" Savoy's voice cut through the room.

"Equipment failure, sir. May I get spares?"

"Inspecting gear is your responsibility. The battle started—make do with what you brought."

She met his cold eyes with ice of her own. Verin continued reading roll. Once the entire class knelt in front of the judges, he nodded to Savoy.

"On your feet," their instructor called, wasting no time on speeches. He ordered two students to the front, and all scrambled to obey.

Renee rubbed her arms for warmth and glared at Tanil.

He smiled, bowing to her. He could not see Alec coming up behind him until the larger boy had his wrist folded in two.

Tanil rose on his toes but wisely kept his mouth shut. A fight would disqualify him alongside Alec. Renee shook her head to prevent further damage for her friend's sake and forced her balled-up hands to open. Most likely the cadets would be paired by size; she'd deal with the weasel in the ring.

The first bout ended and Savoy called out new names. Renee's muscles twitched expectantly each time he spoke. During her classmates' fights, she shivered. Between them, she held her breath. At last Savoy cleared his throat and turned in her direction. Bile bit Renee and she rose to answer the call she knew was coming.

"Cadet Alec Takay," Savoy said, motioning him to take a spot in mid ring.

Renee sank back down.

She had just pulled herself together enough to congratulate Alec on a clean victory, when her own name sounded across the salle. Cold gripped her face. It was time.

"Fighters enter the Service of the Crown by the sword," Verin intoned the ritual words for the sixth time that day as Renee and Tanil faced each other across the sand. "The Crown seeks not good fighters; it seeks the best. May your skill prove your worth."

"Salute!" Savoy called on the heels of the declaration. His voice held the steel of war. "Ready blades!"

Renee brought the practice blade forward, raising the tip to eye level and the bevel at the height of her navel. Across the sand, Tanil did the same.

"Fight!"

They moved, circling each other like hungry animals. He swung first, wild and hard. She blocked the blow before it could shatter her. In her side vision, she saw blue mage light dance around Grovener's hand. The Healer's certainty that his services would be needed did nothing to boost her confidence.

Her attack thumped Tanil's chest-pad but failed to wipe the grin off his face. She was stronger than before, yes—but still not strong enough to hurt him through the pads. Any points she scored would be irrelevant if he disqualified her. As if to underline the thought, a missed parry opened her ribs to a strike. Burning pain shot across her chest. Her breath faltered. Panic returned. She had no options. If she attacked, she left herself vulnerable to crippling strikes. If she stayed defensive and, by miracle, blocked every blow, she'd lose on points.

His blade cracked against her sword arm. It went numb. The blade streaked toward her head next, a full swing of polished wood intent on cracking her skull. Tanil's nostrils flared with heavy breaths. His fevered eyes glimmered with full intent to follow through with the blow. Her life rested on the parry. She locked weapons shaft to shaft with the boy's. Her muscles cramped from the strain, and she was forced to kick his middle to win distance. He growled, but she couldn't spare the energy for a reply.

"How long do we let this continue?" an unfamiliar voice asked.

"Until she gives up," Verin answered, with no hint of emotion.

Savoy said nothing.

No, she wasn't quitting. And she wasn't dying. But what was she doing? Sweat dripped from her hair and stung her eyes. Blinded, she reached up to wipe them, and Tanil rapped her bruised triceps. She muffled a cry and sidestepped the next attack. She shook out her arm. It wasn't broken, she realized. It wasn't disabled. It stung. Nothing more, nothing less.

"You don't hit hard," she said, surprising herself with the sincerity of the statement. She survived Savoy's blows. Tanil's were unworthy of the comparison. All she really needed to do was protect her head and *move*. What did it matter that the boys preferred to break bones and sever heads, when a nick of the artery like Savoy had taught her killed just as well? The realization rushed through her like a sharp wave clearing debris from a dammed stream. She didn't need to prove herself as good as the boys. She needed to prove she could kill them.

Renee relaxed her muscles. Tanil thought he'd beat her into submission? Well, he was welcome to his delusions. Exhaling, Renee switched her grip to that of her morning exercises. Her sword flowed around the boy's blade, carving soft lines across his wrists and chest. Tanil's increasingly frantic movements voiced his bewilderment. She fed off his desperation and grew calmer, surer with each of his wild strikes. *It's a sword, not a tree trunk, oaf.* Her tip gently sliced his neck.

"Gods," someone muttered. "She's killed him five times over."

"No," Savoy replied, and raised his voice. "Quit fooling around and finish it, de Winter."

What more did he want? Renee swallowed. In front of her, Tanil cocked his sword and swung. She pivoted from his blade's grandiose arc and waited, letting him lose his own balance. Now she danced inside. With another pivot she circled to his back and, from behind, laid her sword across his windpipe. She felt her blade press into the delicate cartilage and knew with sickening certainty that should she pull, her dull wood would crush it forever, like an egg.

"Stop." His whisper came fast and desperate. "I yield."

She lowered her blade and shoved him away to face the judges, to whom he had to declare his intention.

"Sirs." He took a breath, his blade lowering to the ground. "I—" He spun, bringing his blade around to crack Renee's unprotected head.

The sounds of the world dimmed and returned. She swayed on her feet. Something wet trickled down into her collar.

"Sirs, I claim victory," said Tanil's voice.

"No yield." Renee heard her own voice reply. Her arms brought up her sword and she hoped they knew what to do with it.

"The cadet may not continue," said Healer Grovener.

Blue mage flame touched her shoulder and Cadet Renee de Winter was disqualified.

CHAPTER 21

The salle's sand saw more bouts. Renee watched them through a blur of shock and ache. She was done. Finished. Disqualified. One cadet had to be cut and it would be her. The Academy, Alec, Sasha—they were her home, and in a day's time she'd be alone. She had been granted a chance, a second family in place of the one that had been taken. Now it was over.

The last fight ended. The cadets dropped to their knees once more. Renee was grateful Healer Grovener permitted her to do as much, although her stomach fell as she knelt beside Alec for the last time. He reached out to grip her hand, offering a silent comfort.

Verin picked up a folded sheet of paper and showed it to his table mates. The knot of Savoy's brow suggested the news was neither pleasant nor expected.

"An anonymous member of this gathering brings allegations of misconduct to the judges' attention," Verin announced, pitching his voice over the salle. "This party contends that one or more of today's examinees appeared here under the influence of the leaf of veesi." His eyes swept the cadets. "The cowardliness of an anonymous report speaks of the author. It does not, however, discount the message. Before sunset today, all senior cadets will report to Healer Grovener. The judges will withhold the results of today's examination until appraising the Healer's report. Dismissed."

Disbelief paralyzed her. Renee didn't even feel Alec's hand slip out of hers. When her senses returned, he was gone. A herd of students made their way to the exit, and she was the only one left kneeling on the now scuffed and bloodied sand of the salle. At last Renee stood and walked to the door in a daze, but a hand seized her collar before she made it out.

"We can start with you. Come along," Grovener said, leaving her no choice but to follow.

Renee managed to find Alec two hours later, sitting atop a boulder on Rock Lake's shore. She pulled her coat tighter and climbed next to him. The breath misting from his nose curled to the heavy gray sky.

"Just because veesi affects me differently, doesn't mean it isn't there," Alec said without turning. "I took some this morning—I can't submit to Grovener's exam."

"I'll kill Tanil." Renee's fists tightened. "This reeks of him."

Alec nodded, then offered a wan smile, a mix of deep sadness and deeper determination. "At least you will continue. One student gone. It will be me."

A shiver ran through her. Alec was right. If he was dismissed, she would remain.

No. She refused to accept it. The Academy was Alec's family as much as it was hers. "They've caught you before. You got through it."

He shook his head. "I was twelve, Renee, and Verin thought he got me before I actually tried any. If Grovener tests me now . . . I have a history and enough of that sewage in my body and in my room that the guard will hold me. Then, well, without the leaf it won't be long until I slip and the bigger truth comes out and I wind up at the gallows." He sighed and allowed silence to finish the story.

A lump formed in Renee's throat. It wasn't fair. Alec, who never asked for, never wanted Control, deserved the same rights as everyone else to determine the course of his life. She found no words to say, and no time to search for them either, as desperate barking sounded from below. Peering down, she spotted Khavi clawing at the rock.

"That's not like him," Renee mumbled, wrinkling her brows. "Alec?" He had his hands clapped to his forehead. "What's wrong?"

Alec gasped, still clutching his head. "He's . . . he's forcing through my Keraldi Barrier. Gods, that hurts." He wheezed and shut his eyes. A few seconds passed until he reclaimed his breath. He stared at her. "I think . . . I think Diam's gone."

A search of Academy grounds proved fruitless for Diam and Savoy both. When Renee returned to Alec's room to report her lack of results, she found him stuffing shirts into his travel pack. Khavi whined at his feet. She touched Alec's shoulder. "Any more luck?"

His eyes flashed. "I can't read the dog's mind, Renee! That I got a few images is a small miracle in itself. I didn't know even *that* was possible unless one was bonded, and until this year, I thought bonding itself little more than my grandma's tale."

Renee winced. "Sorry, I didn't mean..." She climbed onto his bed and, propping her elbows on her knees, studied the stitching on his blanket. The sense that something very bad had happened settled around her shoulders. "Do you think Savoy and Diam left together?"

"No. The images Khavi gave me felt... wrapped in cotton, all blurry like." He rubbed his head. "I think Diam followed me to Atham when I went to buy... what I need. People, kids especially, have been disappearing off Southwest streets for months. They say night gangs abduct them in the darkness and sell them to Vipers. If Diam went exploring because of me—"

"It wasn't because of you." Renee pressed her finger into Alec's chest. "It was *not*. This is Diam Savoy we speak of. There's nothing in the Seven Hells that could scare that boy into staying put." She bit a loose fingernail and felt her thoughts snap together. "Khavi can follow Diam's trail, right?" Renee waited for Alec's nod and stepped toward the door. "Good. Let me know when you finish packing," she said, leaving his quarters before he could stop her.

By gods' grace, she found Sasha in their room. It was rather impossible to overlook the boy's relation to Savoy, and something Sasha once said now bothered Renee.

"I need a favor." Renee pulled out her travel pack and started to fill it. "Do you recall the beginning of the year, when you said Savoy was here because somebody wanted it so? I need to know who and why, and whether it had anything to do with Diam."

Sasha sat down and crossed her legs. "What happened at the exams?"

Renee didn't answer for several seconds. Her world, which had been turning in chaotic, nauseating circles for several months, now screeched to a clarifying halt. "I followed the rules," she answered. "I did. I followed the code exactly, and . . ." Renee's voice trailed off as she stared into her travel pack.

Sasha's brow furrowed. "Are you being dismissed?"

"No." A chuckle escaped her. No, she wasn't going to be dismissed. This time. To enjoy her good fortune, all she had to do was abandon Alec and leave Diam's fate to others. To buy herself another half year in the Crown's Service—a service that was ready to choose the cheating Tanil over her—all she had to do was shut her eyes and disavow those who mattered most at their moment of greatest need. And if she did *that* to protect the possibility of a career, either the career was not worth having or she was not worth a Servant's title.

"No, Sasha, I haven't been dismissed. I'm dismissing myself."

CHAPTER 22

Armed with travel packs, Renee and Alec followed Khavi eastward through the woods. Broken branches and prints in the snow lent credibility to the route—someone had passed here recently. Around them, a light snow fell, dusting the ground and crunching underfoot. Although the sun reflecting off the crystal flakes brightened the afternoon, a darkening sky foretold foul weather to come.

The sword hanging off Renee's left hip chafed with each step and taxed her balance. She squirmed, readjusting the steel. Savoy had been right. The blade, once meant for Riley, was too long for her.

Alec was quiet, his gaze veiled. Renee made no mention of the hanging threads on Alec's jacket where he'd ripped off the Academy seal. They had left their uniforms behind, but Alec had no other winter coat to take. She snugged her Academy scarf—the one piece of memory she permitted herself to bring with her—around her neck.

Three hours into the journey as the gray skies set loose their blizzard, her initial excitement began to fade. Footprints disappeared under the snow.

"Joining the Crown's Service was your life, Renee," Alec said suddenly. "It isn't too late to go back."

She stumbled. "And get cut the next chance that comes?"

"No." He blocked her path and faced her. "You can—"

"Make my own choices. I chose you and Diam. It's done." She walked around him and continued down the trail, locking her mind against further assaults of doubt. "I do wish we knew where in the Seven Hells we're headed," she said, her boot sliding off a stone hidden beneath the snow. At least Diam's captors had to be on foot by now—between the weather and the poor footing, any horse would have to be hand-led. Her stomach growled. Anxiety had kept them hiking through dinner and now it was late, the dimming sunlight about to vanish completely. They needed to make camp, should have made it before now. Renee stopped walking, raised her forearm to fend off the wind, and evaluated the terrain.

The terrain seemed to stare back. A chill gripped her spine. Renee shook her head, her hand resting on the sword's hilt. Her pulse quickened. Someone was watching them. A bandit, lurking behind snow-burdened evergreens. Or, an injured traveler, too cold and hurt to call out for help. Or, a Viper scout, mapping another approach to Atham. Or . . .

Khavi whined.

"Halt!" A familiar voice commanded from behind them. "Remove your hats."

Renee twisted around to find Savoy's steel pointing at her

head. It remained there until both her and Alec's faces were bared, the sharp wind biting their cheeks.

"Is Diam . . ." He caught her eyes and did not bother finishing the question. "There was a note in my room." He sheathed his blade and motioned for them to follow him off the path. Fifty paces from the trail, a camp, complete with Seaborn, Kye, and a tent, sprung from hiding. Savoy glared at the sky, then at her and Alec. "What are you two doing here?"

Pleasure meeting you as well. "Same thing you are," Renee replied. Savoy was no longer her commanding officer. She owed him no military courtesy.

He snorted and turned away.

Renee ground her teeth. "Khavi has Diam's scent."

Savoy paused and scratched the dog's chin. "I hadn't thought of that," he told Seaborn, without bothering to look back at Renee and Alec. "Good. The bloody blizzard wiped the tracks." He squinted at the sky. "We'll send the kids back to the Academy once the weather clears."

Renee blinked at the gall. "You will not." She stood her ground. "We quit."

Savoy did turn then and cocked an eyebrow, but Khavi's sudden howl halted the conversation. The dog shied as if struck and cowered to the ground, his tale between his legs. Howls turned into desperate whimpers.

Renee's gaze shot to Alec, who shook his head. He knew no more than she did.

Savoy squatted, pulled off his glove, and reached toward

Khavi's muzzle. "What's wrong, boy?" he asked softly, and sighed when the dog cringed away. Savoy stood up, his hand dropping limply to his side. He drew a breath. "Takay and de Winter, you will go back." His voice grew hard. "At best you'll get in the way out here. More likely, I'll get you killed."

"No." Renee stood her ground. Alec shifted uncomfortably behind her.

Twisting, Savoy caught her arm and threw her into a snowbank. "Which of my words confused you, girl?"

Renee gasped from shock and cold.

He pulled his sword. Metal whispered against the sheath. "Staying with me will get you dead. If you have a burning desire to be cut to shreds, I will oblige the curiosity right now and save us both the trouble."

"Seven Hells, Korish!" Seaborn's voice pierced the storm. "You've made your point. Stop now."

Renee's breath misted, adding dramatic effect to the unfolding theater. "You won't kill me."

Savoy chuckled without humor. "No, I won't kill you." Renee prepared to push herself up, but Savoy's blade remained at her throat. His free hand stopped Seaborn's approach and his face grew calm. On the sword's hilt, Savoy's fingers adjusted their grip. Renee realized her miscalculation a moment before he nodded his agreement again. "But I will hurt you enough to prevent travel."

She didn't doubt him now. And she knew he was granting her precious seconds needed for escape, but her body refused to move. Her hands scuffled in the snow and defiance fueled her waning courage. She stayed where she was, locked in a contest of wills. Somewhere nearby, Seaborn repeated his friend's name. The wind whipped the words away.

"Brace yourself," Savoy said softly. Not a threat, a recommendation. His muscles tensed. The rising point of the blade tripled in size.

"Get away from her."

Savoy's eyes grew and his sword snapped away from Renee toward Alec's voice.

Renee scrambled up on her elbow. A gasp escaped her as she saw what her friend had done.

A chaotic blue blaze engulfed Alec. He shook with effort but his focus remained on a shimmering tentacle that extended from his hand to Savoy's sword. The steel heated, glowing a bright orange red that spread down the blade. When it reached the hilt and touched skin, something sizzled, like frying bacon.

Savoy gasped but permitted himself no more than that. He shifted his weight, like a panther readying to pounce. "Mage." The surprise that flickered in his face yielded to discipline and the word came as a simple statement of fact. He clenched his teeth and stepped forward.

"Stop!" Renee scrambled to her feet.

Without breaking his line of sight, Savoy reached out with his free hand and pulled her behind him.

Alec's body quivered at the center of the blue flame. Savoy, in contrast, was poised and still. Perhaps he had not yet decided whether to strike. Or else he had, and only awaited the right moment.

Panic pounded Renee. "Alec! Stop! He'll kill you."

Alec's voice was strangled. "I can't."

A streak of white fur leaped from the snow. Paws hit Alec's chest and followed him to the ground. The mage flame died. Triumphant, Khavi wagged his tail and licked the face of his fallen prey.

Pushing past Savoy, Renee rushed to Alec. She found the opening in his jacket lining and placed orange leaves to his lips, wishing she knew what dose to offer. Given the circumstances, more was probably better. His tunic and hair were drenched in sweat and he wheezed softly, struggling to steady his breath.

"I see." Seaborn's voice was uncharacteristically flat.

Renee tightened her hold around her friend's shoulders. "He's . . . good with animals. He can track with Khavi better than you can. You need him." She took a breath. It wasn't good enough. *Seven Hells, Khavi is a mage too!* she almost shouted, but swallowed it down. The secret was not hers to tell, nor had she any proof for the outlandish claim. But she needed the men to listen. She had to give them something more than vague skills or wild legends. "And, if you turn him in now, you'll both be tied up with authorities instead of out searching for Diam."

Several paces away, Savoy lowered his blade at last.

"Understood," he said, his face unreadable. A crimson drop fell on the snow beneath his right hand. Another drop joined it. Khavi trotted up and prodded his wet nose into the sleeve obscuring Savoy's fingers, then gave a reproachful look when the hand pulled away.

"I'm sorry," Alec whispered.

Savoy turned and walked off into the woods alone.

Shame ambushed Renee in the dark. Being tossed into a snowbank had kindled unwelcome memories—it seemed Savoy was turning knocking her about into a habit. Her last glimpse of the Academy, with white flakes circling the peaked gate, floated through her mind each time she closed her eyes. Alec stayed silent and twitched in his dreams. When they started out early the following morning, Renee had no trouble waking; she hadn't slept.

According to Seaborn, the note that appeared in Savoy's room after the exams directed him to the Yellow Rose in Catar City. There was no signature. The fresh trail the men had followed, until the storm destroyed the tracks, confirmed recent travel toward Catar, the Vipers' home turf. Any legitimate business went by road. Renee rubbed her arms. Savoy was the true target of this mess. He had to be. No other reason to leave the note in his room. Someone had issued Savoy a challenge, and named the battlefield. And, of course, Savoy was answering it.

None of which was reason to patronize *her*. Renee bloody well wasn't the kidnapper.

She coughed as cold air bit her lungs, and tightened her scarf. They trekked on. Tree limbs sagged under the weight of their white burdens. Long, sharp icicles hung from the thicker branches. Kye, whose velvety black coat shone in dazzling contrast to the white world, picked an unfortunate moment to snack on the vegetation, shaking snow from a pine onto Renee's head.

Gasping, she jumped sideways and cringed at the small clump of wetness that made its way into her collar and snaked down her spine. Savoy's eyes flickered in her direction. Depriving him the satisfaction of watching her squirm, Renee made no comment. To her irritation, the man showed no discomfort in the freezing weather. He strode along, leading his horse and scanning the landscape, as if his body long ago negotiated a truce with the wind and the chill. And he never called for a break.

"Korish, stop a few minutes," Seaborn said after they crested another hill, having marched several hours upward to get there. He looked like Renee felt, exhaustion slumping his shoulders.

Savoy regarded him, then Alec and Renee. His lips pressed together in annoyance but he said nothing, and slung off his pack.

She restrained a sigh. The man consented to traveling together, so he needed to stop complaining about their inadequacy every ten seconds, however wordlessly he did so. She reached for her canteen. No water came out. A thick slab of ice blocked the vessel's mouth. She stuffed it back with a curse. Everything she touched, it seemed, from the essay to the bout with Tanil to the gods' forsaken water flask, had a whiff of failure to it. Of course, Savoy's canteen suffered no such issues. Taking a swallow, he extended it to her.

"I'm not thirsty."

He shrugged, and after offering a drink to the other travelers, stowed the canteen back in his pack. Upside down. "Ice floats," he said, catching her gaze—just in case she hadn't already noted his superiority.

Ignoring him, she dug a frozen hunk of bread from her pack and contemplated the chances of keeping her teeth intact if she bit it.

"Forget that, make a fire." Savoy looked to the sky. "We'll camp here for the night."

"We'll lose time," she said, despite no longer feeling her toes. The three layers of socks she pulled on that morning failed to do their job.

"We'll lose one of you if you don't get something hot inside." Of course, he excluded himself from that category. Weather and fatigue bothered only mere mortals. If Seaborn and Alec had not already started unpacking, she would have kept hiking. Or tried to.

Renee gathered her waning energy and surveyed their new campsite, building a mental list of chores.

Savoy eyed her with condescending concern. "Gather firewood, de Winter," he ordered, as if making such decisions was beyond her. "Alec, animals and gear. Connor, you and I will put up the tents. You have a problem, de Winter?"

The words left her mouth before her brain filtered them. "Yes. It's blond, green-eyed, and thinks it's a god." She shifted her weight under the penetrating stares. In for a copper, in for a crown. She glanced at Alec and Seaborn. "We're not daft. I just said what everyone's thinking."

"Not me," Seaborn said quietly, and turned to his work.

Savoy ran a hand through his hair, his face as indifferent as his tone. "Do whatever you want, de Winter."

"I thought you liked him," Alec whispered when they'd turned to their chores.

"I thought you didn't."

He shrugged, not meeting her gaze. "I don't. But disliking him doesn't bother me."

Unsure what he meant, Renee began setting up camp, fast realizing that firewood remained the only outstanding critical task. Damn the man.

Once the fire was started, she savored its warmth for several indulgent minutes before surveying the rest of the setup. Alec brought over kitchen gear and started compiling ingredients for some sort of stew. Seaborn, armed with a small shovel, piled a windbreak mound by the first tent. Savoy anchored the second. Well, tried to anchor the second. She watched him struggle to tie a knot one-handed.

Walking over, Renee inserted herself between him and the rope. She drew it taut and secured it with easy motions. Permitting herself a content smile, she met Savoy's eyes.

Instead of thanking her, he reached down and pulled loose her bootlaces. "You'll freeze your feet tying them so tight. Blood can't move." He shook his head. "How many socks did you cram in there?"

Right. Courteous conversation was clearly beyond his skill set. She was neither his student nor his soldier. She was a friend of his brother's and trying to save the boy's life. And she was done with his bullying. "What's your problem?"

"Beyond a novice crusading for democracy? A kidnapped eight-year-old boy."

"If you bothered to mind him, we would not have that issue," she said, knowing she went too far. And not caring.

His eyes flashed. "We don't. I do. You are a tagalong liability who can't tell reality from grand adventure."

She went to slap him. He caught her wrist in mid-motion. The next instant, he released it with a hiss of pain, cradling his bandaged hand to his chest. It was not funny at all, but Renee smiled anyway and walked away.

After cooling off enough to be passable company, Renee went to inspect Alec's kitchen adventures. He was not there, but Seaborn, sitting on a fallen trunk near the fire, extended a mug of tea to her. He held up another one and called to Savoy, but the man shook his head and headed to the opposite edge of the clearing.

Savoy dug out a small jar and braced it between his knees to open the lid, then unwrapped the bandage. When the salve touched the lesion, he closed his eyes and rocked over the cradled palm for a breath, before refastening the dressing.

"Do you think burns hurt more than arrow wounds?" Renee asked Seaborn, who glanced over at Savoy and winced.

"I think no one should be that skilled at tying a bandage one-handed."

"If he behaved like a normal human being, he wouldn't have to," she mumbled. After making certain that Savoy showed no signs of listening, she turned back to Seaborn. "Was he different as a cadet?"

"He was the Seven Hells' personal representative to the mortal realm. Gods, I don't know how the Academy survived us both." Seaborn's smile faded and he stirred the fire with a stick. "I left for a while at fourteen. When I returned, Verin had him on a leash and he wasn't talking much to anyone, me included."

"He still doesn't."

He shook his head. "Relatively speaking, he does."

"You stopped being friends after the horse incident?" When several seconds passed without an answer, she looked up to see Seaborn watching her, his brows raised. She tried to cover her words.

He shook his head. "Too late. When did he tell you what that essay was really about?"

The heat rising in her face had nothing to do with the fire. "After what he did to me in the salle."

"After what he did to you in the salle?" Seaborn sat back and looked at her incredulously. "Renee, what he did to you in the salle was save you from getting thrown out of the Academy on the spot. He and Verin went head to head for half an hour over it. And then another quarter hour because he would not let Verin touch you."

She swallowed. *Thrown out on the spot.* Bloody gods. Her face burned despite the cold. She was on probation, yes, but in combat arts, not academics. "Expulsion for one mistake? My first?"

"You chose a poor time for it." He spread his hands. "Verin *had to* cut a senior cadet in a few weeks anyway. You were making a difficult decision very easy, Renee."

She hadn't considered that. She glanced at Savoy. "Why didn't he just tell me I was getting off easy?"

Seaborn tilted his head back. "I would wager," he said, emphasizing the last word, "he did not wish to make excuses for his actions."

Renee's stomach twitched in familiar frustration. *His* actions. Exactly. They were back to that. "Master Verin handles such things in private. Why did Savoy wish to humiliate me?"

Seaborn chuckled. "Is that what you think?" He braced his elbows on his knees and cocked his head at her. "Humiliate you how, Renee? By besting you in a sparring match? I doubt there is anyone in Atham who could hold his own for more than a minute with the man."

She looked at Savoy and back. "He had wanted to deliver the blows himself. If it wasn't to prove a point, then why?"

Seaborn glanced at his friend. "He's a fighter, Renee. He'd wish to face what comes with a sword in hand, even a battle he could not win. Perhaps he believed the same true for you?" He wrapped his hands around his mug and lowered his already quiet voice. "Plus, Korish is not one to let others handle his dirty work. He considered your fate his fault."

"That's—" Seaborn's hunched shoulders made her swallow the word *ridiculous*. She frowned. "Does . . . Does he hold himself accountable for your injuries in the riding accident?"

"I believe he always has." Seaborn snuffed out a stray ember with his boot. "I also believe having to hurt you reopened that wound."

Renee rose before dawn the following morning. Savoy had the watch and was in the midst of morning chores, flowing through the camp like a dancer across the floor. A pot of stew was already heating on a makeshift stove and a stack of fresh wood waited by the fire. On this miserably cold morning, in the middle of the forsaken woods, he looked more at home than she recalled ever seeing him at the Academy.

"What should I do?" she called out, searching for unfinished tasks.

He unbuckled Kye's hobbles and stowed them in a saddlebag. "Whatever you wish."

A log cracked in the fire, lighting the silence. Savoy lifted Kye's heavy hoof, awkwardly balancing it atop his right forearm while his other hand worked the hoof-pick. His sword hung from the wrong hip, a change Renee had failed to notice until now.

She lowered her head and bent to pet Khavi, who slept curled in a ball. The dog lumbered up in greeting, moving with uncharacteristic stiffness. She furrowed her brows at his lethargy and had just reached out to pet him when a snow-laden branch broke from a tree and crashed to the ground beside Savoy. The stallion jumped in place, despite Savoy's arm still supporting a hoof. Gasping, he dropped the hoof pick and cradled his bandaged hand before leaning on his horse for support.

He turned his head before Renee could look away and their eyes met across the campsite.

"Enjoying the show?" he asked.

She shook her head.

Savoy returned to his task, leaving her to stare at his back and regret her smile of the previous evening. It was time to mend things.

Ten minutes later, Renee sat atop the fallen tree trunk by the fire and filled two mugs with steaming coffee. She took a second to savor the rising steam and called to Savoy, "Peace offering?"

"There isn't a war." He did not sit, but at least he took the coffee.

"How's your hand?"

"What do you want?"

She looked at the fire. It was easier to watch the flames than his face. "Our best swordsman can't grip his blade. My teacher's worried about his brother. And . . ." She gathered herself. "And my friend's hurt, and no one will even help him tie the bandage."

He said nothing for a while, and the crackle of the burning wood filled the silence. "I'm not your friend," he said quietly, long after a thick log charcoaled in the center and broke in two. "And you wouldn't wish me as one."

"I understand the risks." She smiled tightly, then drew a breath. "Seaborn told me that Headmaster Verin had wished to dismiss me." She didn't look at him still. In retrospect, she was daft to not have at least suspected the truth. Dafter still to have done the deed, but it was too late for that line of thought. Her head bent over her cup, the hot fumes warming her face. *It was gentler on my pride to blame you than to thank you. I'm sorry.* She opened her mouth, but the words would not come. She nodded at his bandage instead. "Does it hurt?"

"Yes."

"Good." She smiled at him.

Savoy blinked, then chuckled back.

She set her cup down into the snow, regretting the loss of heat. "May I see?"

He shrugged wearily but sat beside her and surrendered his hand. The muscles on his forearm coiled when she pulled away the layers of cloth that stuck to the wound. The unveiled raw, blistered flesh made Renee suck in a breath and turn away. Blood rushed from her head. She lifted her face to the sky and counted to ten until the wave of dizziness passed. "Gods."

He pulled his hand back and flexed his swollen fingers. "It looked better yesterday."

"Maybe Alec can—"

"Meddle within my Keraldi Barrier without any training? No." Savoy pulled the small jar of salve from his pocket and opened it. Seen up close, the viscous white liquid inside was tinged with a pale blue shimmer. "Mage-made." He answered her unspoken question. "They say it fights off corruption. Seven Hells, it should fight off bears the way it stings."

She peered inside and recoiled from the rank smell. The salve had to cost double its weight in gold. Meanwhile, Savoy braced his forearm against his knee and fumbled in his pocket for a clean strip of linen.

"Do you want help?" She made herself sound steady. Even a pair of inexperienced hands had to be better than changing a dressing one-handed.

"No." He paused and then his good hand halted her rising. "But I will take the company, if you do not mind."

CHAPTER 23

Catar drowned in green. Dirty green coats on loitering young men. Thin green headcloths on girls who winked and purred on street corners. Mismatched green store signs. The shades varied from one ragged cloth to the next, but the color itself was there, slithering through the narrow streets. Viper color.

Growing up in the countryside, Renee learned the Family's game. Their veesi dealers titled themselves merchants, their thugs claimed the name *private guard*. Even nobles like Lord Palan feigned legitimacy. Calling a tribute a donation made little financial difference, but compared to the naked disrespect for the law that the Vipers showed, it was genteel.

"The Family sprung from nobility." Seaborn's voice had a classroom cadence that made Savoy roll his eyes. Ignoring him, Seaborn added, "Overt crudeness would upset their more delicate maneuvers. The Vipers breed in prisons and slums—their approach is bludgeon."

Bludgeon. Like shooting arrows into the palace and setting mage buildings aflame. Renee sighed. Bribing the Crown at a time of barren treasury, like the Family was doing, was certainly more refined—and more devious as well. "Doesn't the Madam realize that brash actions push King Lysian toward an alliance with the Family? He would save face if nothing else."

"The Madam rose to her place through blood and must champion her cause in a manner her people approve. Her Vipers crave to see men cower and break in the Predator arena and the streets alike. To hold respect, the Madam must make the Crown capitulate from *fear*, not from some mutually beneficial arrangement," said Seaborn.

"And the Family?" asked Renee.

"They desire coin. All else, from veesi sale to extortion and blackmail, is but a means to that end."

A rat of a man with an unshaven face made a kissing noise at Renee. She cracked her knuckles but kept her pace steady. Frosted sewage crunched underfoot, the cobblestones as foul as the gazes upon her.

Alec, who had developed a habit of keeping pace at the fringe of the group, stepped toward her. Savoy started in the same direction, and Alec veered back to his place, looking straight ahead.

"Take off your scarf." Savoy stepped up beside her, Kye shouldering away Seaborn.

Her fingers touched the woolen scarf hugging her neck. Wide bands of blue and red, representing the Academy's two tracks, stood proudly against black wool.

"Do it," he hissed into her ear.

Biting the inside of her cheek, she unwound the cloth. The wind invaded her collar.

"Throw it into the sewage, not into your pocket."

She jerked her chin up toward his face, the symbol of Tildor clutched in her fist. Her nostrils flared. "No."

"Then get the bloody hells away, before you expose me as well as yourself. Or did you plan to stand in the public square and demand Diam's release in the Crown's name?"

She stepped away from him but let the wool slip from her fingers. Her eyes closed to avoid watching Kye's hooves trample the scarf. When she brought herself to turn back, she saw that the expensive cloth was buried in filth. How could a Tildor city have so forsaken the rule of law that a flag of justice became a liability?

Seaborn put a hand on her shoulder. "I doubt the Seventh blows trumpets before an assault. We would likewise do well to keep our loyalties hidden."

She took a breath of rank air and let her heart catch up to her mind. Lady Renee and her entourage traveled on personal business. They were no one to the Crown, useless as political hostages, pointless as symbols for vengeance. Shivering, she maneuvered over to Alec and they walked in companionable silence.

At Seaborn's suggestion, the group lodged at Hunter's Inn. It was a modest place in a clean part of town, the type of place suitable for a visiting young noble. The innkeeper apologized for a lack of private quarters for the lady, but offered two adjoining rooms where tall walls tried to compensate for stingy floor space. Nonetheless, after five days of a winter march—the

191

storm had doubled the usual travel time—they had real rooms and real beds. A silver coin even bought connection to a courier who'd bring a note with Renee's location to Sasha.

"You're quiet, even for you," Renee told Alec while she readied for bed. Her friend had spent the day mumbling to Khavi, who had staggered along at his side. He hadn't volunteered an explanation for the dog's lethargy, and she had feared to ask. Now, still in his travel clothes, Alec lay atop his bedspread, fingers interlaced behind his head. Outside their window, stars glistened against a moonless sky, twinkling like fireflies. Navigating between the two narrow beds to a small wash table, Renee poured some water from a chipped pitcher into the basin. She touched it and sighed. "It's cold."

Alec looked at her, his eyes as distant as the outside stars. His gaze shifted to the basin and his hand flicked forward, a blue glow hugging his fingers like a glove. A moment later, a hair of light extended from his palm toward the water. It touched the basin for several heartbeats before melting away into nothingness. "Try it now."

Swallowing, Renee dipped a finger into the wash water. It warmed her skin. She frowned and wiped her hand on her nightshirt. "Don't do that."

"Why not?" The indifference in his voice chilled her. "You know what I am. As they do." He frowned at the closed door separating the rooms. Since the incident with the sword, neither Savoy nor Seaborn had brought up Alec's nature, but neither did they go out of their way to speak to him. To be fair, Alec avoided them as well, especially Savoy.

"You said you didn't want to be a mage."

"I don't." Alec sat up and crossed his arms. "I gave half my life to the Academy, did all the Crown asked of a Servant." His voice rose. "You were there. You know. They bleed your soul until you can hardly move and then discard you if you trip. I didn't trip. I gave all they wanted. And do you know what? They'd have shackled me anyway, for being born as I was, for not wishing to let some Mage Council decide whether to train me into a Healer or a weapon or whatever else." Alec's nostrils flared, his face darkening with unbridled anger that Renee had never seen in him before. "I thought I could win, prove that I could make my own choices! I couldn't. If Tildor will always treat me as a mage first and a person second, why forfeit the few advantages there are?"

"Because you can't have it both ways, Alec! If you want to Control, then register and follow the rules. Else, don't use it absent an emergency."

"Register?" His eyes flashed and he rose from the bed. "Forfeit my life to the council? You know why they burn the registration symbol over a mage's heart. So you couldn't amputate the marked body part if you wanted to. Once they brand you, they can find you anywhere. They can make the symbol kill you."

"Which the Crown orders only if you turn murderer or something of similar nature," Renee pointed out.

"I don't need a death threat to keep me from hurting others," he shouted. "I've never done it and never will!"

"Seen Savoy's hand lately?" she yelled to match his tone.

"Savoy." Alec rolled his eyes. A moment later, his jaw clenched tight. "I kept him from stabbing you, Renee. And I touched his sword, not him." He paused. "Why do you stare?"

Renee stepped back from the blue mage flame that ravaged the air around Alec's palms, seemingly without his knowledge. Her heart sped. When attacking Savoy, Alec had been unable to stop the assault without Khavi's help. "Alec."

He advanced toward her. The flame encircling his hands pulsated and intensified with each breath. "What's wrong with you?" he growled.

"Stop!" Renee's back struck the wall. She slid along it toward the door. "I had it wrong." She forced calm into her voice and extended her hands in front of her. "You are right. You are right."

His flaming hand extended and blue flame shot forth. It struck the wall beside Renee's head, leaving a scorch mark on the reddish plaster. She gasped.

The door connecting the rooms crashed open. "What goes on?" Seaborn boomed.

Alec jerked from the noise and stared at his hands, eyes growing wide. "I . . . I'm not certain," he stammered. He looked from the scorched wall to Renee, froze a moment, and backed away. "Gods." Retreating to his bed, he drew up his knees and cradled his head on them. His body twitched.

Renee let out a breath and licked dry lips. She was exhausted, as if she had just run for leagues, and her knees threatened to wobble. A hand touched her shoulder. Savoy watched Alec, but leaned against the wall by her side.

Seaborn fished veesi from Alec's pack and put several leaves to the boy's lips, whispering something soothing about Control taking time to harness. Alec cringed, but she felt no sympathy for him now. An untrained mage was like a child with an armed crossbow. *Now I wish him to chew veesi?* Alec could not keep himself drugged all his life. She rubbed her face and leaned toward Savoy. "Could you walk with me?"

"You should care for your friend," he answered for her ears alone.

The men left the room, leaving Renee and Alec to their soup of shame and confusion.

Alec sat cross-legged on his bed and stared at his feet.

She sat next to him, rested her elbows atop her knees, and watched her fingers interlace in meaningless patterns. Perhaps she had done something to trigger the episode. Did it matter if she had? Alec had to bear responsibility for his power if he did not wish the Crown to take up that burden.

He spoke first. "You like him, don't you?" he said quietly. "Korish Savoy."

Her heart paused.

"You know he's twenty-three and you still like him, even when he was our instructor . . . In a way you don't like me."

Blood drained from her face. Seven Hells, curse her blindness. Alec's protectiveness, his hatred of Savoy and Cory, his post by her side growing stronger each year. She touched his arm. "Alec, you're my best, dearest friend." Her mouth tripped over the words. He was more her family than her father had ever been. She loved him in a way no other attraction could diminish. "You are . . . my brother. Savoy cannot compete with that."

"He doesn't have to." The words came under his breath. He shook himself and slid off the bed. "My apologies for earlier. I've not tried living veesi-free before. The energy currents get . . . overwhelming."

"Alec . . ."

He shook his head to cut off her words and spoke quickly of Catar and its streets. They tortured the conversation for a quarter hour before declaring surrender and claiming their beds. Renee drifted to sleep pondering the unnerving nature of friendship, and what exactly she felt about Korish Savoy.

CHAPTER 24

In Hunter's Inn's stable the next morning, Savoy poured a scoop of grain into Kye's feed and reached for a currycomb. Care for animals, then gear, then self. The burn on his hand slowed his progress, but with a wild mage in their midst, Savoy was lucky to have gotten off as lightly as he did. Renee's decision to keep her friend's confidence and all but blackmail him and Connor into doing the same was an interesting one, displaying the kind of calculated recklessness Savoy was prone to himself. Which was not a compliment to either of them.

A stable hand shuffled his feet nearby, disturbing Savoy's thoughts. "The stable boys can—"

"Get their ribs broken."

A mare whinnied nearby and Kye kicked the wooden stall partition, shaking the housing. The hostler disappeared.

Savoy patted the stallion's neck and went back to his work, letting the facts roll across his mind. Although the growing Viper presence in Atham led to many crime-of-opportunity kidnappings, Diam's abduction was deliberate. A means to force Savoy to Catar. *Why?* Unknown. Regardless, the boy—or someone who knew his whereabouts—was somewhere in this city. At least that was the operating assumption. Alec had promised to take Khavi on a sweep of the terrain and Renee planned to mingle in what passed for Catar's noble court. This left him free to walk into whatever ambush Diam's captors had planned for him at the Yellow Rose Inn, wherever and whatever that was.

"Riding out?" Connor frowned from the stable's entrance and made his way forward. The ease with which he had navigated to Hunter's Inn the previous day belied more knowledge of Catar than books and documents could account for. "I thought to accompany you for fear you'd start three fights by sunset."

"Afraid I'll lose?"

"Afraid you'll win."

Savoy snorted, then remembered the original question. Connor would have made an exceptional swordsman, but a fighter could ill afford to fear horses. If the fear even stopped there. *And whose fault lies at the root of that?* Savoy busied himself with the task at hand. Kye's slick black coat had grown to rich velvet in cold winter months. "I'll walk."

Seaborn leaned against the wall. After several minutes of silence, he crossed his arms and looked out toward the court-yard beyond the stable. "I disappointed you when I quit the fighter track."

Savoy lifted Kye's water bucket with his good hand and hung it on a hook inside the stall. There had to be a worse time for this conversation, but one did not come to mind. He fed the horse a stashed apple and stepped past his friend to replace the borrowed brushes.

Connor cleared his throat. "You think fear guided my choice."

The brushes clacked against each other. "Yes. Did it not?"

There was a pause. "It did. But it was the right choice nonetheless."

"A fear-forced choice is not a choice at all." Savoy spun around. "Why do you speak of this now?"

Connor opened his mouth, then shut it. "No reason." He shook his head. "My apologies."

"Hand me a flake of hay."

Connor did, but unsaid words charged the air like a knocked arrow in a ready bow. He may have laid the subject of their careers to rest, but he was not done speaking things Savoy did not wish to hear. Savoy rested his elbows on the gate of Kye's stall. "Say it, Connor. Or don't."

Connor motioned to the bandage on Savoy's hand. "If you need a mage Healer . . . it can be arranged."

Savoy's brow rose. Seeing a Crown's mage posed too great a risk of exposure to chance, which meant the man Savoy accused of cowardliness a few breaths ago meddled in affairs that bordered treason. "For a magistrate, Connor, your relationship with the law leaves enough leeway for a herd of horses to pass abreast."

Connor shook his head. "My personal opinions do not affect my work, and I've made no secret of disliking registration."

"Mmm. I am certain you report contact with your . . ." Savoy paused to find a fitting term for dangerous felons. ". . . acquaintances, to Atham."

"Atham benefits from my contacts well enough."

Savoy paused in mid-motion, then chuckled. So Connor, whom Savoy once accused of real-world ignorance, dabbled in whispers. It suited him. "You've always found no less trouble than I did, you know. You were just better at not getting caught."

"You covered for me," said Connor.

Savoy shrugged. "When you couldn't sit comfortably, you did a poor job on my homework." He straightened and glanced outside. It was time to go. "Diam first. Then we'll visit your friends." He clapped Connor's shoulder. "Come. An ambush awaits."

The storm's passing left piles of snow on Catar's already narrow streets. The houses huddled together as if seeking warmth, but succeeded only in blocking the sun. If the nobles' estates at the city's fringes touched woods, no hint of vegetation survived in the city center. Even Atham's worst slums welcomed trees; Catar wasn't Atham.

Savoy walked, keeping one hand on his sword and the other on his purse. Although he wore nothing to identify him as a Servant, he was still a stranger here, and that alone made him conspicuous. He nodded toward the sword hanging on Connor's hip. It was Renee's, but noble ladies seldom strolled about armed to the teeth. "Can you use it?"

"We will find out."

Savoy stifled a sigh. "Try not to stab me."

"I'll—" Connor's retort cut off as an adolescent girl, scantily clad for the chill, stepped out from a small alcove, gripped his sleeve, and trailed a finger down his forearm.

"Cold today," she purred.

"Go for a run." Savoy removed her hand from Connor's sleeve and continued walking. He made it three steps before a large youth blocked his path. Frustration bubbled inside his stomach and crept upward. He looked the roadblock in the eye. "Move."

"This here be a paid street. Extra for touchin' the girl." A malicious smile played across the youth's lips.

Savoy rolled his eyes, stroking the hilt of his sword. "This here be a sharp, pointy thing. Move."

"Korish, don't." Connor gripped his shoulder. "What will you do if the guard comes?"

"Run," Savoy and the youth said simultaneously.

Connor huffed. "It delights me that you found a playmate, but perhaps you could delay your amusement until after we find the Yellow Rose?"

The youth whistled, his smile dissipating. "Yellow Rose? Mayhap I'll sell you what you need right here. Prime seats too. Good for any fight with new pups this month. Take your bets now too. You be lucky meeting Mot today."

Savoy took a gold crown from his purse and twisted the coin in his fingers. "We're looking for a boy."

Mot's smile returned, showing a mouth of teeth. "That be premium, after the fight. What age?"

Savoy had to master his voice to coolness before daring to answer. "A particular boy. Where is the Yellow Rose Inn?"

He laughed. "Mot thinks you best buy the tickets."

Ignoring Connor's pointed looks, he tossed the coin into the air. The youth caught it, handed over two round chits, and disappeared into a nearby doorway.

"Predator tickets." Connor raised his brows. "Your notion of recreation?"

"No, I simply can't walk past a law without breaking it." Savoy examined the newly acquired round bits of painted metal, his stomach clenching as if struck with a blow. "The Yellow Rose isn't an inn." He turned the cold chits in his fingers to display the markings that confirmed beyond a hope of doubt what Mot had implied. On the other side from the strokes indicating the fight time, shone a painted rose with lush yellow petals. "It's a Viper Pit."

Connor let out a breath. Collecting the chits, he slipped them into his pocket. "I'll get you details. Give me a few hours."

Savoy narrowed his brows. "Lead on."

The tightness around Connor's lips suggested that Savoy's company had not entered his plans, but he was smart enough to avoid futile protests. Shrugging, he led the way down a busy street and ducked into a taproom. Savoy followed through the door to find his way blocked by the guard. By the time he shoved the larger man aside, Connor had disappeared out the back. Bloody hero proving his courage.

Savoy cursed.

"A Viper Pit?" Renee turned the chit over in her hands, as much to examine the specimen as to distance herself from the storm of Savoy's fury.

The target of the assault, bruised and cut, sat shirtless on one of Hunter's Inn's beds. From what she gathered since the shouting started, Seaborn had taken the initiative to disappear into Catar alone and ran into trouble that concluded with a loss of purse, cloak, and Renee's sword. To her surprise, Renee found the loss of her family weapon didn't distress her. The blade had been a poor fit. She'd get a new one.

"What in the Seven Hells were you trying to prove, Connor?" Savoy raked a wet towel over the shallow grazes on his victim's side. "The vastness of your stupidity?"

Seaborn gritted his teeth and stared at the wall. The lacerations were shallow, more ugly than serious. In fact, of the two men, the pale Savoy looked worse.

Renee found a long strip of cloth to wrap Seaborn's torso.

He smiled at her before reaching for his shirt and wincing. "Thank you." He started on the buttons. "Cease yelling, Korish. I'm all right. You've hurt me worse sparring."

"You don't risk death when we spar." Savoy hit a washbasin, which shattered against the floor into a fountain of water and porcelain debris. Staring at the destruction, he ran a hand through his hair and moved away to perch himself on the bureau. By the time he spoke again, his voice was collected. "Very well. What did your birdies tell you?"

"The Yellow Rose is a local Viper lair. They run Predator fights and deal in human trade. A boy matching Diam's description came in a few days ago from their dealer in Atham—a viper-tattooed man named Vert—to be held for ransom, or sold if none is paid. Not unusual, except for the ransom itself, which is Lord Palan's head."

Savoy leaned forward. "The Vipers want me to go after Palan?"

"Not the Vipers." Seaborn shook his head. "The Vipers do not seem to know Diam's name, much less his relation to you personally. Someone delivered the boy to Vert, left ransom instructions, and said no more. Probably the same someone who left the note in your room. Everyone believes the ransom to be a joke, but they have nothing to lose."

"*Someone.*" Savoy crossed his arms. "*Someone* wanted me out of Atham, or hunting Palan, or both. So he used my brother as bait, and the Vipers as jailers. Who?" He leaned his head back against the wall and closed his eyes for a moment. "Not the Family, since Palan is a target, and not the Vipers, since they neither know who Diam is nor would they want to draw my attention to their home base . . . No, whoever he is, the bastard who arranged this game knows me well enough to know my relatives. If I were still heading the Seventh, I'd suspect a plot to sabotage the unit, but . . ." He shook his head, then straightened, pinning Seaborn with a stare. "Your birdies sing well."

"They do." Seaborn ran his hand over the bandage and sighed. "Unfortunately, it would be unwise to contact them again. For everyone's sake."

Renee suppressed a shiver.

Savoy tapped his finger on the windowpane. "What happens if I visit the Rose and start smashing heads?"

"You get dead; Diam becomes a liability and also gets dead," Seaborn replied dryly.

In the corner of the room, Alec cleared his throat but gestured to Renee when faces turned toward him.

She nodded. "Khavi found Diam's scent near Duke Leon's estate. The place spans several acres, complete with guards and walls."

"We can scale the wall at night," said Savoy.

"Or, perhaps, walk in through the front door." Renee's face heated as she forced herself to meet Savoy's eyes. "Do you dance?"

"What?"

"I went to the governor's manor, where the nobles assemble to share news." Seeing Savoy tense, she shook her head quickly. "No one thought twice of it. De Winter is a minor house, but an out-of-town visitor is a novelty. It would raise greater questions if I *didn't* go."

"Then why do you look as if you fear I'll strangle you?"

"Duke Leon is hosting a ball tomorrow night." Renee took a breath. It was better to just say it. "I've committed to going, with a guest. Thus . . . do you dance?"

Savoy blinked while Seaborn's laugh filled the room. "He dances, Renee. And if he doesn't, I'll teach him myself."

It wasn't that Renee disliked dresses; it was that the trio in the other room had never seen her in one. Worse yet, she couldn't reach the back ribbons. She ran her hands over the recent purchase, smoothing the slippery rose-and-white bodice that tapered out to a sea of skirt. In the Academy, she all but stripped in front of the boys, yet the walk to the other room now daunted her.

"Are you done yet?" Alec called through the closed door.

Adjusting a hair tie, she contemplated appropriate retorts to the inevitable jests. Conjuring none of value, she sighed, commanded her hands to stop fidgeting, and opened the door.

They stared.

Her cheeks heated as she fingered the skirt, clutching the material like a dolt. Her eyes studied the worn, wooden floorboards.

Clapping startled her. Lifting her head, she saw the three of them lounging around the room, grinning like ten-year-olds and applauding. Savoy, sitting atop the bureau, radiated juvenile amusement. Someone whistled.

Renee retreated, her eyes beginning to sting. *I enjoy being a girl,* she yelled inside her mind while pleading with the gods to make her disappear.

Savoy hopped down and caught her elbow before she reached the door. Mirth she did not share danced on his face. "Renee, you look . . . feminine."

"I *am* a girl."

"Figures," he said dryly. "I thought there was something odd about you."

He held her gaze until her mind resolved to smile at the boys' stupid humor. She twisted, turning her back to the crowd. "Will one of you tie this, please."

At first, nothing happened. Several seconds later, she felt pointless tugging on the back lace, and losing patience, turned her head.

Savoy winced. "Must it be tied?"

"I think that hooks there," Seaborn suggested, while Alec came up to lend a third set of hands. She twisted back around and endured more tugging. On the fourth "let's try this," Renee thanked them for their efforts and went in search of a female. *Any* female.

She returned to find Savoy dressed in flowing black pants and a dark shirt that she and Seaborn had picked out for him. The outfit accented his athletic build and blond hair, which brushed the back of his shoulders. Wearing a suffering expression, he listened to Seaborn's lecture.

"Connor, shut up, please." He massaged his temples. "A description of a waltz won't help. I'll manage." He faltered and looked toward Renee, his face growing serious. "Plus, I don't believe we'll be spending much time on the dance floor."

She picked up the cue. "The hosts will expect you to dance with me at first and then yield me to other gentlemen. You'll have free rein for a while before you come back to ensure my well-being." Ignoring his rolling eyes, she continued. "When you do, I'll feel faint. We'll make our apologies as you take me to get fresh air, at which point we'll enjoy minimal scrutiny while walking the grounds. We can't bring swords in, but perhaps Duke Leon's halls have something to . . . borrow."

He repeated the instructions back to her and rose, addressing their companions. "We'll see you later tonight. Alec, if you find a way to release Khavi inside the estate gardens, it would help narrow the search."

Alec nodded but kept his hands buried in pockets and eyes on the floor. Renee swallowed a sigh. It wasn't as if this was a courtship outing or one to which Alec could come instead. Nodding a thank-you to Savoy, who opened the door, she headed out of the room.

Walking to Duke Leon's estate, Renee tingled with excitement. This was *her* plan. Even Savoy had listened, approved, and now heeded her lead. In a way, she had done the job usually reserved for him, and they were about to test how well she had done it. She opened her mouth to bring up the topic, but the tension in his face deflected her thoughts. "Are you nervous?" She touched his arm. "I can back-lead you in dance, and since you're but my escort, no one will pay attention to you. It all sounds grander than it is."

Steering himself away from her touch, Savoy gave her a sidelong glance, but kept silent.

The seductive voice of a violin escaped through the gilded doors. Beside them, a tall, weedy butler examined invitations.

"A pleasure, my lady." He bowed without so much as looking at her companion.

She murmured her thanks and glided into the marbled

hallway, noticing that Savoy's were the only footsteps making no sound on the glistening stones. In the ballroom, flickering candle and lantern light reflected off the polished dance floor. Flowers poured from wide vases, bright ponds of color amidst the green velvet drapes.

Renee shook her head to reject a boy's offering of honey wine, and glanced at Savoy. His face was void of emotion.

"I need to thank the host," she whispered.

"Of course." Savoy bowed and stepped back at once, while she navigated among dresses and long coats, many of them green, to make the prescribed greetings. The noble guests unlikely belonged to the Vipers directly; the choice of color was tribute. Was the tribute offered in respect or fear? She marked the thought and, her introductions made, held her hand out to Savoy.

He materialized by her side and bowed again. "If I may," he said, and led her forward, dignity filling each motion.

The music started. Renee felt the strength of his frame the moment she laid her left palm on his shoulder. She smelled the soap in his hair. His hand gripped hers and pushed away, engaging a gentle tension between them. He swayed, weight changing from foot to foot.

One, two, three. One, two, three. The music called in high, flowing notes.

Savoy shifted his weight once more, and with the next strong beat, stepped through her, propelling them down the dance floor. The chandeliers spun, the room swaying to the song while they circled, rising and falling with the pulsing rhythm of the waltz. Renee's heart pounded, exhilaration filling her chest.

Humility claimed her when, several songs later, they returned to the sideline chairs. Savoy's eyes, on the other hand, sparked with impish amusement.

"You did that on purpose." She glared. Dance instruction was typically limited to noble circles; it had been reasonable to expect Savoy ignorant of it. "Where did you learn?"

"My father. I don't know where he learned it. Did I spoil your fun?" A small smile tugged at the corners of his mouth. "You were enjoying having the upper hand on me."

Recalling the comments she made earlier, Renee blushed and stroked the velvet armrests. While she searched for a way out of her self-dug hole, Savoy moved on to a different topic.

"You seem at ease here." He waved his hand to encompass the room. "Why the Academy?"

She brushed the velvet again, used to the question and embarrassed of the answer. "I wish—*wished*—to make a difference. To keep Tildor safe." She squirmed and flickered her fingers in dismissal. "Just a childish fantasy."

Savoy snorted. "Horse shit. *Why?*"

She sighed. "The Family destroyed a wagon carrying my mother and brother when my father refused to pay tribute. I should have been in that wagon . . . " Her fingers touched the scar and she clamped her hand shut around it. The career she pursued to honor their memory was gone now. "I don't wish the likes of it to happen again, anywhere in Tildor." Holding her breath, she awaited his laugh at what her father dubbed delusions of self-importance.

Savoy leaned his chair back until it teetered on its hind legs. He studied her, his face unreadable. "Don't let yourself feel shame for living," he said quietly, glancing at her closed fist. "As for changing the world, that begins with deciding you can."

She lowered her face and nodded. The night was bowing to introspection. "What about you?" she asked. "Why do you do it?"

"I fit. I like the freedom of running missions in the middle of nowhere." He paused, shrugging, then jerked his chin toward the dance floor. "You better go meet some suitors. It's getting late."

She rose but paused and spun toward him. "Horse shit, sir," Renee whispered. "Why did you become the Crown's Servant?"

The corners of Savoy's mouth twitched. "Because otherwise," he said, letting his tipped chair return to the floor, "I'd be its criminal."

CHAPTER 25

"Preened-out peacocks," Savoy said under his breath as they stepped into the snow-covered gardens behind the ballroom.

"They didn't see you come out?" Renee waited for his nod and let out a breath of relief. "Here comes Khavi." The approaching dog's white fur reflected shimmers of moonlight. She fingered her pale pink dress and cringed at her color choice. Dark fabric better melted into the night.

Savoy pushed her into the shadows and wrapped his black cloak around her shoulders. His blond hair disappeared under a dark hat he produced from nowhere. His hand reached for a sword that was not there and he looked at Renee. She shook her head. There was no way to steal one from the manor. They'd have to do with the knives they brought. Savoy nodded once, and slid out to follow Khavi, whose paws crunched on the frozen grass.

Manicured grounds gave way to an untamed forest. Renee's initial indignation at the duke's careless abandon of his backlands changed to suspicion. The dense, wild vegetation, an inky black tangle in the dark of night, discouraged trespassing. Leafless branches struck Renee's face and snatched at her clothes.

She pulled her knife from under her dress and cut away the underskirt.

A quarter hour into the hike, the dog stopped at what seemed a random clearing in the woods and scratched at the frosty ground.

Renee crouched and felt a prolonged crack. "It's a door." She pulled up on a wooden edge.

Steep, slippery stairs led them underground. The air, heavy with mold and moisture, hung like fog. Renee lowered the hinged cover over their heads, shutting away the moonlight. The door clicked shut and flashed with a small speck of blue.

Cursing, Savoy tried in vain to reopen the exit. They were trapped.

Darkness hugged them. Savoy's breath warmed the back of her neck. "Wait." He halted her with a hand on her shoulder.

She felt him crouch, then heard a muffled crunch, like glass breaking beneath cloth. Savoy moved in front of her, a small pouch glowing blue in his hand.

"Light sac," he whispered. "The Mage Council divined them for the Seventh last year."

The stairway spiraled down, yielding to a lantern-lit corridor. A pair of leather bracelets lay discarded on the floor of a small alcove to their left. On closer look, Renee saw blue tinted metal strips interwoven with the leather bands. Mage work. She tossed the thing back into the corner.

Khavi jogged forward, his claws ticking against the stone. The walls were uneven here, far enough apart in some places for several men to walk abreast, in others so narrow that only one person could pass at a time. After a while, Renee and Savoy spilled into a wider, main corridor.

"Memorize the layout," Savoy whispered. His voice was calm. "Keep it basic. Count the paces. Note odd markings."

She repeated his words in her head. She and Alec had practiced mapping this past autumn—she shook her head; was it truly so recent?—but basics were easier at the Academy, when her heart wasn't pounding in her chest and she wasn't counting footsteps that echoed against underground walls.

Savoy's hand halted her again. He pointed to his ear, then forward to where another hall joined the main artery from the east. Stuffing the light sac into his boot, he pulled out his knife.

Renee had to close her eyes to catch the approaching footsteps. Once she did, they seemed deafeningly loud. Several paces ahead, Khavi froze in his tracks, turned his head, teeth glowing with reflected light.

"I heard you taming the wild child," said a gruff, self-satisfied voice.

"Life's small pleasures," answered a baritone. "I told 'em months ago that market's ripe for eight-yearers, if you train 'em right."

Savoy, expressionless, held up two fingers.

Renee's hands curled into fists. Gripping her knife, she stepped forward toward the junction. It was two on two, with surprise on their side. The footsteps grew louder. The speakers were nearing. Little longer until confrontation. Renee looked at

Savoy, realizing that she had passed him and now held point.

He motioned her behind him.

Renee's heart sped. Someone close cleared his throat. She took a quick breath and found Savoy's eyes. "Let me," she mouthed.

His lips tightened—and Renee's heart sank. Was he recalling her loss to Tanil? Or her panic over a *paper*? Or her struggles during the Queen's Day dinner? She waited, motionless, and had just resigned herself to rejection when Savoy raised his brows and nodded, flattening against the wall behind her. Renee grinned. She twisted the knife in her hand, aligning the blade parallel with her forearm. She could hear rough breathing closing from the right. An instant later, two sloppy, bearded men stepped out, one of them scratching his armpit.

Now! Renee pushed away from the stone and gripped the first guard's tunic. They crashed into the opposite wall, the wood baton falling from his belt and skittering away. The man's wide eyes grew larger still when her forearm pressed against his jugular. The knife felt hot in her other hand. All she had to do was plunge it into her immobilized prey. She hesitated. His lip curled.

A thud against her back slammed through her. She twisted around to see Savoy pull the second guard off her back and snake an arm around his neck.

Renee's opponent used the moment to wrench himself free and now circled her. She cursed silently, watching his shoulders. He was unarmed but carried twice her weight. This fight she'd win on speed—she knew enough to understand that now. She feinted with her knife. He recoiled and swung his fist, raising his elbow too high and exposing his ribs.

Renee saw the opening, saw where her blade must plunge into real, living flesh. And wavered once more. Flesh was a far cry from the pads they used in the salle. The opening vanished.

"Get it done," Savoy's voice demanded. "Or I will."

The guard rushed her, pinning her against the wall, his toothy snarl catching the dim light. Decayed breath hit Renee's face. He grabbed her wrist and slammed it against the stone. She cried out. He grinned, prying the weapon from her fingers. Now armed, he trailed the point of her own knife down her body. The blade stopped at her chest, pressing until a small crimson circle soaked the cloth by the blade's tip.

Blood drained from her face. Her eyes jerked in search of Savoy.

He met her gaze with a challenging one. Letting his now limp victim slide from his grasp, Savoy crossed his arms and leaned back against the wall.

Renee swallowed.

The guard holding her smacked wet lips together. "I like fiery kittens," he hissed, leaning closer. A smile distorted his mouth. He licked her cheek. "Salty."

That did it. Renee's knee shot up between the pervert's legs, sending him yelping to his knees. He groped for her, the knife slicing the air in wide, clumsy strokes. On its downward swing the blade bit into her arm.

A surge of anger roared through her. Her hand grabbed the

guard's wrist and snapped it backward. Her fingers forced the knife from his. She flipped the blade parallel to her forearm, twisted around, and slit his neck.

The world stopped. The silence of finished battle settled around her. The knife in her hand was wet. A man dead.

"Clean off the blade," Savoy said.

She crouched over the body and wiped the blood off against her dress. Bile rose in her throat.

"This is what you signed up for." Savoy took her shoulders and turned her toward him. "Let me see to your arm."

She frowned at the gash he was wrapping with a ripped hem of his shirt. "It doesn't hurt."

"At the moment, I doubt you'd feel an amputation." He secured the knot. "If it's all the same to you, I'd rather we not leave a trail of blood."

They moved on. With two bodies behind them, time pressed. Khavi ducked into a side passage and led them, by Renee's sense, eastward. Twists and intersections grew more frequent. Savoy stayed ahead, jogging the straightaway, pausing before corners and turns. She caught his rhythm. Stop. Look. Clear. I go. You go. Count the paces. Remember the turns.

The underground network rivaled the city above in its complexity. Specks of blue glow shimmered at several junctures, betraying amulets tucked into the walls. The Crown could never afford such a setup, not with the materials and mage hours involved.

The corridor bent right again, this time revealing an alcove similar to the one they saw earlier. Metal bars stretched across the stone opening. Inside, a small blond boy hugged his knees, rocking himself with slow, shaking movements. The dirty blanket on which he sat was the cell's only furniture.

"Diam!" Savoy sprinted to the bars.

The boy scrambled forward to the barred door. "Korish?" he whispered, as if unsure of what he was seeing. Then his eyes widened. "Korish. Korish!" he cried, certain that now he was here, Savoy would purge all evil from the world. Renee felt a pang. She used to think Riley omnipotent too.

She shook away memory's shadow and returned to work examining the cell. She saw no lock, but a blue light shone around the door's edges.

Savoy threw his weight against the bars. No result. He pulled. The metal doorframe remained immobile. He rubbed his shoulder and stepped back.

"I don't like it here," Diam said. Favoring his left side, he lowered himself to the floor.

"Neither do I." Unsheathing his knife, Savoy traced the outlines of the metal door. He found the glowing amulet twisted into the metal and pounded against it with the hilt of his weapon. The knife vibrated on impact but made no dent in the construction. He glanced at Diam and pounded harder, the growing violence doing little beyond making a racket.

Renee touched his shoulder. "It's not working."

"And you know what would?" He shook her off. His hands jerked the bars.

A slide of white fur caught her attention. Looking down, she saw Khavi crouching. Diam sat on the floor beside him. Their gazes locked.

The hair on the back of her neck rose. "Savoy, move." She caught his wrist and pointed at the pair.

The intensity growing between boy and dog dried her tongue. She stepped from them. Somewhere far away, footsteps ticked against the stone. Renee's fingers tightened around Savoy's wrist, whether to comfort herself or to keep him at bay, she did not know. Echoes of voices—many voices—joined those of footsteps, still too distant to discern. She opened her mouth to ask Diam about the coming patrols, but clamped it shut. Khavi shimmered with a pearly, blue glow.

"Gods," Savoy whispered.

Renee gripped her arms. She knew what Khavi was, but knowing was as far from seeing as the tap of a wooden sword was from a knife in a man's throat. Even now, watching the event unfold before her, she was unsure she believed, much less understood, its nature.

Khavi's glow pulsated like a beating heart. The amulet's light brightened in reply. Two mirrors feeding each other. The blue glow grew painful to watch, flared, and died.

Savoy jerked the cage door. It opened. Rushing inside, he put a hand on his brother's shoulder. "Imp."

"Korish!" Diam clamped skinny arms around Savoy's waist. "What's wrong with your hand?"

"I'll tell you tonight." He motioned Renee forward. They

needed to stay ahead of the coming patrol. "Diam, there is another ward locking the exit. Can Khavi open it?"

"We'll try." The boy stumbled. Khavi's tongue lolled from his exhausted muzzle.

Savoy sheathed his knife to scoop up his brother. They hurried back the way they came, staying ahead of the approaching footsteps.

They ran hard. The now familiar twists of the underground tunnels, the still-splayed bodies of the two guards, the lanterns lining the walls, all disappeared in a streak behind them. Renee had not expected they would get far. But they had.

Just not far enough.

Less than a hundred spans, a hundred running steps, to the exit remained when a horde of guards burst into the corridor behind them. Swords glimmered in the lantern light like fireflies in the night's darkness. Even if they made it to the door, there was no time to disarm the ward.

Savoy's jaw tightened. "Over there." He pointed to a narrowing in the passage, twenty paces ahead. Thrusting Diam into Renee's arms, he pulled his knife and herded them forward.

She sprinted for cover, Savoy's footsteps tapping the stone behind her. Reaching the target, she lowered the boy to the ground and turned in time to see Savoy convert a rushing enemy into a human shield. He relieved his victim of a quiver and crossbow and leveled it at the oncoming wave.

Renee drew a breath. The corridor narrowed enough here

to allow Savoy to block the passage. Realizing they could not approach en masse, the advancing guards slowed. Renee put a hand on Savoy's back to guide him as he retreated toward the safety of the exit. He loaded the weapon while he moved. They had a chance. A small one, but a chance. She focused on that.

"Halt." A voice boomed through the corridor.

The guards stopped.

Renee could not see who had spoken and continued moving until, from behind a wall of men, a ray of blue flame crept through the air. A mage.

Savoy's arm extended the crossbow. His muscles tensed and an arrow shot into the crowd. Despite someone's shout of pain the ray kept extending. Renee's gut dropped. Savoy had guessed wrong.

The mage fire approached Savoy, cleared his head, and arched toward Diam.

Renee shoved the boy back and Khavi leaped into the air, throwing his body into the coming stream.

Diam screamed.

The dog, shimmering in a blue glow, fell to the floor and whimpered, continuing to absorb the mage's assault.

"Fighter, toss the crossbow into the walkway," the booming voice commanded. "Or I will kill your party."

Savoy turned his head toward Renee. "He can't." His voice was calm, almost bored. "Get them out."

Her fists tightened. What the mage couldn't do was kill them all at the same time. Savoy had as much chance of holding the passage and escaping as she did of flying. "You can't—"

"We came for Diam. Get it done or he'll die." Reaching into his boot, Savoy handed her the light sac. And then he turned around, reloaded the crossbow, and presented his chest to a bolt of blue flame.

A few heartbeats later, his body thudded down to the stone floor.

CHAPTER 26

Back at Hunter's Inn, Renee leaned against the wall, arms crossed over the front of her blood-soaked dress. The bureau on which Savoy liked to sit was empty. His sword hung by the door. Outside, it had started to rain, the drops pounding the window.

"We could speak to the governor." Alec stared at his hands, which glowed and dimmed like flickering candles. Renee lacked energy to ask that he stop. "Tell him about the tunnels and—"

Seaborn shook his head, his gaze never wavering from the stormy window. "The governor bows to the Vipers. Korish would not survive if the Madam discovered his identity. Official help must come from Atham and the Seventh."

Renee caught the hesitation in his voice, glanced at Diam, and knew he had heard it too. The Seventh would uproot the world to retrieve Savoy. But they could not bring back the dead.

"Korish is gonna come back for his sword." Diam scrubbed his sleeve across his dirty face and limped to where his brother's weapon hung on the wall.

Seaborn took down the sword and squatted next to Diam. "I think someone should take care of this for him."

Diam grasped the hilt and wrestled the shining weapon into

ready position. Savoy took care of his tools. "It's heavy." The blade's tip brushed the floor. Diam's lips pressed together. Then, jerking his chin up, he thrust the hilt toward Renee. "You take it."

She looked over her shoulder at Seaborn. "When can you leave for Atham, sir?"

"In the morning." His eyes narrowed. "I thought you wished to pledge to King Lysian, Renee. If you returned, given the circumstance, perhaps . . ."

She took the sword from Diam, slid it into its sheath, and adjusted the buckle at her hip. If Savoy was alive, she would free him. And if he wasn't, she would bring his captors to Crown's justice. King Lysian had called on his champions to guard Tildor's heart. She did not need a uniform to do that.

At dawn, Seaborn decided to kill himself. He was riding to the Academy, and he was doing it mounted on Savoy's horse.

"I don't have time to hike to Atham," he said, clipping Kye into the crossties and ignoring all pleas for sanity. His hand narrowly escaped Kye's snapping teeth; undeterred, the stallion laid his ears back and awaited the next opportunity.

They had agreed to let Diam stay in Catar, for now. Theoretically, this was to allow Seaborn faster travel and because returning the boy to the place from which he had already been abducted once was arguably a bad idea. Privately, Renee feared Diam would simply run off if they tried. The speed with which Seaborn agreed to the plan suggested he had similar worries.

"Great gods." Renee stepped back as a hoof flick caught Seaborn's thigh. He grunted, his face pale and sweaty, set his jaw, and picked up the bit.

Never mind the beast's pastime of destroying people who *weren't* afraid of riding.

"Find nobles who bet on Predators." Seaborn's fingers fumbled a simple girth knot. "If Korish is alive . . . he's prime for the cages. Hells, the lunatic might actually enjoy it."

She forced a chuckle. "How long until you have news?"

He rubbed the bridge of his nose. "With clear weather and a mount, I'll be in Atham in two days. I'll need a day or two after that."

Renee nodded, adding another two days for the messenger to return. Under a week, then. Better than she dared hoped. "Get the Seventh here, sir. I'll find Savoy."

Seaborn returned the nod, as if he believed her, then stepped back from the horse, who now stood ready for the journey. Provided the rider managed to mount. "I don't wish an audience," Seaborn said quietly.

"Gods' luck." Renee bowed her farewell and withdrew inside the stable. Her ears strained for signs of trouble as she leaned against the wooden wall. Savoy's sword, too big for her, weighed down both her hip and heart. In a week's time, her world had morphed from theory to reality. Just months ago she cringed at push-ups, agonized over rebuke-filled glances, and sobbed over strikes from a wooden practice blade. *They are but bruises,* Savoy had told her at Rock Lake, but only now did she understand his words. A hill feels like a mountain until the real thing laughs in your face.

Renee reconvened with Alec and Diam in their Hunter's Inn room. The adjacent chamber, where Seaborn and Savoy had been staying, now housed other guests. Her impulse to return to the underground entrance at Duke Leon's estate met with raised brows from Alec.

"In daylight?" He shook his head. "That's crazy, Renee, even for you. Plus, Diam needs a Healer. Seaborn gave me a name."

She crossed her arms, looking from Diam to the forest of stone buildings that hid the estate from view. That Alec was right did little to soothe her stomach. Each moment they waited worked against them.

"Wait for sundown." He touched her shoulder and steered her toward Diam. "Then we'll go."

Despite matching Seaborn's descriptions, the old, cracked streets and sad-looking buildings did nothing to inspire confidence. People scurried about the slushy roads, sharp eyes full of scrutiny and warning. Even the sun shone more dimly, as if the clouds conspired against the neighborhood. Renee pulled her coat tighter. "Alec, you sure about this?"

He nodded, guiding her around a pile of dog excrement on the sidewalk. At least she *hoped* the excrement came from a dog. "Scouted this morning and made inquiries on top of that." A hint of excitement fueled Alec's voice. "I don't know how Seaborn knows old Zev, but the word on him is . . . reverent."

Beside her, Diam struggled to keep up with Alec's too-fast stride.

"Slow down," she told Alec for the third time and frowned at Diam. Despite gripping his left side, the boy gazed around all too curiously. Renee fought down burbling panic. Neither his brother nor the Academy instructors had been able to contain Diam's wanderings through Atham. How were she and Alec to manage him in Catar? The weight of the world gained several stone.

Old Zev lived in the basement of a run-down shack, which threatened to collapse under a bout of hard wind. The bald, sagging old man who cracked open the door refused to let them inside until hearing a whisper of Seaborn's name. Even with that he hesitated, yellow eyes piercing each newcomer until his gaze found Khavi and his pupils widened.

"A unique pleasure," Zev murmured, letting the quartet inside.

The mage's apartment smelled of sweet herbs. Piles of wide pillows lay on the tattered carpet in the center of the room, where Renee expected a couch. Zev settled himself on one of the pillow piles and crossed his arms, his eyes growing hard as he stared at her. "You don't belong here." He shook his head. "Not like Connor to forgo warning."

"Our apologies." Kneeling on a pillow next to the little man, Renee sketched the story of Diam's abduction. "Will you help him?" she asked upon concluding the tale.

Zev smiled. "Which one? The little lad with the hurt side or the big one without a rein on his power?"

Her eyes darted to Alec in time to see him startle and hide a blue-glowing hand behind his back.

Zev's grin grew. "Young idiots. You think Connor sent you here for a few bruises when you have a brewing disaster walking among you?" A scowl replaced self-content mirth, and he glared at Alec. "Stupid, careless boy. You will kill someone. What in gods' realm possessed you to hide your head in the sand?"

Alec stuffed his hands in his pockets and said nothing.

"He didn't hide." Renee stepped in for him. "He chose. Chose to become a fighter Servant for the Crown."

"He does not get to choose!"

"Registration—" Alec began, but Zev cut him off.

"Is a Crown-forged set of whips and shackles. And it still exists because of self-centered hooligans like you."

Zev's accusation ushered in silence. Renee glanced at her friend, but saw no more comprehension on his face than she felt.

The old man climbed to his feet and fed a log into the fire. "Young mages speak of choices," he said quietly. "But the energy we feel grows like this flame. If we fail to control it, it will consume us. And the house. And everyone inside." He turned, pinning Alec with his eyes. "Learning to rein in the energy flows takes years. And years more to make something useful of your skills. Unschooled mages harbor disasters. As long as those like you think they have a right to forgo training, neither I, nor Connor, nor anyone else battling registration has a leg to stand on." He shook his head.

Several seconds passed before Renee remembered to breathe. To her left, Alec's sad eyes watched the fire, his head bowed. Old Zev limped over to Diam and said something into the boy's ear before laying a blue glowing hand on him. The boy cried out, fresh tears leaking down his cheeks, but quieted quickly, and the room returned to silence.

Khavi curled at the boy's feet.

"We should get back," Renee said, placing a hand on Alec's shoulder.

He ignored her touch. "May I stay here a little longer, Master Zev?"

The old man nodded and, that evening, Hunter's Inn was emptier still.

CHAPTER 27

An hour after the midnight bell echoed through Catar, Renee headed to Duke Leon's estates alone. And this time, she came better prepared.

She wore dark clothes, Alec's sword, and a pack with a lantern. She had extracted Diam's promise to lock himself inside the room, but welcomed the company of Khavi, who trotted beside her, their breath visible in the frigid night air. It was a scouting mission. No more than an hour. Descend underground, map the passages, get out. Unlike her last visit here, she would leave no bodies, take nothing, stay hidden. If she found Savoy on this first foray, she would memorize his location to give it to the Seventh. She would not attempt rescue by herself. She knew better than that.

Renee repeated the last instruction to herself again and again until it stopped feeling like a cold hand clamping her heart. Having a plan was her only advantage.

They had snuck into the estate from the forest side, staying clear of the duke's mansion with its guards and lanterns. She had counted her paces when making her escape with Diam, and now retraced the steps, planning to enter from where they had last exited. Khavi stayed close in what Renee hoped was approval of her route.

The ground under her feet shifted in texture. Khavi pawed it, wagging his tail and whining softly. Holding her breath, Renee crouched down and ran her hand over the cold dirt, feeling for the crack of the trap-door edge. It was there.

And it was locked. Bolted shut, from the feel of it.

Khavi sniffed the ground and gave Renee a *something's there* look. That was all. She sighed. Diam had done his best to explain Renee's intentions to Khavi, but whether the dog failed to understand or saw nothing he could do, she didn't know. *Not that it matters*, she thought, giving the unbudging door another pull and cursing. Either way, she wasn't getting in, not through here.

Next morning at Hunter's Inn, Alec took a book from his pack and climbed onto his bed. "It does make sense they'd lock it after you and Savoy snuck in, Renee," he told her. "Or change the lock. Or add a dead bolt. Or whatever they did." An aura of contentment clung to him, something Renee had not seen in some time. Alec ran his fingers down the book's cover before setting it on the bed. "You should have waited for me last night."

"I did."

"I . . . ran late." He shifted his weight. "Zev introduced me to some people. Others, like me." Alec stared out the window. "Catar isn't like Atham. No one here thinks mages are property or dangerous animals to be broken to saddle."

"They *aren't* like you. They never wished to serve the Crown."

"I wished to choose my own path." His contentment vanished. "It didn't work at the Academy. Here, it may."

Renee poured water into the basin and washed what little sleep she got from her face. A day and a night had passed with nothing to show for it. "I need to find Duke Leon."

"And do what?" Alec leaned back against the wall, interlacing his fingers behind his head. "Inquire as to what he knows about a secret passage to a Viper prison that you found in his back woods?"

She slammed the water jug down. If Alec could offer none of his own solutions, he could at least support hers. "I don't know!" She wheeled to face him. "What would you have me do?"

"I'm sorry." He held up his palms. Whether the apology was for upsetting her or his limited interest in Savoy's fate, Renee could not tell. He picked up his book. "You are right—try the nobles and Duke Leon again. It helped the last time."

The nobles attending court at the governor's manor welcomed Renee with courteous but reserved bows. Her novelty was spent, her house a minor one, and her disgruntled-Academy-reject tale unverified. Putting on a demure expression, Renee stalked the edge of the gathering and awaited the chance to engage her prey, whose green neckerchief she spotted in the crowd.

"The curtain is setting on Lysian's nonsense," Duke Leon told a group assembled before him. "The Devmani empire nips Tildor's western border but instead of addressing it, the king arrests his own subjects and threatens to assault Catar! He's tasting the Family's coin, you mark my words. Tildor monarchs have long pandered to wealthy merchants instead of seeing to those in need. Whatever quarrels some have with Predator competition, none can deny its role in holding Catar's economy."

"Catar's economy or Madam's coffers?" The man beside him stroked his mustache. Several of the guests' lips tightened into lines. A woman excused herself to the privy.

Taking a breath, Renee strode up to fill the gap before it closed. "Both, my lord." She curtsied to the mustached man and continued quickly, before they could parry the intrusion. "Shops, inns, taverns, even the meat pie carts, all rely on the fights to bring business," she said, hoping she guessed true. Her eyes found Duke Leon. Whatever his connection to the Vipers, it likely touched his purse. "Would you agree, Your Grace?"

He tilted his head. "Lady . . . Renee. It is a pleasure seeing you again." He bowed. "I fear your keen mind puts mine to shame. Perhaps my daughter would prove more entertaining company? It would please me to introduce you."

Too hard, too fast. Renee cursed herself. "I beg you forgive the brash intrusion, my lord." She curtsied again, spreading the skirts of her dress. "It was only that I heard you discussing Catar's economy and hoped you'd consider indulging my curiosity. My father's estate breeds goats, you see, and his view of trade is somewhat narrow, unlike yours."

"Kind words to an old man's ears, but I would not presume

to take advantage of a maiden's good manners with my tedious musings." A smile that stopped short of his eyes signaled the end of discussion.

Swallowing both the polite dismissal and the colorful words she'd picked up from the Seventh, Renee glided away. She kept her pace slow, but the men refrained from conversation while she was in earshot. Whatever they knew of Catar's dark market, they did not mean to share.

Returning to Hunter's Inn, Renee sprinted up the stairs and slammed the door to their room. Alec was gone. She tore loose the laces on her dress and jerked open a drawer, flipping through its contents for a shirt and beaten trousers. The underground entrance was locked. The nobles said nothing. She knew no one in the city to query. And Seaborn wouldn't have news for days yet. By then, Savoy might be dead. Where in the Seven Hells did that leave her? Or Savoy?

"Who peed in your oatmeal?" Diam's voice speared her to a halt.

She looked up, startled to find the boy sitting atop her bed, two paces away. "Who did *what?*"

"Peed in your oatmeal." He repeated the words as if trying them on for size.

Closing her eyes, Renee counted to ten. "When did you start talking like that?"

"This morning."

"This morning." She stared at her new eight-year-old responsibility. He needed a change of clothes. And tutors. And structure. And another dozen things she couldn't think of, much less make happen. Her eyes found her practice sword and her hand ached for its feel, for the clarity of the world when viewed over a weapon's edge. "Do you know where Alec went?" *And why he left you alone?* she groused silently.

Diam shrugged and jumped off the bed. "The Underground, that tavern near Zev. Same as yesterday." Diam blocked Renee's way and opened a grubby fist to display the contents of his palm. Predator chits. "Found 'em in Korish's coat. Alec said Korish bought them."

"He did." Her shoulders sagged and she reached to take the chits from Diam. "But it wasn't for sport. He was looking for you."

Diam jerked his treasure from reach. "I wanna go." His chin set. His hands gripped the metal bits as if they were a message from his brother. "Korish bought these. He bought them, so we have to go."

Renee was about to reject him again, but Diam's desperate eyes halted her. She took a breath. He asked for so little. Yes, the scraps of information a spectator could gather from watching the pointless killing would be meager, but there was little else she could do. And if . . . "Will you promise to stay within sight of Hunter's Inn and mind the innkeeper's wife?" she asked, and was rewarded by immediate head bobbing. "Very well." Renee squatted down to the boy's level. "But you must keep to your word. Your brother offered his life for yours. Don't squander his sacrifice."

Diam's green eyes widened and he nodded again.

Renee prayed to the gods that was enough.

The Underground took time to find. Hidden in plain sight, its facade blended with the crumbling brick of the rest of the block. Inside, it bustled with youthful energy. Adolescents crowded the mismatched tables, shouting and laughing over one another.

Renee expected to find Alec in a corner and swallowed surprise at seeing him amidst a thick crowd. Several girls around him leaned forward in their seats, their eyes glued on his moving lips. Smiling, Renee wondered whether her friend even noticed the attention. His muscled body, so typical among the fighter cadets, here drew admiring gazes.

When she approached, a boy with skinny shoulders and black curls smiled a greeting. His eyes traced her curves, and he blushed when she raised an eyebrow. Hers was a fighter's body too. The corners of her mouth twitched.

The boy grinned. "I'm Ivan. What's your name?"

"Renee," Alec answered for her. He sounded more startled than pleased. "Good to see you." He gave her his seat and pulled up another chair for himself. A pause stretched several heartbeats. "Uh, let me introduce you. Renee, uh, meet Ellina, Sheri, Ivan, Jasper, Timon . . ." He motioned to each companion in turn, continuing around the dozen people at the table.

She forced a smile, infected with her friend's discomfort. The group smiled back. The boy with black curls held out his hand, a tentacle of blue glow snaking its way to her. She frowned, looking at Alec for clarification.

Her friend blushed, and a light stream of his own swam out, meeting the boy's. "No, she isn't, uh—"

The boy's glow and smile died together. "She's a blinder?"

Alec's lack of answer ushered in a heavy silence. Her skin crawled. Blinder. Under their scrutiny, Renee scraped back her chair, collected her dignity, and faced her friend. "I found practice swords and came to see if you wished to spar."

"Sure," Alec answered too quickly and bid the table farewell, promising to return.

"Nonsense." A pretty boy with peach-fuzz cheeks and glasses rose with Alec. "We'll watch. I love a fight."

Shushing the warning bells in her head, Renee headed for the door.

The small clearing they found offered privacy from pedestrians, but felt wrong nevertheless. Backs of buildings surrounded three sides of the patch of dirt, and a small fence in the corner blocked the pile of trash, but not its stench. The handful of youths who followed them from the tavern gathered near one of the walls. Standing with her back to them, Renee brought up her blade in salute, and let her body's cry for exercise drown out all else.

Alec secured his stance and engaged, the weapon dancing its way toward Renee's abdomen. She parried the attack easily. Too easily. Then again. The strikes labored to pick up speed, the rolling beat of wood on wood growing in cadence, yet stopping short of climax, as if dulled by invisible cotton. Renee lunged toward his head. Alec missed the parry and, unconcerned, reset for the next bout.

Blood pulsated in her temple. "Are you paying attention?"

"Mage zero, blinder one! Scary." The sideline jeers rose between them.

Alec rolled his eyes. She glared, and his gaze chilled in reply. When he attacked, his blade sailed full force. Renee redirected the strike moments before it could welt her arm. Her breath stilled in surprise, but he granted her no time for reflection. A second attack followed, and a third, each pregnant with power. She switched her stance to favor the speed-based game Savoy had taught her, staying ahead of the blows whose force she couldn't match. The fight morphed from dance to death match. Pouring her frustrations into action, she met him step for step, countering his strength with angles of her blade. It was exhilarating. And frightening.

Pivoting from another savage strike, Renee wondered who this cold-eyed boy was, and whether his emerging new world had space left for her. Contemplation led to a misstep. Unable to redirect his attack, she raised her sword to meet the blow straight on. The blades locked above her head, his pressing down, hers up. Renee's arms trembled against the pressure until, slowly, Alec overpowered her with brute strength.

The swords touched her head. The audience cheered. Alec studied the ground, his face a stone.

A cold wind ruffled Renee's sweat-soaked hair and stung her eyes. Wiping a sleeve across her face, she took a moment to readjust her blade, unwilling to feel anything beyond the chill air and slippery wood. He wanted to play this game? Very well. Let him. Looking up, she saw him backing away. "Exhausted?" she demanded.

"Ooooh! Challenge!" shouted the ever-helpful sideline. But this time its rally wasn't unanimous.

"It's cold," a voice complained.

"Agreed. Enough toying with the blinder, Alec."

The stillness of her face faltered, her knuckles went white. Renee twisted around and pierced the spectators with her eyes. "Toying?"

The black-curled boy, Ivan, shrugged. "It's too cold for this game." When she continued staring, he rolled his eyes. "You're waving a wooden stick around."

"Want to try?"

"Renee, don't." Alec stepped beside her. "You don't understand."

Her heart pounded in her ears. "No, *he* doesn't understand." *Nor do you.* Plucking the practice sword from Alec's hand, she tossed it to the challenger. "Come play."

The boy's smug grin grew wide when he caught the blade. He stepped out in front of her, mocked a salute, and stumbled into a semblance of a fighting stance. His sword wavered, threatening to crash from his hand. Bringing up her weapon, Renee decided to start with disarming the bastard.

Her attack never happened. The moment she moved, the boy's free hand shot a stream of blue flame that turned Renee's sword into a torch. She dropped the burning wood while Ivan hooted and laughed, his mirth spreading to the audience.

"I tried to warn you," Alec said quietly.

Renee caught amusement dancing across his face. The betrayal pierced like steel. She backed away, one step, then another, unsure where she had left to go. The sounds of the world blended and muted. She saw the other mages' lips move, but couldn't spare the effort to make out the words. Turning on her heels, she fled the yard.

Renee sprinted through Catar's streets. When pedestrians shouted at her back, she chose emptier corridors, heedless of direction, heedless of everything but the pounding of her feet and the cold air filling her lungs. A bend took her down a dead-end street. She shifted to run back and froze.

"Looks like I got me lucky," slurred a man whose wine-stained shirt hung half-tucked from his britches. Behind him, a half dozen others cheered agreement. Patting one another's shoulders, they spread across the width of the corridor, blocking her route.

The man advanced.

Renee retreated until her back hit the wall and the stench of cheap spirits filled her nostrils.

CHAPTER 28

Awareness brushed Savoy like a puff of wind. His body ached with a deep, nagging pain that seeped into each muscle fiber. The burn on his hand had disappeared. He pushed himself up, panted from the exertion, and looked around.

He sat in a cage, two spans square—scarcely tall enough for Savoy's height—that stood inside a larger room. He wore only white drawstring trousers and, around his wrists and neck, flat bands of leather interwoven with blue-tinted metal strips and rings. The leather chafed, but in light of a previously certain death, he lacked grounds to complain.

"I've neither time nor desire to break a new pup, Jasper." A large, muscular man carrying a coiled hemp whip at his waist entered the room. He was in his mid-thirties and hard, the kind of hard that grows from experience. Crossing meaty arms, the man weighed Savoy with his eyes and scoffed when Savoy returned the look glare for glare.

"Make time," said the man's partner, a scrawny adolescent whose peach-fuzz cheeks had unlikely yet met a razor. "Mother said I could have him." The boy adjusted his glasses and squatted to Savoy's eye level. "Hi, Cat. I'm Jasper, your keeper. That's your training master, Den. Don't be frightened."

Cat? Savoy studied the smiling youth who saved him the trouble of creating an identity and hoped he had found the weaker link.

"I named you for your green eyes," Jasper continued.

Savoy glanced at Den to measure his reaction, but the man showed none. Instead, he and Jasper began to back away. Something was about to happen. Savoy tensed. Jasper smiled and raised his hand.

It glowed blue.

Savoy's bracelets shimmered in reply and started to pull.

A wave of foreboding washed over him as the glowing bands dragged his wrists up and back, gluing his arms to the back of his collar. Savoy fought the restraints, but the invisible force sheared through the struggle, twisting joints and muscles into compliance, tearing the skin beneath the leather to blood.

Jasper's hand flashed once more, the light reflecting off his glasses. The three bands dragged their prisoner backward, forcing him to move his feet or fall, and slammed him against the metal cage. Savoy glared at Jasper and gritted his teeth.

Den entered the cage and clipped a rope to the bands holding Savoy. Immediately, the glow coming from Jasper's hand died, releasing the strain on Savoy's wrists.

"You going to cause a problem?" Den growled into Savoy's ear and, arching him backward, marched him out and down a corridor, similar to the one that once led to Diam's cage.

They came to a large room where two rows of cots lined the

walls. Six men, dressed in identical white pants, pinned him with hate-filled glares.

"You sleep there." Den pointed to an empty cot next to a bald, mountain-sized man. Then he retrieved a piece of chalk from his pocket and wrote "Cat, evaluation care" on the slate affixed to the footboard.

A man with a scar running down his face cleared his throat. "We already got six."

"Don't you worry, Pretty. We'll return to six soon enough." Den unclipped the rope and left without further word.

Savoy crossed his arms and regarded his cellmates. Predators. "It usually takes people longer to dislike me."

"How long?" Mountain Man asked with surprising sincerity.

"Shut up, Boulder." Pretty looked Savoy up and down. "You really this clueless?"

"No, I enjoy putting on shows of ignorance."

"White Team has six slots and, now, seven pups," said a third man, joining the conversation. The sign on his bed named him Farmer.

Pretty bared his teeth. "Which means, little blond boy, one of us awaits a death match."

"My sympathies to you then, Pretty." Savoy sat on the thin, blanket-covered mattress and tugged at his wristbands, careful of the raw flesh beneath.

"Don't bother," Farmer mumbled, motioning to Savoy's wrists. "There's only one way out of here."

"Death?"

"Two ways out, then. The Predator who wins fourth tier finals gets his freedom. If you need a delusion of hope to cling to, use that."

Looking up, Savoy found the man's eyes and nodded his thanks, adding the new scrap of information to his pitifully small pile.

A few hours later, Savoy was herded into a training salle. *Beautiful.* That was the only word for it. Equipment shone with polish and begged for use. Clean, raked sand covered the floor evenly. Cords marked off sparring rings. Ropes, pull-up bars, free weights, punching bags, leather strike pads, all emanated maintenance and care. The Academy's salle, one of the finest the Crown had, paled in comparison, like a starved pony next to Kye.

Boulder, the large, slow-witted man, paced beside a pile of rocks.

"Don't touch Boulder's stones." Farmer caught Savoy's arm. "He'll wail all morning."

The giant did look attached. Every few seconds, he stopped pacing and squatted down, stroking one rock or another as if they were puppies. Watching him mumble and brush stray grains of sand from one gray pet, Savoy thought of Diam, who used to play like that, turning twigs and pebbles into horses and warriors. The man looked up, eyes full of innocence and caution, and grimaced at Pretty, who swaggered in his direction.

"Don't hurt 'em." Boulder stood guard in front of his pile.

Pretty grinned. He reached down and gathered a handful of sand. "Sand's just a bunch of dead rocks, did you know that?" he asked, while Boulder shuffled from foot to foot, wringing large hands together. Without waiting for a reply, Pretty cocked his arm for a throw.

Savoy caught it.

"Cat, don't!" Farmer called out, but Savoy already twisted Pretty's wrist and drove him to the ground. He straddled the man's chest and cocked a fist, ready to reshape Pretty's nose.

The blow never connected. Instead, the instant before his fist descended, the bands around Savoy's wrists tightened, shimmering with blue glow.

"I see we have a problem." Den's voice said behind him.

Turning, Savoy saw the training master a few yards away, pointing an amulet in his direction. A line of light stretched like a leash, from the amulet to his bands. Den jerked the leash, ripping Savoy off Pretty.

Savoy landed face-first in the sand and sat up, spitting the grains from his mouth. The next moment, his wrists pulled up to the collar, and the leather pieces glued together. Savoy met Den's gaze and threw a dirty look at the amulet. "Coward."

"Idiot."

"One doesn't negate the other."

"Don't try me."

"Don't worry. I'm tied up at the moment."

Den tapped his hand against his thigh and stared at Savoy, who braced himself for a blow. No strike came. Instead, the training master squeezed the amulet and the glow died, releasing the restraints. Den shook his head and pointed toward one of the sparring rings. "We'll do this once, Cat. And only once."

Savoy rubbed his wrists and rose, aware of the silence settling around them. His hand reached for a nonexistent sword and he covered the misstep by dusting sand off his trousers. Den's invitation reminded him of how he himself handled rookies, which suggested that one of the two of them was in for a surprise. Meanwhile, Den unhooked the rope-whip from his waist and rested it on the ground. When he stepped into the ring, boredom played in his eyes.

"Begin."

Savoy brought his right leg back and bladed his body into a fighting stance. His weight shifted, and his hands rose to protect his head. Den crouched and shot in, moving faster than Savoy had expected from a large man more than a decade older than him. Savoy sprawled back from the attack, shoved Den's shoulders, and danced away. Den came at him again, an odd frontal assault that would have gotten him skewered had Savoy had so much as a toothpick. But a weapon he did not have, and Den cut him at the knees.

Savoy slapped the ground as he fell, landing without injury. Newfound respect formed in his mind. The man knew his sport. Fighting for top position, Savoy tried to rise, but Den twisted him onto his back and knelt atop him, driving his knee into Savoy's stomach. The effect was immediate and miserable. Pressure on his midsection made each breath an effort. Savoy looked up, knowing that little stopped Den from punching his head. Den returned the gaze. But he didn't strike. Instead, the knee cinched tighter and tighter each time Savoy exhaled. Fighting for air, he struggled to twist his body out from underneath his heavier opponent. He succeeded only in relocating the knee a hand-width higher. It now pressed on his floating ribs. Savoy could draw air now, but the agony of straining bone overwhelmed the joy of breathing.

Collecting his strength, Savoy braced his hands against Den's knee. He twisted sideways and out, shoving himself free from under the other's weight. Maintaining momentum, he rolled to his feet and kicked. Den rocked back, a trickle of blood tracing his chin. Savoy's chest heaved as he circled, looking for his next opening. He saw it and kicked again, aiming a roundhouse at the man's temple. Had the blow connected, its impact would have knocked Den unconscious. It didn't happen that way.

Den blocked the strike with the point of his elbow and wrapped his arms around the leg. He twisted, jerked Savoy off balance, and forced him back to the ground. This time, when Savoy slapped the sand to disperse the force of the fall, Den attacked the outstretched arm. The pressure on Savoy's shoulder came sudden and hard, like a door slam. Den torqued the joint again and fire raced through limb. Savoy had no escape but to tear his own rotator cuff. He drew a breath.

"Tap out, moron."

The pressure increased, muscles and tendons straining from the pull.

"I said, tap. Unless you fight better with severed muscles."

Swallowing his pride, Savoy raised his free hand and struck the ground. The pressure ceased, but the fire remained. Shaking out his shoulder, Savoy hopped to his feet, determined to improve his performance in the next round.

Den shook his head, the look of bored indifference never wavering from his eyes. "I said once." He stepped out of the ring and took a leash from the wall. "Hands behind your head."

Faced with the choice of a voluntary compliance or a mage-forced one, Savoy gathered his remaining shreds of dignity and obeyed. The metal clip clicked as Den hooked it into the rings on the wristbands. A hated sound already. He stared straight ahead as Den led him toward the wall where another metal loop protruded from the stone. There was nothing special about that loop, just a common metal circle like hundreds of others found in any city. Found wherever people needed to tie up a horse.

Den threaded the leash through the ring and tied it off at a height too low to allow Savoy to stand, yet high enough that it stretched his joints when he knelt. He looked up to see Pretty's content gaze and Boulder's frightened one and hoped that his own reflected an indifference he wished he felt.

It was hours before practice ended and the line of fighters trailed out of the salle. Left alone, Den strode to Savoy.

The promise of relief inflamed the deep ache in his arms and back. The overpowering stretch of his abused shoulder made

Savoy count time in breaths. He had kept his face still, and now silently counted down from a hundred to maintain composure through the final moments of punishment.

Den hooked his finger under Savoy's chin and tipped up his face. "Are you through being cocky?" There was no malice in his voice. Den had disciplined a green boy, no more, no less, and that routine chore evoked no more emotion in him than tiring out an unruly horse would have for Savoy.

Whatever Savoy's eventual escape would entail, showing up Den in his own salle would not be part of the plan. "Yes."

"Good." A moment of silence hung in the air.

Savoy held his breath.

"See you tomorrow, Cat." Meeting Savoy's eyes, Den turned away and walked out of the salle.

Savoy's labored breaths violated the silence of the night. In the darkness of the salle, his arms, back, and shoulders were aflame, his wrist rubbed bloody against the bands.

He struggled against the ropes. Not from hope of loosening the knots—he knew that was impossible—but because he couldn't do otherwise. Not in the depth of night, when the remembered smell of blood and piss in a dank dungeon cell filled his memory. Not when fear of something long over visited once more. He struggled, throwing himself against his binds. The hours crept on.

Eventually, he took hold of himself and stopped. A faint blue light from an amulet in the stone cast his shadow onto the sand, keeping him company until morning. A sagging man tied to a wall.

The door to the salle opened, admitting two men. Den carried a lantern, Jasper a bowl.

"Gods, Den, it was his first day." Jasper set the bowl down and patted Savoy's shoulder. Behind his glasses, the boy's large eyes danced. "Poor pup."

"Unbroken pup. He'll live."

Jasper reached toward the wall and untied the rope holding his wristbands. Relief rushed through Savoy's arms. He collapsed to the floor and cradled his shoulders. Smiling, Jasper pushed the bowl toward Savoy's knees. Inside, a spoon drowned in a brown mush, stinking of fat and overcooked, saltless meat. A pool of gooey, half-coagulated egg crowned the breakfast's center.

Food. Savoy grasped the spoon in his fist, ready to swallow without tasting. Cramped muscles trembled. The spoon shook, spilling its contents on the way to his mouth. Globs of warm fat, egg, and meat plopped off and streaked down his chest.

Jasper chuckled. Den did not.

"This won't do." Jasper squatted down in front of Savoy, as if addressing a child. "I can Heal. Would you like me to?" Blue glow ignited around his hand. His breath quickened. He was eager.

Den caught the boy's arm before it extended.

"He can't train like this," Jasper said, his voice rising. He stood, fingers curling into a fist simmering in mage fire.

"Yes, he can."

Savoy tensed. The choice he was about to make, however ignorant, would gain him an enemy. He pushed himself to his feet and stepped toward Den. "I can train fine, sir."

Den's eyes flashed, but his hands and voice remained calm. "Begin by shutting up."

Jasper's lower lip trembled. He swallowed and turned away. "*I'm* the keeper," he whispered toward the floor. "I decide when a pup needs Healing." When he turned back, his face was dark. The flame around his hand grew brighter and he gripped Savoy's bicep.

A rush of energy invaded Savoy's mind, smashing over his Keraldi Barrier. Savoy didn't fight it. Experience with Healers had taught him not to.

Jasper's magic lacked Grovener's finesse. The young mage didn't nip Savoy's barrier as much as rip through it as if with a dull blade. A cry caught in Savoy's throat, but he clenched his fists and remained silent.

The energy scorched down his nerves, mending the pulls and tears in his shoulders. Savoy relaxed and waited for Jasper to withdraw. Instead, he found a cruel smile tugging the corners of the boy's lips. Savoy's mind struggled to raise his Keraldi Barrier, but it was too late.

The boy closed his eyes, and instead of dissipating, the force inside Savoy's body barreled on. It gripped his lungs; Savoy gasped for breath. It cramped on his diaphragm, and he convulsed, unable to exhale. He reached out to grab the damn mage, but Jasper only chuckled and stepped behind him without breaking contact. The next moment something squeezed Savoy's stomach. Bile shot up his throat, filled his mouth, and poured out onto the sand.

"Feeling better?" Jasper asked when Savoy finished depositing the contents of his stomach on the salle floor. Thin scorch marks, like a spiderweb of black silk, streaked from the spot where Jasper's hand had touched him and the mage's energy had funneled into his body.

Savoy had chosen his enemies poorly.

CHAPTER 29

The alley wall pressed into Renee's back.

"Looks like I got me lucky," the man slurred again, wiping his mouth with the hanging hem of his shirt. He approached, reeking of wine, sweat, and tobacco. The light of the alleyway behind him dimmed as the crowd grew—drunkards and gutterscum eager to see a struggle.

Renee sidestepped, but the man's arm blocked her and trailed across her stomach. When she screamed for help, a damp, calloused hand clamped over her mouth and nose. She gasped and twisted, fighting for air.

"You'll purr soon enough, wench," the man slurred. He pushed forward until he sandwiched her to the wall. A pus-oozing pimple on his neck jiggled at her eye level.

"Aw, Nino, we can't see nothin'," whined a deep, unsteady voice. Other shouts joined the complaint.

Nino's free hand grabbed Renee's hair and jerked her toward the middle of the alley. She fell onto packed dirt, the impact jolting the air from her body. The original half dozen spectators had doubled. Still more trickled in. They encircled her and Nino. His hand groped forward, seizing the front of her tunic, and the fabric bit the back of her neck and tore. The sound of ripping cloth triggered hoots and whistles. Cold air brushed the exposed skin of her right shoulder and breast. Nino grinned, sniffed the cloth in his hand, and advanced again, eyes blood-shot and ravenous.

Renee should have died in childhood. But she had not. Death happened to other people. It happened to enemies, like the guard she killed while rescuing Diam. It happened to good people, like her mother and Riley. But not to her. Yet here it was, staring her in the face. She would die not from an army or a bandit's sword, but from a mob of cloudy-witted drunks in pursuit of momentary desire. It wasn't glorious. It wasn't meaningful. It wasn't fair.

The thick, sickening crowd swayed before her, crushing any hope she had of escape.

"You are mine," Nino confirmed, as if reading her thoughts. "And then theirs." He grinned up at his friends and then back down at her. His eyes shone. "And then you are dead."

A memory swam before her eyes. *You are dead.* Her sword arm tightened in remembered agony and disgrace. *That will be the last time anyone here lets go of a weapon,* continued the voice in her head, and cold green eyes pinned her. *Am I understood?*

She recoiled from the memory, suddenly more horrified at finding herself cowering on the ground than by the rotten-toothed men surrounding her. She met Nino's eyes, accepted the impossibility of escape, and rose into a fighting stance, redefining victory. "As are you."

She spun. Her foot gained momentum as it cocked under her body and extended into Nino's gut.

He gasped before roaring obscenities, less imaginative ones than she had learned from the Seventh, and swung at her head.

Ducking the blow, Renee rammed the heel of her hand into the man's jaw. In her side vision, she saw Nino's friends approaching the melee, teetering on the line between enjoying the spectacle and wishing for a piece of it. Her time was short. She struck her elbow against his ear just as hands grabbed her from behind. They forced her to the ground. She noticed blood trickling down Nino's head, and smiled. Then a ham of a fist jammed itself into her nose, and despite the general shouting, she heard the crack of bone.

Renee swallowed blood and continued kicking until the men secured all her limbs. It took four of them to pin her. Nino towered above.

And then came the growl. A menacing, inhuman growl that spoke of blood and shredded flesh. The sea of drunks froze. The growl came again, and the mob parted before a large, white wolf whose teeth shimmered in the dusk. Renee gasped when she met the animal's savage eyes. For the first time, she truly appreciated what Khavi was.

The dog—no, mage-wolf—stepped toward her. One by one, her captors let go and moved away. Khavi turned and stood guard. Nino too retreated toward the safety of the masses, but the wolf snapped his jaw and Nino froze in place. Renee understood the lout's fear. Grateful as Renee was for Khavi's appearance, not even she could bring herself to reach toward his grizzled fur. Rising to her feet, she held closed the flapping tear in her tunic and eyed the crowd.

The wolf licked his teeth and settled onto his haunches beside her. The gathered crowd shifted from foot to foot, but remained where it stood. *Maybe they think I'll get torn to pieces*, Renee thought, examining her options. Khavi stretched his nose to the sky and howled.

Time stretched on in impasse until, without warning, Khavi rose and trotted away. Renee swallowed and started after him, but someone grabbed the back of her shirt and by the time she twisted free, the wolf was spans ahead. The mob opened to let him through and closed behind him, all gazes trailing the animal. All except one. Nino's eyes remained on Renee, his expression contemplative.

The silence that had settled on the alley was short-lived. Within moments, grunts, hoots, and obscene exclamations reclaimed the air. The drunks returned to Renee and she raised her fists, ready for action.

"Renee!" Diam's high voice ripped through the crowd, sending fresh panic through her. The bloody bond! He had seen through the wolf's eyes and was now rushing into a drunken mob. She shouted for him to leave, but his voice grew closer and louder.

Her heart raced. The frustration and stupidity that had spurred her sprint through Catar's alley now endangered the boy it was her duty to protect. The mob would wreck him for sport. And it would be her fault. "No! Go back!" she called. "Run, Diam! Please!"

But the crowd shifted again.

Khavi returned. With Diam.

The boy panted and clung on to the scruff of his wolf's neck. In his other hand, he clenched a sword much too large for him. Savoy's sword. "Here. Brought. This." He gasped the words one by one.

Renee grasped the hilt. A coolness from the steel seeped into her nerves as she examined the alley from behind the weapon's tip. The circle of unsteady slobs resumed meaningless motion. Nino melted into the crowd and now issued his threats while safely wedged between two well-chosen gorillas.

"Diam," Renee said, not taking her eyes off the crowd. "Hold on to Khavi and walk out of here just like you walked in."

"I wanna stay."

"Me too." Alec's voice carried over the dull roar. Elbowing men out of the way, he emerged at Renee's left and stood by her. Blue flame hugged his hands and wrists, bright against the grim sky.

The departing sun cast long shadows onto the alley ground. Silhouettes of beast, fighter, and mage extended in a triangle in front of Renee. A gust of wind swept her bare skin, but she made no move to cover herself. Her spine lengthened and shoulders settled square atop it, while the rhythmic beating of her heart filled her ears. Drawing a breath, Renee stepped forward and extended her sword to Nino's throat.

The man attempted to retreat, but the thick crowd left little wiggle room.

"Nino," she said, enunciating the syllables through the muffle of her broken nose. The sword tip nipped the tender skin over his trachea, and droplets of blood snaked down his neck.

"Who are you?" he whispered.

"She's a wench no better than she 'ot to be, you sod," sneered a man beside him. The certainty in his voice faded when she turned to him. He reached toward his pocket, but Renee's sword caught the underside of his wrist. She kept her touch gentle and precise, just as Savoy had taught her, the razor edge of her steel poised along the man's veins. He froze in place. The wind blew, bringing a whiff of ammonia so potent that even Renee smelled it. Glancing down, she saw urine soak the man's shoes and trickle into a puddle on the ground.

Shaking her head, she withdrew and sheathed the blade. "Master Nino." She turned to him. "If we may leave now."

He blinked twice, then wheeled around on his fellows. " Out of the way, you sods!" The bodies partied and he turned to her, his knuckles touching his forehead. "Will that do, m'lady?"

"It will do just fine." She nodded to him, and walked past. Once out of earshot of the crowd, Renee looked down at Diam, her heart pounding once more. "You promised to stay at the inn."

The boy shrugged with no shred of remorse and Renee

sucked in a long, slow breath, the image of what could have been turning her stomach.

At the mouth of the alley, beyond reach of the recent fighting ground, Alec's mage friends, Jasper and Ivan, feigned invisibility. The latter had turned her practice blade into a torch. Renee eyed him suspiciously.

Alec crossed his arms. "What happened to you two?" His large body dwarfed the two twig-like mages. "You claimed to stay behind me."

They both looked down, shuffling their feet.

"Well?" Alec leaned against the wall.

Ivan said nothing. Jasper pushed his glasses higher on his nose and pulled off his jacket, offering it to Renee. "Please take it," he said when she made no move toward it. "It's the one useful thing I would have done all day."

"Coward," Alec confirmed, and Jasper shrank like a kicked puppy.

Renee took the coat still dangling from his hand and slipped it on. "Why didn't you two turn them all into charcoal?"

"Control in the midst of that mess?" Jasper shook his head. "One knock on the nose like you got and Ivan'd be useless."

"Can't you stay far away and . . ." Renee made a vague motion with her hand.

Jasper snorted. "He might if he were battle trained. But Ivan here's studying mostly thermal work—can help forge any weapon you want, so long as he doesn't have to be around when you use it."

"Didn't see you rush in either, Jasper," Ivan shot back.

"I'm a Healer!"

"So am I," Alec countered. Anger flashed in his dark eyes. "What's your point?"

"The point"—Renee stepped between Alec and the boys— "is that they are not fighters, and I am not a mage. You're the only one who wants to be both. Live with it, Alec." She turned to Jasper. "Thank you for the coat. I just realized I'm freezing."

He smiled and stood straighter, spirit returning to his crimson face.

"Archers keep their distance too," she continued in a voice her broken nose muffled. "And my old roommate, she couldn't fight off a mosquito, but I'm sure she'll preside over half of Atham one day. And I really could use a Healer more now than ten minutes ago."

It was Alec's turn to blush. "You want Jasper." He cleared his throat. "When I called myself a Healer . . . I meant that's what I decided to study. Right now, your nose is better off without my help."

She turned to the quiet boy. "Would you mind?"

He nodded and stepped forward. Blue flame danced about his hand.

"Don't worry, blinder." Ivan made the title sound affectionate. "Jasper's good. And he wants to show off anyway."

Jasper put a hand on her shoulder, nipped nimbly through the Keraldi Barrier and poured his energy into her, urging the tissues to heal. It was nothing like Grovener's magic, but the pain did lessen and air started to trickle through the passage. She thanked him sincerely and the boy seemed to grow from the praise.

"I'm hungry," Diam announced, his fingers brushing Khavi's fur.

Jasper sighed, adjusting his glasses. "It grows late. I need to get home before Mother gets furious, and I've got pups to feed besides."

They walked him home, or at least close enough to hear his mother shout for Jasper to get his useless ass into the house. The boy sagged.

"Jasper . . ." Renee let the words trail off. A pigeon or courier with a message from Sasha if not yet Seaborn might have arrived at Hunter's Inn by now. Doubtful, but she couldn't help longing to check. Pressing her lips together, she looked from her new friend to the mansion looming behind him. In the open doorway, a tall, slender woman with striking blond hair puffed a tobacco stick. The smoke snaked around her like a living shroud.

"Mother is . . . Mother." Jasper forced a smile. "I'll fare all right."

Renee raised her hand in a guilty farewell. "Feels wrong to just leave him."

The odd stare Ivan gave her chilled her chest.

CHAPTER 30

Savoy braced his palms on his thighs and gasped for breath, staring at Jasper's receding back until the closing door cut him off from view. It took the mage longer to tear through the barrier each time he tried. But Savoy's attempts at defense carried their own consequences.

Rubbing a new spidery black line on his chest, Savoy frowned at the barracks' door. Around him, the men debated the lineup for an upcoming fight, the first since Savoy's arrival and his first chance at contact with the outside world. Unfortunately, their discussion offered in obscenities what it lacked in information.

The outside world. De Winter. The girl's image invaded his mind again, vying for a place beside Diam and Connor. He saw her meeting him glare for glare in the snow-filled forest, then striding across the ballroom floor as if the Vipers crawling upon it were nothing of consequence. She was a good kid. No, not just a kid, a rising fighter and ally, a younger sister who had somehow snuck into his life. His fist clenched. Being a part of his life was not a safe place to be.

"Dreaming of the Freedom Fight, Cat?" Farmer's voice shook him from his thoughts.

"There is no Freedom Fight, Farm. It's an illusion to maintain order." Savoy rose to his feet to check the door. "No one is letting anyone go."

"It exists. Den used to be one of us."

Den won his freedom? Savoy turned.

Farmer chuckled bitterly. "Might as well not exist, right? Would need to train a dozen years to get as good as him."

Savoy offered a noncommittal grunt, but it was not the dozen training years that bothered him. It was the question as to why someone supposedly free would choose to stay. Frowning, he twisted the handle and felt his heart contract. "It's open."

Instead of rustling excitement, he heard only Pretty's chuckle. "Shall you escape for a bath?"

Shrugging, Savoy stepped into the hallway and learned at once what the others already knew. Beyond the bathing room and the salle, all other doors in the small corridor had the blue glow of mage locks. He memorized the passageway regardless.

The door to the salle hung partially ajar, and lantern light spilled out. Savoy halted by the doorframe and slowed his breath, his body falling into the trained rhythm of surveillance.

At the far end of the room, Den stood with his back to the door. In his right hand, he clutched a sword as if it were a club, and stumbled around the floor. Every few steps he stopped to examine a book lying open on the ground. It took several minutes before Savoy recognized the crude movements as a torturous imitation of a beginner swordsmanship pattern. What kind of fighter doesn't know one end of the sword from another?

Den paused, perspiration soaking his shirt, and cursed under his breath. When he put down his blade and bent over the book, Savoy slid into the room. A glance at the text confirmed the pattern Den was butchering that evening. Savoy picked up the discarded blade.

"Step north, block, lunge," Savoy said, summoning the form drilled into him in childhood. His crisp words filled the salle. "Turn south, block, lunge." The sword swooshed, slicing the air. "East. Same thing. Then west. If you don't finish where you started, your stances are off."

Den turned. Stared. Tension stretched taut between them. Their breaths sounded loud in the empty room. Then the startled look on Den's face morphed to cold rage. The temperature seemed to plummet. Shame and fury flashed in the large man's face, and his hands trembled in clenched fists. "Drop. That. Blade." The trainer repeated his demand, his voice growing louder with each retelling, as if the piece of wood in Savoy's hand would explode if not released. A vein pulsated across Den's temple and he shifted his weight from foot to foot. In moments, his treasured wall of calm and control had crumpled to dust. "Drop it! Drop it, now!"

"Drop? No." Savoy twisted the sword and held the hilt out toward the other man. He took care to give no sign of mockery or even acknowledge the gash he had opened in Den's armor. He had stripped the man of his pride; adding salt to the injury would be indefensible.

Their eyes met.

Savoy shook his head. "Don't."

With a jerk, Den ripped the blade free and threw it across the room. The wood crashed into some padding and thumped onto the sand. The trainer's hand fumbled in his pocket and extracted the amulet. It slipped in his fingers, but he caught it and aimed at Savoy.

The leather bands obeyed, flashing to life and pulling together.

Den gripped Savoy's hair and forced him to face the wall. He pulled on the rope, securing Savoy high to the ring. "Who in the Seven Hells do you think you are?" he growled in his ear. "You think you've had it hard till now? You're an idiotic, useless, unbroken pup."

Savoy's forehead pressed against the cool wall. He held his breath. Behind him, heavy breathing and rustling filled the air and then a crack echoed through the salle. He tensed. The next moment the crack came again, and a stripe of fire ignited across his back.

The blows rained with thunderstorm fury, growing harder and faster until, like a flash of lightning, they ceased to exist. Trails of blood trickled down Savoy's back.

Savoy breathed deeply, drawing comfort from the stone before him. Pain was a familiar companion in both fighting and training. He worried little for it. The inability to defend himself scorched worse.

He took another breath to collect himself and turned his head, unsurprised to find Den staring at the ground. The hemp, red likely for the first time in its life, fell to the sand.

Den's shoulders slumped, shame filling the void of exhausted anger. In the minutes just passed, Savoy lost skin, but Den lost more. And they both knew it. Savoy remained silent, letting the trainer simmer in disgrace. From fighter to irate bully was a long way to fall.

"Papa?"

Bloody gods. Savoy's head snapped toward the child's voice at the door. He froze at the sight of a curly-haired little girl clutching a blanket in two grubby fists. Her wide eyes glistened in the lantern light, and darted between him and Den, growing more frightened with each trip.

"Papa? Look. Someone hurt that man." She stepped into the salle and hugged the blanket to her face. "Who did that?"

Den's mouth moved but produced no words. Once, twice, three times. The child repeated her question, her small hand touching Savoy's skin and coming away wet. Den swallowed.

The soldier inside Savoy demanded he keep his mouth shut. Cursing himself, he spoke nonetheless. "A stranger wanted to hurt me," he told the girl, "but your papa found us and chased him away."

"Oh!" The fright in her eyes turned to awe as she gazed at Den, her face full of worship and pride. "You won't let the stranger come back, will you, Papa?"

Den shook his head and scooped up the little girl. "I won't, Mia." Over her head, his eyes met Savoy's. "I won't." He touched his forehead to the child's. "What are you doing out of bed?"

She mumbled something about a nightmare and the pair left. Savoy was alone. He twisted in his binds, seeking some comfort.

A body adjusted to anything. He focused on breathing, and the world had just started to dim away when footsteps roused him. Den pulled free the rope and stepped away while Savoy got his feet under him.

"Go to bed, Cat," he said quietly. "I'll make sure Jasper doesn't bother you."

Savoy massaged his shoulders and straightened, holding Den's gaze before walking to the door.

"Her mother died." Den's voice paused behind him. "I have nowhere else to leave her."

"No business of mine."

"You're stupid, you know." Den's words dripped bitterness. "You should've left me to stumble with her. Broken me."

"I know." He resumed walking.

"Who are you, Cat?"

"An idiotic, unbroken pup," Savoy replied, shutting the door behind him.

It was two days before Den spoke to Savoy again, demanding he stay after training. The others left in a hurry, as if afraid to be named accomplices in whatever offense Savoy was about to answer for. Shrugging, Savoy knelt by the wall and awaited the coming festivities.

Den closed the door behind them. The bolt clicked as it slid into place. That was a first. His gaze remained on the lock. "You needn't kneel. You're not in trouble."

Savoy rose from his usual penalty spot beside the ring in

the wall and crossed his arms. This was certainly a first. Den needed something.

The trainer shuffled his feet once and turned, staring at the ground. His jaw clenched and loosened. It seemed an eternity of silence passed before he spoke. "Will you teach me?"

Ah. "No."

Den jerked straight. "Not the answer I expected." His brows narrowed, and he tilted his head. "Not the brightest one either."

"I'm rarely accused of an overabundance of brainpower." Savoy paused. "Or of making a fine pet."

"Ah." Den tilted his head the other way and ran a hand through his hair. Silence reclaimed its hold over the salle. A thoughtful look flickered in his eyes, and Savoy held his breath. Minutes passed before the trainer spoke again. "All right. Not a favor. An exchange? What is it that you want?"

"To get out."

"That'd be slightly counterproductive to my cause, would it not?" Sarcasm left Den's face and he added more quietly, "I don't have the power to do that, Cat. I could get you food, perhaps a girl or—"

"Very well. You train me, I train you. Lesson for lesson."

"Train you beyond what we do every day?"

Savoy nodded.

"You've lost your mind. You'll collapse from exhaustion."

Savoy shrugged again. "Can't argue either point. The deal stands."

Den frowned, opened his mouth as if to say something, but closed it and shook away the thought. "Accepted."

Savoy bowed, idly wondering what brilliance inspired him to better arm his own captor.

CHAPTER 31

No message came on the fourth day of Seaborn's absence. Or the fifth. Or the eighth. Not even a note to explain the silence. Renee alternated between worrying for him and vowing to dismember the man. Alec had no theory to contribute, except to add that it was doubtful any combination of him, Diam, and Khavi would be able to open the door to the underground tunnels now that the Vipers had strengthened the lock. *Bloody helpful.* Following their run-in with Nino, Alec had invited Renee to visit the mage tavern more than once, but despite welcoming words, his tone lacked enthusiasm. Although Jasper and Ivan liked her well enough, she made most of Alec's other mage friends—unregistered, outlaw mage friends—uncomfortable. He seemed to avoid the inn and private conversations with her.

Renee paced the room, kicking any object in foot's reach. At the writing desk, Diam bent over a sheet of paper.

"How did you get nabbed in Atham?" Renee asked, stopping beside him.

"You asked me that already. Twice." He cupped his free hand, shielding his work from view. "Someone stuck a smelly cloth over my face while Khavi hunted." He tilted his face toward her, his eyes wary. "Are you gonna break things again?"

Renee sighed. The week had been rough on them both. "I'm sorry." She forced a smile. "What are you writing?"

"It's a secret."

"Shall I guess?"

His eyes widened and he shook his head. Before Renee could fix the security breach she'd created, Diam stuffed the paper into his back pocket and scurried out the door, Khavi trotting in his wake.

"Diam!" Rubbing her temple, Renee headed outside after him, although experience proved such attempts fruitless. Catar failed to intimidate the boy any more than Atham had, discussions of Savoy's sacrifice brought nods and tears but no results, and locking the door yielded little beyond broken windows. Acknowledging the truth that she could contain Diam no better than the Academy had been able to, Renee was left with trusting Khavi to protect the boy until she could conjure either Savoy or a way to contact his parents. At least Diam kept his vow to return home before dark each day.

As expected, Diam had slipped out of sight. The wind flung droplets of thin rain into Renee's face as she stopped in the street and buried her hands in her pockets. The foul morning had driven a meat-pie merchant and his cart under cover of an overhanging rooftop. Despite the aroma, Renee knew better than to purchase the pastries, which had doubled her and Diam over with stomach cramps two days back. Nothing in this gods'-forsaken city could be trusted. An elderly woman, her head bent against the wind, stepped around Renee. A young lad trotting at the woman's heels carefully cut her purse. A pickpocket. And this was the nice part of Catar City.

Renee ground her teeth together. Her frustration at all the wasted days of inactivity boiled over. She inserted herself between the culprit and his victim. The youth, a half-starved lad with angry eyes and torn clothes, snarled.

"Give it back." Renee gripped his arm.

The boy spat.

She wiped the saliva from her cheek and folded his wrist, raising him up on his toes. "A Healer will cost more than what you got from her. Give it back."

He swung at her face. Dodging the blow, she twisted his hand until he howled. Gawkers gathered around, willing to endure the weather for a bit of entertainment. She held fast. Let them look. She released her breath, but not the pressure. "How long do you want to keep at this?"

"This would be long enough," said a gruff voice. Someone grabbed the scruff of her shirt and jerked her aside. "I don't need vigilantes in my city."

Looking up, Renee stared at the uniformed Servant of the Crown who had seized hold of her. Several paces away, his partner growled something to the pickpocket. She licked her lips and met the Servant's eyes. "I'm not a vigilante. I'm . . ." The words caught in her throat. She was nothing. Her career had ended before it began. "I'm . . . " She looked away. "I'm sorry."

The Servant's eyes softened. "This is no place for you, girl."

She nodded, the Servant's words salting her wounds. There was no place for her. Not in the Crown's Service, not at her father's estates, not at her friend's side. The Servant patted her shoulder and walked away. The old woman was nowhere to be seen. Renee stood alone.

Closing her eyes, she seized the emptiness filling her heart and tucked it from her mind. She was done waiting for news. If tomorrow arrived without a message, she'd go to Atham herself. Right after the cursed Predator match she promised Diam.

Savoy rose the morning of the fight to find tension cracking the air and his own excitement morbidly elevated. A fight for sport. A brush with the outside world. A crowd with hundreds of eyes that, for however vile a reason, could appreciate the art of combat.

And, Savoy admitted, it was amusing to watch Jasper trot in useless anxiety-ridden circles.

At present, the boy mage was supervising the bathing, as if the fighters might drown if left unattended, or else strangle themselves with the towels, which the boy already passed out and collected three times. The apparently complex task finished, Jasper invited a woman with an expression as tight as her hair bun into the bathing room.

"She's here for the bookies," Farmer whispered. "Can't field an injured Predator without disclosing, so they can adjust the odds." He jerked his head at the examiner. "She caught Jasper trying to pull one over her last year, so he's on notice."

Savoy tensed. The woman was a mage. Nausea crept up his throat.

Despite Savoy's genuine attempt to cooperate, it took the examiner a dozen tries to pierce his Keraldi Barrier. His body fought her like it fought Jasper, and his heart pounded long after she walked away.

Jasper's face dripped venom. Savoy was certain that only the bell calling all fighters to the arena saved him a private conversation with the boy. Or, at least, delayed it.

"What in the bloody hells were you pulling?" Den growled into his ear, holding him back from the others as they headed down the corridor. "Did you lose your mind?"

"Years ago." Savoy's gaze locked on the passage they turned into, recognizing the pattern of tiny blue amulets wedged into the stones. It was the main corridor he and Renee briefly navigated when coming after Diam. Walking in their current direction, they came to the arena.

"Find it. Now." Den shot a glance toward the arena door. A team of trumpets roused cheers, which escaped into the corridor. The *boom-boom-boom* of a large drum vibrated through the tunnel. "You're not facing a death match, but lose and you might be. Someone has to go soon. We have seven fighters and six slots. The Madam will not long tolerate feeding an extra mouth. Understand?"

Savoy stretched his back. "It's not my first fight, Den."

"It is here."

The gravity of Den's voice made Savoy pause. He nodded, pulling his mind to battle.

The arena overflowed with people, shouts, and ale. Rows upon rows of wooden benches rose high to the ceiling. With no windows to let in daylight, the light from blazing torches and lanterns gave the hall a furnace-like feel. In the center, at the bottom of the pit, stood a roofless cage where the fighting would take place. The design offered a prime view to the top seats, but would seal all inside if the exits failed. Savoy followed his group out of the tunnel and directly into a holding pen, while the opposing team made itself comfortable on the other side. The ripe reek of too many unwashed bodies in a closed space filled his nose, almost but not quite concealing another smell: the copper tinge of blood and fear.

He looked at the spectators. They seemed so close, just a few paces away. But they weren't close. Seven-span-high bars, topped with barbed wire, separated him and them.

"Boulder, weighing in at twenty-two stone!" shouted a voice deep in the crowd. "Place your bets on the human animal!"

Green-clad young men gripping notepads scurried about the rows, stopping and making notes whenever a spectator beckoned. Women in clothing that revealed more than it hid carried trays of drink. The smell of stale wine mixed with sweat and tobacco settled over the place like a dense cloud of fog.

Savoy frowned at Den. "All I've seen Boulder do is move stones. Who pays to watch him fight?"

"No one." Den's flat voice set Savoy further on edge. "They pay to watch him kill."

Ah. Savoy nodded, tightening his jaw. "And if he kills the ref?"

"He won't." Den looked toward the sand. "Jasper trained him not to."

Savoy digested the thought while trumpets sounded and the crowd's voices quieted to a dull roar. It was almost time. Squaring his shoulders, Savoy raised his face to challenge the room. And his heart froze.

In the second row of the middle section sat Renee and Diam.

Renee stilled her foot's tapping. Yes, she was wasting time. And yes, the hours spent supporting Vipers' sport were hours taken from her mission. But she had made a promise to Diam and it would not do to sulk over keeping her word. She was here. She might as well try and learn something.

Diam jerked forward, startling Renee from her train of thought. He pointed down, jostling a serving girl who scurried by with a mug-filled tray. Stale dark liquid sloshed into his lap. "Korish!" he yelled.

"What?" Renee threw her arms around the boy to keep him seated. The pounding of her heart drowned out the din of cheering drunks as her eyes followed Diam's extended finger. She gasped. It was impossible. No, it wasn't.

Savoy stood in the right-side holding pen, his eyes stoically sweeping the room. Centuries stretched on until all at once, their gazes met. She tensed, holding her breath. It lasted no more than a second, but then his head gave a small shake and turned away.

Beside her, Diam yelled for his brother. Renee clamped her hand over his mouth until he quieted. And then she cursed herself, digging her nails into her thighs. She should have known. Or speculated. Or found a bloody bookie and beat him into speaking. There was no better candidate for the Vipers' games. Hadn't Seaborn told her that? In all gods' names, the Yellow Rose in Diam's demand note was the same bloody Viper pit that sold fight tickets. She scrubbed her trembling palms over her face.

In the seat beside her, Diam regained all the self-control his eight-year-old self could muster and sat on his hands. "Why do they put barbed wire on the bars?"

Renee reined in her silent tirade and looked down through smoke-filled air to where vertical metal bars separated the fighters and spectators. The smooth rods rose seven spans—almost four times a man's height—into the air to a crown of tangled barbs. The Vipers took no chances. "So no one climbs out," she told him.

He squeezed her hand.

Music bellowed again while Renee wiped the sweat from her free hand on her thigh. Announcers shouted names and measurements, prompting bookies to close the records. A man holding a knotted rope's end entered the cage, bowed, and pointed to the holding pens. Another roll of the drum. From Savoy's side, a large man in white pants stepped onto the sand and gazed at the cheering crowd. On the left, a scrawny fighter in blue was shoved out, skidding to a halt in the sand.

The man in white, a bald behemoth, stopped walking and gazed about. His hand came up to his mouth and he sucked his knuckle. The referee bounced his rope-end. Once. Twice. Shouts of "Crush him, Boulder!" cascaded from the stands. The third time the referee raised his rope, he brought it down hard across the man's bare shoulders. Boulder flinched and advanced toward his opponent.

The small man trembled. He covered his head with his hands, stretching skin taut over protruding ribs. Unlike the other Predators awaiting their turn, this one looked pitifully underfed.

"Excuse me, what are the odds?" Renee asked the spectator beside her.

"Three to one," the woman answered.

Renee's eyebrows rose. A one in three chance of Scrawny's victory sounded beyond optimistic. "And if, er, Boulder wins?"

She frowned. "Of course he'll win."

"But the bet?"

"Can you not see it's a death match? Boulder only fights death matches. Three he kills before the five-minute bell, one, after. On you go, Boulder! Move!"

Gods. Boulder now towered over his opponent, and still nothing happened. The growing din of the crowd encouraged the referee to use his rope's end. Boulder roared, cocked back his ham of a fist, and waited too long. The small man launched forward, like a rabid cornered rat, aiming his fingers at Boulder's eyes.

That was a mistake.

He missed the eyes, and Boulder's massive hands closed around the man's arm. He broke it, snapping the bone to a hideous angle. Then, wearing an expression of a pouting child, he struck his knuckles against the man's nose. Again. And again. The wound opened wider with each blow. Blood gushed down Scrawy's chin, onto his chest, and dripped out to the sand. Renee smelled the copper.

"I gotta be sick," whispered a voice at her elbow. Even in this light, Diam's face had taken on an unmistakable green tinge.

Grabbing hold of his arm, Renee ushered the boy toward the stairs, ignoring the curses of the spectators whose view they blocked as they passed. She should never have agreed to bring him.

They just made it. Khavi pounced on Diam the moment they emerged outside. The boy clutched his wolf's fur—she could no longer think of Khavi as a dog—took a breath, and jerked away to retch onto the ground. Renee rubbed a circle on his back, grateful they left before he could see his brother pushed into the cage.

"Renee? Are you well?"

She jumped and turned at the sound of Jasper's voice. The skinny mage closed the door behind him and adjusted his

glasses. Khavi let out a low growl, but Renee welcomed a familiar face. "A bit more gruesome than expected. What brings you
here?"

"You didn't see me?" He looked disappointed when she shook
her head. "In the right pen," he prodded. "With the white pups.
I'm their keeper."

Renee's mouth dried, as much from Jasper's words as from
the fear that Diam would blurt out Savoy's identity. The child,
however, remained silent and held Khavi's fur in a death grip.
She cleared her throat. "I wanted to see them fight, but . . ." She
jerked her head at Diam, and Jasper nodded in understanding.
"What's a keeper?" she asked.

"Me. I take care of them. Feeding, vet care, all that. I keep the
trainer in check too, you know, or else he'd run the poor pups
into the ground. If not for me, Den would've killed the newest
one."

"Amazing," she managed. A thunderstorm after a week of
drought. Gods, she should have considered Predator fights days
ago. "That's, well, unbelievable."

"It's true," Jasper continued eagerly. "The new one, Cat, he
won't stop thanking me. Den's hard on him, but that's the trainer's job, too, to be hard. I ensure it keeps under rein of reason."

She cleared her throat. "Is Cat the blond-haired one? I wished
to see him fight. He's . . . pretty."

"He is, isn't he?" Jasper gleamed as if discussing a prized
horse. "He's fighting now, though, if you wish to hurry down to
the pit."

Renee pointed to Diam and turned up her palms. "I wish." She took a breath. Nothing to lose. "Jasper? Do you think I could meet him, the pretty one? Can you do that?"

The boy smiled. "I can do most anything here. Take the wee man home and meet me here after the fight."

Jasper wasn't there when she returned. She waited. A quarter hour after the last of the spectators left the arena, a large man calling himself Den appeared at her side. He weighed her with his eyes, but beckoned her to follow.

"Did Cat win his fight?" Renee asked her escort.

"Yes," he grunted, and said no more.

They walked down past the arena, through a door on the right, and into a corridor she recognized from her foray underground. At a juncture where she and Savoy had once headed east to find Diam—the stones where Renee first took a life were forever branded in her mind—they now turned west. A few more turns brought them to a closed door. Renee sketched the map in her mind.

"In there." Den pushed the handle.

She faked a smile and moved past him. Then stopped. The thick rug on the floor and a bench with scented candles said the small room was meant for visitors who paid to enjoy the fighter's company. Inside, Savoy knelt on the floor, his hands tied uncomfortably high to a ring in the wall. He was still shirtless from the fight, with drawstring pants hanging on his hips. Green eyes betrayed no sign of recognition. Den loosened the ropes—enough to give Savoy some movement while permitting Renee to step out of his reach, should she wish to.

"I promise not to damage him," she told Den, glancing pointedly from him to the door. Her heart pounded in her ears. "Will you untie him for me?"

A hint of surprise flickered across Den's face, but he schooled it away and complied. "Call out if you need anything."

Savoy massaged his shoulders and stared at the man's receding back until the door closed with a click. His eyes flowed to Renee. She thought she caught a momentary warmth in his gaze, but if it was there, it disappeared in a blink. He did not smile.

"Commander—"

He put a finger to his lips, cutting her off. "Cat. And you shouldn't be here."

She hugged her arms to her chest and lowered her voice to match his. "Neither should you." It wasn't the reception she'd imagined. She took a step toward him, and Savoy stood. Exhaustion shadowed his face and he favored his right knee when rising, likely a souvenir from his fight. It had to be bad if he let her see it. She avoided looking down, pretending not to notice the limp. She could not, however, ignore the leather bands on his wrists or the fading welts covering his back and shoulders, crisscrossing the ones Verin's old discipline had left. Her hand reached out toward him but she stayed its course, sensing he did not wish to be touched. She could do that much for a friend. "Are you well, then?"

Savoy followed her gaze and turned to hide his back from

view. "Not my first beating. Nor last." He sighed. "That is a hazard of being me. I also happen to be alive, which trumps other details. Agreed?"

She nodded. "How do we get you out of here?"

"You don't." He braced his hand on the wall beside her head and bore down with his gaze. "You stay clear. Understood?"

"You are in a poor position to issue orders."

He grasped her shoulders and twisted her roughly toward the western wall. "That way are cells they call barracks. Is that where you wish to be? Or do you imagine Vipers make use only of boys and men?" He looked pointedly at the candles and rug.

She stepped away and turned to him. Her life was hers to risk, but there was no reason to add more weight to his conscience. She would do what she must. "No, of course not. A captured rescuer would be of little help."

His brows tightened in suspicion.

Renee hurried on. Better to keep her words confined to truths. "I will go to Atham and inform Verin of your exact location. Seaborn's already there, laying the groundwork." *Although gods know what's keeping him.* "Is there something else I might do?"

Approaching footsteps echoed down the corridor. Savoy looked at the door and spoke quickly. "Diam?"

"Healthy. He misses you. He'll be safe with Alec while I'm gone."

The steps grew louder. Savoy nodded. "The man who brought

you here is named Den. If I had to trust someone here, it would be him. Not yet, though. If—"

The door swung open to admit Jasper. The boy's smile dissolved to alarm. "Gods, how did he get loose? Are you all right, Renee?" He came up beside her and extended his hand toward Savoy.

Savoy retreated. His shoulders hunched defensively and Renee's heart squeezed at the sudden paleness of his face. A blue glow sparked at the tips of Jasper's fingers and Savoy's wrists twisted behind his head, as if the leather bracelets overpowered twisting muscle.

Something felt very wrong, like a bow straining in the distance, arrow poised. "Jasper?" Renee touched the boy's shoulder, hoping her voice betrayed nothing of her thumping pulse. "I . . . I want to leave. Will you lead me out, please?"

For an instant she feared he'd refuse and the bow would loose its arrow, but he nodded at her and held open the door. Her shoulders relaxed and she preceded him out. Just before the door closed, Jasper paused to bid Savoy farewell.

And Savoy flinched.

After the arena, Renee stopped at Hunter's Inn only long enough to check on Diam. She needed Alec, and there was no point in looking for him at the inn anymore. She hugged Diam and, by silent agreement, said nothing about his brother's fate.

"A message came for you," Diam said, unburying himself from

her shoulder. He extended a strip of paper he'd been clutching, unabashed at having read Renee's mail.

She unrolled the strip and read its single word. *Palan.* Written in Sasha's hand. Renee's skin crawled.

Diam slid down and peered at the ink. "What about Uncle Palan?"

"I asked Sasha to discover who was responsible for your brother's assignment to the Academy this year." She tossed the paper into the fire. "Why do you call him Uncle, Diam?"

The boy shrugged. "'Cause he asked me to."

Renee frowned. Why in the Seven Hells would the head of the Family do that? She shook her head. Time enough to worry about it later. For now, she had to be off to Zev's.

Renee pounded the door with more abuse than the aging wood warranted.

The door opened. Letting her inside, Alec marked his place in a book with his finger and looked over his shoulder. "Sorry, Master Zev, no more visitors, I promise."

"Mmm," Zev grumbled, sparing a nod for Renee before frowning at Alec. "Did you pick up the tea, boy, as I asked?"

Alec winced. "No, sir. Renee and I can go now, though."

Renee stiffened.

Zev waved his hand and limped out. "Never you mind. I will buy it myself."

Instead of sighing in relief, Alec blushed and frowned at the closing door. "He's just saying that. We should fetch it."

Enough. She stepped into his line of sight. "Quit worrying about tea. Jasper . . . " She stopped. The words she expected to pour out refused to do so. She had never seen Savoy afraid. "Your friend Jasper, he's—he's a Viper."

Alec leaned against the wall. "Yes, I know."

Her eyes widened.

"I thought you knew. Most everyone in Catar is a Viper." He rubbed his face. "Did something happen?"

"I found Savoy."

Alec froze, then sat on the floor, pulling her down beside him. The scent of sweet spice, like Zev's, drifted from his shirt.

Leaning against him, she started at the beginning. The words tumbled out now, detailing the arena, the fights, the meeting in the carpeted room. "I think Jasper is hurting him," she said at last, resting her forearms against her knees. "I cannot explain it otherwise."

An impatient sigh rose beside her. "Being a mage doesn't make him evil, Renee," Alec bit out. "Just because you can't do something doesn't mean those who can are diseased. You said it yourself—the man had welts. That isn't mage work."

Renee's eyes narrowed. "You saw Grovener cut an arrow from him, Alec. Savoy isn't afraid of bruises. You didn't see . . . " She shook her head and sat upright. Alec hadn't seen, and her proof amounted to analyzing pallor. She breathed evenly to douse the fire in her blood. "I never called Control a disease. But it's not an assurance of virtue either. Will you agree that we each know too little about Jasper to judge his integrity?" She thanked the gods

286

when Alec nodded. "All right. If a mage, some mage, was hurting Savoy, could he shield himself?"

Alec's face reclaimed it usual introspection. "Break a mage's concentration and he's useless. Pain, fear, distraction, anything like that and, well, you saw Jasper and Ivan in that alley. As for shielding . . ." His eyes scanned a large bookshelf and returned apologetic. "The Keraldi Barrier provides natural protection, but it's no better against force than skin against a knife. Not much help there."

"Better than nothing." Renee rested her forehead against her arms.

"I don't know. It's like holding off a sword by gripping the blade with your bare hands; the steel will win anyway, just later and more painfully."

The description nauseated her. "If Jasper were registered—"

"The Crown could ship him off to disarm Devmani mage traps. Or kill him." Alec's shoulders tensed. "Good solution."

Her temper gave way at last. "If he were registered, the threat of punishment from the Mage Council would keep him from puppeteering people to begin with!"

Alec rose. "People commit crimes every day, Renee. It's not fair to single us out for special penalty."

Renee looked at him for several heartbeats before shifting her gaze to the fire. "*Us* used to mean you and me, Alec."

Alec said nothing.

CHAPTER 32

The stallion Renee had hired for her ride to Atham snorted his discontent as she reined him to a walk on the Academy grounds. Gray clouds dimmed the late afternoon sunlight, washing the color from buildings and people alike. A cool breeze lifted Renee's sweaty hair and dried the foam hugging the horse's flanks. Patting the stallion's neck, Renee yielded him to a stable boy's care and rubbed her face.

Palan. Sasha's message had gnawed at her for the last two days' ride. So the fat lord was the one behind Savoy's return to Atham. Who did Palan manipulate to get the leader of a specialty unit pulled from the field? And why? And how? Did Palan's labors to befriend Diam have anything to do with it? Renee's skin felt tight. Rubbing her arms, she made her way to the main courtyard. For now, she would focus on the facts she had. She knew where Savoy was. All she needed was Verin's help to get him out.

The courtyard rolled out in a crunchy carpet of frozen yellow grass. Renee looked around. It was strange to be back. Stranger still to have cares beyond school walls. Despite having braced herself, the sight of the Academy's grounds squeezed her chest. She could practically hear the fire crackling in her room, could see Rock Lake's glass surface, could smell the mix of sand and sweat in the salle. All was the same and yet . . . Renee frowned.

Something was off.

The cadets moved faster between buildings, and uniformed guard seemed to have tripled in her fortnight away. It was fortunate she knew most guardsmen by name; their faces suggested they'd have evicted a stranger.

Seaborn was not to be found, either in his office or his quarters. A sentry guarding the cadets' barracks, another novelty begun in her absence, hesitated to let her inside.

"Very well," she told the young guardsman. "Could you tell Cadet Sasha Jurran that I would welcome her company out here?"

His gaze dropped to the ground.

"You know me, Chad."

He shook his head. "It is not that, Re—" He cleared his throat. "My lady. It's . . . " His voice faltered again. "Sasha will not leave her room. Or let anyone in."

Renee jerked straight. "What?"

"A few days ago . . . She . . . " The guard took a breath and collected himself. "I was the one who found her. Beaten half conscious and discarded naked at the Academy's gates. Someone had broken three of her fingers and carved a pair of puncture marks on her neck."

Renee's face went cold, as if doused with ice water. She pushed past the guard to the door.

His hand gripped her shoulder. "There is more. The following day, King Lysian's little cousin disappeared. A wee toddler."

"Claire?" Renee rubbed her eyes, remembering the giggling girl rocking her chair at the Queen's Day dinner. It seemed the Vipers were finishing what they started, terrorizing the royal family until King Lysian had no choice but to turn a blind eye to their business. Twisting on her heels, Renee found the guard's eyes. "Let me by, Chad. The Crown's cousin cannot spend her life hiding."

He glanced from her to the building he guarded and stepped aside.

Renee strode down the long corridor of the Academy barracks, each stride a painful echo of the life she'd left behind. She trailed her fingers along the uneven walls and stopped beside the door that once held her name. She knocked.

"Leave, please," came a voice from inside.

"Sasha, it's me."

"Great gods." Sasha opened the door a crack and stood frozen for a moment before grasping Renee's hands and pulling her inside. Her left eye was swollen, the purple bruises pushing against her hairline. A bandage swathed her right hand, a silk scarf her neck. Sasha opened her mouth, cringed, and instead of speaking, buried her face in Renee's shoulder.

"It's all right," Renee said, steering them to the bed. But it wasn't all right. It was as wrong as having Alec as an opponent instead of an ally. As wrong as seeing Savoy in shackles, flinching from Jasper's glance. Perhaps worse. Sasha wasn't a fighter.

She reasoned and discussed and debated, and she never hurt anyone. The thought of a Viper—of anyone!—abusing Sasha made the blood heat in Renee's veins. Nostrils flaring, she smoothed her friend's hair. "Do you wish to speak of it?"

"No." A sob escaped. "The Vipers took Claire."

"I know," Renee whispered.

"Who's next?" Sasha's voice broke. "My aunt? My mother? What if the Vipers get my mother? What if—"

"It will stop." Renee pulled back to look Sasha in the face. "Lysian is a good king. He will *make* it stop."

Sasha shook her head, wiping her eyes. "No, Renee, it won't. The Madam does not have armies, but she has mages. If Lys marches on Catar with too few soldiers, he'll be impotent. If he brings many, the fighting will turn the whole city to blood. The whole city." Her words shook. "And then the Family will press for *its* advantage. And when Tildor's neighbors in the Devmani Empire find out, they will attack us in our weakness. Tildor will be back at war. And"—Sasha's words poured faster, each one upsetting the next—"and if Lys does nothing, the Vipers will keep coming after my family."

Renee drew a breath. Sasha was likely right. She usually was. "And will staying locked in the room change any of it? The Vipers want you terrified. Don't aid their quest."

"I'm not like you, Renee," she whispered. "I can't just order myself unafraid."

"Neither can I. But we can try."

Sasha studied the bedspread. "You found Diam," she said finally, and straightened. "Then you can stay a while, here with me?"

Renee sighed. "No." Taking a breath, she described what took place since she left, leaving out only Alec's mage nature. If the story implied that veesi use spurred his decision to leave, it was the lesser of the evils. As she spoke, the fear in Sasha's face dampened, and became focused on the dilemma at hand.

"Seaborn is at the palace," Sasha said when Renee finished speaking. "Lys has him in chambers with other officials, divining options for the crisis. Perhaps that sheds light on his delay."

Renee frowned, opening her mouth to protest Seaborn's failure to send word, but halted when Sasha sighed.

"Don't be angry, Renee. For better or worse, Lys settled the weight of Tildor's safety on Seaborn's shoulders."

Renee nodded. Seaborn was a Servant on active duty with birdies and connections in Catar, the Vipers' stronghold. He could not have ignored the Crown's call at a time like this. "Still, he could have written," she said.

"He may have. The couriers have been . . ." Sasha's lips pressed together, warding off fresh tears. "We've had trouble with messages."

Renee sensed it was time to shift the topic. "How did you learn of Palan's hand in Savoy's assignment?"

Sasha forced a smile. "Because Lys had a hand in that too."

Renee frowned. "Since when does the king get involved in the field orders of a mere commander, even if it's one as good as Savoy?"

"Since the leader of the Family offered to barter said orders for the location of a major Viper veesi shipment." Sasha leaned forward, resting her elbows on her knees. "Verin and Lys had a row over it. Apparently Verin didn't wish to do it, saying that Palan was manipulating the Crown into attacking the Family's rival, and that allowing Palan to influence military assignments, no matter how minor, was a dangerous path to start on. Lys argued that removing veesi from Tildor's streets and gold from a crime group's purse had to be done, and that one man's assignment mattered little on the larger scale."

Renee nodded. "I'm with Lysian. Plus, the Family would have nabbed the veesi for itself otherwise."

Sasha nodded. "Lys said that as well. He overruled Verin, had the Seventh take down the shipment, and cut orders for Savoy's reassignment. What confuses me, though, is why. How does Savoy's presence at the Academy benefit Palan?"

"I don't know." Renee shook her head. "In fact, I think it backfired—Diam's kidnapper wanted Savoy to kill Palan in exchange for Diam's life." She paused. It was a mess. How had Lysian put it? *A disease of crime.* She thought back to the speech, the dais in the courtyard, Fisker yelling at Diam to clear the grass. It seemed an eternity ago. "You know, there is one person who despises Savoy and Palan both. Fisker."

Sasha's lips pressed together. "Palan is part of the Family—I understand Fisker's grudge there. But why Savoy?"

Renee raised her hand, wiggling the finger Fisker was missing.

Sasha tipped her head back, then shook it. "No, no, I don't see it." She waved. "Oh, I believe there's bad blood—that much was clear from the Queen's Day fallout—but Fisker . . . Gods, you remember what he was like at the Academy? The man's addicted to his notion of law like a veesi crony to the leaf. Yes, he'd pauper the treasury to track a pickpocket, but he wouldn't arrange a kidnapping."

Renee kept silent. Fisker attempted to lock a teenage Savoy in the dungeons and then saw him whipped as a consolation prize. He was capable of more than Sasha thought. But maybe her roommate was right—hurt pride was not reason enough for the guardsman to *break* a rule.

"Something else I found odd," Sasha added, interrupting Renee's thoughts. "Palan withdrew Tanil from the cadet roll shortly after you left."

Renee hissed, her fists tightening in a renewed wave of fury. Cheating, dishonorable, Predator-betting Tanil. Then a thought struck her. "Could Tanil be behind the kidnapping?" she asked slowly, tilting her face to look at her friend. "He had little love for Savoy and might have expected to rise in the Family hierarchy if his uncle were dead. He knew enough from the fight at Rock Lake to separate Diam from Khavi." The arrow in the wolf's side had likely been Tanil's first attempt to do so. "He had a Viper connection from all his Predator-betting to whom he could pass Diam, and it would serve him well to keep the sew-

294

age he was creating out of his backyard by having Diam shipped off to Catar."

Sasha rubbed the back of her neck, looking past Renee. "And then Palan found out and removed Tanil from the Academy to address the treason?" She nodded, refocusing on Renee's face. "Possible."

"It still doesn't explain why Palan wanted Savoy in Atham to begin with, though." Renee paused for a moment, wondering which was worse—having the man who ordered her mother and Riley killed now in charge of the Family, or the vileness that was Tanil calling the shots. She sighed and looked out the window to check the sun's position. If she wished to speak with Verin before the day's end, she needed to go. "Shall we meet in the mess for dinner?" she asked, touching Sasha's arm, then realized with chagrin that her mess hall privileges had ended when she quit school. "Or at a tavern?"

Sasha shook her head. "I'm tired," she said, retreating to her bed.

Renee bit her lip. In a just world, she should have been able to stay.

As Renee closed the door, she saw her friend disappear beneath the covers, and sighed. Sasha had every right to be frightened no matter how much Renee wished it otherwise. And, although Renee knew she had exhausted what she could do for her friend right now, the weight of Sasha's fear stayed with her.

CHAPTER 33

Renee already had the Administrative Building in her line of sight when labored breathing alerted her to an approaching presence.

Turning to see who accosted her, Renee found herself looking at a well-dressed, sweaty-faced man. Dark eyes set deep in a fleshy face sparkled with intelligence. Her shoulders tensed as she bowed to the man who she had spoken much about, but never before spoken *to.* "Lord Palan. Good afternoon."

"My lady." Lord Palan fell in step beside Renee as if they had known each other for years. He gestured at the gathering clouds, but what he spoke of had little to do with weather. "Is the phrase 'The enemy of my enemy is my ally' familiar to you?"

She squinted at the graying sky. The leader of a major crime group did not approach sixteen-year-old ex-cadets with talk of alliances unless said ex-cadets had something he wanted. Renee rubbed the scar on her palm. Whatever she had was not for sale to her mother's killer. "Your Family murdered mine, my lord. Are those words familiar to you?"

He blinked. "Yes, quite so. But they are not accurate in your case." Palan rubbed his chins. "We've had no dealings with the de Winter estate besides collections for the road guards."

Renee frowned. If the man was feigning surprise at the charge, he was doing it well. "My father spoke otherwise."

"Hmm. When tragedy strikes, peace of mind is sometimes gained by believing an accident to be the work of evil. Although . . ." Palan squinted in thought and unbuttoned the top of his jacket. The material was plain, but Renee could see the expensive tailoring and cut. The lord cared for his looks. "Before her death, did not the de Winter lands belong wholly to your lady mother?" He waved his hand as if casually accusing Lord Tamath de Winter of murder was nothing of consequence. Perhaps, to the leader of the Family, it wasn't. "Forgive me. That implication was offensive and, I'm sure, baseless." Reaching into his coat, he pulled out a folded sheet of parchment. "Now, a gesture of good faith."

The shift in conversation shoved Renee off balance once more. Better to keep her mouth shut until the ground settled.

Palan made a show of adjusting his ring. "For the past year, your lord father has petitioned me for a contract for sale of wool and goat cheese. You know enough of my organization, I think, to predict that a contract with me has very little chance of failing to generate profits."

She nodded. The nominal wool and cheese loads would carry veesi or perform another service for the Family. In either case, Lord Tamath would collect coin even if every de Winter goat died of colic. Renee found her father's intentions disgusting, but, unfortunately, not surprising. "Why do you tell me of this?"

"I wish to give you veto power over the contract."

She blinked. "Veto?"

He raised the folded paper. "I've signed the deal from my side, opposite your father's hand. If you find the arrangement disagreeable, tear up the parchment. Otherwise, pass it to him. As you see, I offer no imposition. Only choice."

Renee drew a breath. Despite herself, she had to bow at the man's skill. She wished no gifts from the Family, but he had given her a gift of knowledge and choice—a gift impossible to reject or return. "Why the generosity, my lord?"

"Not generosity. Only a show of good faith, like I stated before." His smile said he'd say no more. With a small bow, Palan slipped the folded parchment and another, smaller piece of paper, into her pocket and turned away.

Renee stared at the receding back. "Why did you want Savoy recalled to the Academy?" she called out.

The large back paused, silence filling the air for several heartbeats. "Because it was Diam's first year here," Palan said finally, and, tugging down his waistcoat, strolled away.

Renee shut her eyes. Why would the brothers' reunion matter to *him*? And how did Palan expect to benefit from befriending her? She felt the answer scratching the corner of her mind but could not drag it out. Her hand touched her pocket, extracting the small paper scrap. A tavern name and a time. Nothing more. For an instant, she considered turning about and chasing down the conniving lord, demanding that he explain himself. Even as the thought sprinted through her, she knew it was foolish. She could not intimidate Palan into divulging more than he wished any more than she could muscle a sword into the skull of a stronger opponent. And Savoy had already taught her the fallacy of *that*.

Savoy. Sasha's news had distracted Renee for a time, but the simmering panic now returned. She needed Verin and the Seventh, and she needed them fast. Praying that Savoy's men were stationed nearby, she hurried to see the headmaster—and High Constable.

Verin's office smelled of jasmine tea. On instinct, Renee came to attention in front of his desk before remembering that military courtesies were no longer hers to follow. She inclined her head instead.

"A pleasure seeing you once more, my lady." Verin diplomatically failed to notice her misstep and rose. He invited her to take a worn leather chair and waited until she sat before doing so himself. "The loss of your company is a great one to both the Crown and the Academy." His voice was unexpectedly genuine. "How can I be of service?"

She leaned forward. "The Vipers—" The words rushed to her lips and she drew a breath to rein them, and herself, in. "The Vipers hold Commander Savoy captive in an underground Predator lair in Catar City."

He didn't even blink. Renee tensed. Waited. Then she felt her eyes go wide with realization.

He *knew*.

"Is a rescue mission—"

Verin shook his head, cutting her off. "There will be no rescue mission." He interlaced his fingers and laid them atop his desk. "Your words pain me, but the Crown never authorized Commander Savoy to abandon his post and ride off to his brother's rescue. A Servant taking independent action is not entitled to the Crown's army any more than a royal account keeper with personal debts is entitled to the Crown's coffers."

Renee stared at him. Her voice failed for several seconds before she forced it to work. "You are Savoy's family," she said quietly. "You raised him, taught him to fight, guided his life. He will die, sir, and you can stop it."

Verin lowered his face, his lips pressed together. When he looked up, a play of the window's light glistened in his gaze. "I am a High Constable in the Crown's army." He voice was low. "I advise King Lysian on military strategy while overseeing the education of all his champions. The position does not permit the luxury of sentiment."

He would not do it. Good gods. Verin would let Savoy die for the sake of . . . what? Administrative purity that had already been fouled by the Family's agreement with the king? Renee drew a breath. "I know Savoy was recalled at Lord Palan's request. And that Lord Palan controls the Family, for all that he tries to keep his hands clean. With all respect, sir, the Crown has already shown . . . flexibility . . . in regards to Savoy. Could you at least address the matter with King Lysian?"

This time, Verin's brows rose. Tilting his head, he studied her in silence. "I see you are well informed," he said at last, just when

Renee began to expect a denial. "Bending to criminals' demands, no matter how enticing the apparent rewards, is always a mistake. I have already spoken to King Lysian. We will not do it again."

She frowned in confusion. "But no criminals are demanding Savoy's rescue, sir. How would it be a boon to them?"

"An assault on Catar helps the Family." Verin chuckled without humor. "Do you not see, my lady? When the Crown refused Lord Palan's petition to attack the Vipers, he arranged for Commander Savoy's recall from the field. Then, miraculously, Savoy became captive in the heart of Catar's Viper layer. It is not a coincidence. Lord Palan is using the Seventh's leader and High Constable's foster son as bait. The guilt and affection you tried to stir in me moments ago is what the Family wishes of us."

Renee rubbed her temple. Had *Palan* ordered Diam kidnapped and given to the Vipers so his older brother would follow? No, Verin's theory felt wrong. Her fingernails dug into her thighs. "I disagree, sir. This *isn't* a Family ploy. Diam's kidnapper wished Palan himself dead."

"Surely you realize such demand is a jest!" Verin tilted his head. "Very well. Who do you believe behind the events?"

"Tanil."

The headmaster smiled. "Which brings us back to the Family, does it not?" He shook his head, his voice hardening. "I believe I am correct, my lady, and I cannot permit Tildor to continue bowing its head to the Family's strong-arming. Not even for Korish Savoy."

301

Renee's fingers dug into the leather pads of her chair. "King Lysian owes Savoy his life!"

Verin's palm slammed the table. "That will do, Lady Renee." His voice froze her to the seat. "In light of your separation from the Academy, this audience is a privilege you and I extend to each other. I am certain neither of us wishes to jeopardize the possibility of enjoying the other's company in the future. Have I made myself clear?"

Quite clear. Renee left the meeting in a temper to match the growing gale. Verin was wrong and would do nothing. Curse the man. Curse Seaborn and his duties. Curse the entire city. Hunching shoulders against the rain, she went outside, her hands seeking her pockets. Rough paper bent under her fingertips. It was the note from Palan. Taking shelter beneath a tree, she read it again. *Greasy Pig. One hour past dusk.* Why in the Seven Hells not?

CHAPTER 34

"Two! Three! Five!" Savoy called parry numbers as he advanced on Den, but his mind kept slipping to Renee's apparent friendship with Jasper. It had been three days since her visit. Did the girl know the fire she toyed with? How long until Jasper turned and hurt her? "It's a blade, not a club, Den." Savoy pulled the blow, cracking the wood against the larger man's clavicle instead of his skull. "And five protects the head. Which, unless your head is up your ass, makes it a high parry."

Den rubbed the new red mark. "You held back. Don't."

Cocking a brow, Savoy threw him a square pad, let the man brace the target, and focused on a point well beyond the padded leather. His muscles snapped like a whip; hip, shoulder, and arm engaging before the blade. The thump echoed through the salle.

Den stumbled. "Good gods." He gasped, cradling the arm despite the pad's protection. "That is how you fight, then? When the stakes are real?"

"On occasion. I favor speed and precision over power."

"Is it more effective?"

Savoy shrugged. "Preference born of childhood habit. I did not come into my height until my late teens and speed gave me an edge. Your size well complements a strength-based style, however." Den stowed away the abused target.

"The day you found me fumbling with a blade, I didn't see you enter." Den jerked his chin at the pad. "You could have split open my skull, dull wood or not."

"An error in judgment I am fast regretting."

The corners of Den's mouth twitched. "The girl who came here last week, she knew you."

Savoy twirled his sword to ease the clench in his stomach. "Harness your brain to your sword."

"No wench in her right mind risks remaining alone with an unrestrained Predator." Den parried a blow. "Not unless she knows him." The man's self-satisfied amusement faded to a serious tone. "Better she keep away. It's not safe for either of you."

"That wench will fillet you from crotch to chin if you get a blade in her hand. And if you call her that again, I'll grant your wish of not pulling strikes." He realized his knuckles turned white in their grip and relaxed his hold, focusing on the clack-clacking wood. "Want to worry about a girl? Worry about your daughter."

"Why do you think I'm here?" Den shook his head. "Have you ever been hungry, Cat? The kind of hungry when you resent a stray dog his bone? Or lived on a street so violent that each time your mother stepped from the house, you feared she'd not return?" He twisted the blade. "The Madam is a harsh mistress, but she keeps order. The Vipers, and only the Vipers, rule Catar now. So long as I obey, the food I buy is mine to keep and Mia is safe even from the guards with a taste for children. It was not thus before she took the Viper throne and tripled its influence."

Savoy shook his head. "You're a slave."

"I'm a slave with the whip instead of the shackles. It could be worse. *Was* worse."

"There are cities beyond Catar." Savoy rubbed his wrists. "The others say you won the Freedom Fight."

Den snorted. "The Madam needed a trainer around the time Mia was born. They killed her mother for trying to escape and came to me, knowing I wouldn't risk leaving. We put on a show and I traded my binds for my daughter. No one leaves the Vipers, Cat. Not alive, they don't."

CHAPTER 35

Renee felt the note rustling in her pocket as she obeyed Lord Palan's neatly penned summons. A card and dice pub at the juncture of the Mage District and Southeast, the Greasy Pig was an establishment that Lady Renee wouldn't consider entering and Cadet Renee wouldn't dare to. It was long and dark, like a candle-lit cave, with a small stage in the back where a scantily clad girl danced and sang. The patrons clustered around tables, shouting to each other over the din and mugs of ale. Bumps ran up the length of Renee's spine, but she straightened it nonetheless and surveyed the room.

Guardsman Fisker looked up at her from a tankard, his eyes glassy. Beside him sat Seaborn, sourly sober. His eyes widened upon meeting hers. So she wasn't expected. *What in the Seven bloody Hells is Palan up to?* Renee elbowed through the crowd to the small side table the two occupied and slid into a chair. "I thought you were at the palace," she told Seaborn by way of greeting, biting back other questions.

"I received an invitation this afternoon that seemed wise to accept." He paused. "I thought you were in Catar City."

Renee frowned. "Lord— Someone went through a lot of trouble to arrange for us to see each other."

Seaborn shook his head. "Not each other." He jerked his chin at Fisker, who was trying to thread the stump of his missing finger through the tankard handle. "Him." Seaborn grasped the guardsman's cup and pulled it away, rousing the guard to sputtering fury. "Speak."

The man scowled. "Nothing to say."

"Very well." Seaborn rose. "I'll inform our *friend* you had a change of heart."

"Curse your eyes." Fisker grunted and demanded the return of his ale, which the other man slid across the table. He drank deeply, belched, and drank again. "Tell me," Fisker said finally, finding Renee's gaze. "Tell me, do you think a Family man or a Viper can be trusted?"

"No." Renee's brows narrowed.

"And is it a guardsman's job to keep such filth clear of the Crown?"

She glanced at Seaborn, then back at Fisker. "Of course."

He nodded and spoke to his cup. "Nine years ago . . . Nine years ago, a man offered me a heavy purse to ensure that Cadet Korish Savoy never graduated."

Renee's shoulders tensed. "Did you take it?"

"No." Fisker slammed the tankard on the table. "I did not take a *bribe*. Cadet Savoy was both a menace and a liability, but I left him be and guarded the Academy he made a farce of. As was my duty." He bared his teeth. "The man returned with a larger sum. I threw him out once more."

A silence followed, lasting too long, but Renee gave Fisker

his time. The man was loyal to the Crown. He valued law and duty both. Yet something had pushed him into tormenting a fourteen-year-old boy and seeded the vendetta that stretched to present day. She stared at Fisker's mangled hand.

He caught her gaze and snorted, holding up the stump. "No. This was a folly of pride." Fisker sighed. "The man returned a third time. With documents." He scowled. "There once were three brothers heading the Family." He held up three fingers to illustrate so great a number. "One rotted in prison like he deserved." A finger bent. "Another—Lord Palan—took charge." A second finger went down. "The third? The third, oldest, brother, who had a liking for killing, he heard that a warrant for his arrest was to be drawn, and fled like a frightened dog. He changed his name, married a mercenary, and, as I was told, was too cowardly to speak of the poison his blood carries." He leaned forward. "Now, would you wager a guess as to who that was? Whose identity those papers held?"

Renee's mind churned, arranging and rearranging the pieces as her heart quickened. A mercenary soldier teaching his son courtly dances. Palan's longstanding interest in Savoy. His efforts to recall the man to the Academy the year Diam started it. The way Palan asked Diam to call him Uncle. That he told her about this meeting at all. Fisker's Justice Hall rant about evils of criminal seeds. The last nail slid into place. Blood drained from Renee's face. "Savoy's father," she said quietly, ignoring the sudden hot sear of Seaborn's gaze. "He was the third brother, wasn't he?" She nodded to herself, following the thought to its end.

"Which makes Savoy a Family man—an offspring of criminal blood—in a Servant's uniform. *That* is why you hate him so."

"He is disease." The guard's eyes flashed. "I came to Verin with the news, but he refused to expel the pestilence and forbade me to take any action." Fisker took a chug of ale. "So I held my tongue and I waited. Waited for the young bastard to put his own neck into the noose."

Renee leaned toward him. "Did you bait Savoy into taking the Crown's horses?"

Fisker grinned, showing his teeth. "It was a matter of time—with evil in his flesh, he courted trouble every moment. And when he slipped next, I made certain the festering pig got what was coming to him, didn't I? Bloody Family scum. Should have died in that rotting jail cell."

Leaving Fisker to his cups and curses, Renee and Seaborn went outside. The fresh air was welcome, despite the icy drizzle, and helped clear Renee's head. Lord Palan had gone through some trouble to ensure the insight was both delivered and believed. Why? What was his angle? Was Renee to believe that, given their blood ties, Palan's desire to help Savoy was genuine? She pulled her coat tighter. Perhaps it was, but the head of the Family surely had more than one motive. Renee spared a moment to consider what kind of leverage the lord had exerted on Fisker to force his tongue and, to her shame, discovered that she did not much care. "Did you know any of this?" she asked Seaborn.

He leaned against the side of the building, tilting his head up against the stone. "Not before this meeting. I am likewise confident of Korish's ignorance."

Renee nodded. How much did blood matter? To Fisker, who condemned Savoy for his lineage, it mattered beyond all reason. It mattered to Palan, who patronized his estranged nephews and looked after Tanil, as useless as he was. To Verin, who let Savoy earn a Servant's uniform despite his father's crimes, bloodlines appeared irrelevant. And to Renee herself? How much blame did she bear for her father's Family dealings?

Her shoulders sagged and she pressed her hand against the wall for support. Could she blame Fisker for what he did to Savoy when the guardsman's motives, like Verin's, stemmed from a sense of duty? Yes. Yes she could. A wrong done in the name of right may be understandable—but it wasn't acceptable. "I despise the Family, sir, as Fisker does," she said finally. "Them, and the Vipers, and the rest of the criminals haunting Tildor. But Savoy *isn't* a Family man, no matter who his father and uncle are. He is my friend and that will not change for all the bastards combined."

Seaborn nodded and relaxed against the wall next to her. "It isn't supposed to."

They stood silent while the rain picked up, the droplets bouncing in the forming puddles. After several moments, Renee pressed her lips together and tilted her face up toward Seaborn. "I received no word from you."

"I was beginning to fear that when nothing returned from

you." He sighed. "Several of the couriers carrying palace messages have faced trouble. No matter now. Verin—"

"Refused aid, I know." She sketched the details of their conversation. "Not bowing to Palan counted for more than Savoy's life. What of the Seventh?"

"Stationed a few days' ride away. I've found a way of getting a message to them, but without a code word to authenticate it, they won't believe it." He shook his head. "They're too well trained to abandon their mission for what could be a poison pen message. At best, they'd contact Verin."

Renee jerked away from the wall and faced him. "Verin can't be the only one with the code. Savoy must have it too." She hurried to update him on developments in Catar, leaving out only Savoy's reaction to the boy mage.

Seaborn leaned forward, nodding at her words. He listened to her like he did to Savoy, Renee realized. She was not his cadet anymore. Renee cleared her throat. "I will talk Jasper into arranging another meeting with Savoy. If I succeed, how do I ensure my message reaches the Seventh?"

Seaborn recited a set of instructions, which Renee repeated several times until they both were confident of her memory. Then good humor faded from Seaborn's face. "You know of the royal kidnapping?" He waited for her nod and dropped his voice. "King Lysian will come to Catar in ten days' time."

"To attack?"

"To rule." Seaborn spread his hands. "The presence of the

Crown with his guards and magistrates does not eliminate illegitimate activities, but it does increase costs and headaches."

"You think the Madam will back down if only to make him go away?"

Seaborn put his hands into his pockets. "No. But the next step spills blood."

CHAPTER 36

Savoy pushed open the salle door to attend what the others thought to be another penalty workout and found Den leaning against the wall, a book in his hands.

"Forgive my unpreparedness," said Den, looking up. "The reading absorbed me." He twisted the book to reveal its cover. *Battlefields of the Seventh.*

Savoy moved his feet to gain better purchase on the sand. His heart quickened

"Please," Den said quietly. "I suggest nothing." He locked the door and remained with his back turned to Savoy. "Nine years ago, the Madam ordered me to antagonize a guardsman at the Academy of Tildor against a cadet who attended school there. The boy was a runt with blond hair and green eyes, but he wielded a sword like he was born to it. Even my untrained eye saw that much."

Savoy's brow rose with an ease he didn't feel. "The Madam?"

"Yes." Den paused, his next words coming with care. "She . . . The Madam takes interest in certain youngsters. She has her reasons."

Savoy stood motionless. The Madam and Lord Palan both. "Was your mission successful?"

"No." Den turned, shaking his head. "I found the guard, a nine-fingered man who disliked the boy to begin with, and I fueled his dislike until it turned to hate. Nonetheless, the lad still graduated to become a Servant of the Crown and thwart many Viper projects." He held up the book. "It is unfortunate the book has no pictures. I wonder what the man looks like grown. Is it not curious that many people may know of a man's deeds without ever learning his appearance?"

A breath escaped Savoy's lips. If Den had meant to capitalize on his discovery, he would have done so before now. Even so, Savoy's life lay in the other's hands.

"No one leaves the Vipers." Den tossed the book to the sand.

"So you said."

Pursing his lips, Den drew the amulet from his pocket.

Savoy spread his wrists to show that no resistance would be offered.

Den hesitated. "You know why the men pretend the Freedom Fight is real?"

"Hope."

Den nodded. "I read the book. If anyone can get out . . ." Licking his lips, he threw the amulet into Savoy's hands and spoke quickly, motioning to the wristbands. "It can't disable your binds, nor unlock most of the doors. But it will open those on the path to the arena. And from the arena to the street. I'll discover it stolen in ten minutes' time. Go through the bathing room, down the corridor to the Pit." He paused. "If you can climb the bars . . ."

Savoy looked Den in the eye, and knew the courage the man's decision had taken. "Should you leave Catar, you'll find welcome at the Academy of Tildor in Atham. If I'm not there, a man named Connor Seaborn will care for you."

"Thank you." Den held out his hand. "Don't get caught."

Savoy paused before undoing the lock on the door. "What did you tell Guardsman Fisker about me?"

"It would be better you not know. Gods' speed, Commander."

"Gods' luck, Den."

Savoy slid into the corridor, his bare feet silent on the cold stone floor. He hesitated at the barracks, listening to Pretty's boasting voice escape through the closed door, and continued to the bathing room. Ten minutes. His heartbeat kept the time.

True to promise, the door obeyed the amulet, unlocking at the touch of the blue stream of light. Savoy paused to listen, heard nothing, and entered. Rows of bathtubs and towels greeted him. The air hung heavy with moisture and soap, and the never-quite-dry floor was slippery, even to bare feet. He looked at the two doors on the opposite wall and, recalling his previous trip to the arena, approached the rightmost.

"Is the laundry finished?" asked a voice outside.

Savoy grabbed a small towel and twisted it into a cord. Another step brought him flat against the wall on the hinge side of the door. He quieted his breathing.

"Marcy?" the same voice called. "I said, are you done with laundry?" The door opened and a plump woman stuck her head inside.

Savoy's hands tightened on the cord. *In or out, mistress, make a decision.*

The woman sighed and retreated, closing the door. Savoy released a slow breath. Dying was in the guards' job description, not the servants'. He pushed away from the wall and reached for the door handle.

It swung open before he touched it.

The plump woman returned. Muttering on about dirty towels, she stepped into the room and headed for a basket of linens in the opposite corner.

Seven Hells. Savoy slid in behind her and looped the twisted towel over her head. Reconsidering at the last moment, he pulled the cloth taut over her mouth instead of her neck. She squealed through her nose, like a piglet at the market, forcing him to tighten the gag. "Keep quiet," he whispered into her ear.

The squealing ceased, replaced by flailing. She twisted about, scratching the air and huffing. Behind her, Savoy sighed, and pulled back on her shoulders until the woman's balance wavered, and he could settle her onto the floor. When he came around to face her, her eyes grew as wide as her cheeks pale.

"No, gods, no, no," she pleaded softly, hugging her arms across her chest.

Savoy crouched. "Do nothing to harm me, and I will reciprocate. Understand?"

She nodded.

"Good. Who else works here tonight?"

She tried, and had Savoy's mission been to procure contraband soap or breach the security of the laundry room, he would have extracted some value from her words. "All right, that's enough." He reached for a spare towel and started binding the woman's hands behind her back.

"Please, sir, don't do that," she begged, her voice shaking and eyes full to the brim. "Leave me, sir. I won't say nothing to nobody."

Of course, and I'm a princess disguised. He held the thought to himself. If he was letting her live, better depart on a sympathetic note. Securing the wrist binding, he wrapped the gag back into place. "If I leave you untied," he whispered into her ear, "you'll be punished for not raising alarm."

The bathing room fiasco concluded, Savoy continued into the corridor. The openness of the passage made him uneasy. Time ticked on. Den had granted him ten minutes. By now he had used them all. Praying that the guards took time to muster, Savoy hurried forward. He stayed close to the wall, ears alert for footsteps and creaking hinges.

A faint blue glow shimmered about the edges of the arena door. He jogged to it, the amulet at the ready. Once more the door's glow died under the amulet's command, and Savoy pulled at the handle.

It refused to budge.

He pulled again. No result. Sweat beaded on his forehead.

The open corridor was ill suited for delay. Resisting the urge to continue yanking the handle, he made himself retreat from the door and look at it anew. Haste wouldn't quicken progress. He took a breath.

The tap of footsteps approaching from a side passage spun Savoy around. The closest concealment, another small passage that fed into the main corridor, lay twenty spans back. Could he make it? He sprinted, bare feet pushing off the hard stone, and spun himself inside. A moment later, a man with an oil jug stepped into the main hall, refilled one hanging lantern, and moved to the next.

Flat against the wall, Savoy tightened his jaw. The workman would be at his task for a quarter hour at best. By then, the search for Savoy would on in full strength. Savoy had to engage, right in the middle of the open corridor, *right now*.

Lifting a small pebble off the ground, Savoy skipped it against the floor.

Five paces away, the workman startled and turned toward the noise, his back exposed. Savoy pushed away from the wall and lunged at the man's legs. He grabbed him at the knees, collapsed them together, and shoved. The man fell. Savoy followed him down.

The oil jug shattered. The man twisted; blood running from his nose soaked his shirt. His eyes widened, meeting Savoy's. And he screamed.

Elp! Elp! Elp! the stones echoed.

Seven Hells. Savoy's stomach clenched.

The man struggled, splattering blood. His mouth opened.

Savoy couldn't permit another scream. His fist struck the man's temple. There was no more noise.

Lowering the unconscious body to the ground, Savoy found himself with his original problem. The amulet had disarmed the mage glow of the arena door. It hadn't opened it. He jogged forward and stopped a pace away, examining the wood.

The Vipers kept the facilities in excellent shape. If a door would not budge, it was locked, not stuck. *Find the second lock.* His eyes tracked the crack where the door met the wall, and worked methodically around the frame. There. A simple sliding latch glittered at the top right corner. He slipped it free and the door opened.

The arena was empty. Rows of wooden benches rose like stairs from where he stood. At the top, two blue, glowing doors led to the street. He was so close now, he could taste the free air. A fence of barbed-wire-topped rods, rising up only four times his height, was all that separated him and it.

Experience checked his excitement in favor of caution. Savoy surveyed his route. The fence blocked the pens and fight area from the spectator section. He was in a cage—a cage without a ceiling, but still a cage. Den had been right, the only way out was to climb.

Savoy approached the metal bars, spaced hand-widths apart. No footholds. He'd have to rely on his hands alone. The barbed wire at the top would cut him, but if he ripped some cloth from his pants to lay over the burrs, he might avoid fatal gashes. The amulet would unlock the door.

He repeated the plan and tucked the amulet into his waistband. Satisfied, he grasped the bars and hauled himself up.

Unlike the climbing-ropes hanging in the salle, the smooth metal slipped in his grasp. For each span of gained ground, he slid down by half. The problem increased as his hands grew damp with sweat. He wiped his palms off on his pants each time he switched holds, all the while wishing for chalk. Why not wish for rope while he was at it? Gritting his teeth, Savoy climbed on. The door to freedom lay in sight.

He paused for breath upon reaching the barbed wire and snaked his hands between the razor coils to hang with both hands from the bar topping the cage. Gashes appeared on his forearms, leaking blood. Savoy's arms shook now, slipping in sweat and screaming with strain. He tried ripping his trousers for a bit of cloth to throw over the bars, but couldn't manage it one-handed. No, he'd have to swing his body over the top and pray the burrs didn't shred him to pieces in the process. He hung loose, took a breath, and started swinging his body side to side like a pendulum. *One. Two . . .*

"Eh!" a voice bellowed below. "Loose pup! Loose pup!"

More voices joined the shouting, but Savoy continued swinging his legs from side to side to gain momentum. The door beckoned. *Three.* On the upswing, Savoy flung himself over the top.

His legs cleared. His torso didn't. Barbed wire and the bars' sharp tops cut into his abdomen. He twisted and the metal dug farther into flesh, biting and ripping. On the ground below, cursing guards gathered on both sides of the bars. Savoy ignored them. Once he was over, he could fight his way to the door.

Setting his jaw, Savoy let his stomach endure the abuse, while he worked to reclaim handholds on the blood-slicked bars. He was halfway over. Just a little more and he could slide down. Hells, he could jump down and sort out the broken bones later. He tensed and passed an arm over the top, getting a shallow cut as reward. Then the other arm. When he breathed out again, it was done. He was dangling safely on the spectator side.

He surveyed the ground before descending. The Vipers gathered there had stopped shouting and now stood calmly on the sand below. One of them, a tall, icy blonde he had never met, bounced an amulet in her hand. A sudden cold seized him as he glanced down at his waistband.

His amulet had fallen. It was all for naught.

"All right, Cat," the woman called. "Even if you sprint for the exit, you can't unlock the door. Take a breath and slide down now."

On the ground, he awaited his captors. They arrived at his side within moments and clutched his arms. A weedy mage energized Savoy's binds, which obediently pulled together. He clipped a leash to the restraints and patted Savoy's shoulder. "Easy, boy." He yelled for a towel and another lead rope.

The blonde with the amulet stood rod-straight, puffing a

thin roll of tobacco into the crowd encircling her. She watched the white, perfect rings of smoke as if they carried infinitely more importance than the people whose gazes beheld her. Beside her, a mousy man with paper and pen hung on her words. ". . . not a day without disaster," the woman said, her white teeth vivid in the lantern light. "Let us see what he has to say for himself."

Savoy drew himself to attention and stepped toward the woman.

The mage holding the leash pulled gently. "Shhhh, easy now," he repeated over and over until Savoy realized that it wasn't him being hauled front and center.

It was Jasper.

"What, might I ask, is the meaning of this?" the woman demanded, glaring at the pale-faced boy. His disheveled hair and clothes suggested he'd been roused from sleep. A trickle of sweat slithered down his temple. The woman inhaled her tobacco stick and continued. "Are you incapable of keeping a rein on a handful of collared pups?"

"H-h-he found an amulet," Jasper stammered. His hands gripped his pants, and his eyes sought refuge in the ground. Savoy had dressed down enough recruits to know the look.

"He is a pup!" The edge in the woman's voice could cut steel. "It's your job to make sure he doesn't find an amulet, or break his neck, or choke on mashed turnips. Look at this bloody mess." She jerked her head toward Savoy, who continued bleeding despite the weedy man's attentions with towel and bandages.

"I'll clean him up." Jasper's voice trembled.

"You bet your useless pig brain you'll clean him up. And that's the last new pup you'll see either, since you can't be bothered to care for them." The woman shook her head and turned her disgusted look on Savoy.

He stared back, shoulders square.

"You wish to reassign the pup, ma'am?" asked the small man with the notebook. "Blue team, perhaps? A seasoned keeper there."

"No, no." She sighed, then continued with quiet resignation, "Once they get this far, there's no taming them. Escape attempt, with an amulet no less? Imagine the liability! No, I'm afraid my son ruined this one beyond repair." She took the stick from her mouth and pressed the lit end under Jasper's chin. He yelped, jerking his head up. "Didn't you?" she asked.

He whimpered. "Yes, Mother."

The woman puffed a ring of smoke into his face, then addressed her secretary. "Mark the pup as fodder for that huge imbecile, whatever his name is."

"Boulder, ma'am."

"Yes, that's the one. He can rip him apart next match. And make sure someone keeps this one alive till then."

"Certainly, ma'am." The man made a mark in his notes and looked patiently at his mistress, who blew smoke into Savoy's face and turned toward the door.

"See to him in the south kennel, Jasper," she called over her shoulder to her son. "You've fouled up enough for one night."

Once everyone left, Jasper pulled Savoy into a room the

size of a large closet and tied the leash to the wall. The door slammed shut. The only light came from a lantern, which the boy set on the floor.

"Best hurry, Jasper, before Mother catches you out of bed," Savoy said.

"Brainless pig ass!" Jasper's arm swung out, backhanding Savoy's face.

Nothing more stimulating to courage than Mother's absence, Savoy thought.

Jasper sneered. "You're nothing but fodder now. No one needs you in fighting shape anymore."

The image of the sickly, malnourished fighter who last faced Boulder materialized in Savoy's memory.

"That's right," Jasper said, as if reading his thoughts. "We only need you *alive* for the next fight, so that imbecile can tear your limbs off." His glowing hand reached for Savoy's shoulder.

Before agony overtook him, Savoy saw tears streaming down the boy's cheeks.

CHAPTER 37

In the morning, Renee had to leave Atham. She gripped the doorframe of Sasha's room, holding her travel pack in one hand while her friend tried to hold back tears.

"Don't leave," Sasha whispered.

But Renee had to leave. Another sword in Atham would make little difference. In Catar, Renee was Savoy's lifeline and Diam's guardian. She had to leave. Sasha knew why, understood, agreed. But she had still asked, and Renee, stepping forward to hug her friend, careful of the girl's bruises and broken hand, had to say no.

Another notch in unfairness's measure. Renee bit the inside of her cheek.

Two days of sleet and mud brought Renee, shivering and heartsick, back to Catar, where she rode at once to Zev's to check on Diam. Khavi nuzzled her hand in greeting, his energy subdued to match the boy's, who napped with his head pillowed on an old book. Alec was out. A glance over Diam's shoulder revealed a drawing of a woman and eagle. She traced it with her finger. "I didn't believe bonding existed. No one does."

Zev shrugged. "People don't believe what they don't see. Even I've heard of no other living bonded pairs until now."

Renee looked up, surprised. Somehow she'd thought Zev as familiar with bonding as Savoy with battle tactics. "Do you know why the rarity?"

The old man chuckled. "Most of the truly powerful mages died during the rebellion, taking their bloodlines with them. The Control strength of most who register today rates a three grade. The five-grade mages number a handful in a generation." He nodded to the book. "Our best guess is that Keraldi and her eagle rated a seven each."

Renee stroked the wolf's fur, absorbing the significance of his partnership with Diam. "Bonding is a matter of power, then?"

"That, and trust. They chose to share life energy." Zev lumbered to his feet and fed a log into the hearth. "Could you do that, Lady Renee? Allow another into your mind and body forever? Share your lifetimes?" He looked into the flame. "Do not speak of the boy's bond to others, my lady. It may bring attention the child does not wish."

Renee nodded; the thought had occurred to her as well. "And if a Healer touches him?"

Zev shook his head. "I expect it would be as with any other mage—usual healing reveals nothing of the patient's Control rating, not unless the patient wishes it so."

She drew a breath. *Usual* healing, Zev had said. Was there another kind? "Diam will have questions."

"I will research the texts," Zev promised. "What little is known, I will find for him."

"Thank you," she said, and begged him to keep the boy a few

hours longer. Finding Jasper and, thus, Savoy could not wait till morning; she needed the code word to call in the Seventh. Renee paused in the doorway. "Do you think there are others like them somewhere?"

"If there are, they are smart enough to never let the secret out," said Zev, and busied himself in making tea.

After her trip to Atham, the mass of green filling Catar's streets irritated Renee all the more. Unlike people in the capital, who hurried along with a purpose, here groups simply loitered. Renee quickened her step and kept a hand on her purse.

The mage tavern Alec had introduced her to buzzed with conversation. Renee nodded a greeting to several patrons. The irony of Cadet de Winter's slide from upholding the Crown's laws to frequenting a felons' gathering spot was not lost on her. In one corner, two boys extended glowing hands toward identical water pails, the crowd cheering the competition. Alec was absent but her true target, Jasper, sat alone at a small table. Renee slid into a chair.

Jasper's head hid behind hunched shoulders. He ignored her.

"What are they on about?" Renee pointed toward the now chanting clump of boys.

He shrugged and kept his face down. "Boiling water or similar nonsense."

"What's with you?" Renee asked.

Jasper lifted his head to reveal a fading five-fingered bruise on one cheek and a small round burn healing on the tender underside of his chin. "Forgive me." He brushed his palm over it as if trying to erase the mark. "One of my pups found some trouble this week. Mother blamed me for it."

"Who?" The question was out before she could stop herself.

"Cat." He stared at the tabletop. "It wasn't my fault, Den's the one who lost his amulet. In gods' names, I was sleeping when it all happened!" Jasper shook his head. "I've Healed Cat many times, you know. His hand was burned when I got him and then Den's methods . . . But the pup never so much as gave me a glance of thanks. And it's somehow all my fault anyway." Jasper scrubbed his hand over his eyes and looked away.

Renee's heart pounded. "What's your fault, Jasper? What happened?"

"Cat tried to run." He hung his head, speaking to the table top. "Mother is putting him down at the next fight."

She stared at him, unable to find words. Not only was she without men, she was without time. "When is that?" Her voice shook despite her grip.

"A week or so." Jasper frowned at the opening door and sank deeper into his chair. "Wonderful."

At the tavern's entrance, a boy of about twelve was looking around like a ferret on duty. His gaze came to rest on Jasper and the boy trotted forward. His dark eyes weighed Renee, as if deciding how her presence affected his mission. Shrugging, he turned to Jasper. "Madam says you are to attend to the weeds." An unpleasant smile curved his lips. "Immediately."

Jasper's nostrils flared.

The messenger took a step back, although his smirk stayed

in place. Clearly, he considered himself employed by a higher authority and thus immune to any insult he offered. "If you refuse, I'm to advise her at once."

Jasper's jaw tensed, the only defense to dignity he seemed able to conjure.

The boy snorted and rubbed invisible dirt from his cheek.

"Your message is understood," Renee said, pushing herself away from the table.

The lad stopped smiling and raised his nose into the air. "Madam said—"

"You may go." She lifted her brow. "If you have no other duties to attend to, I am certain some can be found."

The boy swallowed, mulled over the threat for a moment, and scurried away.

Jasper shook his head. "That is twice you've stood up for me, blinder."

She blushed. It was Jasper's connections, not genuine friendship, that brought her to sit at his table. She searched for words that were both true and appropriate. "You healed my nose."

He said nothing, but a spark of pleasure lit his face. It seemed no one said thank you to the boy very often.

And now she had to turn his goodwill against him. Renee swallowed her rising bile. "Could you get me in to see Cat tonight? I'd like to see him again before, you know . . ."

To her relief, Jasper nodded at once.

The Madam was not one to be kept waiting and the weeds had to be seen to first. Renee agreed to come along with Jasper for the company. She had followed him for several blocks before she realized they were heading toward the arena entrance. Sure enough, the boy took her inside the same door Den once had. Apparently, the Viper weed variety flourished beneath the ground.

They entered the main corridor and Renee took her bearings. Savoy and the Predators lived toward the left, west of her position. Diam's old cell lay toward the right—east. Her jaw tightened as they passed the entrance to a narrow tunnel that she knew led to Duke Leon's grounds. Savoy had been captured there.

Jasper turned right into an unfamiliar corridor. In addition to lanterns, specs of blue shimmered in the occasional crevice near the ceiling, such that the space would not surrender to total darkness even if all lanterns failed at once. A professional setup to rival the palace in function if not decor. The tunnel system of Catar's bowels was proving even more extensive than Renee imagined. It was a wonder that the topside structures had not caved in to join their darker cousins.

They took another east-bound turn and the musky scent of stone and earth gave way to stink. Renee's groan drew a nod of agreement from Jasper.

"That's the weeds." He shook his head and returned to discussing the fighters. "Keeping pups is like tuning an instrument. Heal an injury too soon and its lesson is lost. Too late, and you lose training time. Diet is important. Even mood. Den understands nothing of it. Once, he strained Cat's hurt shoulder for pure enjoyment." Jasper frowned at an askew lantern but did not fix it. "Weeding, that's the opposite. No skill. No finesse. Repetitive drudgery any half-trained mage could manage."

The reek increased.

Renee coughed, interrupting him. "Why the stink?"

He shrugged. "That's just the way weeds are." He took a third turn toward the odor. Twenty paces more brought them to a cell similar to the one Diam had occupied. The next step took Renee's breath.

The filth-covered forms swarming within were children.

"Where are they from?" she asked. There had to be thirty of them, all under ten, in a space not four spans square. The slop bucket lay overturned in the corner and one little boy relieved himself where he stood, having no care for whom the excrement landed on.

"This batch came from Atham, I believe." Jasper scratched the back of his head. "The harvesters are lazy there, taking whatever the locals bring instead of doing their job. Likely as not, most of this batch will wither before anything useful can be made of them. The pleasure houses pay coppers unless the product is trained." He sighed. "There's always tunnel work to do, I suppose."

"They are but children."

He shook his head. "They are hungry street urchins who would have frozen to death in the winter if not for us. The ribs show on half the stock and the other half is too dumb to find the slops. Not even a blind noble would buy these."

She turned away before the horror on her face revealed itself. Noble estates, including her father's, often bought children who worked in exchange for clothing and a roof, but those youngsters were orphaned, not *kidnapped*. So this was the fate of the people disappearing from the capital's streets. "What are you to do with them, Jasper?"

"Heal the worms and whatever other corruption they brought with them. The washers will launder the ones worth keeping." He sighed, letting blue fire spread over his fingers. "Pray we catch none of their pestilence."

Renee forced herself to approach the bars and memorize the young faces behind them. A dark-eyed boy with a scar over his brow holding a smaller boy's hand. A toddler girl whimpering for her mother. A five-year-old with a distended belly lying listless on the stone floor.

Getting Savoy out alive was only the beginning of her problems.

CHAPTER 38

The door of Savoy's cell screeched behind Renee and shut with dull finality. She shook her head, pushing the children's faces to the back of her mind. She had little time. Jasper was in the hallway, keeping watch for stray guards while she visited his pup, *Cat*, slated for destruction in perhaps a week's time.

Unlike the guest room where she saw Savoy last, this chamber was dark; a stale, tiny tomb in which the eyes could never adjust. She uncovered the lantern and was relieved at its warm pool of light.

Savoy sat on the floor, his bare back pressed against the stone. His forearms rose to shield his eyes, exposing shivering muscles. Several marks, small webs of black silk, marred his skin.

She crouched beside him. "You're cold."

"The least of my worries." He risked lowering his arm and blinked. "It is too much to hope you stopped toying with fire?"

"Leading by example?"

He chuckled once, then quieted and focused on cracking his knuckles. "You promised to go to Atham."

"I never promised to stay there." She sat on the floor. "Atham has its own problems. The kidnappings and assaults hold everyone in fear. Sentries stand outside the Academy's barracks.

Sasha Jurran ..." Renee lowered her head. "She's the second of the Crown's family to pay the price of relation. Lysian's youngest cousin is the other. The Crown plans to arrive in Catar in a week, but we cannot expect assistance from that front."

Savoy snorted. "You asked Verin for the Seventh and he said no."

She hoped the murk hid her wince. "We have means of contacting them. We need but the code word."

He shook his head. "I will obey Verin's orders."

Her gut clenched. There were enough battles and walls without Savoy arguing against what shreds of solutions they had. "You don't trust me with the code?"

"Did I miss your promotion to High Constable?" His voice was cold. "If Verin believes the Seventh's current mission is more important than I am, then it is. Your own accounts put Atham teetering toward disaster, with the Crown and Vipers galloping at each other to see who flinches first. You want my support of a plan that undermines the entire security posture?"

She rose and leaned against the opposite wall, two paces away. The cold from the stone seeped into her skin. Without knowing it, Savoy was caught in a game between Verin and Palan and gods knew who else. For an instant, she considered telling him, then rejected the thought. He'd only side tighter with Verin's thinking. "You don't know the nuances," she said instead. "The Vipers hold other prisoners in the tunnels. Children." Her nostrils flared. "The Seventh will save lives. If you care little about yours, consider the ... the weeds."

"My point exactly. I do not know the nuances." Savoy leaned forward. "Prisoner rescue is better organized by a man who sees the whole field of battle than one who sits in an underground hole. It is your duty to ensure Verin and the other constables have the information they need, not forge a side mission that answers your own priorities."

"My duty." Her fingers worked themselves into fists. "My duty is my own. I am not in the Crown's Service any longer."

His green eyes flashed. "I am."

Renee's lips opened without sound.

Savoy rose and braced his hand on the wall beside her shoulder, forcing her to meet his gaze. "Please," Renee said. "Don't do this."

"I owe Verin everything that I am." Savoy's voice was gentle. "I will not undermine him. Your coming here gave me a choice. And I made it." He held her eyes until she swallowed and bowed her head. "I'm not done fighting. But should I lose, there is a letter in my pack. Will you mail it to my parents?"

"Of course," she whispered without looking up. "I'll get it to them."

"What now?" Renee asked Alec. She wished he would come sit by her, but he stayed across the room, on what used to be his bed at Hunter's Inn. She told him of Atham's problems and of Verin's refusal, of Jasper and the weeds, of King Lysian's imminent arrival that threatened to spark battle on Catar's streets, of Savoy's death sentence. She told him and he had listened. But he had asked no questions. She dipped her head to better see his face. "Alec?"

He braced his forearms against his knees and looked toward the window where gray buildings blocked the view of the horizon. "You play upon Jasper?" he said after a moment, as if that bothered him the most of everything she had shared. Renee wondered whether he even heard the rest. Before she could answer, he frowned. "It is not like you to indulge in such games. Do you realize who he is?"

She forced her clenched fingers to loosen. Upon hearing the evil brewing within arm's reach, Alec should have rallied with support and enthusiasm. Instead he brooded as if taking action was a matter of debate. She tilted her face toward him. "A mage, a Viper, a fifteen-year-old boy. Which answer are you seeking?"

"He's the Madam's son."

She blinked. The boy's notorious mother led the Vipers? The implication of Jasper's bruised cheek and the odd look Ivan had given Renee beside Jasper's house took on new meaning. As did his weeding chores. "How long have you known?"

He shook off the question. "What I mean, Renee, is that he has no choice in what he does. You manipulate him into crossing her and he'll suffer for it."

"He has a choice. There is always a choice," said Renee. "Mine is to save Savoy and the two dozen of Atham's children the Vipers have trapped beneath the ground."

"What of Savoy's choice?"

"To die?"

"To stop risking others to save his skin." Alec shrugged. "Verin, Savoy, the gods themselves are telling you to leave this be."

She stared for a moment, then drew up her legs and studied him. He sat in the middle of the bed, not the corner of it like he used to. His voice had grown deeper, it seemed, and it spoke more of energy currents than swords. She drew a breath. "Once you knew you could Control, was joining the Academy really nothing more than a challenge you waged against Tildor?"

His face lifted in surprise and he spread his palms, paused. "I'm not certain," he said at last. "My aunt refused the Crown's will and died for it. My mother bent to it and lost all that she was. Yes, I wished to challenge Tildor and win. Was that my sole fuel? I don't know." He shrugged. "It little matters. Harnessing Control is a commitment, not a hobby to be toyed with whenever a free moment arises. I know that now. You can't be a swordsman and a Healer at the same time any more than you can be a blacksmith and a farmer together. Staying at the Academy was a mistake. Becoming a Servant would have changed nothing."

Perhaps he was right, but coming to Catar seemed to have changed everything. Her finger traced the stitching on the bedspread. "You will not help."

"Diam is safe, that's what we left the Academy to do. I have completed my part." Alec sighed, the words rushing out. "Savoy is no friend of mine, Renee. And the people of Atham are the Crown's responsibility. The same Crown who enslaves mages to do its bidding. I owe nothing to either."

CHAPTER 39

No Alec, no Seventh, and King Lysian's impending arrival hung over Catar like a menacing fog. Only for Diam's sake did Renee stop herself from punching the wall. The boy sat beside the window, gazing left and right as if expecting his brother to stroll down the cobblestones below.

Instead, a fine-cloth merchant across the alleyway was boarding up his windows while his sons hauled crates of goods into an awaiting wagon. A few doors down, a crowd gathered around the armorer's shop, purchasing new weapons or sharpening used ones. Renee had gotten a new sword there herself just a week ago.

It had been thus for days, ever since news of the Crown's intentions to ride to Catar had reached the city. Whispers in the inn's common room had grown into currents of unease. Guests who could, paid their fees and packed. Few wished front-seat viewing should a confrontation between King Lysian and the Madam erupt.

Khavi whined and nosed the door. Nodding, Diam climbed down from his perch and, without saying a word, left with his wolf. Renee stared at the closed door, then took down Savoy's sword and ran a sharpening stone along its edge. He'd like his weapon cared for.

The knock startled her. Letting the blade hang at her side, she called out a challenge and frowned at the familiar voice. "Lord Palan." She stepped aside to let him in and hoped her voice betrayed none of the sudden dread that washed over her. "To what do I owe the honor?"

"Lady Renee." He bowed, small eyes and self-satisfied smile the same as ever. "If I may impose on your hospitality?"

You already have. "Of course."

"You still do not trust me, I see." Lord Palan seemed pleased. "My nephew picks his friends well."

"I don't believe Savoy counts you among them."

The smile vanished. Palan glanced at a jug of water and, at Renee's polite bow, poured himself a glass. "Korish still wore swaddle cloths when his parents fled to hide among mercenaries." He settled into a chair. "When the boy started at the Academy, he took a dislike to me. Telling him the truth would not have served his interests. Or mine."

She took a chair opposite him. The man did not visit for his health. She must have something he wanted. What in the bloody hells was it? Renee crossed her legs. "How did Verin learn the truth of Savoy's bloodlines?"

"From me." Palan's lips pressed together. "The boy would not accept a position with me even while locked in the dungeons. I did what I had to do to ensure his future."

"I don't understand."

Palan frowned. "I agreed the Family would not interfere in Academy affairs or sell veesi leaf on the grounds. In return,

Verin was to assure Savoy's career. There is no way to say it more plainly."

Renee paused. Verin fostered Savoy at Palan's bidding? It helped explain the heavy hand the headmaster used in raising him, if the alternative was turning a gifted Crown-trained fighter back over to the Family. "Forgive my indiscretion," Renee said at last, "but I fail to see your advantage in such a deal."

Palan's eyes flashed. "I care for my family, whether estranged or not."

"And does Tanil share your . . . enthusiasm for relatives?" Renee held her breath. If she was right about Tanil's involvement in Diam's kidnapping, the fat lord had a problem on his hands. "It seems your young foster wishes you dead. You and his cousins both."

Palan's lips pressed together again and his dark eyes narrowed on Renee's.

Her heart hastened under his calculating gaze. It was as if he were assessing the value of her continued existence. She would do well to remember whom she spoke to.

Palan shook himself and inclined his head, like a fighter acknowledging the other's score. "Tanil knows nothing of the Savoys' relation to the family. He simply fell into a combination of debt and sloth, which he sought to remedy by pitting his teacher against me." He finished his water and interlaced his fingers over his belly. "The boy thought that if Commander Savoy and I were busy with each other, he'd be free of harsh training and financial oversight both. It worked out poorly for him."

Renee swallowed, suddenly perceiving the reason behind Palan's visit and courtship of her. "You want Diam." She rubbed the back of her neck. "With one nephew a traitor to your blood and another facing death, Diam is the closest kin you have left." But why not simply snatch the boy from the streets? Why all the effort at befriending Renee? The answer echoed from the lord's own words. She smiled, leaning toward him. "You wish for my help in endearing him to you, for fear that he'd otherwise reject you, like Savoy did."

Palan bowed from his seat. "I am Diam's next of kin, my lady."

"His parents—"

"Died several weeks ago, while guarding a merchant foolish enough to deal near the Devmani boarder."

A high-pitched wail cut the air.

Blood drained from Renee's face. She twisted, searching for the source of the cry. It echoed from the hallway. She opened the door and the aghast eavesdropper stumbled inside, bewildered eyes darting from one face to another. "Diam . . ." Renee reached for him, but Khavi blocked her path. When she tried again, he growled, showing his teeth. Renee pulled back.

Diam's small rib cage expanded with drawn air. "It's not true!" he shouted, louder than Renee thought possible. "You're lying! You're all lying!" The wails increased in pitch until they morphed into sobs. The boy fell to the ground, a small shaking ball.

Renee reached out to gather him in her arms, but met Khavi's snapping jaws. Palan's efforts found a similar fate. The wolf paced in circles and whimpered. He maintained his guard until Diam cried himself to stillness.

Then she understood why. Faint wisps of blue flame sparked around the boy's nail beds and eyes.

Palan studied the sleeping child in silence, then pulled a long breath, and smiled.

Renee ran to get Zev and Alec, who came at once, walking through the rustling streets as quickly as Zev's limp allowed. Snippets of conversation, all of a flavor, escaped from loiterers and pedestrians, barmaids and errand-boys. The Crown did nothing for Catar's people. The Family was behind Lysian's trip. The king had been bought and paid for. The Vipers shouldn't—wouldn't—bend knee. The old spoke of blood spilled a decade past, when the Madam wiped away the Vipers' last challenger. The young bought knives. Renee hurried ahead, but a look from Alec returned her to Zev's side.

"It's not as if you don't know the way," she hissed under her breath.

"It's not as if you'll do any good without us," he whispered back.

Zev cleared his throat, a reminder that he was old, not deaf. "The boy's bonded partner will keep everyone safe enough. I come to offer little heroism."

He was right. Flames weren't consuming Hunter's Inn when they arrived. Diam lay curled in bed, sobbing in his sleep. Hints of blue light pulsated gently at the corners of his closed eyelids.

Zev shuffled past Palan to place his hand over the child's shoulder. The last scraps of glow died and Diam relaxed. "His body feels the energy, but cannot Control it yet." Zev smiled a sorrowful smile. "The energy leaks. It's calm now."

"I don't understand," she whispered, and stroked Diam's hair. "Isn't he too young?"

Zev nodded. "Stress does strange things to the body. And he is sensitive. Very sensitive."

Renee glanced at Khavi, wondering if the sensitivity had anything to do with how the pair had found each other. Perhaps the wolf would help buffer the energy currents until the boy's mind caught up to his body.

"Will he be strong?" Lord Palan asked, something lurking behind his eyes.

Zev shrugged. "I'd imagine so."

Lord Palan smiled again, and Renee didn't like it. Her hand tightened around Diam's shoulder. While Savoy remained alive, the child would stay right where he was. As would his secret.

No one said much. The sun dimmed and Palan took his leave. When a bell somewhere outside tolled the late hour, Zev rose painfully from a chair, laid a glowing hand on Diam for another moment, and made his bows. While he labored his way down the inn's stairs, Alec gathered their jackets. Renee stared at her friend, her heart growing heavier each moment. The night had been about neither Savoy nor politics nor the Crown. Maybe he only planned to walk Zev to the Mage Quarter and return. She chewed her lip. "Where are you going?"

"Home." He shrugged into his coat and paused. "Did you need something?"

She shook her head and stared at the door long after he departed.

King Lysian arrived in Catar three days later, and with him Connor Seaborn.

Renee met Seaborn outside the governor's manor where the Crown's advisors and royal court took up residence. "The Yellow Rose's next Predator competition will run in two days' time. I may not know what I'll do, but I'll do something," Renee told Seaborn.

He sighed. "If peace holds that long." Seaborn shook his head, the circles beneath his eyes dark despite the bright day. He'd lost weight since they first left Atham a month ago, and his clothes hung looser. "The Madam and King Lysian harden their positions each day, Renee. She wants the release of the Viper lords and a pledge for the Crown to keep clear of Viper affairs. He wants a complete, immediate cession of all illegal activities and a surrender of the group's senior members. With factions rallying to both leaders, soon neither will be in a position to compromise even if he or she wishes to. And then . . ." He trailed off.

And then it was war. Renee crossed her arms, thinking of the underground network and Atham's children marooned in it. "What if the victory was symbolic? If King Lysian won something precious to him while assaulting something the Vipers hold sacred, but without actually destroying much infrastructure or Viper troops?"

"Such as?" Seaborn ran a hand through his hair and continued, "The Madam is too well-protected, we don't know the whereabouts of the Crown's cousin, and there is precious little as important to the Crown right now, besides. King Lysian is unwilling to wait." Seaborn frowned at her. "Is there something you know, Renee?"

"Perhaps." She turned away before he could stop her. She needed to think.

"I have an idea," Renee told Diam as she stepped into their room.

The boy, sitting again on the windowsill, refused to turn.

"What are you watching for?"

He pressed his face against the glass. "The Seventh."

Renee sighed. There was little to say. "They—"

Diam shrieked and bounced from his perch. Dodging Renee's hands, he scampered out of the room, his footsteps banging down the steps.

She chased after him to the landing, but it was no use. He was already gone.

Renee had just picked up a pen and her sketches of the Vipers' underground passages when voices rumbled in the hallway. Familiar voices. "Gods," she whispered, the pen falling to the floor.

"Good evening," Cory said, leaning his elbow on the frame of the doorway. "We heard you had a wee problem."

CHAPTER 40

"How?" Bewilderment overpowering manners, Renee stared from one member of the Seventh to another. "I mean, greetings. No, I mean how. How in the Seven Hells did you know?"

Cory took a folded sheet from his breast pocket. "Diam's letter." He frowned. "I was surprised to nay hear from you or Connor."

"We had no code word," Renee said, reaching for Diam's mailing. "I didn't think Savoy gave it to an eight-year-old."

"Of course not." Cory sounded offended. "Diam uses his own code. He's written ever since learning how, and sent wee drawings before then." He set the boy on the floor and put a finger under his chin. "Did speaking of this slip your mind, lad?"

Diam's green eyes and set chin looked like Savoy's as he met the adult's gaze. "You never tell anyone a code word. I promised."

"Anyone doubting they're brothers?" mumbled someone from the Seventh.

At the first opportunity, Renee pulled Cory into the stable, where the horses' snorts and whinnies offered an agreeable backdrop to private conversation. She petted the nose of the bay mare they supposedly visited and aimed her words at the ground. "You should know that I did not simply lack the code word needed to send you a message, but that Commander Savoy specifically refused to give it."

The sergeant stiffened beside her. "Do ye know why?"

"Yes." If any reason was enough to make the men reconsider their involvement, this was the one. Nonetheless, they deserved to make their own choice. "Verin declined my request for any official assistance, much less agreed to pull a specialty unit from its mission."

"High Constable Verin?" Cory whistled a low tone. "And what does he make of your own presence here?"

Renee shrugged, but her fingers dug into the horse's mane. "I made my choice."

"Aye, I see ye did. And so did I. Three years past." His hand brushed her arm, the touch teasing. "We spoke of this before, if in a prettier landscape."

Heat gripped Renee's cheeks and she scowled into Cory's grinning eyes. The bruises of Rock Lake were a lifetime ago, when Savoy walked among immortal gods, and Cory was a sergeant who invited her and Alec to partake in the highly dangerous workout that was the Seventh's morning jog. "Seven bloody Hells, this is not a jest, Cory." She stepped away to where she could see his face without having to look up. Responsibility weighed her words, heavier for the fact that someone else would pay for any mistake she made. "You do this, and the Crown can charge you and your men with treason. *Treason*. Ensure that each of your soldiers stands clear on this point or I will burn the maps I've drawn and leave you twiddling your thumbs in wee circles. Am I plain on this, Sergeant?"

The grin faded from his face, and he picked up a brush. "Aye, you are." He shook his hair away from his eyes and slid the brush along the mare's flank. "What I mean to say is that we understood the consequences of answering the summons of an eight-year-old boy. I will gut-check each man if ye wish, but I dinna expect any will have a change of heart."

Renee watched his shoulders bunch and straighten as he worked the road's grime from the horse's coat. She took a breath. "Forgive me, Cory. I gave offense."

He tilted his face toward her and shook his head. "Ye spoke like an officer." With a sigh, he straightened up, letting the brush hang by his side. A hint of a smile touched his lips. "'Tis a job I neither want nor envy. Officers don't get much sleep, so far as I can see."

She touched his arm and returned to the inn, knowing that the simple kiss they'd once shared couldn't be again. Not like that. Not like it was. Not anymore.

The following morning, Renee returned to the governor's manor. The wind following her had lost all courtesy, batting the rain and stench of fish from yesterday's market all over the street. The few nobles braving the weather offered proper greetings, but Renee rushed past with haste that bordered rudeness. Was Catar ever dry and warm? Dodging Fisker with his guard team and a group of masons adding final touches to the Great Hall, she forged her way to where Seaborn and other magistrates bent over a parchment stack. "Master Seaborn!"

Fisker pushed away from the wall and headed toward her.

Seaborn straightened to survey the room. Making what appeared to be hasty apologies to his colleagues, he caught Renee before Fisker could and steered her from earshot. "What's amiss?" he asked, the tone warning that something significant had better account for the intrusion.

"I need to see King Lysian. Alone."

He rocked back on his heels. "Just that? And have you a plan for accomplishing that small errand?"

"Tell him I have maps of the Vipers' underground lair and know the location of two dozen child prisoners, but will only share the information if granted an audience. Would that answer?"

Seaborn looked at her sharply and rubbed the bridge of his nose. "It may." He glanced around the hall. "What have you hid up your sleeve, Renee?"

"The Seventh and a few other details."

Seaborn straightened, his exhausted eyes surprised as she sketched out her plan. "Bloody gods. You're as crazy as Korish."

"And?"

He nodded. "I will try. Wait in the gardens." He lowered his voice further. "And watch your words in the halls. Our friend from the Pig has been skulking around too much for my comfort."

The sun rode low on the horizon when a servant in palace

livery finally appeared to escort Renee to the Crown's chambers.

"He recalls you from Queen's Day," the woman confided, climbing the stairs to the king's private apartments.

Renee nodded. The servant stopped by a carved wooden door, knocked thrice, and, upon receiving permission, announced her charge.

King Lysian sat on the windowsill, one knee drawn up and shoulders pressing into the curved stone. He was dressed simply: a pair of black breeches and a blue shirt, a few shades deeper than his eyes. Embroidery wreathed the cuffs and collar of the starched cloth. A miniature painting of a child's profile rested in his hands. He turned his head toward Renee but stayed seated. "I am given to understand that my once future Servant now holds information hostage."

She tightened her jaw to ward off the sting of his words and considered her next move. "Information is a coy mistress, Your Highness," she said, curtsying. "Once met, she will not leave, even when her presence grows inconvenient."

The king considered her for a moment, no recognition of who she was, beyond a failed cadet, apparent in his eyes. Then a spark of uncertain comprehension. He tilted his head. "You wish to tell me something, yet to have me not know it?"

"My maps of the Vipers' lair are yours, Your Highness. As for the rest, yes, you took my words correctly." She held her breath.

He touched the painted child's cheek and put down the piece, then swung himself to face Renee. His head tilted and his fingers tapped each other for many moments before a grin suddenly lit his face. "Forgive my manners! How could I have failed to recognize my dear cousin's friend?"

Renee tilted her head. Of course he had recognized her. Even the servant who led her here had said so. "Think nothing of it, Your High—"

His hand interrupted her. "His Highness refuses to grant audience to the errant *Lady Renee de Winter*. But it would be my honor to entertain a family friend in my cousin Sasha's absence." He slid to the floor and offered a bow proper for a young man's greeting to a maiden. "My friends call me Lys."

Her face tingled. "An honor . . ." Unable to bring herself to call the Crown by his given name, she hid the verbal stumble in the folds of another curtsy. "I am Renee."

"A name of beauty. May I offer you wine?"

Renee rose to her feet and accepted the goblet, catching the mischief playing in Lysian's face as he presented the drink. Her heart pounded.

He smiled at her.

She buried her nose in the wine. "I fear I'm a terrible gossip."

"Then I shall endeavor to believe none of it, but will listen attentively in the name of good manners. Will that answer?" Despite the jovial tone, the last was not said in jest.

Renee nodded soberly. "I believe it would." She took an offered chair. "I heard rumor that a group of soldiers left their post to assist a friend in peril. Should their mission succeed, I believe it would serve the Crown to have autho-rized it. In fact, it would serve the Crown to claim the whole matter had been a pre-planned covert assault on the Vipers."

Lysian frowned. "And should the mission fail?"

"The Crown knew nothing of it. Soldiers will always find mischief. Such things are sergeants' concerns." She squared her shoulders. "All the men made their choice freely. They understand the consequences."

He hoisted himself back onto the windowsill, setting the cup beside his thigh. "We speak of Commander Savoy." His finger rose to ward off protest. "I pay mind to the fate of the man who saved my life, and I know I have withheld aid that may save his." Lysian lowered his face. "What you suggest will permit the Crown to reap the rewards while taking none of the risk. It sounds unjust."

"It is." She replaced her cup onto the tray and crossed her legs. Lives hung on her words as surely as they did on fighters' swords. "The rescue attempt will be made regardless—during the next Predator match in two days' time. We have no way of knowing where Savoy has been moved in the interim. If it fails, it fails. But at least in success, the Crown's seal would save the soldiers from punishment for abandoning their posts. That is better than nothing. The existence of official orders would also give more weight to Commander Savoy's later testimony against the Vipers, telling the world that no group is beyond a Servant's reach."

"Speak to me of the underground." Lysian sipped his wine while she described the maze of narrow tunnels and mage-locked cages. "There is not room for an army?"

"No."

"But it is a terrain to which a few well trained fighters would be suited . . . if not occupied with rescuing their leader?"

Renee stiffened. Should Lysian order the Seventh to abandon Savoy in pursuit of Atham's hostages, their refusal would buy them a noose.

As if aware of her thoughts, Lysian put up his palm. "I may be new to the throne, but I have learned enough not to issue orders that would not be obeyed. I spoke of a follow-on action."

A breath of relief escaped her. "Yes. They would be both well suited and well positioned for the task."

"Very good." Lysian leaned back against the window and regarded her. "I will write such orders, to be made public only in the event of the Seventh's success. I will also give you a sealed note ordering the Seventh to attempt hostage rescue upon securing Commander Savoy's release. But I set one condition, Lady Renee."

She inclined her head and waited.

"Upon exiting these chambers, you will once again bear the title of Servant Cadet. You will be permitted to remain in Catar until this mission ends, but must then return to the Academy and finish training. Will you accept?"

Heart pounding in her ears, Cadet Renee de Winter dropped to one knee. A warrior's formal salute to a king she served once more, a pledge from the Crown's champion that she would become.

CHAPTER 41

Blood was in the air. Renee could feel it. It was in the eyes of green-clad young men who diced on street corners, in their words as they muttered over cheap ale. The innkeeper at Hunter's Inn tensed each time the king's name sounded in the half-empty common room. Alec said the veesi trade dropped—dealers had other concerns. The armorer's shop stood empty, its door battered open and merchandise gone. The two days since the Crown's arrival had cleared the cobblestones of children and the elderly, drove nobles to visit relatives. Even Diam stayed put without being told.

At the end of the second day, the evening before Savoy's fight, Lord Palan returned to Hunter's Inn. If walking amidst snakes bothered the head of the Family, there was nothing in Palan's face to suggest it.

"Uncle Palan!" Diam grabbed the man's ring-ladened hand the moment he moved past the doorframe. "Come see what I can do! Do you want some water?" The boy carefully filled a large cup, but in his enthusiasm to bring it over, sloshed the contents onto Palan's starched shirt. The lord pretended not to notice and claimed a chair, Diam settling cross-legged on the floor before him. Renee sat too, unnerved by their growing familiarity.

"Watch me," Diam instructed, and closed his eyes. Nothing happened at first. Then, infant wisps of blue flame touched the boy's fingertips, played there, and died away. His eyes flew open. "Did you see?"

"I did." Lord Palan smiled. "You'll grow to quite the mage."

"Yes." Renee forced her way into the conversation. "You can register in Atham. They will have the post rebuilt by that time, I wager," she added for Lord Palan's benefit, although whether registration would be possible given the bond, even Zev had no idea.

Palan smiled again, but it failed to reach his eyes. "Not something to worry about until your thirteenth birthday, my boy. Just stay safe and enjoy yourself for now."

Unable to contradict him, Renee scowled.

Diam looked from his uncle to Renee, and hugged his knees as if smelling the undercurrents of the exchange. When neither spoke, he bit his lip and picked at the rug. "Uncle Palan, why doesn't Korish like you?"

Renee stiffened.

Lord Palan sighed. "Because Master Verin does not like me."

"Why?"

"A difference of philosophies. Yes, yes, I know you're about to ask what kind." He pursed his lips and brought his hands together under his silk shirt collar. Renee leaned forward to listen, but several seconds passed until he spoke. "Imagine that we have ten very sick people, but only one dose of medicine."

Diam crinkled his nose and nodded.

"Who should get it? This is where Master Verin and I differ in opinion. I'd give the medicine to the person I cared for most. For example, you, if you were one of the ten. Master Verin, however, would choose whoever he thought most valuable to Tildor, even if his own mother ailed."

"But what if all the sick people were bad, like bandits?" Diam asked. "What would he do then?"

Lord Palan stroked his chin. "Hmm. Destroy the medicine, most likely."

Diam frowned. "Would Korish do that too?"

"Your brother keeps his own council," Renee interjected, sparing them Lord Palan's assessment of Savoy. "What would you do, Diam?"

He ran his hands through Khavi's fur and looked out to the streets. "I'd make more medicine."

A knock sounded at the door, announcing that Cory and the Seventh had arrived to make final preparations for the following day. The sergeant popped his head in and, seeing the lord, hesitated.

Renee rose. "Thank you for your company, Lord Palan."

Taking the cue, the man lumbered to his feet. "Korish fights tomorrow," he said, stopping at the door. "I do not wish for Diam to attend."

Neither did she, but the gods damn her if she let Palan use

Savoy's fight to snare Diam closer. The boy would wait at Zev's. "We've covered this ground, my lord. Diam stays with me while Korish lives." The words made her wince.

"I do not ask to take him, only that he not watch. In fact, my lady, permit me to recommend your lack of attendance as well."

"My lack?" The hairs on Renee's neck stirred at his tone. "I fear I cannot fulfill that request either."

"Not a request, my lady. Only a suggestion." His bow encompassed her and Cory both. "Forgive my intrusion. I will leave you to your planning." He hesitated, adjusting a ring on his finger. "One more suggestion, if I may. If you do attend tomorrow's festivities, bring water and towels."

Wrinkling her forehead, Renee waited until Cory's companions filed into the room and closed the door. She glanced at him. "Towels? What for?"

Cory's face grew dark. "To clean up blood." He shook his head. "I don't believe yer friend intends to leave the rescue on our shoulders alone." He pulled the writing table to the center of the room and spread Renee's map on it while the other men crowded around. "It will be as it will be. For now, we might review what we do know."

Outside the arena the following day, the crowd, as big as last time, shoved and jostled. Vendors shouted their goods. Entertainment of this sort, it seemed, suffered little from the concerns otherwise plaguing the city. The scent of meat pies and honey sweets nauseated Renee. Beside her, Cory munched a bit of bread-wrapped cheese. "Lure the mage outside," he reminded her quietly, letting her ahead of him into the arena entrance. "We'll handle him there. I want the boy hand-walking us in. If you dinna think he'll go, signal Mag." He jerked his chin at the Seventh's archer hiding a crossbow beneath his cloak. "He'll kill the opponent if the commander can't handle it hand to hand."

She frowned at the cage standing in the belly of the underground while Mag took his post near the exit. "He'll never make the shot."

"He'll make it. But the bolt may pierce bystanders on its way." They pushed their way down the rows. People parted for Cory the way they did not for Renee. He continued speaking. "Dinna worry about Mag. Your mark is the mage boy."

Jasper. She looked around. None of the fighters or staff had yet arrived. Lord Palan's warning of the previous night nagged at her, but before she could give them voice, the trumpets called out and the crowd roared in anticipation.

The trumpets blared. A hand between Savoy's shoulder blades shoved him into the holding pen. He shielded his eyes from the light. His mouth was parched after over a day without water. The Vipers left little to chance.

"Anger Boulder; he'll kill you quicker."

Savoy turned and lowered his arm enough to see Den step into the pen. "Brilliant plan."

The trainer's head bowed. "I told you, no one leaves the Vipers."

"Return to your fighters." Savoy stretched his back.

"In a moment I must." Den hesitated. "Something's wrong with the crowd today. I cannot say what, but something feels off. And your girl came."

Renee. Savoy forced his gaze to the stands. Hundreds of crammed bodies fidgeted in their seats. "Alone?"

"No, with a young man, broad shoulders, dark curly hair. They sit at the top."

Savoy traced the rows of benches rising toward the ceiling. Faces and figures blended together. At the top, a cloaked figure standing beside an entrance raised a hand in signal. *Friend in sight.* Then, another. *Target in sight.*

Savoy turned to the other entrance and found a second sentry signaling his report. Military. Someone he knew? Savoy tried in vain to find who the sentries were signaling *to*. "Be careful, Den," he said under his breath. "I've a sense that Boulder and I won't be the only ones fighting today."

"Mag sees Savoy," Cory whispered to Renee. "He has a shot at the man beside him. Ye know him?"

She leaned forward, squinting over the spectators' heads, and winced at Savoy's worn look. Had the Vipers bothered to give him food? "Den, a trainer. Savoy trusts him. And there is Jasper." She fingered the knife hidden up her sleeve. The boy was herding his fighters into the eastern pen. "He sat with the spectators the last time." Renee frowned at the bars separating the fighters from the public.

A moment later Jasper disappeared from view. He reappeared at a side door on the spectators' side of the bars.

"There is a passage, then." Cory inclined his head toward the door. "But I dinna think it direct. The walk took him a bit of time. Ye ready?"

With a nod, Renee stood and waved like a dolt. "Jasper!"

He didn't look up. A tall blond woman dressed in green and gold—his mother the Madam—was talking to him between blowing thick rings of white smoke from her tobacco stick. Beside her slender, athletic build, the boy seemed a scrawny kitten. A serving girl rushed by them. Like a trained fighter, the Madam shifted her weight just enough to clear the path, while Jasper lurched out of the way. Renee called his name again, but the words lost themselves in the din of the crowd.

"Boulder preys on Cat, first round!" a bookie shouted in her ear. The reek of stale beer drifted from his coat. "Place your bets, place your bets! What does your heart tell you, my lady? Will today pass the five-minute mark?"

First round. Seven Hells. Ignoring the now irritated bookie, she pitched her voice over the arena. "Jasper!" Nothing. She turned to Cory. "I must go down to him. No." She touched his rising shoulder. "Alone."

Ignoring Cory's bristling, Renee picked her way between the benches. Her clean trousers collected stains and spills, her sword's scabbard knocked against shins. She needed to beat the trumpets. She needed to get there before Boulder started tearing at Savoy's limbs. Faster. She pushed past the shouting people, already tipsy with excitement and cheap wine. Curses and catcalls followed her.

"Lookin' for a seat, my kitten? Plenty o' room on my lap."

"Wiggle on over for a kiss, darlin.'"

Other voices joined in with more descriptive offers. Renee kept her focus on Jasper and her feet moving.

A waitress carrying an overfilled tray scurried down the aisle. Renee pressed herself against the spectators to let her by. Instantly, a hand pinched the curve of Renee's hip. Bloody wonderful.

"Ah!" yelped a male voice. "Whaddya do that for?"

Renee turned to find the man behind her, presumably the pincher, holding a bleeding nose. His neighbor lowered his hand. "That be m'lady," he said to the bleeding man. "You touch her again, and you won't need to be watching no fighting. She'll cut you wide open, she will. Isn't that right, m'lady?" He looked at her and grinned.

It took a moment to recognize the man from the alley. "You're right, Nino." She schooled her face to a cool smile. As she let out a breath and moved on, she heard Nino educating his friends.

". . . and then she turns to me, her sword all dripping with blood and I think I'm next for sure. But no, she looks at me and says, you're a great man, Nino. I want you to live! Just like that, and . . ." The story continued, detailing how she summoned a pack of wolves and slaughtered a dozen armed giants.

By the time Renee reached Jasper, the Madam was gone.

Renee glanced toward the west exit and received a ready signal from Mag. She took a breath. "Jasper!"

He turned, his smile lighting with recognition. Then a tightness came over his face. "Cat's match is first," he told her.

"He's but one pup."

"Of course," Jasper said, but there was no heart in the words.

For an instant Renee considered bringing the boy in on the plan. *No.* Jasper was putting down a prize horse. He would mourn the loss, but he would not uproot his life for it. "Would you spare a moment for me?" She motioned toward the door.

"Certainly."

Relief washed through her.

"Just after the first fight," he added. "Sit beside me. This won't take long."

Renee's nails dug into her palm. After the first fight was one fight too late. "No. We must go now."

He shook his head. "I cannot. The trumpet will call in but a moment. Sit."

"But . . ." The words died in her throat. The trumped wailed. People behind her hissed that she stop blocking the view.

And the crowd raised its voice in cheer.

"Crush him, Boulder. Crush, crush! Crush him, Boulder. Crush. Crush!"

Renee barely had time to signal *Failure* before someone pushed into an empty seat.

Savoy watched Renee dance around Jasper, her face dark with

frustration. The trumpet called. The girl's hand rose above her head. *Failure.*

"Cat, wake up!" Den pushed him from behind. "Go!"

Savoy stepped forward, but his attention remained with the signals. He followed Renee's gaze up bench rows. It was easier to see now that people were seated. And he did see. Blood rush to his face. The figure at the door was Mag, who now signaled, *Ready to fire.*

Without time to ponder how the Seventh got here, Savoy accepted the fact and calculated the consequences. Fire at whom? From their perspective, the threat was either Den or Boulder, neither of whom Savoy wished pierced. "Take cover," he called to Den before launching himself at Boulder, trusting that no arrow would fly with him in the line of fire.

Boulder absorbed Savoy's collision without a stagger. The crowd roared, laughing. Boulder scowled at the stands, his eyes filled with hurt, like a teased child's. "They mock me," he whispered. "But I don't wanna fight you, Cat."

Thank the gods for that. In the ample time Savoy had had to think, he'd conjured nothing more brilliant than theatrics. That was, after all, what the crowd sought. "Pretend, Boulder," he whispered, his voice calm. "Pretend to fight me."

"Hit him, you moron," growled the referee. He held a rope's end to encourage action, but had yet to strike.

"Cat?" Boulder sucked his knuckle. He shuddered when the crowd laughed again. "Cat, what do I do?"

Savoy ground his teeth. "Hit me. Big swing, little hit. Now."

The large man shut his eyes tight, raised up his fist, and swung.

Ducking a right hook that would've broken his jaw, Savoy circled around. *Now what?*

The crowd hissed, agitated at the lack of blood. Boulder's eyes darted chaotically. An animal seeking refuge. The referee yelled in his ear, and Boulder flailed his fists. One clipped Savoy's side, stopping his breath. When he could gulp air again, he staggered from the sharp pain of cracked ribs.

Boulder's gaze turned wide and wet. "I did bad."

"Fight!" The referee hefted his rope. When the threat failed, he swung his lash across Boulder's shoulders.

The giant howled.

Savoy took a step back, understanding the danger. Enraged with pain, the already upset Boulder would turn uncontrollable. Deadly. Exactly what the Vipers wanted. The referee hefted the rope again, his gaze sharp; no good to anyone if Boulder turned on *him.* Savoy had to do something. Now.

He shot in, locking one hand behind Boulder's head and the other around his waist. The action momentarily satisfied the crowd. There wasn't much time.

"Boulder. Boulder, look at me." Savoy kept his voice calm. "Good. Can you trust me?"

"He hit me!" Boulder sniffled. "My shoulder hurts."

The crowd resumed restless booing. The moment of reprieve was slipping away. The referee cocked his rope. Swearing under his breath, Savoy spun the pair so the lash cut him instead.

"Boulder, look at me," Savoy repeated. "Can you trust me? I will make your shoulder not hurt."

The giant nodded.

"Good. Be still." While Boulder frowned in confusion, Savoy spun behind him and snaked an arm around the giant's thick neck. He tightened his hold, squeezing the arteries with his bicep and forearm. "Sleep now."

Boulder jerked upright, clawing at his neck. Savoy swore and readjusted the choke to stay clear of the windpipe. This had to be painless.

"Easy. Sleep now," he whispered again, gently tightening the hold. Boulder stopped fighting. Another few seconds passed, and the large head darkened from the diminished blood flow. Continuing to whisper, Savoy walked the dizzying man toward the cage wall and braced against it. Shutting away the crowd's roar, he focused on his task: balancing the risk of Boulder awaking too early and not awaking at all.

"Korish!" An unfamiliar voice just beyond the bars demanded his attention. "Korish!"

He glanced up to see a small, mouse-like man scurry forward. Before the guards could reach him, the man thrust a wrapped package between the bars. He stared Savoy in the eye. "A present from your uncle, Korish." The man hissed and ran off.

"What uncle?"

Savoy received no answer. Because just then, all Seven Hells broke loose.

CHAPTER 42

"Fire!"

The scream tore Renee's attention from the ring.

Fire.

A rain of blazing, oil-filled jars fell over the arena. A new shot of flames burst everywhere the jars shattered. Spilling oil fed the blaze. The fire lapped up the liquid fuel, then jumped to the wooden benches. The scent of tar and burning wood filled Renee's nostrils. More screams. And then another odor; the sickening smell of charcoaled meat. Panicked voices rose around her. Bodies stampeded up toward the exit, pressing, crushing, shoving.

Jasper shot from his seat to the side door exit. A fireball landed at his feet and he shied back to Renee's side.

"Commander!" Renee called.

Savoy turned. Sweat ran from his shoulders. He stood two spans away from her, no distance at all except for the bars. The large man he'd been fighting stirred awake but stayed huddled on the ground, huge hands clamped over his ears. Savoy's chest heaved but his voice was steady. "Your work?"

She smiled. "Not quite." Renee turned to point out the Seventh's men and her smile melted. They were cut off by burning columns that split the chamber in two. Until the fire was tamed, the Seventh could do nothing for either Savoy or the spectators. People darted like panicked rabbits around her. She had made a vow to King Lysian when she agreed to return to the Academy. These people were her responsibility. Turning back she met Savoy's eyes. If he could care for himself a while longer, he'd have to.

He nodded. "I'm all right. Go." He started to turn away when his eyes narrowed. His hand shot out between the bars to grab the front of Jasper's tunic. A jerk of the wrist and the boy's face slammed against the metal. "Keep away from her, mage," said Savoy. "Understand me?"

The rage in Savoy's eyes told Renee the extent of Jasper's deeds. Nausea climbed her throat.

Blood ran from the boy's nose down to his shirt. He extended a glowing hand toward his captor but the pitiful wisps of blue flame died. "I understand," he whispered. His pleading gaze sought Renee.

She grasped Jasper's shirt and yanked him away from the bars. He fell to the floor and stayed there, sniveling. There was no time to address him now. Hundreds of terrified spectators darted in all directions. Fire jumped between wooden benches, ceiling beams, columns. People cursed, shoved, and struck each other. They tripped over their victims as often as they gained headway. One man's shirt caught flame and he flailed his arms, screaming at the gods until someone found the sense to throw a jacket over him. Traffic and debris plugged both exits.

Renee filled her lungs and climbed onto a bench. "Freeze where you are!" she shouted, pitching her voice over the crowd and the crackle of rising flames.

Heads turned. The momentary attention of the mob rested on her. It was drunk on fear. Crazed with it. Above all, Renee tasted the people's indecision; should they pummel her to the ground or tear off her limbs? A burning splinter fell on the bench next to her. "I will cut the throat of the next man who runs." Renee stomped the flame out with her boot. "The doors are still blocked. We need to clear the area of wood and other fuel or the fire will consume us all. The rows below us are empty. You"—she pointed to a large man with a scar in place of one eye—"pick up that bench and—"

"I ain't no lumberjack!" He pushed forward. A vein pulsed in his bald temple, his skin flushed from the heat. "Who are you to cry decrees, wench?"

Shouts chorused agreement.

The advancing man raised his fist.

Renee struggled to keep her shoulders relaxed despite her racing heart. Smoke was filling her lungs. She knew this would happen. She expected it. She knew what to do. Didn't she? Her hand dropped down. The small blade in her sleeve slid discreetly into her palm. The hair on her arms shriveled, singed away by the increasing heat. Renee made herself breathe.

The man lurched into arm's reach. Seen up close, his scar was jagged and messy.

Now! Before the man could strike, Renee spun him around

and pressed her knife to his neck. The metal blade flickered, reflecting the growing flames. The crowd fell silent. Her hand tightened on the knife's hilt. What next? The mob had to respect her over the fire. They had to. And she had to make them.

The man choked out a laugh. "You bluff, chit."

Renee's jaw tightened.

"She ain't bluffin', Gus," said Nino, emerging from the crowd. "M'lady, she don't bluff."

Beneath her knife, the man, Gus, stopped laughing. Seizing the moment, Renee snugged her hold. Gus's voice changed to a high-pitched whimper. Renee pinned Nino with her eyes. "Will your friend here do as he's told?"

Nino and Gus nodded together, the latter nipping himself on the blade and gasping. Renee withdrew the knife and shoved the man to the ground. "Let us get these benches moved, then. You four," she yelled, pointing to men and tasks.

While Nino enforced her orders, Renee folded her arms across her chest, wondering how anyone in the room could miss the deafening pounding of her heart.

Shouts rose around Savoy and spread like the flames themselves. Jars of burning oil continued to fly. Flames burst wherever jars shattered. The fight's spectators were now the fire's prey; some frightened, some injured, some dead. The cage exits blazed hot, forcing the fighters to the center.

Stepping away from the bars, Savoy unwrapped the bundled gift from his mysterious benefactor. It was wet—a soggy face mask coiled around a knife and a clipper tool sturdy enough to cut the crown of barbed wire. The man who delivered the present was long gone. Savoy tied the mask around his face and showed the tools to Den. "From an uncle," Savoy said wryly.

Den's brows rose. "It seems the day favors you."

"Hm." Savoy focused beyond the bars. Renee herded a frightened mob toward the Seventh, who were there despite his own and Verin's orders. Bloody impressive. And suicidal.

He shook himself and touched the bars. Hot but not scalding. Not yet anyway. "Rip your pants for face masks and wet them in the drinking pail." His voice soared above the chaos, but would take time to penetrate everyone's confusion. Savoy pointed to Den and the referee. "You two, make it happen."

Before either could move, Boulder shoved passed them and leaped onto the cage wall. A burn on his shoulder blistered where a hot ember had landed.

"Boulder, stop!" Savoy shouted, but the man's own screaming drowned out the words. Hand over hand, Boulder hauled his bulk up toward the barbed wire. Savoy wondered whether he even saw the razor barbs before he crashed into them.

Boulder floundered like a fish on dry ground. His screams changed from fear to agony to a fit of choking. Smoke gathered thick by the top of the cage. He twisted again and blood poured from his wounds, slicking the metal bars. When he fell, his body sent a cloud of sand into the air. Savoy saw that the barbs had claimed Boulder's eye. Gravity had claimed his neck, and he moved no more.

Savoy swallowed. "Rip your pants for face masks and wet them in the drinking pail," he repeated, this time to a silent audience. "You will climb out after I remove the barbed wire." Taking the referee's rope to attach to the top of the cage, Savoy began to climb.

Renee's troops made headway against the flames. A wide, wood-free wedge of cleared floor reached halfway toward the exit. Cory and his bucket brigade reached them from the other side. Faces she recognized from Atham's guard had joined the cause, dispatching the remaining flames and directing the surviving spectators toward the narrow exits. News of the fire had spread faster than she'd expected. Renee blinked. How much time *had* passed? She didn't know. Bodies lay sprawled, some charred beyond recognition, others crushed by the crowds or collapsed ceiling beams.

"Who started the bloody fire?" said a familiar voice.

She turned, regarded Savoy for a breath, and threw her arms around him. "Your uncle," she said into his shoulder.

"I don't hug," said Savoy.

"Idiot."

He chuckled and pushed her away. "What uncle?"

Cory cleared his throat. "If you permit a wee interruption, rumor seems to have assigned us a bit of a rescue mission. An irrelevant matter of child hostages."

Savoy squeezed Renee's shoulder and moved away, his back relaxing into a commanding presence no less steady for lack of uniform or lost weight. He accepted a flask of water from the sergeant and drained it.

Renee's fingers brushed her sword hilt. The coming hostage rescue rested on the quality of her information, the accuracy of her maps. "I can guide us through the tunnels, sir."

Savoy's jaw tensed and he looked from her to his sergeant.

Cory shot Renee an apologetic glance but spoke to Savoy. "I have Renee's maps memorized, sir. The Crown's forces are already securing the perimeter and the arena."

"Very good." Savoy spared Renee a glance. "Continue clearing everyone out until relief arrives." Without waiting for her reply, he called out something about an amulet to Den, and the three jogged up the smoldering rows, leaving her behind.

Renee stared after them, then kicked a charcoaled bit of wood against the remains of the column.

"You're just as useless as I am." Jasper laughed bitterly.

She turned to the corner where the boy mage still huddled, although not so cowed as before. His color returned as Savoy's receding back disappeared from view.

She stilled her face. Jasper did not realize how wrong he was. He was the son of the Vipers' Madam herself, a boy with insight into vital operations of a major crime group. His usefulness was beyond measure. To the Crown.

Renee tasted blood and realized she had bitten the inside of her cheek. She befriended Jasper to rescue a soldier the world had abandoned, not to turn Jasper prisoner for giving her his trust. Savoy was free. Mission accomplished. Yet her renewed pledge to King Lysian now made the boy her enemy.

Jasper rose to his feet, a sneer spreading over his sweaty, soot-covered face. He turned around to survey the arena. The side door through which he had entered once more had a clear path.

Renee blocked his way.

Cocking his hand, Jasper threw a palm full of ash into Renee's eyes and dashed past her. *Bastard.* She cleared her face in time to see him disappear through the side door. Renee ran after him, following his receding footfalls into the blue-tinged darkness of the tunnel. The abrupt chill of the underground felt strange after the furnace of the arena.

Jasper headed north, where Renee had never been. She sprinted behind him, catching glimpses of his leg or arm turning one corner or another. Twice, only the sound of his feet pounding against the stone helped her keep the path. Her lungs stung.

Jasper's tunic disappeared behind another turn. Renee ran to the corner and stopped. Her target was trapped between her and a locked door. She sent a prayer of thanks to the gods.

Drawing her sword, Renee stepped toward him. The charade of the last few weeks had come to a close. She served law and the Crown. He served a crime group that threatened Tildor's rule. There was no compromise. Jasper was too valuable a hostage. "Commander Savoy and his team are storming these passages as we speak. They will free the weeds and all the other slaves you hold."

The boy chuckled and shifted his weight from foot to foot. "The weeds will die like chickens freed from a henhouse. The slaves too. You'll see." Bits of blue flame crackled between his fingers. "If you touch me, I'll make you scream just like that idiot Cat did."

She halted her advance. "'Cat' is Commander Korish Savoy. You don't wish to toy with him."

"He's a craven loon."

"Your words or your mother's?"

Jasper flinched. The blue fire around his hand flared in wild gasps. "You forget what a mage is, blinder. I can melt your eyes and watch them drip down your face."

Renee tightened the grip on her sword. The sweet, smiling Jasper, who had offered friendship in exchange for words of kindness, was gone. A monster stood before her. Footsteps echoed in the tunnels behind them. She licked her lips. "Join me, Jasper. Come to Atham. I will speak on your behalf."

He sneered. "Why would I trust you?"

The footsteps grew closer. "Have I not stood up for you? King Lysian's little cousin cowers in these tunnels. Her name is Claire. Let us use her to guarantee your safety. Let us use her to stop the coming war."

He hesitated, the flame calming to a simmer. "Stop a war?" He spoke the words as if trying them on for size.

"The Crown brings soldiers to wipe out this Viper nest. We can stop the fighting before it starts."

He tilted his head.

Renee held her breath.

"Of all the brainless vermin lurking in the dark, why does

your useless presence not surprise me?" A cool female voice spoke behind her. The Madam, now wearing a sword across her back, ignored Renee, directing her words at Jasper. The weapon's hilt reflected bits of blue light that matched tiny glowing studs in her ears. "Bloody gods, boy, stop staring as if the door was a novelty and open the lock."

Twisting to place the wall at her back, Renee moved her blade between the two adversaries now before her. The sent of tobacco drifting from the Madam filled Renee's nose. Jasper shied toward the door and extended his hand. The pitiful mage flame flickered and died.

"Impotent idiot." The Madam pulled an amulet from her pocket and strode forward.

Renee raised her blade, blocking the woman's way. The world shrank to a hum. The Vipers' Madam—the woman running a criminal enterprise so powerful, it threatened to throw Tildor into civil war—now stood within reach of Renee's sword. "If you please, Madam."

The woman turned to her with an expression one gave to a pigeon flapping its wings.

With speed that rivaled Savoy's, the Madam drew her sword. Renee did not register the movement until the blade's hilt whistled by her head. A dull pain exploded in her temple and the world turned dark.

CHAPTER 43

"Renee."

The coolness of stone seeped through the back of her shirt.

"Renee," the voice repeated. "Renee!"

She dared a breath. A blaze of pain exploded behind her eyes.

"That's good." Alec spoke with a gentleness he usually reserved for hurt animals. "Take another."

She obeyed while his fingers explored her scalp. Something soft and damp pressed against her temple. "How . . ." She strained to catch words and thoughts that kept slipping beyond her reach. Alec had bowed out, hadn't he? "How are you here, Alec? You foreswore the Crown."

"News of fire spreads fast. Once I heard where . . ." He drew a deep breath. "Friends need not like each other's choices to guard each other's backs, right?" He brushed her cheek. "Do you remember what happened?"

She forced her eyes open but did not attempt a nod. Alec crouched beside her, a blue light around his neck illuminating the creases in his forehead. "The Madam struck me," she whispered. "Went west. With Jasper." She had to catch them. "Can you help me?"

"Others will come soon," said Alec. "Savoy saw you run into the passage. He will bring you to a real Healer. I am certain of it."

"No." She pushed herself up on her arms, head spinning. "I must stay in the fight. As must he. Heal me?"

Alec smoothed the hair from her face. "I came to keep you safe, not help your cause. You'll be safer above ground."

She sniffled blood. "Get away from me, then." Grinding her teeth, Renee pulled herself to her feet. The floor swam beneath her. She focused on a point on the wall, and stepped forward.

Alec caught her mid-fall. His body was warm and tense. "All right. I'll do it." His voice was resigned and seemed a bit deeper than Renee remembered. "I'll try to, anyway. Don't fight."

"I trust you." She fingered his necklace. "You charged your amulet. Your aunt would be proud."

"Mmm." His glowing hand hovered beside her head. "Don't look," he whispered.

She closed her eyes and felt him touch her forehead. Then his energy penetrated deeper, pierced the Keraldi Barrier, and sought out the throbbing. She focused on her breath, on the way her lungs expanded and squeezed. Breath by breath, the worst of the pain dulled. When Alec pulled away, sweat matted his hair and both their chests heaved with exertion.

Renee touched her temple. The pain was still there, but it was different, tame. She laid her palm against his cheek. "Thank you."

He pulled off his amulet and hung it around her neck. "The

Crown's fighters will come soon. Gods' strength keep you, Renee."

She touched his sleeve. "Will you wait with me?"

"I must go." He lowered his face, his voice soft. "I . . . The Crown's fighters are coming." Leaning close, he kissed her cheek and retreated into the darkness.

"Alec," she shouted.

No answer came.

"Alec!" Tears mixed with blood and snaked across her lips. She would find him after this was over. He would be at Zev's or in the mages' tavern. They would sit cross-legged on the bed and argue about the theatrics of the day, of Madam and Jasper and the fire. She would say . . .

"Renee!" A familiar voice echoed from the walls. The voice repeated her name and she heard herself answer Savoy's call. By the time the commander reached her, she had found her feet and her weapon, if not stillness for her thoughts.

Savoy paused beside her to ensure that she could walk unaided, then moved past to peer through the now open door. "What happened here?" he asked over his shoulder.

"Jasper's mother is the Viper Madam." Renee covered the crack in her voice with a cough. "They both went forward."

He glanced at her face and turned back, giving no sign of having noted anything amiss.

She bit her lip in gratitude. "Why aren't you with the Seventh?"

"They are set to their task." He cursed as pounding feet and labored breathing announced a new arrival. "The streets crawl with the Crown's soldiers. Shortly, we shall have enough help to trip one another."

Renee called a challenge to the newcomer.

"Fisker!" a baritone voice answered. A moment later the man himself appeared, a sheathed blade hanging at his hip. His jaw tightened when he saw Savoy.

Savoy blocked the man's path.

Fisker sighed but held out his hands. Professionalism in his voice battled disdain. "I shall follow your lead, Sav—Commander. For this operation."

The thought of Fisker guarding her back gave Renee a foul taste. There was no help for it, though. Nodding to Fisker, Savoy advanced into the passage. Renee jogged to take up position behind him.

Lights, both mage-made and lantern, shone bright. Woven tapestries dressed the stone walls. The scent of fresh bread mixed with the musk of underground air. All was quiet. Then a pair of guards posted at a doorway ahead saw them and drew blades.

"I have the rear," Fisker called.

Savoy, armed with a knife, lowered himself to a crouch.

Renee pulled her sword and engaged the rightmost guard, her blade meeting his in a dance of steel. The guard's short sword suited the tight space. Renee buried her headache. She focused on the tip of her blade, relying on speed and precision to make her cuts. When the guard's too-hard swing pulled him off balance, her sword found its opening and plunged into his chest.

Pulling her blade free, Renee found that Fisker had killed a latecomer and Savoy was standing over his own prone foe. Savoy pressed the bloody tip of the guard's own sword against the man's throat. "Where is the Madam?"

The captive eyed the blade. "She took the girl and left."

"Define *girl* and *left*," said Savoy.

"The Crown's girl. Little. Maybe two." He pointed with his head toward the door he had been guarding. "Was locked up in a cage."

Savoy held his position. "De Winter."

Renee ran to the chamber. A constellation of mage lights illuminated a four-poster bed standing on a thick carpet. A gold-rimmed looking glass hung beside the bed. On the other side of the room, Renee saw a barred alcove. Restraining herself, Renee checked the bed and closet first, ensuring all was clear before approaching the cage.

A woolen blanket covered the jail cell floor. Another blanket lay folded in a trundle bed alongside abandoned wooden toys. For reasons of her own, the Madam had treated her hostage gently. Thinking of Jasper, Renee doubted the motivation arose from maternal instinct.

"The bed chamber is consistent with the man's claim," Renee said, returning to Savoy and Fisker.

Fisker pointed to the prisoner. "He claims there is an exit at the end of this corridor."

Savoy searched the guard. "Will this open the doors?" he

asked, pulling an amulet from the man's pocket. He bounced the diamond in his palm.

The man's gaze caught Savoy's wristbands and collar. "Open doors, charge lights, and restrain unruly pups. Seems I reached for the wrong weapon." His bitter chuckle turned into a grunt of pain.

"The mistake saved your life." Savoy withdrew. "Restrain him," he told Fisker, and moved on down the passage.

Renee stayed by Savoy's side. Behind them, the guard screamed. Renee raised a brow. Continued interrogation had not been part of Fisker's orders.

"If he kills the man, I will deal with him later. We move faster than a woman carrying a toddler, but not enough to spare the time."

Even when that time means a life. Renee swallowed but kept moving.

Fisker caught up to them several minutes later and reported nothing. She considered questioning the man but thought better of it. He either killed the prisoner or he did not. No argument would change that.

The tunnel they now walked through differed from the others. Barely a pace wide, it had no off-shoots, no lights, and seemingly no end. Logical, for an emergency route to a covert exit. Renee took the lead, letting Alec's necklace light the way.

The passage turned and the floor dropped from under her feet. Renee fell. She shouted a warning to the others as her knees banged the stone floor. Glancing back, she realized she had fallen down a tall step into a room that lay a span lower than the tunnel floor had been.

"That is far enough, all of you."

Renee turned toward the speaker. Her heart pounded.

The Madam stood at the far end of the barren chamber, a bound and gagged toddler balanced on her hip. Beside them, a metal ladder rose to a trapdoor in the ceiling. The woman's wrist flicked, smoothly releasing a blade from her sleeve into her palm. She rested the knife against Claire's throat and met the eyes of Savoy, Renee, and Fisker in turn.

Renee drew a sharp breath. The girl was struggling against her binds, her little wrists rubbed raw on the rope and long lashes damp with tears. A few paces away, Jasper rocked over a deformed ankle, likely another victim of the devious entrance. Renee pushed aside their pain to focus on their lives.

Renee, Savoy, and Fisker kept still, their blades at the ready.

"Jasper." The Madam's voice dripped disdain. "Quit whimpering, climb up the ladder, and open the door."

Renee shifted her weight.

The woman pressed the knife into Claire's neck until a trickle of blood ran free, dripping to stain the Madam's loose shirt-sleeve. The child bucked wildly, a wail escaping around the gag.

Renee froze.

Jasper struggled upright. Face contorted and pale, he brought his healthy foot under him, rocked once, twice, and tried to rise. The injury took his weight and he cried out, falling to the floor. "I can't."

The Madam snorted and weighed the ladder with her gaze. Without Jasper to climb first, she would have to open the trapdoor herself. A simple act except for the squirming toddler in her arms and the necessity of leaving her son behind. The latter must offend her sense of security if not morality.

Savoy cleared his throat. "Take your time, Madam. I've nowhere to be."

"Cat, if I recall?" The Madam smiled, flashing white teeth against red lips.

"Commander Savoy."

"So I've heard. 'Tis a shame we lacked earlier introduction." She shifted her stance. "I hope my offspring has not damaged you beyond repair?"

On the floor, Jasper's head sank into his shoulders.

"Draw your blade and test me yourself," said Savoy.

She chuckled. "A professional curiosity I may satisfy later. I fear I'm an assassin, not dualist, by trade." Circling the ladder such that she could watch her opponents while she climbed, the Madam gripped the bars and climbed up. Claire's dangling feet banged against the metal steps.

"Mother!" Jasper reached up toward the woman.

The Madam, now by the ceiling, looked down at her son. Her face still, she released the toddler into the empty air, in the same motion throwing the knife in her hand at Jasper.

CHAPTER 44

Claire shrieked. Dropping her sword, Renee lunged forward to catch the falling child. The girl's weight caught her shoulder, sending them both to the ground. Renee twisted in the air to put herself at the bottom of the falling heap and felt her charge bounce against her as the stone struck her back.

Grunting, she rolled to her feet. The little girl sobbed but pulled against her binds. Alive. Renee turned, steeling herself to see Jasper pierced with his mother's blade. But, he wasn't. Savoy rose from atop Jasper—he had pushed the boy clear. The Madam's knife, intended for her son's heart, skittered harmlessly across the floor. Above them, the trapdoor in the ceiling banged closed, its edges glimmering with sparks of blue flame.

The Madam was gone.

Fisker grunted in frustration.

Renee retrieved her sword and slid it into its sheath before untying the small hostage. Once free, Claire scrambled across the floor and curled up in a corner, tear-streaked face hidden inside her arms. The face of another girl flinching in fear floated in Renee's mind. This could have been Sasha. Almost was. Bloody gods. *It almost was.*

Savoy's foot caught Jasper's side and rolled the boy over like a log. "What did you do to the child?"

"Nothing." His voice trembled. "I swear. I did nothing."

Savoy looked down at the boy. The commander's nostrils flared. A shadow darkened his face. And then he twitched, as if something only he saw unfolded before him. Something that had nothing to do with a sobbing toddler.

"Commander?" Renee called out.

Savoy showed no sign of having heard her. Bending, he gripped Jasper's throat and hauled the mage boy to his feet.

Jasper gasped and struggled against the grip, like a kitten twisting for freedom.

"Can't concentrate in pain, can you, mage?" said Savoy. The cold hatred in his voice chilled Renee.

"Savoy." She forced her voice steady, afraid to nudge a stone balancing on a cliff's edge. Savoy could kill Jasper. Would kill him if given a hair more cause. "Release him. Please. It's over."

Savoy's muscles bunched beneath taut skin and Jasper's eyes shot open. The gurgles ceased.

Claire shrank deeper into her corner.

"He's fifteen," whispered Renee. "He's scared and he's hurt."

Savoy's jaw tightened.

Renee stepped closer. She laid her hand on Savoy's forearm and felt it tremble. "You saved his life minutes ago. Don't take it now."

Savoy's face twitched. He loosened his hold, letting the boy slide to the ground.

Jasper gasped for air, rubbing his neck and staring at the floor.

"Begging your pardon, Commander." Fisker stood beside the waist-high step from which Renee had fallen into the room. He ran his hand along its edge and frowned. "There is something amiss here. Do you still have the amulet?"

"There is no mage work there." Jasper's voice trembled.

Renee rubbed her temple. The boy would do well to keep from attracting Savoy's attention.

Savoy turned the point of his sword on Jasper. "Horse shit. What's in that step, mage?"

Jasper scampered back, the seat of his pants rubbing the floor. "Nothing. I swear, Cat. Nothing."

Savoy looked from the boy to the guardsman. Jasper was shaking his head like a wet dog while Fisker held up his hand, ready to catch the stone. Savoy tossed the amulet to Fisker.

A triumphant smile touched the guard's face. The back of Renee's neck tightened. She cried out a warning, but the guardsman had already turned and pointed the amulet at Savoy. The wristbands came alive at the amulet's order, twisting Savoy's wrists behind his head and pulling him to the metal ladder.

Fisker drew his sword. "Even more useful than I imagined." He pocketed the amulet and turned toward the restrained Savoy.

"What are you doing?" Drawing her sword, Renee barred his way. A drop of sweat escaped her matted hair and stung her eye. She scrubbed her arm roughly across her forehead. Her heart sped.

"You know what he is." Fisker's face was dark, his lips set in a sneer. His shadow fell over her. "Did you not see the charcoaled bodies of those in the arena who died to buy him a few minutes of distraction? He is a corruption that poisons the Crown's blood. He and his kind always have been."

Renee adjusted her stance. The top of her head just reached the guardsman's shoulder. "The Family started that fire," she said, weighing Fisker with her gaze. She could do this, she'd dealt with large men before. "Commander Savoy knows nothing of his relation."

"His ignorance of his uncle does not change it. People died regardless. They will continue dying unless I cut him down. Him, and then the rest of his vile bloodline." The four fingers of Fisker's free hand flexed. "Step aside, girl."

Behind Renee, Savoy growled. "What bloody uncle?"

"Savoy is a Servant of the Crown." Renee moved across the floor, circling Fisker. "Do you put your judgment above King Lysian's?"

Fisker barked a laugh and rotated slowly to keep Renee in sight. "King Lysian wore swaddle cloths when I took up the sword." He jerked his chin at Savoy. "I watched this disease grow, saw as his Family connections bought him escape from justice. But you want proof of your own, girl? Look at his deeds today, choosing to save a Viper boy over capturing the Madam herself." He shook his head and held up his mangled hand. "I know the gods' truth just as I know they chose me to correct their error."

Renee gave up reasoning with a madman and tightened her

grip on her sword. She slid toward Fisker, searching for an opening.

Fisker took the first move, slashing at her neck. Renee stepped in and parried the attack, her arm numb from the force of the impact. Had she moved a hair slower, he would have shattered her defenses. She took a breath to steady herself.

"He swings his blade like a club," Savoy said behind her, a calm confirmation to her own conclusion. "Play—"

"A different game," Renee finished for him.

Fisker slashed with wild fury and no pause, forcing Renee to dance from side to side to avoid getting cleaved in two. The strikes were crude but powerful. Very powerful. Fisker had decided to kill her.

Renee slid right to avoid another attack. She waited until the man's blade whistled through the air, and closed in, crowding him. His greater reach turned to disadvantage in close quarters. Renee's blade nicked his arm.

Blood dripped through Fisker's sleeve. His eyes flashed and he growled like a bear whose wound stirred more rage than pain. Cocking his foot, Fisker kicked Renee. The heavy boot sank into her abdomen. She couldn't breathe. She stumbled backward and lost her balance. Gasping, Renee rolled as she fell, racing to avoid the point of his blade. She got her legs under her just as Fisker's sword struck. It hit the floor where she had fallen a heartbeat earlier. Shifting her weight to her arms, Renee spun with her leg outstretched, sweeping Fisker's ankles out from under him.

Fisker toppled backward. Swinging his sword in savage arcs, he took several seconds to re-settle into a fighting stance. It was unfair that he could buy himself time for composure and Renee could not, but it was what it was. *Fair* was for the training salle.

Renee's heart sped, feeding on her fear. Breaths chased each other in her chest. Another moment and she would be fighting herself as well as Fisker. To calm herself, she lunged in with a combination Savoy favored in their morning drills. Fisker danced from parry to parry, too busy fighting her off to offer an assault, and losing wind with each motion.

The momentum was hers. Renee's hand tightened on the hilt, the tip of the sword aiming into his gut. Savoy shouted a warning but the words drowned in the hum. Renee drew a calming breath and let herself feel the rhythm of the fight. The rhythm *she* was setting. Her grip softened, giving her arm the freedom to adjust in mid motion. The guardsman may have started the bout, but now it belonged to her.

In her mind, she was fighting on the sands of a salle. Finesse returned to her fingers, her breath supporting her moves. The lives hanging on the outcome of the match faded from thought. This was about the song of attacks and parries, the conversation of the blades that was meaningful in itself.

The lunge at Fisker's gut changed in mid-motion. Her wrist bent, tipping the blade up. The steel shaft of her sword sparkled with reflected light and pierced her target under the jaw. Blood bubbled from the wound. Renee watched it without understanding.

A sharp pain erupted above her elbow and she jerked away. Fisker's sword slid free of her arm and clattered to the ground. The guardsman followed his weapon. The fight had ended with both partners hitting their mark. His heavier strike pierced her muscle clear through; her gentle one went little deeper than the skin of his neck, severing the artery that pulsed there.

Renee cleaned then sheathed her blade, while in the corner, the little girl who would prevent a war stuck her thumb into her mouth.

CHAPTER 45

"How do you feel?" Healer Grovener pressed his fingers against Renee's wrist.

"Trapped." She pulled away. In her time out of a cadet's uniform, she forgot the limitations of the rank. Deportation back to the Academy the moment she and Savoy brought their charges up out of Catar's underground had come as a crude blow. Once the Crown's Healer had made the recommendation, not even Savoy stood up for her right to stay in the fight.

"Did headaches awaken you again this night?" Grovener's pen hovered over his notes.

"No," she lied. "Have you news from Catar?"

"I pay no mind to such matters." His pen scratched paper. "Your visitor may know more than I, however."

Visitor. She had been allowed none until now. Renee turned to the opening door. "Sasha!"

The girl hesitated in the doorway. Outlines of fading bruises still marred her face and she wrapped herself with her arms, but she was here, outside her quarters and braving the world. "I'm not so naive as to believe the Vipers castrated, but I don't think they will target my family again any time soon," she said quietly, a ghost of a smile touching her face. "Thanks to you."

Renee vaulted out of bed, dodged the Healer, and threw her good arm around her friend. They held on for several heart-beats. "You're safe now," Renee whispered into Sasha's shoulder before pulling back and guiding them both to the cot. "And Catar? How much blood . . . " She trailed off seeing the other's head shake.

"None. It was beautiful, Renee. The Crown's forces"—she grinned, emphasizing the phrase that once more included Renee—"extracting our cousin from the heart of the Vipers' lair sent a message that a troop of soldiers never could. Lys halted military action as soon as he had Claire, face and blood both saved. And to ensure his intentions sank in, he also seized the infrastructure of Predator competitions."

Renee frowned at the word choice. "He closed the games?"

Sasha bit her lip. "No . . . It's not so simple. Those games—"

"Hold up Catar's economy. I know. If they dissolve, economic chaos will rein until the Vipers think up something equally vile to fill the void."

Sasha's eyes widened. "I see my Lys is not the only one who moved beyond seeing the world in white and black. Your think-ing is right. The games will go on, but under the Crown's man-agement."

"The fighters?"

"Volunteers and convicts."

Renee nodded. As good a solution as could be made.

Sasha went on, "Of course, Lord Palan tried to use his pres-ence in Catar to leverage a larger portion of the veesi market for himself, but that's hardly news. And I understand there is a newly registered boy mage who has provided vital insight into the operation."

"Jasper." Renee made a note to find the boy upon her release. She owed him that much. "What of Commander Savoy and the others?"

"They trickle back. Savoy and Diam should arrive by morning." Sasha played with the bedspread and spoke to the floor. "Your lord father is here. He has been waiting to see you."

A jolt ran down Renee's back. She wished to believe that concern brought her father to her bedside, but the conversation with Lord Palan echoed in her head. He had claimed the Family's innocence in her mother's death. He even dared imply that her father stood to benefit from the accident. It was ludicrous to weigh the word of a criminal against that of her father, but she was yet to catch Lord Palan in a lie. She scrubbed her hand over her face. "Sasha, do you have a ring I could borrow? The bigger the better."

Her face still, Sasha slid a ruby off her finger and laid it on the table beside the bed before leaving. She didn't ask questions.

There was little one could do to make an infirmary look dignified, but Renee tried. She pulled the blanket taut over her cot—a tough trick with one arm in a sling—and changed into a pressed set of shirt and britches that Sasha had tossed through the window. The ruby ring and a folded piece of blank parchment lay on the small bedside table. She hoped to need neither.

Her head throbbed. She leaned against the wall and massaged her temple until a knock brought her to her feet.

Lord Tamath de Winter wore beaten britches and shirtsleeves instead of his typical formal attire. "The Healer permitted no visitors before today." He shuffled his feet. "Are you . . . Good gods, Renee, how do you feel?" Crossing the room in a rush, he touched his fingers under her chin. His mustache twitched.

Renee tensed but stayed still. "I recover well, my lord."

He let his hand fall to his side. "I hear the king himself now calls you friend and shares wine?"

She blushed. "A one-time audience."

"Or the first." He cleared his throat. "I wished to apologize for hasty words spoken without thought. Your home is yours as it has been always."

Renee bowed, but the stone in her stomach remained in place. Lord Tamath did not keep the habit of apologizing. "How fare the estates, my lord?"

He shrugged. "All well. I secured a new contract for wool and goat cheese that will serve us fine."

You have not secured it yet, Father. She smiled. "I'm pleased to hear it."

He waved his hand in dismissal. "I would not trouble you over it, but my colleague may have forwarded the documents to you by error."

And thus the dice settled. Renee was prepared for the wave of disappointment, but was surprised to find it tempered with relief. At least now she understood the game. "If you speak of Lord Palan, there was no error. He gave me the contract for review." She let her gaze slide to the objects on the table. "Are you aware of his Family ties?"

Lord Tamath stiffened. "I am. I am also aware that should I fail to honor his demands, I will see grave ills befall the estate." He reached out toward her. "The last time I refused the Family, your mother and brother paid the price. I fear losing you to the same fate."

Renee's head thumped with each heartbeat. Her father's words directly contradicted Palan's. "You do this deal only for protection?"

"Why else would I deal with a monster who killed my wife and my child?"

She licked her lips and smiled. "Then I have fortunate news. The contract is here." She raised her finger to stay his reaching hand. "But Lord Palan needs a great service from me. In return, he is prepared to guarantee that no Family tentacle will ever touch the de Winter estates. They will collect no tribute and offer no menace. Lord Palan offers his ring as a token of guarantee. You can display it to any Family servant and he or she will let you be."

Her father's mustache twitched again.

Renee gestured to the table. "Which will you take?" She held her breath.

He reached out and snatched the parchment. "You will understand when you are older," he said, and started to the door. Then he stopped, one hand on the doorknob. "What is the meaning of this?" Lord Tamath spun, his eyes flashing darkness as he waved the blank parchment in the air. "What did you do with my contract?"

"What did you do with my mother?"

His jaw shut with a click.

Heat gripped her face. She advanced on him. "The Family did not kill her or Riley."

He bowed lightly as if conceding a match. "No. The coach crashed in a meaningless accident. I thought having a culprit to blame would ease both our souls."

It was plausible. Or maybe Palan's supposition was right, and Lord Tamath had rigged the accident to gain ownership of his wife's lands. Renee was beyond taking her father's words at face value. Fatigue erupted from nowhere and washed over her. She gripped the edge of the table for balance, refusing to sit while her father remained in the room. "I don't believe I will be returning to your estates, my lord."

"My labors on the contract will not be annulled. Where is it?"

"Destroyed." The steadiness of Renee's voice surprised her.

Lord Tamath turned and left without another word, slamming the door in his wake.

~~~ CHAPTER 46 ~~~

Sleep claimed Renee after her father's visit, eating up the rest of the day and the night. The following morning, she awoke to an argument on the other side of the infirmary wall. She rubbed her face and sat upright, recognizing the voices.

"I came for Renee," said Savoy.

"I little care why you came, boy. Your ribs are broken," said Grovener.

A crash of furniture clattering to the floor echoed through the room, and a door banged closed. Renee scrambled from her bed and into her clothes, adjusting her shirt collar just in time to answer a knock.

Savoy strode in, pulling disheveled hair back into a ponytail. "Still Grovener's prisoner?"

She left her sling on the table and wrapped her arms around him.

"I don't do hugs."

"You need the practice."

Chuckling, he laid his hands on her shoulders and pushed away, his body oddly rigid.

Renee ran the back of her hand down his side, pressing hard against his ribs.

He tensed and caught her wrist. "Don't do that."

Lifting a brow, Renee twisted free from his grip but said nothing. Her point was made.

"Unrest brews on the western border." He moved across the room. "The soldiers the Crown pulled away to attend to Catar return to their posts but their numbers will not suffice. The Devmani Emperor is looking a little too covetously at Tildor's commerce."

Renee perched on the edge of the bed and looked out the window, as if troop movement leagues away could be made out. "War?"

Savoy shrugged. "Perhaps. The temptation to test a neighboring new king is hard to resist."

Renee rubbed her arms. Fighters moved from post to post, campaign to campaign, greeting and taking leave of friends as often as the wind changed. Even if the gods rooted Savoy to Atham, Renee herself would be gone on her field trial before much longer. "When do you leave?"

"One week."

She hesitated, the words balancing on her tongue. "I'm . . . I'm sorry about your parents."

Savoy nodded. "We had little time for each other." His voice asked her not to press and they shared a silence. He looked up after a few moments, catching her eye. "My family is here," he said quietly, "as is yours." He stretched his shoulders. "You'll have the summer cycle to fulfill your missed schoolwork. Connor volunteered to oversee it."

Schoolwork. She wanted to chuckle at the circle life had formed. She cleared her throat instead. "I, ah, I should write to Alec. Did you see him before you left?"

Savoy's face was still. "Alec left Catar with some other young mages. Too many Crown's eyes there now. Zev sent Connor a note."

"That can't be right." Renee frowned. "No, he would've told me. Was there a letter for me with Zev's ..." Seeing Savoy shake his head, Renee focused her gaze at the budding tree branch that swayed outside and pressed her teeth together.

"Renee!" A human arrow shot through the door. "You're awake! Wanna see something? Healer Grovener taught me to glow just one finger!" Diam hurried to demonstrate this feat before throwing his arms around her neck.

"The imp, on the other hand, does do hugs." Savoy backed away to give his brother room. "She's all yours."

Hugging Diam, Renee watched the closing door and shuffled through her memory. Was it her imagination or had Savoy flinched when his brother approached? She glanced at Diam and knew he'd seen it too. Rubbing her nose, Renee began composing a plea for release from the Healer's lair. She had things to do.

Talking her way to freedom took until the following morning. After taking a moment to greet Sasha, her once-again room-mate, Renee searched out Savoy. Finding both his quarters and the salle empty, she tried Rock Lake. Spring rains had softened the down-sloped path, making the mud splotch and stick to her shoes. She cleared the trail and squinted from the blinding sun reflecting off the lake.

"Savoy?" Her voice bounced from the rocks.

"Yes?"

She followed his call to a wide alcove, where he lay reclining against a gently sloping stone. Renee lowered herself beside him. "How fair the ribs?"

"Healing."

Healing, not healed. "A sword may find its way into you in the west."

He turned his head, his eyes shut against the sun. "You lecture me on the dangers of warfare?"

"You avoid mages. One of whom is your brother."

Savoy rose on his elbows and opened his eyes, his voice low. "This conversation is over."

"I was there." She made herself lie relaxed against the stone but knew the nonchalance fooled neither of them. Her heart raced, threatening to trip her words. "I saw. I know. And I'll make this easy for you. You go see Grovener, or I will, and I'll tell him everything. You have until the noon bell two days hence." With that, Renee swallowed and closed her eyes, unable to meet the fury raging in his.

When she opened them, Savoy was gone.

"All packed?" Connor asked, trotting Lava beside Kye. They rode down a wide stretch of dirt road, cooling the horses after a run. Back in the Academy, the Seventh took on supplies and readied to ride out.

Savoy shifted in his saddle. His side ached. "I'm always packed."

"And Diam? If you still seek a guardian . . ." Connor shrugged, silently extending the offer without insisting.

Savoy stared at the tree line. The decision had to be made, but the right answer continued to elude him. Each melting hour made it more urgent but no clearer. "Be his friend, Connor. He needs one as good as you."

Connor nodded. "Of course. Do you plan to ask Verin? I know he'll agree."

"No." The answer came out sharper than Savoy intended. "I don't believe Diam's heart would fit a military life." Dropping the topic, he navigated Kye into the stable and stiffened at the sight of a velvet-clad fat man who awaited him there. "Lord Palan."

"Will you not call me Uncle?"

"No."

"Very well, Lord Korish—stop wincing at the name, it's yours by birth—will you walk with me?"

The news of his father's past still spun Savoy's head, although it explained some of Lord Palan's earlier behavior. Now an odd mix of distaste and curiosity made Savoy leave Kye in Connor's care and fall in step with the man. Lord Palan remained silent until Savoy finally spoke.

"You're a criminal," Savoy said. If the lord expected pleasantries, he was mistaken.

"The Family traffics contraband, yes," Palan answered without hesitation. "Master Verin knew as much when he took you on as a foster. He wanted a swordsman and I wanted to secure your future. We struck a bargain."

A bargain. With himself as commodity. Savoy ran a hand through his hair. Verin had always been up front about taking Savoy in for his sword arm. Did it matter that there was more to the arrangement? Of course it bloody well mattered. It saved him from becoming Tanil. Savoy looked back at Palan. "You orchestrated the fire in Catar."

"Yes."

"That was no contraband trafficking, my lord. That was murder. Dozens died."

"You, however, escaped." Lord Palan's voice flowed honeysmooth, without a hint of agitation or doubt. It was also the controlled, professional tone of a man who stood by his decisions. "But yes, others died. Others who were less important to me. Tell me, have you not killed dozens of enemies? If a man of the Seventh was captured, would you not kill dozens to free him?"

The man twisted words. "You didn't attack an enemy; you killed Tildor's own people."

"Ah, but you define enemies by the Crown's priorities, which, mind you, tend to shift. I define the enemy by my own values. Those people were enemies because their existence threatened you. They were also enemies because they were Vipers, whose business threatens ours."

"I serve the Crown. Do you expect me to endorse your views?"

"Of course not." Palan held up a hand. "But, despite our disagreement on goals, do consider our similarity in tactics. After all, can you not respect a swordsman who fights for the other side? Can you not learn from each other when you step foot on neutral ground?" He twisted a ring. "Speaking of learning, I hope that when you return to Atham next, you will find time for your cousin."

Savoy blinked. "Tanil? I will find a blade for him, my lord."

"The flat of one, if you wish. The boy's discipline does lack." Palan caught Savoy's eyes. "But he is your family and he is young. He will not find a path in the Crown's Service nor in the Family's leadership, but I hope you will help him find his honor in as much as it is possible."

Savoy glared and was still contemplating the words when Lord Palan spoke again.

"Diam—"

"You will not have him."

"Of course. I only meant to tell you he is heading this way. Ride safely to the west." The older man smiled, bowed, and walked away.

Savoy glanced behind him. The boy really was coming. Shaking his head, Savoy started back toward the stable. He'd check on Diam after seeing to Kye. The promise made it to the tip of his tongue when he realized the footsteps had stopped. He turned to find Diam standing several yards away.

"You saw me and walked the other way." The boy narrowed his eyes.

"I was going to brush down Kye. Do you wish to help?"

"No, you weren't. You were walking away from me. You've done it all week."

"Diam—" he started to say, but his brother turned and ran. The receding footsteps remained imprinted in the soggy ground, and for many hours, in Savoy's mind.

The Academy bell tolled noon when Renee approached the Healer's office to exchange Savoy's friendship for his well-being. Her feet dragged in the mud. She watched her toes and stumbled when another pair of boots cut across her path.

"You still intend to carry out your threat?" Savoy crossed his arms over his chest. His voice was cool.

"Yes." She pushed around him and walked on.

"Wait." Light footsteps caught up to her and a hand touched her shoulder. "We go together."

"Have you come to your senses or to destroy more of my furniture?" Healer Grovener peered at Savoy over his glasses. It was the dry, unamused look he granted everyone, but Renee sensed an understanding lurking behind his eyes. He was no fool and, Renee realized, had known Savoy a great deal longer than she.

"Neither. But I did come to you." Savoy drew himself up. "For two separate matters, sir."

"One is your ribs. What's the other?"

"My brother. Would you consider an apprentice?"

Renee drew a breath and held it as long seconds stretched on before the man replied.

"What of his page and cadet studies?" Grovener removed his glasses and cleaned them with the hem of his shirt. "A boy cannot answer to two masters."

"I will withdraw him from the Academy rolls. He's years away from registration, and even then your tutelage would fulfill the mandate."

Grovener steeped his hands in front of his chest. "You are a fighter, Commander. I will neither teach the boy combat nor arrange for such lessons."

"Understood. I ask only that he see Master Verin once a week." Savoy paused. "And the same with Lord Palan."

"An interesting combination." The Healer's fingers tapped each other. Another eternity came and went. "Very well. I will take the child." The glasses returned to his face. "And now, finally, will you remove your shirt and sit still?"

Savoy obeyed, stripping to the waist and pulling himself onto the table. Dark bruises covered the left side of his chest but Renee knew that the tension in his shoulders had nothing to do with physical discomfort. She stepped closer and heard him draw breath.

"This may not go as smoothly as it should, sir," Savoy said quietly, running a hand through his hair.

"Mmm." Grovener washed his hands in a basin. "Do you trust the girl?"

"Yes."

The mage turned, a blue flame playing around his fingers. "Then she will stand guard over me as we work."

Savoy flinched once at the sight of the mage fire, then schooled his face and turned to Renee. "Will you?" he asked, his voice carefully neutral.

Renee's hands gripped together behind her back. Saying nothing, she took up a stance beside the wall. It didn't matter that she trusted Grovener, or that Savoy was the better fighter, or that they were on friendly grounds. A friend asked her to stand watch. And she would.

Beyond the infirmary wall, the din of cadets' voices blended together. The Academy was moving on—it paused neither for Renee's departure nor her return. In two days, when Savoy took his leave, it would not pause for him either.

The morning of the Seventh's departure, the mess hall, as usual, swarmed with uniforms. Cadets shouted over the heads of their friends and shoved closer to the food platters. Renee snatched a piece of bread and cheese and headed to a small table in the corner where Savoy and Seaborn sat together. Like her, both men wore full uniforms, an odd change from their days in Catar. It would be odder still in a few hours, when Savoy and his team rode out, leaving Renee to reclaim her spot in the classroom.

As she approached Savoy's table, students shot Renee questioning looks. Cadets stayed clear of instructors and officers. She hurried to pull out a chair and sit.

Savoy stole her cheese.

She kicked him under the table.

He chuckled, but there was a finality to the laugh, as if it were the last to be shared. The commander pins on his collar loomed over the table, casting an invisible shadow. A moment later Savoy pushed himself back. "I must check on the men. Connor, de Winter." He bowed to each and strode away, the mob of cadets parting before him.

Renee picked at her bread, spreading the crumbs over her plate.

"A burden of the uniform." Seaborn took a drink of his coffee. "You will grow used to it."

"Friendship subject to wardrobe?"

"Only the display of it." Seaborn moved back his chair. "The commander left a sword for you. He said you wore it to the palace on Queen's Day. Pick it up at your convenience."

Renee's brows arched. "Was it not from the armory?"

"No, it was his throughout the Academy." Seaborn rose and took his plate. "I will see you in class, Cadet de Winter." He tilted his head at her. "And, if memory serves, you owe me a paper."

Commander Korish Savoy guided his horse beyond Atham's

city walls, toward the awaiting group of fighters. "Fall in!" he called, and the men formed their columns.

Cory trotted up on his bay, his gaze lingering on the city behind them. "She's quite a lass, isn't she?"

Savoy chuckled. "Spare the efforts, Sergeant. De Winter is out of your reach."

Cory raised his hands. "I've a rule not to court friends and siblings of anyone who can skin me alive." He paused. "Ye think we'll work with her again?"

Savoy nodded his head. "That one, Cory, will one day command us all."

ACKNOWLEDGMENTS

A humongous thank you to:

Crit partners SM Blooding, Ralene, and Jay,
for staying with me chapter by chapter.

Agent Leigh Feldman, for always giving me perspective.

Editor Jess Garrison, to whom King Lysian owes his life.

Assistant editor Claire Evans for all the quiet things she did.

The Tildor Herald Cadets, the best novel street team ever.

The Lucky 13s for shared trust.

My husband, who put up with my
"need to go write" disappearing act.

Bloggers who revealed my cover and re-tweeted my news.

All of you who've let me bounce ideas, talk writing,
and run scenes by you "just real quick."

THANK YOU, TILDOR TEAM.